7,000 CLAMS

A Novel

7,000 CLAMS

A Novel

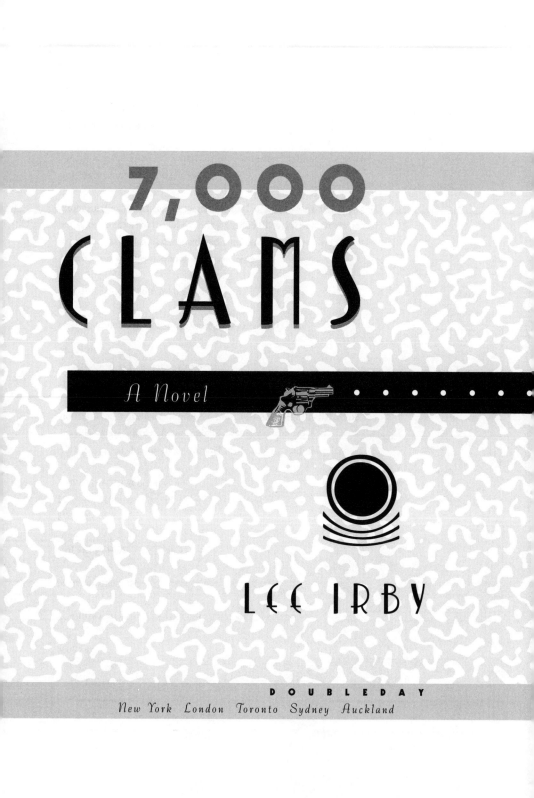

LEE IRBY

DOUBLEDAY

New York London Toronto Sydney Auckland

PUBLISHED BY DOUBLEDAY
a division of Random House, Inc.

DOUBLEDAY and the portrayal of an anchor with a dolphin are registered
trademarks of Random House, Inc.

Book design by Donna Sinisgalli

Library of Congress Cataloging-in-Publication Data

Irby, Lee.
7,000 clams : a novel / Lee Irby.—1st ed.
p.   cm.
ISBN 0-385-51189-2
1. Ruth, Babe, 1895–1948—Fiction.   2. Saint Petersburg (Fla.)—Fiction.
3. Promissory notes—Fiction.   4. Baseball players—Fiction.
5. Prohibition—Fiction.   I. Title: Seven thousand clams.   II. Title.

PS3609.R47A6177 2004
813'.6—dc22
2004045578

PRINTED IN THE UNITED STATES OF AMERICA

August 2004

First Edition

1 2 3 4 5 6 7 8 9 10

FOR BETH

Acknowledgments

I cannot say thank you enough to my editor, Jason Kaufman, and my agent, Nat Sobel, whose belief in and support of this book hopefully will not get them fired. Jenny Choi answered all of my silly questions. Jack Davis went above and beyond to cleanse the manuscript, and Suzan Harrison helped me get over some early hurdles. Mike Burke and Shannon Burke contributed valuable critiques at a crucial juncture. Scott McDonald guided me in the right direction when I was lost in the wilderness. Joe Szymanski's fingerprints can be found on almost every page, and his advice was invariably on the mark.

Gary Mormino and Ray Arsenault opened up an exotic world for a budding novelist to explore. Gary never failed to encourage me and freely shared his archival treasures. Ray's work on St. Petersburg in particular fired my imagination; I plundered it with gusto.

7,000
CLAMS

A Novel

A DEPARTURE,

1925

The staircase cascades down to the platform like a black waterfall of steel and rivets. At the foot stand three porters wearing thin cotton jackets, no match for the stabbing cold that has tormented New York since Christmas. The last passengers of the southbound Dixie Flyer have boarded, men in long wool coats and ladies garbed in fur, headed off for pleasant weather elsewhere. The porters have loaded their considerable luggage, leather bags neatly packed with golfing britches, tennis togs, and foulard dresses, something for every occasion on their holidays in Hot Springs and Palm Beach.

"White folks be headed south," says one porter in a rich baritone, "and black folks be headed north." Heads bob in easy agreement; coins jangle restlessly in deep pockets, the tips garnered for loading the suitcases of the well-to-do. They've all made more in an hour at Pennsylvania Station than a sharecropper makes in a week.

Steel columns reach up to cambered arches that support the lattice of windows in the glass ceiling high above. Some days it seems like the arches hold up heaven itself, the way shafts of light shine down. But not today. The sun has disappeared, and as soon as this train departs, the porters will disappear too, back to a small room beneath the stairs where they can pretend to be warm for a few minutes, before the arrival of the 83 at 1:06.

A whistle sounds, shrieking through the station. "All aboard!" a conductor shouts, beefy hand cupped to mouth, eyes red and watery. Suddenly, bounding down the steel stairs comes a ticket clerk, spectacles pinched to a thin nose and in danger of flying off as he waves his arms wildly trying to get the conductor's attention. "Wait, now! Hold the train! Hold the train!"

Somebody important must be on the Dixie Flyer, the porters decide, curious now as the spectacle unfolds. A few seconds later they see a huge man appear at the head of the stairs, surveying the platform below as a lord would his minions. He begins his descent at a leisurely pace, obviously in no hurry. He knows the world will wait for him, so there's no reason to rush. He walks with a cocksure swagger, a great garish blue coat pulled tight against his massive chest. The wind has whisked a curly lock of black hair onto his forehead, giving the man a boyish look, the disheveled appearance of an untamed lad forced to put on his Sunday best. Behind him trails another hapless porter, struggling to carry the man's mountain of luggage, including a set of brand-new golf clubs. At the foot of the stairs some sportswriters catch the big man, who stops and allows a photographer to snap off some shots, the bulb popping loudly like a small gun.

"Hey, Babe!" a reporter shouts. "How much you tipping the scales these days?"

"Counting my pecker?" The big man snickers, then reaches into his blue coat and pulls out a cigar. "Boys, I've never felt better in my life." He pauses, lights his stogie, and immediately falls into a fit of coughing, which reddens his face. "The Yankees don't pay me to model no swimming trunks. Hey kid!"

George Herman Ruth motions to a little boy hiding behind a column, calling him over to the impromptu news conference. The kid at first appears to be too stunned to move a muscle; he's been tagging along ever since he saw the slugger out on Sixth Avenue. The kid's eyes grow wide and somehow his body begins to go forward. The crowd of reporters parts to make way for the youngster. The Babe kneels down and puts his big, meaty arm around the child's thin, small shoulders.

5

The boy quakes as if palsied by the cold, so vivid and palpable is his excitement.

"Listen, kiddo," the Babe sings, "how 'bout you taking this here sawbuck and going up to that Kraut selling wieners by the newsstand and picking up five for the Babe? Can you do that for me?"

The boy nods eagerly, eyes bugged in disbelief.

"Good. And run back as fast as you can." With a final pat the boy scampers off, his little feet pattering against the steel steps as he hurries to the terminal. Ruth stands up, a bright smiled fixed on his lips. "The Babe gets hungry, he eats. He gets horny, he screws. You swing big, you live big. It ain't as complicated as you make it sound, you dumb eggheads."

The reporters laugh, as they usually do at Ruth, but they also know that the slugger doesn't look especially well. He seems to be about thirty pounds overweight, and his face, jowly at the best of times, swells from a bloated chin. Every year he makes a pilgrimage to Hot Springs, Arkansas, to pull himself together before spring training starts in Florida, but this year he'll have to redouble his efforts to get in condition. Can he do it? Can he continue to find success through excess, live like he doesn't care about tomorrow only to seize the day and conquer? It doesn't seem possible, but neither did hitting fifty homers in a season, a feat he's already accomplished twice.

"How many homers this year, Babe?" a reporter calls out.

"A hundred. Hey, any of you scoffers ever been to St. Pete? What kind of burg is it anyway?"

"It's swanky, Babe. Real swanky."

"Is it wet?"

"All Florida is. So I hear."

"All aboard!" the conductor shouts as again the whistle splits the frigid air.

The smile quickly fades from the Babe's face. "Where'd that kid go with my franks? And my ten smackers?" The reporters all wheel around; the staircase is empty. The kid is nowhere to be found.

"The hell with it!" Babe Ruth chuckles merrily, unperturbed by the grift. "And I was hungry, too. They got food on these trains." He gives a wave as he springs over to his Pullman car. "See you in St. Pete, boys!"

The reporters know Ruth was slapped with a paternity suit six months ago, although the case had been dropped. They know he consumes women and food with equal fervor and equal indiscrimination. They know he likes to spend time at the racetrack, where, when he won, he won big. Though he lost even bigger, and they know that, too, these reporters huddling at the train station on this cold winter day in February 1925. They know facts about the man, and facts are like stars, hovering above us in fixed constellations that guide our lives through eternal blackness.

"How long you give the bastard to live?" asks one wag as the train begins to pull slowly away from the station.

NOBLE
· · · · · · · ·
SAVAGE

The floor is so cold against his feet that it feels like he's walking on ice. The fire went out last night, but he didn't start feeling it until he sobered up. Now not even his companion for the evening, the lovely Ginger DeMore, can keep him warm anymore.

"Hey, you!" she calls out. "Come back here."

Frank Hearn grins at her, revealing a set of perfectly straight teeth. A few are chipped, though, like old china. His nose is crooked, and one cheek sits flatter against his face than the other. But he's got wavy brown hair, a cleft chin, and bright hazel eyes, making him a ruggedly handsome sort. He stands well over six feet and is sturdily constructed, thick in the chest and broad in the shoulders, solid like a gnarled oak tree, with the same sort of markings. A few scars, some bumps, a broken limb or two over the years, but still impressive.

"I'll brew us a pot of coffee," he tells her. There's not a stick of wood left to feed the stove, so he'll have to trudge downstairs to borrow some more from the landlord. But this will be the last time. You don't need firewood in Florida, and that's where he's headed. The Sunshine State.

"I'll be right back," he says, sitting on the edge of the bed to get dressed.

"Where're you going?" asks Ginger sleepily, propping herself up on her elbows. "You sick of me already?"

"No, I'm sick of the cold. I need to get some wood." He pulls on a pair of wool socks. His toes poke through a few holes, and he wiggles them. These won't be making the trip south. You don't need wool in that heat.

Ginger falls back onto a pillow like she's been shot. "Get me some Bromo-Seltzer while you're at it. My head is spinning like a top."

"How about some hair of the dog?"

"Hardware for breakfast? I like how you think, sport."

Now dressed, Frank strides over to the closet by the front door. He opens it and stands back to regard what's inside: 117 bottles of Hennessey Three Star scotch, straight from the Canadian shores of Lake Erie. Frank just got back to Asbury Park yesterday, and he can't help but marvel at his handiwork, the neatly stacked cases, the block printing on the sides, so official looking, so perfect. Name-brand booze, more valuable than gold.

"If that ain't the cat's meow!" Ginger purrs once she sees the haul. "Some bootlegger you are!"

"They're pretty, huh?" He reaches in and grabs a bottle out of an already-opened case. This is the last one he'll take for himself. He gave two last night to Murray Redd, photographer and Frank's good buddy. Murray took pictures of naked women—models like Ginger, whom Frank met last night. It sure pays to have friends. Frank has gorged himself on Murray's skirts the past three years. He'll miss those parties at the studio, but all good things must come to an end.

"I've never seen so much booze," gushes Ginger.

"You won't be seeing it for very long. I got it all worked out. Somebody's buying the whole load." He examines the bottle of scotch he's holding, his attention drawn especially to the label. That's what makes it so beautiful: people love labels on their booze. They'll pay dearly for it, too.

"Aren't you a smart boy. Pour me a drink already."

He finds a glass, one of two he owns, and fills it up halfway. For himself, he takes a quick swig off the bottle, then another.

"I'll be right back," he says, teeth rattling from the cold. "I gotta get a fire going."

"Hurry up already. It's lonely in here all alone."

He smiles down at Ginger, reclined naked on his bed, barely covered with the blanket. She is just what the doctor ordered, a woman plump in all the right places, with a full bust and strong thighs she could wrap around you like she was breaking a mustang. She also speaks in a low, gravelly voice that puts you in a naughty frame of mind, and after six nights in the freezing cold on a smelly fishing boat, Frank had plenty on his mind when he brought Ginger home last night. Very quickly those long, lonely nights on the Hudson River faded away.

Frank gathers an armful of wood, quietly, keeping an eye on his landlord's door. No need to wake him up. He'll ask for the rent and Frank won't have it to give. Not till later today, after he sees Ed Callahan. That's who's buying the booze. And when Frank gets a stake this time, he won't blow it. No sir. He won't be that stupid again. He ran through a thousand berries last summer like it was nothing. And for what? Showing some dame a good time. Dinners, movies, drinks, new clothes, you name it, and Frank bought it for her. The thing was, she was a poor little rich girl, a millionaire's daughter. What a soak he was. No, he won't be that stupid this time. He learned his lesson. There'll be time aplenty for skirts once he gets to Florida and gets set up in the real estate game.

"I'm back," he announces, closing the door with his foot and hurrying over to the stove. Heat is all he wants. "Let me light a fire. I hate this cold."

"Why don't you let me warm you up?" asks Ginger, peeling back the blanket to show a little more of her bust. She's got his attention now. Frank breaks into a wide grin, like a kid who's just found a silver dollar.

"Let me get this started. I'll be right there."

He holds a match to an old newspaper and then puts the flame beneath a few small logs.

"Hurry up already," she coos.

The logs begin to crackle as they catch on fire.

•   •   •

"I gotta get going," he tells her. "I'm not giving you the bum's rush or anything. I got business to take care of." He untangles himself from her nude body. He's supposed to meet with Callahan at noon, and he wants to get this squared away, since he invested almost every penny he had in buying the booze.

Ginger sighs theatrically. "Men and their business. It's all work, work, work. You sound like my husband."

"Husband?" The word gets stuck in Frank's throat like a chicken bone. "You never said nothing about a husband."

"You never asked."

She starts collecting her clothes, which are strewn on the floor around the bed. Frank stands and watches her with a new suspicion. Married? She doesn't act too married, and there's no ring on her finger. Somehow he missed it. Must've been blinded by her slinky cocktail dress.

"Ah, don't get balled up, Frank," she sings merrily, pulling on that same cocktail dress with the studded rhinestones that unglued him last night. "I left him. We're separated and getting a divorce."

"Yeah? Why's that?"

She shakes her head like she's warding off a fly. "Lots of reasons. Do you really want to know?"

"I just don't want some rube showing up here looking to kill me."

She snorts a derisive laugh. "You won't have to worry about that. You seen my purse anywhere? I need some lipstick. I can't go out looking like this. Oh, there you are." Her purse is resting on a chair. She picks it up, and starts looking around.

"Mirror?"

"Don't got one."

She shrugs, and walks over to the chifforobe, where she begins applying makeup, humming to herself as she does. She's almost dressed now, and soon she'll be heading out the door and out of his life for good.

"There. How do I look?"

"Swell."

She's got a purse in her hand, and when she spins around, something heavy falls out of it and crashes against the floor. A pistol, .22 caliber by the looks of it, snub-nosed. She stoops and gathers it up.

"Why are you packing heat?" he asks her. That's the last thing he expected she'd carry around.

"A girl needs a friend."

"I guess it ain't my business to ask."

She's not smiling anymore. Her body starts to sag like she's got a boulder on her back, and she sinks to the bed. "I'd tell you, Frank. The whole story. But I can't. The less you know, the better."

"Look, cheer up. I seen plenty of guns in my time, used a few myself. I don't care about that. But if you're in some trouble, I could help." Immediately he regrets these words. Don't get involved with some dame, he reminds himself. Not now, when you're so close to leaving.

"Will you come see me tonight, Frank? I'm staying at the Allison, on Deal Lake."

He shakes his head. "I would if I could. But I'm leaving for Florida."

"Florida?" She tries to act like she couldn't care less but he can tell she's feeling rejected. Like he's blowing hot air just so he can give her a kiss-off. "Funny, you never mentioned it before."

"You never asked."

"How silly of me."

"It's true. I'm not high-hatting you. I am going to Florida. Wait a minute, I'll prove it." It's important to convince her he's not fibbing. He'd help her if he could. But he can't. So there he is, on his knees, looking under the bed for a shoe box. In that shoe box are scores of brochures and pamphlets he's been collecting over the past twenty months that show how, with just a little bit of accumulated capital, a person could make a fortune investing in Florida real estate. He's gazed at these documents countless times, especially the one featuring a certain Maynard Thompson, who arrived in Miami with just ten dollars and is now a millionaire. There's even a picture of Maynard standing in front of his brand new Dusenberg, a beautiful gal draped on each arm. He's an unremarkable-looking man, a drooping mustache and sad eyes. He doesn't seem to have any pep. But he made it big in Florida.

"Here," he says, standing up. "Look at these."

But Ginger is gone. The room is empty, and only her smell remains. He walks over and closes the door, first looking down the hall. No sign of her. She's not too keen on good-byes, seems like. Maybe it's better that way.

He walks over to the stove. There's one more log and he drops it in the fire. As he squats at the stove, holding his hands close to the flames, he feels warm for the first time in a long time. Not just from the fire, either. No, this booze is going to do good things. It will get Frank to Florida, at last, after too much futzing around. First he'll have to split the loot with Enrico, who owns the fishing boat they took to Canada. He needs the dough, since he's got a wife and a couple of kids. They'll be in good shape now. Enrico said he'd pay the note off he owed on the boat. Never will a load of booze bring as much happiness as this one. Frank down in Florida, Enrico out of hock.

Then the windows start rattling like a train is going by. But there's no train around here. Frank looks up, alarmed. The entire building begins shaking. An earthquake in Asbury Park? Then he hears the footsteps, and they sound like the thudding approach of a herd of stampeding buffaloes. He springs to his feet just in time to see the front door crashing in, and behind it, a streaming phalanx of men in long wool coats, guns drawn.

"Hold it right there!" a man shouts. A small man, with protruding ears and thinning hair the color of rust. Frank recognizes him at once: Dwight Yoder of the Prohibition Bureau. He is egg-shaped in head and body, one a miniature of the other. Both seem fragile and delicate, like blown glass. One punch would crack either. "Don't move a muscle, Hearn."

"Who sent you?" That's the first question that pops into Frank's head. This smells like a setup.

"The power of the federal government, Frank. The Volstead Act. Haven't you heard of it?"

"Look here, boss." One of the goons waves everybody over, and now they're all gawking at the Hennessey in the closet. Yoder barks out some instructions, and two men shoo Frank into a corner, guns pointed right into his face. Frank's jaw twitches angrily as he watches the cases of booze being carried away, rapidly, with a military precision, as if this group has done this kind of raid plenty of times before.

"How was Canada, Frank?" asks Yoder derisively, his owlish mouth forming a childlike look of joy. Frank doesn't answer, because there's nothing to say. The last of the cases has been carried out, but still Yoder is there to enjoy the satisfaction of seeing Frank taken down a few notches. Years ago they both worked for Ed Callahan, who always gave the hardest jobs to Frank, because Yoder just didn't have the muscle. You could tell it ate at Yoder, and maybe that was why he left to go work for the Prohibition Bureau in Trenton. Callahan said he planted Yoder there for protection, but this didn't seem like protection.

"It's been a pleasure, Frank," he sneers. "We'll have to do this again real soon."

"Go to hell, Yoder."

"You want me to take you in? Huh?" Yoder always liked sounding tough, and the badge gave him plenty of chances.

"Yeah, take me in," Frank says calmly, knowing it won't happen. Yoder doesn't have a warrant, doesn't have the legal authority to be in here at all. But that's not the point: the point was getting the booze.

"Maybe next time I will, Frank. You better be careful, because I'm watching you. Come on, fellas. Let's scram."

It's **been** a very bumpy ride.

For four hours Irene Howard has ridden in the back of a cab, all the way from Trenton, where she disembarked from her train. Yesterday she was sitting in her logic class, and today she's as far away from logic as a person can get.

There's no going back now. The last time she did this, slipped off campus to go see Frank Hearn, the dean of students was adamant: should Irene again leave school without written permission from her parents, she would be expelled from Pearlman College, no questions asked. And her parents were equally determined: if you pull this stunt again, young lady, you shall find yourself on a slow boat to China—literally.

So Irene knows her life will never be the same after this. Maybe she and Frank will run off together somewhere and see the world. After all, she turns twenty-one this summer and that's when she can start using her trust fund. It's her money and she can do whatever she wants with it. And what she wants to do is be in love with Frank Hearn and go on a safari. Ride camels across the desert. Sail on the Adriatic. Have lunch in Paris. If he's alive, that is. She hasn't heard a word from him in a long, long time. But that's a trivial detail.

"Where to?" the driver asks in heavily accented English.

"Dunleavy Street," she replies.

"Where's that?"

"I'll find it, don't worry. Keep on this street, it's Ocean Avenue."

The surf pounds the shore from the onslaught of wind, spraying spumes of salty mist into the heavy air. The beach is empty, except for a cluster of sandpipers unafraid of the cold. Birds mate for life, they say. When one mate dies, the other soon follows. That's as much as Irene learned from biology last year. But maybe that's as much as anyone needs to know. Life is love is devotion. Up ahead she sees a big yellow building with huge, arched windows offering vistas of the wide sea. The arcade. Its windows are shuttered now, but seeing it fills her with happiness. The arcade, where they first kissed on the Fourth of July, beneath the exploding fireworks overhead. She knows the way now. She tells the driver to turn right and they head west up Fifth Avenue, past Sunset Park and her aunt's little house—but there's no time to see Tillie now. After a few more blocks the cab crosses Main Street and then bounces over the railroad tracks.

"Turn left, turn left!" she barks, sitting at the edge of her seat. The grand hotels and opulent homes have given way to a congested area of little houses built close together, the humble residences of what Irene fondly calls "the working class," the artisans and laborers and maids who toil to keep Asbury Park functioning. Their gathering place is Asbury Avenue, where in the summer crowds swell on the sidewalks, and smells of strange foods fill the air.

They pass Looper's filling station. They pass Yelverton's store, where Frank used to work as a boy. He had a terrible time growing up. Father left when he was two; mother passed away when he was thirteen. Then he was on his own, fighting and clawing to stay alive. He dropped out of school and started running errands for the local henchmen. Most such unfortunate souls end up dead or in prison, but Frank is cut from a different cloth. Had he been born in Greenwich, he'd be a young executive on the rise, given his natural talents.

"Next left," she chirps excitedly, sitting up close to the front, arms perched on the seat. Her heart pounds like the surf as the cab swings off Asbury Avenue onto Dunleavy Street. They pass a vacant lot where the boys played ball, and then—

"That's it! That one right there!" Irene points to a two-story wood-frame building. Its paint is flaking off in huge chunks, having been gnawed by the sun and salty air. The cab stops, and Irene unfurls her long, thin body from the backseat. "I'll be right back!"

"Hey, wait!" The driver chases after her. "You owe me ten dollars!"

"Oh, can't you wait for me? The person I'm looking for might not be in."

Her voice begins to crack as she speaks, and she feels a flood of tears ready to pour forth, tears she's shed on countless nights the past month as the letters she wrote him over the Christmas holiday started coming back, marked Current Address Unknown. It was like a form of torture, having those slices of her soul go unnoticed and unread, as she imagined him in the arms of another.

"How do I know you're not creeping out the back way?" the cabbie asks suspiciously.

Irene reaches into her black leather handbag, and fishes for a velvet purse with gold tethers. In it are bills of various denominations. She hands him a twenty, without paying much attention. "Here, please wait for me."

The driver clutches the bill, and Irene flounces toward the building as if being pursued. Her short black hair, bobbed in the latest Clara Bow style, bounces with each long stride, and the bells of the dog collar around her neck jingle lightly. A wristwatch is wrapped around each ankle, just above where her crossword-style stockings are rolled down. An expert tennis player and golfer, she possesses the easy grace of a natural athlete, but she stopped going to the country club after the tedium of the members became unbearable to her. The sons of millionaires fleering in cocksure derision. The daughters of millionaires locked in vapid conversation. No, this is more to her liking. This place, this desolate, forlorn place.

Down a narrow, drafty corridor, past piles of termite dust and sand, she makes her way back to number four, where he lives. Frank Hearn. The name itself sends a shiver down her spine. Mrs. Frank Hearn. Irene Howard Hearn. Her notebooks at school were covered with these signatures, so easily did she drift off into daydream during a dull lecture. She approaches the door with trepidation, as she always did whenever they came back here together.

"You did the right thing," Irene mutters to herself, left arm raised, ready to knock on the cracked door—cracked from a bout of passion she'd never forget. It was that night they saw Douglas Fairbanks and Mary Pickford in *Fly Away Home* at the Paramount. Afterward Frank and she went dancing at Izzy's blind pig on Ridge Avenue, and she drank too much rum punch. She told Frank she needed to clear her head, so they went walking on the beach. The moon was shining bright, its reflection sparkling on the calm waters of the ocean, creating a lighted path to eternity. How she wanted him: his strong body next to hers, soft lips on her neck, warm hands caressing her. Back to his apartment they raced—she was too bashful to make love on the beach—and they tore at each other as soon as they got there. Right at the front door. He lifted her up as if she weighed nothing and somehow the door cracked. She doesn't remember it cracking. But her mind was otherwise occupied with different impressions.

But that was in early August, a lifetime ago, a world away. Now it's winter, and the summer has long since faded. But not the wild emotions, not the fervid longing. None of that has receded. If anything, Irene feels more strongly now than she ever has. *By October, he'll be a distant memory*, Aunt Tillie had told her in September, when Irene left Asbury Park sobbing uncontrollably, her body heaving in great spasms of sorrow, to return to the leafy college campus that more properly resembled a manicured jail, to live with a roommate who took no effort to be friendly, to study subjects so boring as to defy comprehension. A more insidious form of torture has yet to be devised, than placing a young woman in love a hundred miles away from her inamorata.

She knocks twice, the first knock barely a tap, followed by a more definitive rap. Silence ensues; she presses her ear against the door and listens. Somewhere in the building she hears a baby crying, but inside number four, nothing stirs. She tries again, much harder now, using the considerable strength she possesses. She was arm-wrestling champion in her neighborhood until her mother forbid her from wrestling with boys.

"Frank?" she calls out to no one, embarrassed by the timber of her voice. Too husky, makes her sound like a stevedore or something.

She waits a few minutes in the silence of her longing, head bowed, mind spinning like a top. Where is he? Why isn't he here? Has he left town? Is he dead? Like a zombie she starts walking back down the long corridor.

Should she wait for him to come home?

No, of course not. It's too frigid to be outside for very long. There's one person who'll know the latest news about the elusive Frank Hearn: Murray Redd, the photographer who introduced them.

Outside, the space where the cab once sat is now empty, but the driver didn't rob her. Her midnight-blue valise, with the Cunard Line tags still hanging off it, sits on the sidewalk, waiting for her like a faithful pet. She gathers it up and starts walking toward Main Street.

The streetcar comes to a stop in front of a cavernous two-story building painted a pale lime-green. Palace Amusements, reads a sign painted in huge black letters across the windowless brick facade. Frank Hearn hops out, hands dug deeply into the pockets of his worn pea coat. A cold wind blows in off the ocean, sending bits of garbage tumbling up empty streets. In the summer the Palace is the place to be, where couples journey down the Tunnel of Love to grope in the cool dark, but on a frosty day in late winter, the boardwalk is desolate.

Why did Ed Callahan stab him in the back? That's what Frank can't figure out. Only two people knew about the shipment from Canada: Enrico, his best buddy and partner in the scheme, and Callahan. Three, if you count Ginger, who didn't know anything until this morning. So that leaves Callahan. Callahan had to have tipped off Yoder. The two of them, they're probably dividing up their booty right now. But where? Frank's been bouncing all over town looking in all of Callahan's usual spots. It's like the man has disappeared into thin air, like he's Houdini for God's sake.

But sometimes Callahan sits in on the card game at the Palace. And if he ain't up there, then . . . then . . . Frank can't finish that thought, because he has no idea where to look next. Yoder is probably

on his way back to Trenton already, and Callahan—he could be anywhere. He liked to go into the city, he liked the steaks at Delmonico's,
he liked the Stork Club, and most of all, he liked some broad named
Hester, who used to be a dancer. Frank met her last summer. Callahan
had the guts to bring her out to the shore even though his wife was still
in town. Love can make you stupid. It wasn't like Callahan to be so
blatant. But it wasn't like him to stick a knife in your back, either.

Frank walks around to the back of the sprawling building and
then up a flight of stairs to Howie Turner's office. Howie doesn't own
the Palace but he takes care of the place in the winter, making sure nobody breaks in and makes off with the junk stacked everywhere, the
games and gambits of summer that entertain the hordes. Howie runs
his own booth, Knock 'Em Down, a bowling game no kid can ever win
because Howie weighted down the pins with melted lead washers,
making them so bottom heavy not even Walter Johnson could muster
enough gas to topple them over. As a kid Frank spent many a nickel
trying, showing such determination that when Frank got old enough,
Howie started giving him odd jobs and introducing him to the right
people. Like Ed Callahan, who took one look at the hulking man-child
and knew Frank Hearn would make a hell of a slugger. At fifteen Frank
already stood over six-four and weighed two hundred pounds, with
fists of steel and a mean streak a mile wide. Right away Callahan used
Frank to help him collect debts, and usually Frank didn't have to slug
anybody. One look was enough to convince most people to come to
terms. Callahan became like a father to Frank, which makes this all
even harder to take, like swallowing down a belt of castor oil.

Frank can hear the voices echoing down the hall, the shouts and
curses of men playing poker. Usually the stakes are small, but sometimes not, depending on who's sitting in. Frank presses his ear against
the door before he knocks, listening for Callahan. But it's impossible
to tell who's in there. His pulse starts racing with anticipation. What if
Callahan's in there and denies it all? What then? Somebody owes him
something besides an explanation. No way he's gonna tell Enrico the
booze is gone.

Frank knocks three times, pauses, then raps twice more quickly, the signal to Howie that all's clear. Not that Howie worries about cops busting up his game. One or two flatties are usually right there with him.

The voices grow silent. The door swings open. Howie takes one look at Frank and waves him on in. A thick fog of smoke hangs in the small, cramped room. Two men sit at the card table with chips stacked by their elbows. One is Detective Malcolm Wise of the Asbury Park Police Department, with whom Frank's had his share of dustups over the years. The other is someone Frank's never seen before. By the looks of it, he's some kind of flattie, in an ill-fitting pinstripe suit that hangs on him like a flour sack.

"Frank Hearn," booms Wise, "just the man we're looking for."

Howie pats Frank on the back. "He knows plenty of dames. Maybe he's seen her."

"My thoughts exactly, Howie. My thoughts exactly."

"Seen who?" Frank is confused by the good cheer Wise is displaying. After all, he's arrested Frank five times in the past eight years. They haven't exactly been sending each other Christmas cards.

"Frank, this is Sal Chiesa."

Sal Chiesa doesn't stand up to shake hands. Instead he nods solemnly like a priest administering last rites. Already Frank doesn't trust the guy.

Wise keeps talking. "Mr. Chiesa here is from Chicago and he's investigating a case. He's trying to find someone. A woman, obviously, and since you know a lot of women, it's a good thing you showed up when you did. Maybe you'd like to help Mr. Chiesa."

"Sure he would," Howie says, again patting Frank on the back. His small, trembling hands feel weightless, like the touch of a ghost. Howie's spooked by these apes. What the hell are they up to? "Frank's a good boy. He likes to help when he can."

"There's a reward," Sal Chiesa intones, before puffing on a long cigar. "Five hundred bucks."

"Not bad," says Frank. "I doubt I can help, though. I've been away on business." He flashes Wise a petulant glare, to show him he's not going to smooch him the way Howie does. Howie gets along with flatties. Always has. And they leave him alone, too. Frank knows he needs to be like Howie but it's hard, especially when men with badges come crashing through your door and take your booze.

"Show him the picture."

Sal Chiesa reaches into the ill-fitting jacket and produces a photograph. He hands it over to Howie, who then holds it up for Frank's inspection. It's a head shot of a pretty woman, pouting at the camera with a pair of full, moist lips, and a spit curl dangling on her forehead. "Appearing nightly at the Moorhaven, Miss Sally Serenade," Frank reads the caption. Sally Serenade? That's the twin sister of Ginger DeMore, is who it is. There's no doubt in his mind. But instead of saying so, Frank squints and shrugs his shoulders.

"She's a looker," he whistles. "I can see why someone would shell out five hundred plunks to get her back."

"Have you seen her around town?" croaks Sal Chiesa.

"Nope. I'd remember her if I did, too."

"Looks can be deceiving, I'm afraid. She might look like a tomato but the truth is she's really a rotten apple."

"Yeah? What she do?"

Sal Chiesa grimaces and shifts in his seat uncomfortably. "Let's just say she's a dangerous woman."

Frank nods his head in apparent agreement. "They're all dangerous, you ask me."

"She's bad news, Frank," Wise counsels him, sounding like he's really issuing a threat. "If you happen to run into her, you should beat it fast. Call me, and we'll come get her."

"Oh, I will, detective. I'd like a shot at those five hundred simoleons." He pauses a moment, as the men regard him. There's nothing left to say anymore. Either they think he's lying or they know he can't help them. It's impossible to read Wise. He's always smiling, no matter what the situation. But he's also a liar, and he's lying about Ginger or Sally or whatever her name is. She's no more dangerous than a fly. She's running from something and they're trying to find her. Well, at least Frank did his part to help her. But that's not why he came. He came for Callahan, and he's not here.

"Thanks for your time," croaks Sal Chiesa. Frank nods and pulls Howie out into the hallway so they can have a chat. Howie limps along, dragging his bum leg that went numb a few years back when some bad Jamaican rum got brought into town. People will drink whatever they can get their hands on these days. Another reason why that Canadian booze is solid gold.

"What's up, Frankie?"

"Who's the ape?"

Howie looks back at the closed door. "Some triggerman from Chicago. Works for Johnny Torrio, same as Wise."

"You seen Callahan?"

"No. Not lately."

"I need to find him."

"You look mad, Frankie."

"Damn right I'm mad. Yoder milked my load from Canada this morning. I think Callahan set me up. I know he did."

Howie digests this news for a second, his eyes contemplating the floor, like he's ashamed to look at Frank. "He owes people money, Frankie. Bad people. I hear he's in deep, on account of that broad of his. Hester."

"That don't give him the right to steal my booze, does it?"

Howie sighs the sigh of a man who's lived long and seen many injustices go unpunished. "No, it don't. I'm just saying. He's in trouble."

"Where is he hiding, Howie? I need to straighten this out with him."

Now Howie's old, tearful eyes search the ceiling for an answer. He's got a problem with his ducts, and sometimes he'll start weeping for no reason. Leaking, he calls it. He's leaking now, except it looks real. He's known Callahan a long time. Frank doesn't want to put him in the position of ratting Callahan out, but life isn't fair sometimes. Sometimes you have to choose sides.

"He's at the beach club, Frankie." Howie reaches out and grabs Frank's arm. "Go easy on him. He ain't himself these days. It happens to people. They screw up. Even the good ones."

"I just want to straighten it all out. I just want to know why he did this to me—you know I trusted him like a brother." Frank feels something catch in his throat, like he might leak out of his eyes, too. "Callahan, of all people."

"I know, Frankie."

Frank turns to leave, but feels a ghost hand on his arm.

"Stay away from that girl." Howie's voice is barely above a whisper, like they're sharing a secret.

"What girl?"

"The one in the photograph. I could tell you were lying and so could they. Be careful with that one. Wise said she killed her husband and took all his money."

"That's a lie."

Howie slaps Frank playfully across the top of his head. "Do what I tell you! There's a million broads in the world. Find a nice one. Like that college girl you were with this summer. Irene, wasn't it? What happened to her?"

"That's ancient history."

Damion Irvine is just finishing a lengthy disquisition on the sexual impulses of women when the knock at the front door startles the membership of the Asbury Park chapter of the Havelock Ellis Society, all three of them gathered around a felt-covered card table in the book-lined living room of society president Mathilde "Tillie" Howard. Tillie excuses herself, mumbling "I'm not expecting anybody" as she pushes away from the table and breezes toward the foyer.

Each of Tillie's movements and mannerisms seems vapory and ethereal, the way she tilts her head when she listens, the way her feet glide when she walks, her long, sheer dresses floating behind her like gossamer wings. Tillie has long cultivated this image of being an emissary from a spiritual realm unreachable to most mortals. Until she reached fifty, she delighted the best company in Greenwich Village with her unconventional ways. But then came the war, followed by Harding and Coolidge, and her favorite people started disappearing. Bill Haywood to Russia. Emma Goldman and Alexander Berkman went to Europe, too. Marie Ganz got married. Adolph Wolff, the Hobo Poet, died in California. More and more, Tillie Howard found herself enjoying the solitude of the New Jersey shore, the familiar patter of her life there. It's a place where old radicals can lick their wounds.

She throws open the front door, its hinges squeaking, and there stands a man wearing a Western Union shirt and cap.

"Hello, darling," she rasps, batting her eyes at the rather manly specimen who nods and hands her a telegram. She examines the envelope. "It's from my sister-in-law. When will you marry me?"

"I'll have to ask my wife first," comes the nervous response.

"Wife! Listen to you! Let me get you some money." She rummages through a drawer in a table on which sit stacks of unanswered correspondence. She finds some change and hands it to the delivery man, her fingers brushing against his palm. "This better not be bad news. Or you're in trouble."

"Yes, ma'am."

He departs, and Tillie stands in the foyer, nervously opening her telegram. Despite her brave and flirtatious demeanor, she knows that no telegram from Lauren Howard will contain cheerful tidings.

She can't read the telegram because her glasses are back in the living room, where Damion Irvine is telling his wife, Paula Lash, that soon technology will allow photographs to be sent over telephone wires. He stops when Tillie floats back in. "Is anything the matter, love?" asks Damion, smoothing his bushy mustache.

"I don't know. Yet." She puts on her spectacles and begins to read:

TILLIE: IRENE MISSING FROM COLLEGE. LOOK IN
USUAL PLACES. ARRIVING AT 3:47 P.M. LPH

"She's done it again!" Tillie exclaims, touching her cheek with her
jewel-bedecked hand. "That foolish child! Oh, what have I done?"
Tillie slumps back into her chair. She looks soulfully at the other
members of the Havelock Ellis Society.

"What's wrong, dear heart?" Paula asks, slipping an arm around
Tillie's thin shoulders.

"Irene's run away again! And it's all my fault!"

"Your niece? The one visiting last summer?"

"The same. She fell in love with a bootlegger."

"Who? Tell us more."

"You may know him. Frank Hearn."

"You mean that brutish chap with the square jaw? Murray's sup-
plier?"

"That's him."

"My, my. Your niece is slumming it."

"She thinks she loves him."

"She obviously has very strong sexual feelings for the man,"
Damion offers clinically, trying his best to sound like Dr. Ellis himself,
a man who understands the science behind sexual attraction. "They
must share a passionate intimacy based on mutual attraction—nothing wrong with that, is there?" Tillie just sighs at this appraisal, because
it's all too accurate.

"In marriage, dear, such intimacy is beautiful," Paula corrects her
husband, "but I believe the problem here is that this Frank Hearn is no
match for Irene Howard. Wanton lust without commitment is bestial.
It is no reason to wed."

"Who are we to judge their passion? Or anyone's, for that matter?
Are you disagreeing with Dr. Ellis?"

"Perhaps I am."

"They'll blame me. Is it my fault?" Tillie looks toward the ceiling
for answers, and finds instead serpentine cracks in the plaster around

the brass chandelier. "Somehow she got into her head that he was no-ble. I kept thinking she'd grow bored. Had I said anything to protest—you know how young women are. She'd have eloped there and then!"

"She fell for a noble savage," quips Damion, who then chuckles at his witticism.

"Yes!" Tillie's eyes grow wide in agreement. "That's it exactly! A noble savage."

"But what young girl doesn't covet such men?" muses Paula. "No-ble savages make the best lovers."

Damion snorts in derision. "Here we go. More adulation heaped upon her immigrant teamster. What was his name again? Roberto?" Paula and Damion openly speak of their lovers, past and present. Shunned by most society, they have found refuge in Tillie's beach cottage. Usually their badinage cheers Tillie, reminding her of days long gone, when revolution seemed possible. But this matter is serious. Lauren Howard is on the warpath, her breath hot with vengeance.

"I must find her." Tillie stands up, still holding the telegram as if it contains detailed instructions on how to negotiate these troubled waters. "She's at Murray's. That's where she'll go. That's where she went last time."

"Would you like us to help you?" offers Paula, standing up as well. Tillie begins looking around for her hat and coat, her keys and purse, items in perpetual obscurity, hidden in the shadows of her dreamy life.

"No, I'll find her, thanks. I'll call the police if I must." Tillie's tabby cat, Puddles, comes purring into the room, and Tillie bends down, scoops her up. "Oh, Puddles, we're in a fine mess. Little Reenie's flown the coop. There, Puddles, there." Like many aging spinsters, Tillie seems more comfortable cooing at animals than talking to people. Puddles starts pawing playfully at the telegram, which Tillie lets drop to the floor. The cat watches it float down, eyes alert to each swoosh. "Get it, Puddles! Get it!"

"Tillie, are you sure you wouldn't like our help?"

"No." Another sigh. "I told her she'd forget him. All sorts of nice young men are interested in her. College boys from good families. Oh, listen to me. I sound like my sister-in-law. You know what I hope? Deep down? I hope they elope. I mean it. I hope they run off together and never come back!" A tear streams down her cheek, and she nuzzles her cat for comfort. "If they love each other this much—they should never be apart. Right, Puddles?"

"So why all the hurly-burly then?"

"Because they'll blame me, that's why. They allowed her to live with me last summer. Her mother sent me a letter: 'If anything should happen to Irene, I'll hold you personally responsible.' As if I can stop love! Poor Irene. To have such a mother as Lauren Howard. And she's coming here. Oh, my. This is most dreadful. I don't know what to do. No: I must find Irene. I must try, at any rate."

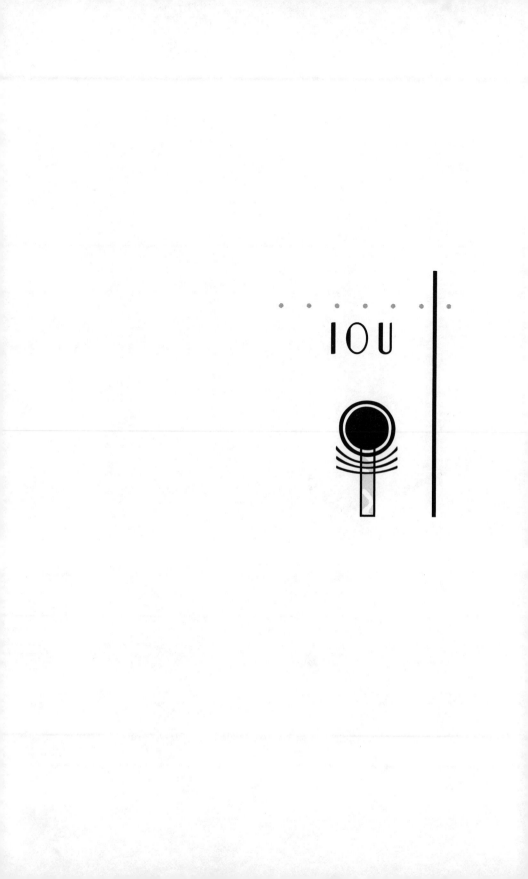

IOU

The surf is pounding the shore with furious waves. The tide is high so even on the boardwalk Frank can feel the cold spray of the ocean's anger against his face. Despite the chill, the beach reminds him of summer, of being with Irene Howard, the millionaire's daughter. She loved to walk up and down the boardwalk, and talk about the people they passed. *He's a pervert,* she might say or, *You can tell she's easy.* She didn't care about clothes or perfume or the stuff most women blabbed about. She was different, that one. She talked about psychology and evolution and Teapot Dome, and Frank didn't understand much about any of it. But he listened. It made sense that men came from apes. People got upset thinking about it, but monkeys don't seem so bad. And face it, some men acted just like apes.

But there's no reason to be thinking about her. She's back at college and probably engaged to some rich kid in a raccoon coat. The likes of Irene Howard don't marry the likes of Frank Hearn. They had a few laughs and that was that.

Up ahead he sees the beach club, a small, wooden building with arching windows seemingly shuttered for the winter. A lone figure stands sentinel by a side door. It's Scraggin, a big burly brawler Frank's known for years. And that's a very good sign. Because if Scraggin is standing guard, chances are Callahan is inside.

As Frank gets closer, a wide smile breaks out on his wind-burned face. "Hey, Scraggin," he waves to his replacement. When Frank decided he'd had enough of collecting debts a couple of years ago, Callahan hired Scraggin for some muscle.

"Hiya, Frankie," Scraggin whistles through the gap in his front teeth. "How's beeswax?"

"Not bad. You?"

"It's cold, huh?"

"You shouldn't be outside, fella. Let's go grab us some coffee." Frank pats Scraggin on the shoulder.

"Not now, Frankie."

"You said you were cold! Come on!" Frank's laying it on thick, knowing Scraggin can't leave if Callahan is in there.

"I'm fine." Scraggin sniffs and wipes his runny nose.

"You don't look fine. You look cold."

"I'm fine."

There's really only one way into the beach club, through the door Scraggin is guarding. It's been a while since Frank has had to use his fists, so he's not sure he can overpower this big hunk of lead. Maybe there's another way.

"Is he in there?" Frank nods toward the door.

Scraggin sucks on his cheeks. "Who's that?"

"Callahan. Come on, Scraggin. Help me out."

"He don't want to see nobody."

"I ain't nobody."

"He said he don't want to see nobody."

"Is Yoder in there with him?"

"He left a couple hours ago."

"He left." Frank lets these words sit like venom in his mouth, then he spits downwind, his lips feeling chapped and his face grown red from the frigid air. "I really need to see him, Scraggs. I ain't got no piece on me." He holds his hands aloft so that Scraggin can frisk him. But Scraggin just keeps standing there, hands wedged in the pockets of his coat.

"Sorry, Frankie. You know how he is."

"No, I don't know, either. I thought I did. But people change on you. Let me ask you something: Does he pay you?"

Scraggin scoffs at the question. "He knows better than that!"

"He owes you, though. Huh? Said he'll get it soon?"

"Something like that."

Scraggin is the kind who does what he's told without asking too many questions, the perfect foot soldier. Planting the seeds of doubt might work in time, but Frank doesn't have much of that left. He's got to get in that building, although the handle of Scraggin's .38 is poking up from his belt. This might not work.

Frank sighs and wipes his nose. "So that's how it's gonna be?"

"Afraid so."

"You ain't letting me in?"

"Nope."

Scraggin still has his hands in the pockets of his coat, because he's been standing out in this cold for too long, waiting on Callahan's orders for this moment should it come. Now here it is and Scraggin has left one small fissure that Frank could possibly squeeze through. Scraggin must think he can get his hands out in time to grab the piece, but what if he can't?

"Well, I guess that takes care of that," whistles Frank. Then he adds, in a voice dripping with innuendo: "I don't know about you, but I don't feel like standing out here freezing my sac off. I think I'll head over to Murray Redd's and see if he's got any new talent he wants me to meet."

"You still hang around with Murray?" Scraggin breaks into a smile, revealing the gap in his front teeth, the gap that added ugliness to his ugliness and made him repugnant to most women. He was always wanting Frank to take him by the studio.

"Sure. We could go over there sometime. You shoulda seen the dame I was with last night."

"Yeah? Did she have a set of knockers?"

"For the love of Mike, did she ever!"

Scraggin has let his guard completely down, deflated like a balloon a week after New Year's. So with one swift motion Frank brings his leg up into Scraggin's groin, and then unleashes a vicious uppercut as the burly man doubles over, hands still wedged into his pockets as he falls to the ground. Another three kicks to the ribs, and then Frank reaches down and grabs the .38 Special from Scraggin's belt. Blood is gushing from his broken nose, and he gasps helplessly for breath as Frank stands over him, hot breaths turning to thick puffs of steam in the swirling winds of the shore.

"Sorry, Scraggs. I told you I needed to see him."

Frank hops away and enters the beach club. He steps into a room filled with men sitting around card tables, a thick haze of cigar smoke heavy in the air. Voices collide, chairs scrape against the floor, matches flame and expire. A bunch of geezers is playing pinochle for one dollar per hand. Frank runs past them, and the old men only give him a cursory glance. They know when to mind their own business.

Frank doesn't know where he's going, but he sees a door marked "Private" adjacent to the small stage in the back corner. He hustles over to it, not sure where it leads but he doesn't have time to think of anything else. He busts through the door, and now faces a narrow hallway. He keeps on running, growing more confused with each stride. What kind of nutso building is this anyway?

At the end of the hall is the janitor's closet. Frank regards it with suspicion, and then reaches down to turn the crystal knob. Right then Scraggin appears at the other end of the hall. "Don't go in there, Frankie," the big man rasps, his face and torso covered with blood. His broken ribs seem to cause jabs of pain with each respiration. "He'll can me."

Frank doesn't say anything. He turns the knob and goes in, gun gripped tightly in his right hand.

When he enters, he sees Callahan busily stowing away bottles of Three Star Hennessey in a cabinet that then gets hastily locked. Four bottles remain out in plain sight, glinting like flasks of amber.

"Frank, nice to see you," the nattily dressed man calls out, sweeping his left arm in a gesture of expansive welcome that is as dramatic as it is forced. It's Callahan's manner to be overly polite in situations beyond his immediate control. His smile becomes pained and his round face seems to grow flat as if pressed on by two boards. A thin bead of sweat appears on his furrowed brow, creased by worry lines running from his bloodshot eyes. On his better days Callahan more resembles a village parson, squat, compact, soulful, with salt-and-pepper hair that lends him an air of easy friendship. But today he looks hassled, like someone with one foot in the grave.

"Those bottles look familiar," says Frank steadily, slamming the door shut with his foot, gun pointed straight and steady.

"Yoder dropped them off this morning."

"Did he? What a coincidence—I saw Yoder this morning, too. Him and his apes stopped by." He can hear Scraggin fumbling at the doorknob. Frank steps back and allows Scraggin to enter the room, grabbing him by the arm and putting the gun to his temple. "Take a look at his face, Callahan. Your mug'll look worse than him unless you start singing me a song."

"Calm down, Frank. I know you're mad. Just don't go off half-cocked."

"I told him not to come in here, boss," offers Scraggin lamely.

"He's bleeding on my rug! Can't we call an ambulance?" Callahan hands the injured man a handkerchief.

"Not till we're done here." Frank guides Scraggin down onto a chair, the gun still against his head. "Yoder took my booze, and I want it back."

"I don't blame you," Callahan warbles, smiling unctuously like a kind grocer with a light scale. "Frankie, I know you're steamed about it. I would be, too, if it was me."

"It was you, you prick! Why'd you sick Yoder on me?"

"Because, Frankie, I was a dead man if I didn't."

"You might be a dead man now. Did you think about that?"

"You're gonna kill me in front of Scraggin? And then what, kill him, too? And then walk past the twenty witnesses who saw you come in here? You're smarter than that. Come on, Frankie. I feel bad about this whole thing. I want to make it right."

"Three thousand berries, that'll make it right. That's what you owe me for the booze."

"Frankie, if I had it, I'd give it to you. How do you think I got in this mess? I'm in deep to the wrong people. Harry Lichtenstein is no one to mess with. They had me by the short hairs. I'm in trouble, Frank. Serious trouble."

"What, you don't come talk to me? You send Yoder over?"

Callahan shakes his head woefully. "It was either that or take one to the brain. I had no choice. I know I did you wrong. I'm sorry, Frankie, I'll make it right once I get everything keen. I swear I will."

This is a pathetic sight, Ed Callahan reduced to a double-crosser pleading for time and making promises he can't keep. Frank lifts the gun from Scraggin's temple and levels it at his old mentor, the man who took a boy under his wing and protected him from some of life's worst lessons. "I don't got time to wait for you, Callahan. I need that money now. If you don't got it, then Yoder does. Or Lichtenstein. Where are they?"

"Frankie, come on. I'm in enough trouble already."

"Where, goddamn it! Tell me one place to look. You owe me that much."

Callahan thinks for a minute. He looks up at the ceiling with heavy eyes, like the answer to all his problems is written above his head.

"Try Regina's." It's Scraggin, voice hard as an anvil. "I heard him say something about going there."

"Regina's?"

"Yeah. Tell him Callahan sent you." Scraggin stands up and points a finger. "You lied to me. I want the money you owe me, you liar." He reaches across the desk and picks up one of the bottles of scotch.

Callahan's face has grown a ghostly shade of white. Fine particles of dust float and twist in the air, a million mad dancers swirling around his head. He doesn't talk. He doesn't need to. His eyes say everything. They are two protruding globes of fear.

"Don't kill him until I leave!" shouts Frank, grabbing Scraggin's arm.

"He's a liar, Frankie! He told me you owed him!"

"Shoot me, okay?" Callahan has raised his arms in the air, almost like he's been crucified. "Put me out of my misery. I know I'm a bum, but let it be a lesson to you both: don't cheat on your wife. It'll just get you in trouble."

A rt Studio, the sign reads, in simple block letters that convey a certain understated elegance in contrast to the mercantile clutter of Cookman Avenue. For the past three years, Murray Redd has maintained his photography studio in the heart of Asbury Park's shopping district, snapping pictures of young women in varying stages of undress. Then he sells them to outfits in New York, who in turn sell them to outfits in Holland and France.

But it was never his intention to peddle these flesh shots. No, Murray Redd began with the purest of motives, the simple love of watching a photograph emerge from the magical mix of chemicals in a darkroom. He left his family's homestead in Seldom Seen, Montana, when he was eighteen and headed east to New York in 1898 with a burning desire to become a photographer. He had twenty dollars in his pocket, a Brownie camera in his satchel, and his mother's moist tears on the lapels of his pinstripe suit ordered through the Montgomery Ward catalog, where he'd also purchased the one-dollar camera. The suit, he realized, made him look absolutely ridiculous on the streets of the city, like a wan mortician, and this initial feeling of not belonging, of being a stranger and possibly a fraud, never left Murray, as he pursued photography with passion mixed with fear. No newspaper would hire him, and he didn't know enough people to open his own portrait studio. Murray was chased out of the most reputable gallery in town, the Camera Club run by Alfred Stieglitz. *American Amateur Photographer* turned down each of his submissions.

Failure haunted him, the specter of returning to Montana with nothing to show for himself. New York was cruel and devoured the weak with the bloodless savagery of a Bengal tiger, but then Murray got an idea. In the sordid section of the Bowery where he lived, he got to know a few women of the night. Perhaps they would undress for a dollar and a bottle of wine. Somebody in New York was bound to pay good money for these shots; he'd heard rumors to that effect anyway. So he tried it, and thus was born a career. Murray Redd would never return to Montana nor would he let the city eat him alive.

Twenty years later, having established himself with several dealers and publishers, Murray left Gotham. The Jersey shore was his new love, the sand and the breeze, and Asbury Park rollicked with lascivious energy. And since he's been here, he's made some exciting discoveries. Like Ginger DeMore, who just strolled into his studio two weeks ago and dropped into his lap like manna from heaven. Said she was friends with Fingers Finley, the piano man, and Murray's old pal from his earliest days in New York. But then Fingers went back home to Chicago, and that's where Ginger met up with the old goat. But, like so many of his models, Ginger hit upon some hard times. Murray asked her about her troubles in the Windy City but she never came out and told him straight. She hemmed and she hawed, which meant it had to do with the coppers. But he's used to that by now, listening to the oblique half-truths, the mostly fabricated tales of woe, the partial stories of How I Ended Up Taking My Clothes Off for Money.

But none of that matters to him. What matters is the photograph, capturing a slice of reality and rendering it beautiful. He's standing in his darkroom, watching photographs of Ginger DeMore develop in a shallow tray of solution as if being summoned by some unseen force. He hangs each photograph up with care, lost in the riotous oblivion of each small task, feeling like some kind of nocturnal, cave-dwelling monster toiling in slavish devotion to appease a master he's never seen. Usually Murray keeps a professional distance from his models, but this Ginger is different. Something about her is just so alluring— the way she looks into the camera like she's looking into the eyes of her lover, totally uninhibited, completely at ease, ready to explode with passion—what man had the power to resist?

So of course Frank Hearn had to ravish her.

He always scoops up all the girls Murray finds, because they seem drawn to his animal magnetism like bees to honey. Plus, since Frank always carries a bottle, he can get them pie-eyed drunk. That guy is a one-man wrecking crew. He doesn't care about Ginger, he'll forget her by next week. Look what happened between him and Irene Howard, a situation Murray still feels bad about.

Irene was Tillie Howard's niece from college and just the sweetest girl you could ever imagine. Did the camera ever love that one, a face with features so strong and delicate, aquiline nose and roseate cheeks, a bright, warm smile, perfect posture, long legs, nice bust—he even talked her into a few topless shots, a secret he'd take to his grave. Because he'd promised Tillie he'd take care of her. Irene was thinking of becoming an actress and wanted to practice in front of a camera. But instead she got all mixed up with Frank Hearn.

It was love for her, that much was obvious. Frank Hearn was all she could talk about, and as the summer wore on, Murray saw them together everywhere, on the beach, at the arcade, even at Izzy's place at three o'clock in the morning, when Murray knew Irene was supposed to be at home because no way Tillie wanted her out that late. Now Tillie was an unbroken mare herself and would spit the bit in a heart- beat, but three o'clock in the morning with a bunch of Negroes and bootleggers? And Frank didn't care. Not one bit. She's old enough to decide for herself, was his attitude.

But did he love her? Did Frank Hearn love anybody? You couldn't tell. Not with him. Maybe because he looked like such a brute. But one thing about it: that whole summer, Murray never saw him with another woman. Not one. So maybe there was something deeper, something he kept hidden away and showed just to Irene. Who almost didn't go back to college. Said she wasn't going. Said she wanted to stay at the shore, which meant she wanted to stay with Frank. Murray and Tillie had to sit her down and beg her to go, because if she didn't, her parents would probably lock her away for the rest of her life and she'd never see Frank again. Tears, yelling, more tears—but she went.

And thank goodness for that. Because it would've been his fault, Murray's fault, and he didn't want that on his record. Murray always feared that Irene would do something stupid to ruin her life. Like marry Frank Hearn. Sure, Frank's somebody you can have a good time with, but Irene Howard should marry the next president. Or a senator. Somebody with some class, and Frank, when you get right down to it, is just another thug on the shore looking to make a quick buck.

He hears a knocking. He ignores it at first, because he's put the closed sign out. But the knocking persists, in fact gaining in intensity, as if the knocker knows he's in there—a close friend, someone who knows his tendencies, knows he loves getting lost in the darkroom. So he stops and takes off his white cotton lab coat, stepping into the light with trepidation. Why would someone force him out of his cave?

At first he doesn't believe who's standing there—because he was just thinking about her. And all of a sudden, she appears. At first he's too shocked to move. He just stands there gawking. Irene Howard waves, smiling that thousand-watt smile.

"Open the door, Murray!" she yells. "I'm freezing."

He does as he's told. But it's still too strange, that Irene should show up today of all days.

"Why aren't you in college?" he chides her playfully. Inside he feels queasy, like he's just ridden one of those roller coasters at Luna Park on Coney Island. It happens when you drop from the top to the bottom.

"College is for suckers, Murray."

"Don't be ridiculous."

"Aren't you going to kiss me hello? I came all this way."

"Not to see me you didn't. Come here, you." He gives her a paternal hug and a kiss on the cheek. She feels cold, like she's been trekking across the tundra. Her nose is red and runny, and he regards her with worry. "You're one big ice cube! What's the matter with you? Here, let's get you warmed up."

"I walked all the way from Frank's apartment. I didn't see one taxi." He notices the suitcase, and slaps his forehead in mock incredulity.

"Oh my God, you're still pining for Frank Hearn? Have you lost your mind? Here." He gives her his raccoon-fur coat, and she wraps herself in it. Even on her worst day Irene Howard could stop traffic. But she shouldn't be here. He told her never to come back. She left for school in September, and it seemed like the worst was over. She wasn't going to ruin her life over Frank Hearn. But then she came back in October. And here she is again, in February. Some people never learn.

"Have you seen him?" she asks breathlessly. "Because I think he got evicted from that place on Dunleavy Street."

"That's because he's a no-good bum and you shouldn't give him another thought." He needs to get word to Tillie Howard, that crazy loon aunt of Irene's who still thinks the world is worth saving.

"I thought you two were pals. What happened, Murray? He's not in jail, is he? Is he in trouble?" She's on the verge of tears, her upper lip trembling in anguish. Murray shakes his head firmly.

"No, he's not in jail. Truth is, I don't know where he is. I haven't seen or heard from him in months." These words come spilling out of his mouth and surprise him. Maybe what she needs is some strong medicine, some castor oil.

"I love him, Murray. I know you're lying to protect me. And that's really sweet of you."

Serious situations call for serious measures. It's obvious the fantasy she's living in is all bunk, but she'll never admit it until it's too late. And since he's the one responsible for bringing them together, he's the one who's got to break them apart—for good.

"You think I'm lying?" he barks. Her eyes grow wide at this most unusual tone: Murray's voice hardly ever gets mean. "I'm not lying about this: Frank Hearn doesn't love you because he doesn't love anybody. He's taken up with some cheap floozy and they've headed off for California so she can be in the movies. I hate to be the one to tell you that, kid. But every word is true."

"He's in California with another woman?" Irene sounds like a lost little girl asking a stranger for directions. Murray feels his heart leap into his throat, but it's for her own good. She was ready to crash her boat into the rocks for no good reason.

"That's exactly right. And you should turn right around and go back to college and forget you ever saw Frank Hearn."

"He said he loved me," she whispers, looking at nothing, face devoid of emotion.

"Don't believe it. Just get on with your life. Look at you, all twisted up in knots over this bum! Dropping out of college!"

"Who is she?"

"Who's who?"

"The woman he left with."

"Some garden-variety dame. Who cares anyway? Look at you! You're still freezing! You need a hot bath. Let's get you over to Tillie's." He tries to pry her up from the stool she's sitting on but she doesn't budge.

"He said he loved me and I asked him if he meant it and he said he did."

"Forget about him! A swell broad like you! You should be marrying a lawyer, you know, a real classy chum. Tell me I'm wrong. Have I ever been wrong?"

Finally a smile breaks out, but it's not a mirthful one. More like the kind you get when you feel so bad that crying's not possible. He pats her on the back. "I know it hurts, kid. But you're better off knowing the truth." Then, out of the blue, Tillie Howard comes bounding into the shop, her skirt hiked up so she can try to run, looking all worried and fretful, but then relieved when she sees Irene.

"There you are!" she gasps. "Thank goodness. Reenie, dear, are you okay?"

Irene doesn't answer.

"Everyone's worried sick about you. Reenie? Can't you say something?" She looks at Murray, who shrugs and pulls Tillie Howard close, and the two of them have a private conversation by the front door.

"She ain't so swell," he whispers. "I told her Frank was with another woman."

"Oh, dear."

Tillie looks back at Irene. A tear rolls down her niece's cheek, and Tillie scurries over to brush it away. "It's okay," she purrs, "you can tell me all about it over a cup of tea. A nice cup of hot tea. That does the trick every time. Huh? Would you like that?"

"Only if there's arsenic in it," replies Irene acidly.

A Model T glides to a stop along Heck Street, in front of an ordinary-looking house with bay windows and gingerbread molding along the fascia. Walking past it, you wouldn't look twice. The lawn is neatly landscaped, handsome drapes hang in the windows, and the paint job is new, a bland mixture of beige and brown: nothing to arouse suspicion. In short, nothing to indicate that within is Asbury Park's most notorious bordello.

"He's in there?" Enrico asks Frank, voice quavering a little once he pulls up on the parking brake.

"I don't know. We'll find out soon enough."

"Before you go in there, promise me, swear on your mother's grave, that you're not going to kill him. The money doesn't mean that much to me, Frank."

Frank frowns at his nervous friend. He's already promised Enrico a hundred times he's not going to lay a finger on Yoder. Maybe one, but no more than that. "Just put your mask on, will ya? I don't want him to see your face."

Enrico shakes his head emphatically. "I know you got that gun. Don't use it, Frank."

"I didn't off Callahan, did I? I won't off Yoder, either. I'm just getting what's ours, is all. I'm just gonna grab him and then we'll drive out to Marlboro."

"And then what? That's what worries me, is what happens once we get out there."

"You're a pinhead. Just put your mask on and keep the car running."

Frank hops out. It's been a while since he paid Regina Royal a visit. Probably last summer, before he started up with Irene Howard. That's when he was rolling in dough, after that first trip to Canada in June. Enrico paid off his house with his cut; Frank bought a night with a cutie named Tina and an eyeful named Tanya. They were like a pair of bookends, tall, willowy skirts with shiny black hair, ready smiles, French perfume, and soft hands. It was a night he'd never forget, well worth the C-note he dropped. With that kind of bankroll, a man felt like he could do no wrong. It was a great summer, but it's been a cold winter.

He rings the bell twice quickly, waits, and then rings twice more, a signal to Regina that a former customer has come back. She throws open the big front door and greets him with a wry smile. "Frank Hearn, what a sight for sore eyes," she beams, taking his hand in both of hers and leading him into the parlor. She's wearing her trademark kimono and bright red slippers, a ring on every finger, and strands of pearls that dangle to her waist. She's not a bad-looking landlady for someone her age and she's got a sharp eye for the numbers. Word is she's put all her money in stocks and is the richest woman on the shore, save a widow or two in Deal. There's not a cop in Asbury Park who'd bust her joint, because one of her best customers is Chief of Police Byrum himself, who likes to do it Greek style, if any of these girls can be believed. Since the average hooker is more honest than the average flattie, why wouldn't it be true?

"Are you paying us a social call, Frank? Please sit down." She motions to a chair, but Frank keeps standing. "There's someone I'd love for you to meet. Her name is Karen and she just turned eighteen. She's lovely."

"I don't doubt it, but that's not why I came. Callahan sent me."

"Ed?" She begins to pout and puts her hands on her hips. "I'm mad at him and you can tell him I said so. He hasn't stopped by in the longest time."

"I'll get on him about that. But this is the jig: he needs to find Dwight Yoder. I heard he might be here. It's real, real important. I wouldn't ask unless it was."

Regina brings a hand to her lips. Her policy is never to interrupt her clients while they're engaged, a rule Frank understands full well, but since he's known Regina for the better part of a decade, he's hoping she'll bend the rule just once.

"I can wait outside, even, if that'll make things easier," he offers in an eager, compliant voice. "Just get word to him to meet me out front, you know, whenever he's finished."

She reaches up and brushes his face with her index finger. "You're a sweet kid, Frank. I've never heard any of the girls say a bad word about you."

"Why would they?"

"Let me see what I can do, darling."

"I'd appreciate it. And Regina, one more favor. Don't tell him it's me. Just say it's Callahan downstairs."

"Oh, Frank, you know I don't run a creep-joint. I can't get mixed up in something. Yoder works for Lichtenstein now, and I don't like that man and he doesn't like me." Regina looks scared. Frank takes a deep breath and gazes at the stairs. Yoder is up there, it's just a matter of flushing him out.

"Regina, this isn't something I enjoy. But if you don't get him down here, I'll go get him myself. I know you don't allow rough stuff in here, but Yoder hijacked a hundred bottles of scotch from me this morning."

Regina nods as she soaks in this information. She doesn't like Yoder, no one does. That's got to count for something. But it quickly becomes a moot point. From upstairs comes that unmistakable, high-pitched titter Yoder makes whenever he gets excited. Frank pulls out the revolver and waves Regina away. She disappears through a door leading to her living quarters, and Frank leaps into the corner formed by the stairs and the wall near the foot, making him invisible to Yoder as he traipses down, chortling good-bye and so long to his paramour. Frank can see their legs above his head, Yoder's plus-fours and two-tone shoes and her skinny calves and yellow slippers. He waits until Yoder reaches the bottom, and then springs forward with the quick-ness of a tiger felling its prey. He grabs Yoder by the neck and presses the cold barrel of the gun to his egg-shaped head.

The girl screams, but, no fool, turns tail and charges back up the stairs and out of harm's way.

"We're going for a ride, Yoder. The first stupid thing you do will be your last."

"You're making a mistake, Frank," Yoder squeals, offering no re-sistance as Frank drags him outside and down to Enrico's waiting flivver, the gun now sticking him in the ribs. They pile into the back-seat. Frank pats Yoder down and finds a .9mm Mauser, the kind the Krauts used in the war. Best semiautomatic there is. He gives it to En-rico for safe keeping. Then they take off.

"I don't have your money, Frank," Yoder pleads earnestly. "You should talk to Callahan about that."

"Shut up."

"You know I work for Harry Lichtenstein now?"

"I said shut up."

Enrico is driving a little unsteadily, swerving around the crooked sections of Cookman Avenue, nearly running off the street and onto the sidewalk. Luckily, not many people were out shopping at Stein-bach's, or there would have been a catastrophe. Maybe it's the mask messing up his sight. He's got to keep it on, though, for his own protection. On Main Street Enrico starts to gather himself together as they pass by Neptune High School. Some kids are loitering on the stairs. How simple and uncomplicated they seem. Nothing to do but hang around and talk about what the girls were wearing and how stupid the teachers are.

Neptune, Bradley Beach, Avon-by-the-Sea, across the Shark River, when the road splits and they head west, out toward the wilds of Marlboro and the old state insane asylum. Yoder hasn't said a word for fifteen minutes, which is fine, because he needs to stew in the uncertainty of his fate like a roasted pork. Maybe then he'll stop with the smart lip and come on the level. It seems to be working. Once Yoder realizes that they're headed out to the middle of nowhere, he begins to grow agitated. He looks out the window, over to Frank, and back out the window. A few more minutes elapse. He turns to face Frank, his lower lip quivering in fear.

"I'm a Fed," he croaks. "You kill me and you'll hang. If Lichtenstein doesn't get you first, that is."

"I don't care about Lichtenstein. What I want is my money. Or my booze, whichever, it doesn't matter."

"I told you I don't have it. The booze is in Atlantic City right now."

Without saying a word Frank slugs him in the nose with the base of his palm. Yoder cries out and grabs his face. Blood begins dripping down his chin and onto his twill knickers. "I don't have it! Goddamn it, Frank!"

"Where's Lichtenstein?"

"Atlantic City, I told you. Callahan owes Harry money. This was how they worked it out."

"With my booze?"

"I was just following orders, Frank."

Frank considers this explanation. Maybe he's telling the truth, and maybe he's not. Either way, there's an easy method of finding out. "Take your clothes off," Frank tells him.

"Here's all the money I got, Frank." Yoder fishes out his roll and hands it over to him, the way an altar boy might proffer a communion wafer. "That's all I got left of my cut. Two hundred bones, give or take a blow job."

"That's your cut? You're a lying mutt. Take off your clothes."

"I didn't make you for queer, Frankie."

"Are you poking fun at me, Yoder? I said get undressed."

"Ah, come on. I don't got the money, I told you that already."

Frank seizes up as if to hit him but Yoder has learned quickly and covers his face. Instead Frank presses the gun right to his temple. "You barged in my place this morning talking tough," he growls, eyes two slits of fury, "but you didn't figure I'd find you so soon. I don't care about no badge and I don't care about Lichtenstein. I'll blow your brains out right now and take your clothes off myself. Then I'll let the buzzards pick at your body for a week or so."

"Okay, okay. I'll show you I ain't got the money if that's what it takes."

A few minutes later Yoder is down to his union suit and socks. Frank goes through every pocket and doesn't find any money. But he does find something else: a piece of paper with chicken scratch written all over it.

"What's this?" Frank scans the paper quickly. A few words catch his eye. " 'I, Babe Ruth, owe Edward Callahan $7,000. June 10, 1924.' What's this all about, Yoder?"

"Something between Callahan and Lichtenstein."

"I'll say. It's an IOU for seven thousand clams that Babe Ruth signed over to Callahan. Well, well, well. Babe Ruth, huh?"

"Frank, don't get in the middle of this. Lichtenstein wants that real, real bad."

"Does he? That's a shame."

By now they've arrived to the gates of Marlboro, an imposing Victorian edifice of granite and brick crenellated walls. The asylum closed ten years ago, and all that remains is the weathered husk of the facility. No one comes out this way much anymore, except kids on a joyride looking to spook their girlfriends. A hundred yards past it the paved road ends, leading back to a sweep of desolation that stretches almost to the outskirts of Trenton, forty miles away. Enrico bumps down this path a bit further and then stops.

"Here we are," sings Frank.

"What do you want, Frank?"

"I want my dough, three thousand bucks. That's what the booze is worth."

"You got seven in your hand right there."

"No, I got a piece of paper in my hand. It's worth seven if it gets collected."

Yoder rolls his eyes in exasperation, like he's a teacher and Frank is the stupid kid who can't add. "What do you think Lichtenstein wants to do? He won't be happy, Frank. He was counting on that IOU."

"I was counting on my money, too. But things happen sometimes, don't they? He can have this back when I get my three thousand bucks."

"You're making a mistake."

"Maybe I am, but who cares? I'm done talking. You know what I want. Get out."

"What about my clothes?"

Frank reaches over, opens the door, and then shoves Yoder out like a newsboy dropping off a load of Sunday papers. Yoder goes spilling out head over heels, wearing only skivvies to ward off the cold. He ought to be good and frozen by the time he walks back to town.

Enrico throws the car in reverse and speeds backward over the bumpy surface, his eyes wide with terror. Frank puts down the gun and starts to count the money. A lousy one-eighty. He peels off four twenties and a sawbuck. Enrico backs into the front drive of Marlboro to turn around, then floors it down the paved road.

"Here," says Frank, leaning over and dropping the money in Enrico's lap.

"What's that?"

"Your share."

Enrico reaches up and tears off his mask. "How much is it?"

"Ninety bills."

"Jesus, Frank. What're you gonna do now?"

"I'm working on it."

He watches the landscape blur past, the dead, leafless trees and the brown grass. Usually when you start the day off getting laid, things work out better than this. A load of booze worth three thousand bucks has turned into ninety and an IOU from Babe Ruth. But it could still work out. The next move belongs to Lichtenstein. "They'll make me an offer for this," says Frank, waving the IOU. "If they want it bad enough."

"What if they don't?"

He looks at the IOU once again. "Maybe the Babe'll pay to get it back. Something like this floating around, he don't want that."

Enrico cranes to look at Frank. "But it's Babe Ruth we're talking about! Not some wally."

"I know. But if he ran up some big gambling debt, he won't want that in the papers. Callahan and Lichtenstein, those are some bad characters."

"You're gonna blackmail him?"

"I don't know, but I'll figure something out. I promise you I'll get our money."

"Frank, I don't want you doing anything dumb."

"Have I done anything stupid so far?"

"Yes! What's stopping them from killing you and taking that IOU? Have you thought about that? Yoder already took our booze. He'll do the same thing again, except next time he'll kill you. You left him out there with no clothes. It's freezing."

Frank scratches his neck. Enrico is a born worrier, but sometimes he brings up a good point. "I guess I can't stay here," Frank muses quietly. "I was headed for Florida. You knew that."

"Florida?" Enrico sounds excited. Frank leans forward to hear. "I saw something in the paper today—that's where Babe Ruth is headed!"

"What?" Frank scrambles into the front seat. "Say that again."

"The Yankees, they're having spring training down in Florida. St. Petersburg, Florida."

"They are?"

"I saw it in the paper."

Frank slaps his diminutive friend on the shoulder. "I should go pay him a visit then. Huh? How's that sound? I'll show him the IOU and ask three grand for it. Hell, I'll make him pay the whole thing, all seven thousand clams!"

"Don't get greedy. Just take the three."

"Why not? It's a debt like any other. The Babe won't know any different. I'll say I work for Callahan, and if he don't pay, it'll be in the papers."

Enrico shakes his head, but his admonitions bounce off Frank's sudden thrill. Florida is back in the picture, just when it seemed far, far away. The sun, the sand, the girls in bathing suits—what's not to love? And speaking of girls, this job might require the services of a curvy blonde, who could worm herself into some important information. And he's got the answer for that, too.

"Drive me by the Allison," he chirps at Enrico. "There's somebody I want to see."

"Who's that? Another one of Murray's sluts?"

"Not exactly. This one's different. I think she might be willing to help us."

The doctor descends the stairs slowly, carrying a weathered brown case with his initials inscribed in gold below the handle. The two women wait at the foot of the stairs, watching him with a careful intensity. Lauren Howard stands erect, arms folded across her chest as if held in place by glue, while her sister-in-law seems to stoop beneath a great weight pressing down on her, hands drawn to mouth to suppress a moan of lamentation. The doctor betrays no hint of his diagnosis, face remaining impassive beneath a well-tended mustache and bright silver spectacles. He is the sort of slender, dour man whose mirthless demeanor makes him immediately trustworthy in a time of crisis. And crisis this surely is. Irene Howard has promised to kill herself.

"Doctor, how is she?" asks Lauren Howard coolly, her mouth barely moving as she speaks. "Did she speak to you, I hope?"

"She did."

"What did she tell you, if I may ask?"

"She said, 'You can't help me.' "

"That's awfully rude, not to speak properly to a doctor."

"Ma'am, she's not well."

"And what's ailing her, do you think?"

"It seems to me like a classic case of neurasthenia. Do you mind if I smoke?"

Dr. Umber produces a pipe from his tweed jacket, then fishes out a pouch of tobacco.

"I'm afraid I'm not familiar with that term, doctor," says Lauren Howard. "Is it curable?"

The doctor strikes a match and lights his pipe, which he then waves about the air as he talks in a mellifluous baritone. Quickly the room reeks of Prince Albert tobacco. "It's a kind of nervous exhaustion that attacks women in highly vulnerable states and incapacitates them. They grow too weak to eat, and begin to become cachexic, which is a kind of withering. This weakness is spreading rapidly, it would seem—"

"Oh no!" gasps Tillie, tears welling in her eyes.

"What can we do?" asks Lauren Howard evenly.

"In this case, I recommend taking her to a salubrious climate, where she can regain her strength through some physical culture and a regimen of sanatives from a health spa expert in such matters."

"Can't she just rest?"

"Ma'am, it's more serious than that. She might deteriorate rapidly without the proper treatment."

"Lauren, for goodness' sake, do what he says!" blurts Tillie helplessly, knowing she should remain silent, and earns a withering glare from her sister-in-law, who above all else detests unbidden displays of emotion, the enemy of polite and cordial relations.

"I am merely inquiring about my daughter," comes the icy response. "Like any good mother should."

"Ma'am, if I may," the doctor interjects. "There is one especially prominent facility in a place most medical professionals regard as the healthiest climate in the United States—St. Petersburg, Florida. The city maintains its own spa and solarium. There she can breathe clean air, sit in the sun, and get physical culture so that she might regain her energy. That's my gravest concern at the moment, her energy. When young women grow weak, it is hard for them to recuperate fully. She's young yet, and appears capable of bearing many children. I'd like not to jeopardize her fecundity."

"I see."

"If you wish, I can contact the spa myself and arrange for your stay. She'll need no less than a month in that climate."

"A month?"

"Indeed. I gave her a tincture of laudanum, so she should be resting comfortably. But I can't urge you enough to depart soon. Tonight, if at all possible. Your daughter needs the curative powers of a strong sun and clean, refreshing air. Only then will she regain her strength."

"She'll get better then?" asks Tillie, reaching out to lightly touch the sleeve of the doctor's jacket. It feels prickly, like the stubble of an unshaven lout, like the face of Frank Hearn. "Is that your opinion?"

"Irene will be fine," Lauren Howard answers with that unshakable confidence in the power of her own will that Tillie finds so off-putting.

How can she always be so sure of herself? Has she never doubted? Has she ever exerted every ounce of her soul only to discover that it wasn't enough? Not a hair out of place, not a wrinkle in her clothes.

It's all Tillie can do not to fling herself at Dr. Umber's feet and beg him to stay, stay and watch out for Irene, sit by her, whisper to her, tell her the simple truths that so escape us in times of trouble. Tomorrow's another day. The sun will rise again. This too shall pass. "I'll make sure of that. Thanks ever so much for coming, doctor. You've been an extraordinary help."

"Shall I call the spa in St. Petersburg?"

"That won't be necessary. I can make all the arrangements."

"Very well then. Please send for me again if she should take a turn for the worse." He pulls on a long black overcoat, doffs a knit cap, and, with a polite bow, leaves the two women alone. Tillie watches him walk down the stairs, gingerly stepping over the ice, carefully gripping the handrail so he doesn't fall—how much sense it makes to approach life thus. Grabbing ahold of a rail to prevent slips and tumbles.

Tillie can feel the hot eyes of Lauren Howard burning a hole in her back, like the sun in August at midday, when the morning mist cedes to the full fury of summer.

"Who taught her to collapse like this, I wonder?" Lauren says, her angry tone leaving no doubt as to the answer. "Who filled her head with such rubbish? Because a man is unfaithful? Because a man disappoints? Certainly not I. I couldn't afford the luxury of neurasthenia." She pauses for a moment. "Whatever that is."

"Irene's not like you," Tillie says to the door.

"No, she's twice as beautiful, twice as alluring. She could have any man in the world fall in love with her. But where is she now? Ruined! Ruined in a bed in this dreary town! Do you know this summer she was to make her debut in Greenwich? Have you any idea how hard I've been working on the arrangements?"

Tillie reaches up and brushes away a tear. She won't cry in front of this woman; won't give her the pleasure of seeing the flood of sorrow she's been holding back ever since she brought Irene home from Murray's studio. No matter what Tillie did or said, she couldn't get Irene to snap out of it, to become that happy, bouncing young woman who attacked life with confidence. Sure, to have your heart broken is like having surgery without any anesthetic: they cut you open and slice away at your inmost parts. And the wounds never heal. Tillie knows that all too well. But this behavior of Irene's is so unlike her; this bizarre quest to find Frank Hearn; her decision to drop out of college when she excelled at school; her talk of suicide—there must be more than some man involved in all this—but why can't Lauren Howard see that? Something's wrong with Irene that goes far beyond Frank Hearn. Something Lauren Howard would never understand: a soul-sickness common to the sensitive few with ideals they won't carve like giblets.

"I know you have high hopes for Irene," says Tillie, carefully picking her words, finally turning to face her sister-in-law. "And I know as well she's seldom if ever disappointed you. She's in all ways a lovely young woman. Clearly there's something wrong—"

"There certainly is. And it began, I'm afraid, last summer."

"I know you blame me for all this," Tillie begins, sniffling as she goes, "but it's impossible to stop nature, Lauren. She fell in love."

"Love?" Lauren Howard presses her hands against her skirt, straightening out its folds. "She was allowed to run wild, just as I feared she would be."

"I did not allow her to run wild. I gave her room to express herself—and she fell in love, Lauren, just like we both have."

"If you let a purebred out of its pen, it will be mating with mongrels in no time. And that, my dear, isn't love."

"It's love to her! That's all that matters, Lauren. And she's in trouble. You heard Dr. Umber, she's weak and could suffer permanently if you don't take her to Florida."

"I'll do as I see fit."

These are the last words Lauren Howard speaks before turning away and walking up the narrow staircase, picking her skirt up as she climbs in mincing steps. While Tillie stands watching her in tearful sorrow, she wishes that her brother, Seddon Howard, were here, because Seddon wouldn't allow any of this. He loves and dotes on Irene, and would have booked passage on the first train south. But Seddon's in Africa, hunting elephants, having left his wife in charge.

●   ●   ●

Lauren Howard taps on the door leading into the room where Irene, her beautiful daughter, is lying in a bed. Lauren turns the knob slowly, hinges creaking when she gently pushes the door open. She peers in; Irene's eyes are closed, and her arms are resting across her chest as if she's deeply pondering some mystery.

"Irene? Can I come in?"

It's like talking to a wall. How could her beloved daughter have developed such a brooding, unreachable temperament? A thirst for self-destruction? It makes no sense at all. Usually Irene bubbled with such joy. She had her moments, to be sure, when she could get downright bratty, but Lauren liked the way Irene went after what she wanted. Unlike her brother, Ben, who still needed toughening. "Do you feel better?"

"I feel nothing." Voice as flat as the windswept plains, matching the doleful eyes that hardly blink.

"Are you hungry?"

"No."

"Thirsty, perhaps? A girl should drink plenty of water to keep her complexion clear."

"Says who?"

"Oh Irene, won't you bathe? You'll feel so much better if you did." Lauren pulls a rocking chair closer to the bed, and reaches out to clasp her daughter's soft arm, which feels lifeless at the touch. So cold, and face and hair so unkempt.

"I don't care what happens to me or my complexion."

"You don't mean that."

"Of course I do. I don't say anything I don't mean, Mother."

"Come on, there's a nice washing bowl over on the dresser and all you must do is move your feet a little." She tries to pull on the arm gently but Irene doesn't budge. She's still got some strength, so the doctor perhaps has overstated her condition. A part of Lauren still wants to believe that this episode will resolve itself expeditiously.

"I need a cigarette," announces Irene, pulling her arm away. "That's what I need."

"That's perfectly awful. But I can't say I'm surprised."

"I'm being honest. I know you disapprove of honesty."

"Stop being ridiculous. Please wash your face. I can see acne starting to form. You're so lovely, Irene. My precious daughter."

"I should've married him last October. I almost did, you know. We were going to drive to Indiana but his car wouldn't start. Oh God, this life, this world. We're all just so stupid and blind and ignorant. I should just jump off the roof."

"Don't you say that!" Lauren shouts. "Don't you dare say that!" She grabs her daughter and begins shaking her, but Irene pushes her away and Lauren nearly tumbles down. Irene breaks into a deep sob, curling up into a ball, and Lauren, speechless, stands watching her as one would a performance so horrific as to defy description. Tillie's footsteps patter as she runs up the stairs, then down the hall. She throws open the door, her eyes meeting those of Lauren Howard, and for the first time Tillie could recall, she saw in them something she's never seen there before: fear.

"Please call that doctor," rasps Lauren Howard, "and have him contact that spa in Florida. We'll be leaving tonight."

"Should I wait for you?" Enrico asks, stopping at Emory Street. The Allison is a block off Deal Lake, but the street is one-way so instead of driving around the block, Frank said to drop him off here, at the corner.

"No, I might be a while." Frank grins and claps Enrico on the shoulder. "She might need some convincing."

"I guess you'll leave after that?"

"I'm not staying here one minute longer than I have to."

"So I guess this is it."

"Yeah, for a while anyway. Looks like I'm finally getting out of this town." The two men shake hands across the seat, boyhood pals with both feet in the adult world, one a husband and father, and the other getting ready to embark on an adventure that will lead God knows where. Frank can see the worry in Enrico's eyes, like he's sure nothing good will come of any of this. Enrico was always wanting him to learn a trade, settle down with the right girl, and watch their kids grow up together. That's probably never going to happen.

"Take care of yourself, big stupid mick."

Frank gives Enrico's hand one last squeeze. "I'll get your money. I won't let you down. I swear to God I won't."

"It's not worth dying for, Frankie."

"Who said it was? I ain't gonna die, unless this Ginger dame accidentally fucks me to death."

One last laugh, then Frank steps out and watches the car pull away. It wasn't supposed to be like this. They were going to get their money and have a nice good-bye dinner, with Paula and the kids, nothing rushed, nothing panicked. A happy time. Not this. But what can you do? What's done is done. Now it's time to push on and get the hell out of town before Yoder makes it back from Marlboro. An hour, tops, is the lead Frank has.

It's another savagely cold night, and Frank walks briskly down Emory Street, hands stuffed into the pockets of the pea coat he'll burn as soon as he steps foot in Florida. It's not a long walk to the Allison, but he should be good and frozen by the time he gets there. Ginger will thaw him out. She'll wrap those thighs around him and in no time Frank won't feel the cold. Yeah, it'll be aces if she wants to tag along. Ginger DeMore can get a dead man's blood pumping. Babe Ruth'll take one look at her and it'll be like waving a red cape in front of a bull.

The other hotels Frank passes by stand in shuttered darkness, empty of life. In winter the only time people go in them is to rob them.

There's been a string of break-ins lately, with the thieves jimmying a window and making off with linens and silver. Doesn't seem worth the trouble of getting caught, but winter can be brutal around here, especially if you run out of cash. The Allison stays open year-round, one of the few boarding houses in Asbury Park to do so. It's a three-story building with a widow's walk on the roof and an inviting front porch crammed full of rocking chairs. A German woman runs it and she keeps it spic-and-span. You hardly ever see her without a broom in her hands and a frown on her face.

A half-block away Frank notices the huge black nickel-plated Jewett sedan parked on the street in front. It's got Illinois tags—isn't Chicago in Illinois? The car itself looks like Sal Chiesa, long and dark and cold. Frank is shivering now, finally overcome by the frigid air and a sudden bout of indecision. Should he stick his snout in the middle of this? He could easily keep on walking. But how could he let them kill her? He can't. It's as simple as that. He's got to help out Ginger DeMore. Sal Chiesa is a triggerman, as sure is the day is long. He's going to take Ginger for a ride in that Jewett, then it's lights out.

"Goddamn it," he mutters, pulling out the .38. "When will something go right today?"

A frontal assault won't work. If Sal Chiesa is here, Detective Wise can't be far behind. That's two guns against one. But where are those guns? Frank creeps up the front stairs, trying not to make a sound. He needs to peek through the big plate-glass window by the front door, to see who is where. Quietly, stealthily, like a big leopard, Frank haunches up the stairs, keeping low to the ground. He slithers across the porch on his stomach, making it to the window. He rises up slowly, until he gets a quick view inside.

Wise is talking to the German woman who runs the place.

Frank ducks back down. If Wise is watching the front door, he deduces, then Chiesa is upstairs looking for Ginger. Which means Frank better get upstairs pronto.

He gulps down some frigid air and feels the hard dread of the swimmer who's strayed too far from shore. This is going to be a tricky proposition. How can he figure out which room Ginger is in? Frank crawls over to the side of the porch and leaps over the rail, careful not to land in a boxwood. He runs back down to the sidewalk so he can see the whole building. As far as the windows go, only a few are illuminated. A fire escape runs down the east side of the building. Frank runs over to it and tries to hoist himself up to the landing. It's about ten feet off the ground so he's got to stand on a wooden crate he finds behind some bushes. Still, he can barely climb up, because the metal is rusted and hard to get a good grip on. Plus, he doesn't want to make a racket, because one of the illuminated windows is right there by the landing on the second floor. Hot puffs of steam come from his panting mouth as he pulls a leg up, and then the rest of his large frame. He waits for a few seconds, then creeps forward, inching toward the window. The fire escape creaks and groans at each of his steps, making Frank wince. The whole thing seems like it's about to collapse.

But he makes it to the window. The curtains are drawn but not tight. He can see between them. There's a woman reclined on a bed, reading a book. It's not Ginger. Just some lonely old crone. Time to move on up to the next window, on the third floor. The climb up is a noisy one. The stairs seem angry at him for stepping on them, and cry out in agony at each footfall. It's the salty air that makes everything corrode so fast. It doesn't take long in this town before you get rusted in place. And then you break.

The window he wants to peer into is located toward the back of the building, a corner room facing the ocean some six or seven blocks to the east. Again Frank squats down and crawls along the wall, trying not to make noise, but that's impossible. He manages to get into position so he can see into the window at a severe angle, a vantage that reveals only a portion of the room. He can't see much of anything, just the bedside table and the top half of an unmade bed.

Then he hears a gunshot.

A single blast, and a body falling to the floor. He springs up and stands so he can see directly into the room. There's Ginger standing motionless with a snub-nosed revolver in her hands, looking like she's been frozen into place, and at her feet is the lifeless body of Sal Chiesa, his gaudy pinstripe suit now sullied by a hole through the breast pocket.

Frank knocks on the windowpane. Ginger looks up and points the gun at him.

"Don't shoot me!" yells Frank as he ducks out of the way. Then he hears footsteps and he lifts his head in time to see Ginger at the window, opening the latch and pushing open the casement.

"He was going to kill me," she tells him in a soft voice, the way a child might explain how a teddy bear got shoved under a chair. Frank folds his body into the room. He rushes over to Sal Chiesa and feels for a pulse. There isn't one. Frank reaches inside the dead man's jacket and pulls out a billfold. There's a good amount of green in there, and no badge. Just as Frank figured, Sal Chiesa was no cop.

"What are you doing?" asks Ginger gently. "Are you robbing him?"

"He doesn't need money where he's going, but we sure do."

"We?"

Frank stands up. "That's right. You're coming with me to Florida." She shakes her head, like she doesn't understand what he said. She's in shock, and isn't in the condition to think. She holds the gun tightly, staring down at the man she just killed.

"Let's go! There's another one downstairs!" He takes her by the wrist and leads her to the window.

"I can't believe they found me. How did they find me?"

"We can't talk about it now. Come on."

Right as Frank is about to jump through the window comes a tender knock at the door, followed by a querulous voice. "Miss DeMore? Are you okay?" It must be the old woman who was reading the book.

Frank nods his head to Ginger, urging her to reply.

"Yeah, I'm fine, Gertrude," Ginger answers, her voice sounding unsteady and hesitant. Gertrude presses on.

"I heard a noise. It's so frightful in here at night."

Frank has made it out to the fire escape. He waves for Ginger to join him. There's shouting in the hallway: Wise is yelling at Gertrude.

He runs up the stairs faster than Frank thought he could. Frank practically pulls Ginger through the window, and then they both start running down the creaky, wobbling stairs of the fire escape. They make it to the bottom landing and without hesitating they both jump down to the ground, rolling when they hit.

Wise fires a shot from the window but misses. Frank pushes Ginger over to the corner of the building with one hand, and with the other takes a mostly blind shot up at Wise. The cop cries out, clutching his knee, crumpling to the grated surface of the fire escape. Finally something went right. That was the luckiest shot in the world. Probably shattered his kneecap, since it was a .38.

"You're a dead man, Hearn!" Wise bellows like a bear. "You hear me! Dead!"

"Let's go!" he says to Ginger, taking her by the hand and leading her into the night, down Emory Street and over toward the frozen lake.

"Where are we going?" she asks, panting heavily, and sounding like she's not sure about anything. Not that he blames her. He's not sure what he's doing, either. But if he acts scared, she won't trust him. And right now, she's got to. For better or worse, they're in this together.

"I told you: Florida. I hear it's nice this time of year."

"Are we gonna run there?"

"If we have to, yeah."

LOSING
· · · · · ·
WEIGHT

A woman sits perched on each arm of the large leather chair the big man occupies, one dressed in canary-yellow satin, the other wearing puce bengaline crepe. Each displays a sly, abstracted smile and strands of gleaming pearls that swing against Babe Ruth's ruddy face whenever they lean down to kiss him or whisper in his ear. He calls them both Dora, after the heroine of the comic strip *Dumb Dora,* but they don't seem to mind that he regards them as interchangeable. In return they fondly call him Walt, after the down-in-the-mouth character from *Gasoline Alley* who can't find true love.

"That Walt's something, huh? Couldn't get his dick wet in a monsoon!" the Babe roars in delight. "You think I look like that chunk?"

"No, honey. You're danged pretty."

"Real southern belles! How about these gals!"

A huge cigar is wedged in his mouth, so that he has to talk through his clenched teeth. But no one at the table is actually talking, not while the cards are being dealt; all yell over the music provided by a trio from Memphis, each of whom will be well-paid for their efforts. The Babe's made sure of that, because he wants music playing during his party in room twelve of the Fordyce Bathhouse in Hot Springs, Arkansas. It's his last night in town, and he wants it to be memorable.

Tomorrow morning he leaves for St. Petersburg, Florida, and the start of another season of baseball.

Waiters have brought in a dozen pans of barbeque ribs, six whole chickens, countless trays of oysters and clams, mounds of fried potatoes, every can of Russian caviar that was to have been served the next night at a party for the Gorries of Philadelphia, in Hot Springs celebrating their twenty-fifth wedding anniversary. The Babe paid the waiters fifty bucks each to break out the stash of fish eggs, and then personally knocked on the Gorries' door and insisted that they join him in his room, where already assembled were the Babe's golfing and gambling buddies and a fresh supply of girls from the Southern Club, a gaming palace that catered to man's enjoyment of life.

The Gorries didn't stay at the party long. They left after the Babe wagered that he could eat an entire chicken in five minutes without belching. Having performed this feat, he then stood on a chair, roared like a lion, and bellowed: "Any women who don't want to fuck, leave." The only member of the distaff to do so was Mrs. Gorrie, whose plump face turned crimson with shame at hearing this hero to children, who was married at that, use such unspeakable vulgarity. Mr. Gorrie hustled her out, but before they left, the Babe hurried over and thanked them for coming, a woman draped on either side of him. "It's been real swell," he said, shaking Mr. Gorrie's sweaty hand. Then he kissed Mrs. Gorrie on the cheek, slapped each of his female companions firmly on the flanks, and carried them back over to the band, where he stood gyrating as he picked up a bottle of whiskey and sucked down a good portion of it. Then the card game started, a game still in progress, a game the Babe is losing badly.

"Looks like you'll owe me next year's salary too, hoss," crowed Edmund Ruffin Taylor, part-owner of various Hot Springs establishments, including the golf course he and the Babe and whomever else played each morning, the dew on the grass sparkling like a field of diamonds. The Babe usually showed up late, half falling out of his clothes, a sheepish grin on his face telling the rest in his foursome that his night had been long and enjoyable. "Got to get the blood flowing, boys," he'd say excitedly, before taking out his driver and teeing his ball up. He'd swing from his heels, in a long, loping way that resembled the mighty cut he took at a baseball, feet close together but somehow perfectly balanced, totally in control of his body. But not his appetites. The Babe had showed up at the resort nestled between the Zig Zag Mountains weighing exactly 256 pounds, and yesterday, before he jumped in the hottest spring coming from the ground (142 degrees), he weighed 238 pounds, after four weeks of jogging and calisthenics he'd been doing with Ritzman, the expert on physical culture at the Fordyce. He was still twenty pounds over his playing weight.

"It ain't over, Ruf!" the Babe growls, pointing his cigar for emphasis. "Not till I says it is. I'm getting my money back, sure as the sun rises in the east."

"Well, deal then, cowboy. I ain't got all day."

Already the slugger feels the cold coming on, his throat scratches and hurts a little when he swallows. His eyes are watery and his nose is runny. Maybe he's running a fever, his face is flushed enough for one. Probably got it a couple days ago when he had to rush out of the steam bath without taking a shower first to gradually cool down, and then went right outside where the cold air disturbed the natural flow of his temperature—and Ritzman trailed him all the way out of the building, imploring the Babe to come back and allow his body to adjust to the extremes. "Sir, you can't be hot one minute and cold the next! Sir, your body can't take it! Sir, I beg of you, ten minutes, that's all I ask!"

But it was too late, the Babe had to be at the Ohio Club for a date with a fascinating broad who understood she was supposed to get on her back. Lord, she was sweet as apple pie on a Sunday afternoon. Long and thin, shaped perfectly, with an ass that seemed to wink at you— What time is it? he wonders suddenly, seized by a panic so severe that he stops shuffling the cards, causing Ruf and the others to look at him cockeyed.

"What's wrong, slugger?" asks Ruf, himself pawing at a showgirl, a dancer from Texas on her way to Broadway. The Babe had been with her last week, but now he's glancing nervously around the room, oblivious to all.

"What damn time is it?" he shouts at the ceiling.

"Two," comes an answer.

"Shit!"

The Babe drops the cards and stands up without warning the women draped on him, who go tumbling away as he rises up, a look of fear etched on his usually amiable face. "Stop the blasted music!" he shouts, waving his massive arms. "Stop, stop!" The band puts down their instruments, shrugging at one another. The Babe sweeps across the room, saying: "Everybody get the hell out! I got something to do!"

A muttering breaks out, sounding like the hushed whispers of conspirators engaged in a secret plot. People stand up and begin rummaging for belongings.

"Not you," the Babe barks, pointing at the woman with the puce dress. "You stay. Everybody else, go."

The Babe turns his back on the party and walks over to one of the tall, arched windows that overlook the Grand Promenade, a bricked path that winds through the parterre gardens to the various springs and surrounding forest. From behind approaches Ruf, with an arm around his date, who has trouble maintaining her balance. She breaks free from Ruf and begins to attempt a pirouette.

"What's wrong, slugger? What's got your gizzard?"

"I got to call somebody," comes the curt answer. The dancer nearly falls into a piano, but grabs the keyboard to right herself. Clanging notes issue forth. The two men look at her, and she giggles to herself, sitting down as if to compose a song.

"Oh. And I was winning, too." Ruf chuckles, knowing not to press too hard whenever the Babe slips into one of these moods, a veritable darkness that contrasts starkly with the usual glow of his omnipresent smile. "Well, take care, big boy, and have yourself a great season with them damn Yankees." Then Ruf extends his hand and, turning, the

Babe clasps it and they share a powerful shake. Finally a small smile returns.

"I hope none of your broads gave me a dose of the clap, you cracker."

"Ah hell, a little mercury never hurt nobody. Clear you right up. You come on down next year, and we'll whip you back into shape!"

The two men enjoy one last laugh, and then Ruf walks over to the piano to collect his companion, who's drifted into a closed-eye reverie as she softly taps on the keys. "We got to go, sugar," he says, but she keeps on playing a sad song, almost gentle in its sadness. The Babe closes his eyes and thinks about what he must do. What he must say.

"I just made that up," she says, throwing back her hair as she stands up. Soon she is gone, along with everyone else, except for the woman in the puce dress, who slumps into a loveseat and begins flipping through the latest edition of *Photoplay*. The Babe walks over to the big, round table where the food sits; it's been mostly decimated but a few morsels remain. He picks up a clump of chicken skin and pops it into his mouth, then wipes the grease from his lips with the back of his hand. He scoops up some potato salad with two fingers and licks them clean. "I got to make a call first," he says to the woman. "I won't be long."

"Okay." She never looks up from the magazine.

The phone sits on a bedside table. He eases his body down onto the mattress, and for a moment he thinks about just drifting off to sleep. His face feels hot, and his mouth is parched. He remembers Ritzman yelling at him about the extremes, in that high-pitched voice of his. A good egg, Ritzman is. Babe sniffles as he picks up the phone, placing the receiver to his mouth and the cup to his ear. "Operator, yeah, connect me with New York. The number? Yeah, it's, ah, Bryant-6743. Okay. You have a nice night, too."

He smiles over at his guest, sitting with legs crossed over the arm of the black-and-white checked loveseat. Her eyes are closed; has she fallen asleep?

"Hey! You!" The Babe whistles, a piercing screech that could wake up a bum sleeping in the rafters of Yankee Stadium.

She jerks herself up, startled.

"You still with me? Come on over, toots. What's your name anyway?"

"Dotty."

"Come on over. You're awful pretty." He pats on the mattress, indicating the spot where he'd like her to sit. She walks over, her face still sleepy, and sits down right as the person on the other end of the line answers. The Babe drapes an arm around her and winks. "Why don't you slip out of that dress? Can you do that for me?" Then into the phone he shouts:

"Hey there! Did I wake you up? I'm sorry. Yeah, it's late."

Dotty stands up and kicks off her shoes.

"We had a little party, a few eggs dropped by, we played cards. I miss you, too. I know. Yeah."

Dotty pulls the dress up over her head and lets it drop to the floor.

"Nothing's wrong. I'm just tired. Got to leave tomorrow for St. Pete. Yeah, she'll be there. I can't tell her to stay home, can I? Claire, I thought you understood. She's still my wife. Can you hold on a second? I got to do something real quick. It won't take long, toots. Trust me."

The Babe pulls Dotty over and gives her a kiss, as his hands explore beneath her beige camisole.

"You still there?" he asks. "Nothing. I just had to do something. Sure, I'm alone. Claire, I'm alone. Ruf was here and some of the other fellas, and we played cards. I lost. I been losing a lot lately but my luck'll change. It always does. Hey! I got another letter today from that shylock, Lichtenstein. Saying I owe him seven thou. I don't know what he's talking about, Claire. Soon as I get to St. Pete, I'll tell Barrow to look into it. That pencil-necked soak don't do squat as it is."

Dotty now stands before him completely undressed. Babe grabs her and pulls her onto the bed. "Well, I better put myself to bed. Gotta hop on the train at the crack of dawn. I know. I can't help it, Claire. She's still my wife. I love you. Okay. Bye now, sweets."

He hangs up the phone. Dotty is examining the cuticles on her long nails, like she's bored and waiting for a bus.

"Now that I'm warmed up," the Babe says, "how about we play a real game?"

DREAMS
· · · · · ·
IN A BOX

The lights of Manhattan glow in the distance like fool's gold, sitting bright on the horizon of vast blackness. It's nearly three o'clock in the morning. Enrico's trawler has plied the rough waters of the Atlantic for the last three hours, and it hasn't been easy on any of them. After all, it was just a couple of days ago that Frank and Enrico made this same perilous trip, and here they are doing it again, getting lashed by the icy winds and tossed about by the angry swells. Everyone is bone tired, hungry, and angry. Enrico is mad at Frank for making him take this midnight run, but what choice did Frank have? How was he supposed to know he was walking into such a mess at Ginger's boardinghouse? They had to leave as soon as possible. Taking a train was too risky. Same with traveling by car. So that left the fishing boat.

From the small cabin Frank looks back to the stern. Ginger has been seasick since they left the Shark River, leaning over a bucket, a blanket wrapped around her heaving shoulders. There's not much he can do for her. Things should get better once they enter the harbor. The swells will die down, and the trip should be smooth all the way to the city.

"It's not long now," Frank tells Enrico, who grunts from his perch at the helm.

"I still got to get back home."

"You should rest a few hours before you go back."

"I got things to do back at home, Frank."

Frank knows when to shut up. There's nothing he can say to make things better—the only trick up his sleeve is getting the money. Only then will Enrico forgive him for this mess. Paula, too. She was mad when he came barging in, a strange woman in tow. She was getting ready to put the kids to bed. Frank could see in her eyes the anger, the disappointment. She was counting on the money, even though she didn't want Enrico to go in the first place.

"Let me go check on her," says Frank, opening the small door and stepping down to the deck. Ginger pushes away from the bucket and curls up in a ball. Frank kneels down next to her and pulls the blanket up to her neck.

"We're getting close," he says, brushing her spray-damp hair. "The ride won't be nearly as rough."

"Aren't you a nice boy," she croaks miserably. "I was just starting to enjoy myself."

"Yeah, this is a real joyride."

She pulls herself up, and falls into his arms like a rag doll. She seems spent, and he's exhausted, too. How are they supposed to make it to Florida? There's a mail train leaving at dawn, and they'd better be on it. It's the cheapest way to get there, and if they miss that train, they'll have to pay double for tickets.

"Don't you get it?" she whispers in his ear. "They found me once, and they'll find me again. Except now you'll get it, too."

"No one's laying a finger on me. Florida is a big state and a long way from here."

"It doesn't matter. You're making a mistake, Frank. You should just throw me overboard."

"Who's looking for you? Who did Sal Chiesa work for?"

She breaks away from his embrace, eyes narrowed in suspicion. From off in the distance comes the thunderous bellow of a steamer, alerting small crafts of its approach. Even at this time of night, the harbor bustles with activity.

"How did you know his name?" she asks.

"I ran into him yesterday. I never seen him before that. He showed me your picture." He pauses a few beats, then adds: "Sally Serenade? Is that your stage name?"

Tears start to stream down her face. She's a total wreck now, and Frank feels like a rube for saying anything. Now how's he supposed to cheer her up? Enrico's mad, Ginger's mad—can't anything go right? He stands up and looks back at the faint beacon from the lighthouse at Sandy Hook. Somewhere in that darkness is the Jersey shore, the only place Frank's ever known. His mother is buried back there. Maybe his father, too. Howie Turner said the old man ended up at Rahway, which is just over to the leeward side. Frank's eyes drift to some random lights. It'd be nice to know where he went. He used to think about his old man plenty. He used to dream that he'd come back to the shore one day, pockets stuffed with money. But not lately.

"I'm sorry, Frank," Ginger says, tugging at his pants.

"It's okay. We're just tired. We'll make it, though. I promise you we'll make it. Everything is going to work out fine."

———

An **Asbury** Park black-and-white and a Chrysler with government tags pull up in front of a dilapidated building on Bangs Street. The Monroe, a sign reads, but it dangles tenuously from a rusted chain, hanging perpendicular to the cracked sidewalk, like a suicide vowing to jump. Most of the shutters also seem ready for the scrap heap. Screens flap helplessly in the wind and a few windows are busted.

A man steps out of the patrol car and inspects the building with disgust. "He lives here now?" Malcolm Wise asks, pulling a pair of crutches from the backseat.

"That's where I found him yesterday," answers Dwight Yoder, getting out of the other car. His nose and several fingers are bandaged from the frostbite he suffered, courtesy of Frank Hearn. He'd be in worse pain except for the morphine he got at the hospital. That's where he ran into Wise. Unbelievable that Frank Hearn would put them both in there on the same night.

Wise hobbles toward the building. "I thought Hearn had more class than this."

"I guess you don't know him that well."

"I don't want to know him at all. It wasn't him I wanted anyway. It's the girl he's with."

"I just want him."

They already know Hearn isn't there; Asbury Park cops sat on the place last night. He never came home. But the question is: Where is he? He never got on a train, and roadblocks set up on Main Street, north and south of Asbury Park, turned up nothing. It's like Hearn vanished into thin air. Both Wise and Yoder feel tremendous pressure to find him, but for different reasons. Although they don't much like or trust each other, they realize they have to work together to get what they want.

Standing inside the front door is a patrolman. Wise tells the kid to go grab a cup of coffee, so he and Yoder can go have a look at Hearn's apartment. Wise eases the crutches down the long, dirty hallway, following Yoder's lead. The doctors said he needed to stay in the hospital for a week. They said he was risking infection if he didn't keep his leg elevated. But you don't send a boy to do a man's job. The only person Wise trusts to search Hearn's apartment is Malcolm Wise. This is just too important to the people in Chicago, especially now that Chiesa is dead and the trail has gone cold. Infection or no infection, Wise wasn't staying in that hospital, getting sponge baths from some hag with a mustache thicker than a Fuller brush. His leg is throbbing; he'll rest once he finishes this.

Yoder opens a door and they step into a typical low-rent efficiency, cold as a witch's tit and dustier than a sawmill. There's a stove, a chifforobe, a sink, a bed.

"Looks like Hearn touched bottom," Wise sniffs.

"Yeah, he liked to spend it as soon as he got it. He considers himself a real Valentino with the skirts."

Wise frowns at this exchange. It wasn't long ago that he was running Hearn and Yoder in for various infractions, but now all of a sudden Yoder has a badge and can act like he knows onions about police work. "Let's just figure out where he is."

Wise starts going through the chifforobe. There isn't much to search, just some moth-eaten clothes and Swiss-cheese socks. Nothing smells very good, either.

He turns around and finds Yoder on the ground, looking under the bed.

"Hey, a shoe box," he calls out. He pulls it out and the two men converge to examine it. Inside are all sorts of brochures and magazine articles about Florida real estate. Now that's a clue even Yoder can decipher.

"I would venture a guess he's headed south," says Wise. "But Florida is a big state."

"Yeah."

"Maybe he's written something down on one of these things. Maybe he's got one city in mind."

Yoder starts scratching his chin. Wise can tell he's got something cooking in that egg-shaped head of his, some information about Hearn he isn't willing to share. "Sure, we should look through it," Yoder replies. Then he picks up a brochure and gives it a cursory glance.

Wise stares at Yoder.

"What's your beef? Why are you looking at me like that?" Yoder's voice goes up an octave.

"You know something, don't you?"

"I don't know where Hearn is, if that's your point."

Wise grunts and picks up a brochure from the shoe box. But he's not paying too much attention to it, because he's trying to remember what Yoder was talking about last night. They were both pretty fuzzy from the medicine and the pain, but Yoder mentioned something about an IOU Hearn stole from him. It's the reason he wants to track Hearn down. It's worth a couple grand, and belonged to Harry Lichtenstein.

"Nothing so far," Yoder offers passively.

"Keep looking."

What was it about the IOU? Wise can't remember and it's driving him nuts. Cops are supposed to be smarter than this. They're trained to observe the smallest details. Things that seem unimportant at first blush might become instrumental in time. That's how he busted up that ring of safecrackers in Old Town. He found a box of matches and tracked it down. But when it came time for promotions, Wise was passed over. That's when he flipped and started working for Torrio.

"You got anything yet?"

Yoder sounds like he's in a hurry, like he's got someplace to go.

"No, just a bunch of snapshots of palm trees. What about you?"

"Same." Yoder tosses his brochures back into the shoe box. Wise hates to do it, but he's got no other choice. He's got to find that girl.

"You know, there's a reward of five hundred bucks for the girl."

"Yeah?" Yoder bites his lower lip.

"Tell me what you know. It ain't Hearn I want. You and Lichtenstein can do whatever you want, and since he shot me, I'll cheer you on. But I need to find the girl, which means I need to find Hearn."

Yoder breathes heavily through his nose, snorting like a bull, as his face twists into a strange smile. "Five hundred, you said?"

"Cash."

"Okay, here's the thing. I think Hearn's gone to Florida to find Babe Ruth."

"The Babe?"

"Sounds crazy, but that's what I think. That's whose IOU he took off me. I mean, it's obvious he wanted to go to Florida. And I just happen to know the Yankees are training down in St. Petersburg. That's the first place I'll look."

Wise reaches inside his jacket and pulls out a bankroll of cash. He peels off five C-notes and hands them over to Yoder. "You going down there, too?"

Yoder shrugs. "It's not that easy, but I've got to find him. Lichtenstein wants that IOU back."

"I'll let you know what turns up. Maybe it'll save you a trip. I'll have some men looking first thing."

"What will that cost me?"

"Nothing. Consider it a favor."

Tears stream down Yoder's chapped face. "This cold—I should go down to Florida no matter what. To get warm and watch some baseball. And I need that IOU. I wouldn't mind taking it off Frank Hearn's corpse."

Wise winces as he stands up. "Shoot him in the knee before you kill him, if it ain't too much trouble."

FLIM

FLAM

Lauren Howard puts down the Edna Ferber novel she's been reading in the several hours since lunch. For her part Irene has done little save stare vacantly out the window, sighing plaintively between periodic catnaps. The laudanum seems to have calmed her nerves. Last night she went without complaint from Tillie's house to the waiting cab that drove them to the city. In Penn Station she slept on a bench until the Orange Blossom Special left at midnight. She continued sleeping as the train plunged southward into the blackness. It's always good when a child sleeps. They can't get into trouble then.

Dark, tormented thoughts continue to hound Lauren like a pack of rabid dogs. What if Irene never gets well? What if she remains in this manic state? Could lying beneath the sun, this so-called "heliotherapy" Doctor Umber spoke of, actually help a person recover lost faculties? What if Irene got worse? And of course there's the ghastly example of Leopold and Loeb, those two well-connected and handsome prep school students in Chicago who last year murdered a fourteen-year-old boy just for the sake of killing. Lauren followed the case closely, confirming as it did her mistrust of a world that could produce such godless monsters. She blamed the parents, who must not have reared those two cold-blooded killers with the firmness children require. Now Irene has veered off the road. Was there any hope?

She looks over at her daughter, still slouched low in her seat, still staring out the window. It is almost time for dinner; Lauren made reservations for 6:30. They'll need to get dressed, and Lord knows if Irene packed anything decent to wear besides her usual assortment of faddish habiliments.

"We'll need to get ready for dinner soon," she announces.

"I'm not hungry," says Irene flatly.

"You need to eat, dear."

"I don't feel like eating, Mummy."

This won't be easy, Lauren tells herself. Be patient. She's a sick child who needs help. The doctor said so. But still, a part of her wants to take Irene by the shoulders and just shake her until she snaps out of this. How could she allow some two-bit ruffian to break her heart? It's monstrous. Meanwhile there's Jimmy Woodman, who's head-over-heels in love with Irene, and she won't give him the time of day. Jimmy goes to Princeton and his father is a very successful banker. He could have his pick of toothsome damsels, and the young lady he chose would be very lucky indeed. But Irene couldn't care less. She fell for a bootlegger. Monstrous.

"I'll use the bathroom first," Lauren says, trying her best to sound cheerful, "and then you may. We older ladies require more time to become beautiful."

Irene doesn't laugh. She just blinks a few times with eyes as wide as marigolds. She looks more alert now. Maybe she's coming to her senses.

Then there's a knock at the door. Lauren steps over to open it. Standing before her is a stocky man in a brown suit. Behind him are two porters. He shows her some identification, proof that he's with the railroad. "Sorry to bother you, ma'am, but I'm letting all the passengers know that we might have a jewel thief on the train."

Lauren brings a hand up to her mouth. "Oh dear."

"A lady has reported some things missing. So we need to take precautions. We do have a safe if you have any valuables you'd like to store."

"I don't, no." She turns to face Irene. "Do you have anything, dear?"

Irene shakes her head no. Lauren thanks the man and shuts the door, making sure to lock it. "A jewel thief on a train," she mumbles. "You're not safe anywhere these days, are you?"

"I wonder if he's handsome."

"Oh Irene! What a dreadful thing to say!"

"He sounds like an exciting man to me. Jewel thief. It has a certain ring, doesn't it?"

"You're trying to provoke me, young lady, and it's starting to work." Lauren can feel the anger rising up in her. But she mustn't show it; she must suffer this insolence, lest she engage her daughter in a screaming match. They just need to get to Florida without any mishaps. An uneventful train ride. Calm nerves. Good food. Rest.

"I hope I get to meet him," Irene continues, obviously enjoying herself. "At least he won't be boring. And think of the jewelry he'll give me—I'll look like a queen!"

"I'm getting dressed for dinner. I suggest you do the same."

"Okay, Mummy."

Lauren steps into the small bathroom where she conducts her toilet. She brought only one dress with her because she had had to pack so quickly to catch the train to Asbury Park. She washes her face and pats herself dry with a soft, plush towel. She applies her makeup carefully, although she has trouble getting her hands to stop shaking. It's like they are obeying some other person. Lauren puts down the lipstick, takes a deep breath, and looks at herself in the mirror. Those wrinkles around her mouth—if she could just get rid of them! The cream she bought isn't doing a thing. Emily Futt went to Mexico for a special treatment. She doesn't look much better, though. She's shriveling up like a prune, too. You're only young and beautiful for a short time, something Irene doesn't understand.

Lauren steps back out. Irene has changed clothes. She's wearing a red satin dress with a scoop neck, her stockings are rolled down to her ankles, a white cloche hat is pulled tight against her head, strands of fake pearls dangle around her neck, and she's wearing a—dog collar? Oh dear God. It's black and leathery, studded with rhinestones, and even has a set of tags on it, which jangle when she sits down to pull on her galoshes.

"Ready whenever you are," Irene sings merrily.

The sound of conviviality ripples across the dining car, its fifty tables covered with brilliant white tablecloths, sparkling Sèvres china, and art moderne ashtrays. Candles flicker and dance as the car hobbles down the rickety tracks, the train attaining a top speed of fifteen miles per hour. Beneath a scalloped ceiling buttressed by mahogany beams, passengers dine on roasted chicken tarragon, oysters florentine, and penuche; many have opened bottles of wine and champagne, or have poured themselves cocktails from elegant silver flasks. Thick velveteen drapes hide them from the strictures of the Volstead Act, which most support in public and violate in private. Attentive waiters roam the aisles nattily attired in white frock coats and black bow ties. Talk of Mellon's tax-cut plan meshes easily with discussions of real estate prices in Florida, like hand slipping into glove. At one table, however, two women are wearing expressions of dolorous incredulity, mouths slightly open, eyes wide. The younger of the two seems almost inconsolable, on the verge of tears. Her dining partner, attired in a soft pink crepe dress with a dropped waist, does her best to offer support.

"That is terrible news!" Lauren Howard gasps, touching her mouth solemnly with a napkin. "I was hoping they'd get him out alive. His poor family! Those miners have a most difficult lot in life."

Floyd Collins didn't make it after all—he'd been trapped in a cave outside Louisville for the past two weeks, following a cave-in at the coal mine where he worked. Frantic efforts to reach him apparently had not succeeded. Terrible, terrible.

"I just had to tell somebody when I found out—I've been praying for weeks—do you think it's true what they say?" Helen Ruth's eyes flash with awe. She seems to be a kind and generous young woman. Lauren leans closer to better hear her. The dear speaks in a soft voice.

"What do they say?"

"That Floyd Collins is really Jesus come back to earth, and that the world's coming to an end."

Lauren Howard sits back up. "I don't know what to believe anymore."

"Neither do I."

"At least he's not suffering," Lauren hastens to add, trying to sound optimistic but not really succeeding.

The waiter comes and removes their salad plates. "Shall I take this one?" he asks, nodding toward Irene's untouched salad. She said she had to use the restroom but hasn't come back yet. Lauren is trying not to worry. But with that jewel thief on board, and her condition—how is a mother not supposed to worry?

"Please," Lauren answers. He picks up the plate and leaves.

"So where is it you are headed, Lauren?" Helen asks, changing the subject away from Floyd Collins.

"St. Petersburg."

"That's where I'm headed, too. It doesn't seem like we'll ever get there. This is the slowest train I've ever been on."

"Yes, this is a long trip." Lauren pulls back the drape and looks out the window. The flat landscape goes tumbling by. It's been hours since they passed any sort of town worth mentioning.

"Is there something wrong?" asks Helen, who's picked up on Lauren Howard's unease.

"Oh, no. It's just the weather is so beguiling and balmy—this would be a lovely spot for a vacation." She lets the drape fall back into place.

"Isn't that the reason you're going to Florida?"

"In a sense, it is. One might say that."

"Isn't that your daughter traveling with you?"

"Yes, it is."

"What a lovely creature! Her cheekbones are remarkable—and so tall! I bet the boys have been flocking to her."

Lauren Howard looks down and smoothes out the wrinkles in her dress as she talks. "Irene has drawn the interest of many eligible bachelors, from outstanding families, but she's spurned them all." Then she looks up, straightening the silverware arrayed before her.

"I bet my daughter ends up just like that. She's a wild one."

"How old is she?"

"Oh, she's four."

"I'll wager she's gorgeous, like her mother."

"Oh, I don't know." Helen forces a laugh. "I miss her terribly. She's staying with my mother back in New York."

The waiter then brings out the entrees, although neither Lauren nor Helen has much of an appetite. Both pick up knife and fork and begin poking at the food, eating little bites and drinking copious amounts of tea. The truth is, both would prefer to be dining alone, but there wasn't space enough to accommodate their requests. So they must soldier on, sturdied by politeness and niceties.

"So how old is your daughter?" asks Helen.

"She's twenty."

"At least she didn't do what I did—run off and get married at sixteen."

"Did your family approve of the match?"

"No, not in the least."

"Did you elope?"

"Practically we did. We got married three months after we first met."

"You married him after three months of courtship?"

"It happened so fast. It was like falling down a flight of stairs."

"If Irene eloped, I don't know what I'd do."

"She won't. She seems like a smart kid. She goes to college, didn't you say?"

"You don't know," Lauren Howard says gravely, holding her knife up as if she intended to plunge it into her heart. "She's already fallen in love with the wrong man—a common bootlegger! She was ready to be his wife, until he took up with another woman. Oh, I shouldn't talk about this. I wonder where she went running off to. Her food is getting cold. Maybe I should go check on her. If you'll excuse me."

Irene Howard stands at the rail of the observation deck, an enigmatic expression etched on her face, as if she might either laugh or cry or both.

"If you must know," she says to a man who's just sidled up to her, "it's a dog collar. And I like it."

"I didn't say I didn't like it. I said: that's unusual."

"What's your name anyway?"

"Ellis Wax."

"Wax?"

"I know, it's a strange name. But it fits me fine. When wax melts, you can make anything you want out of it."

Ellis Wax is a small man, but wiry in the way of an escape artist, someone who can contort his body to wriggle out of handcuffs and shackles. He's got black, beady eyes that belong on a rattlesnake and jet-black hair that's perfectly straight and could serve as a scrub brush. He has a way of smiling that Irene finds a little rude: it's more of a sneer than a smile, like he's openly mocking everyone. But because he's a little rude, she doesn't mind him standing there and smoking a cigarette, as long as he doesn't mind giving her one of her own. Rude people are interesting people, she decides on the spot. They don't care about what society thinks of them.

"Wax also drips and makes a mess," she replies casually.

"It depends on how clean you are when you handle it."

"How droll. Give me a ciggy."

"Sure thing. They sell them inside."

"I'm broke."

He snorts out a laugh and shakes his head. "What, you expect me to buy that? A flapper like you?"

"I'm not a flapper, for your information."

"What, you just forgot to buckle your shoes?"

"Just give me a cigarette or I'll scream."

He reaches into the pocket of his gray flannel suit and produces a silver case with initials that don't seem to contain the letter *E* or *W*. He pulls out a Camel as thin as the fingers that hold it, part of a delicate hand that Irene supposes belongs to someone of a sensitive nature, a surgeon or a pianist. Except nothing about this man seems sensitive. Not that mocking grin, not those black eyes darting nervously around, not that damn-it-all-to-hell voice as rough as the stubble on his face. He's in bad need of a shower, but at least he's not some pretty boy from Yale in a gabardine raincoat with the keys to daddy's Marmon touring car in his pocket.

"Here, Gloria Swanson," he sneers, giving her the smoke. "You know which end to light?" He strikes a match, cupping it expertly so that it doesn't get blown out.

"Very funny. That's no way to talk to a crazy person."

"Who's crazy?"

"I am." She exhales quickly, trying hard not to cough. But her last cigarette was a month ago, so she can't help but hack away like a tyro. He shakes his head to register his I-told-you-so scorn. Through a sudden burst of smoke-induced tears she continues as if nothing happened: "That's why I'm going to St. Petersburg. To get help at a solarium. But it won't work. I'm not going back to college, no matter what. I hate it there."

"What school?"

"Pearlman."

"I knew someone who went there."

He blows smoke up into the air, and it scatters into the passing wind. Then he flicks his butt onto the tracks.

"Who?"

"Who cares? So you're crazy, huh? You need help?"

"Lots of it, apparently. I'm not fit for decent society. Which is fine by me. Do you have any hardware, Mr. Wax? Any panther sweat?"

"Panther sweat?" He gives her a hard look.

"Yeah, booze."

"You are a flapper, aren't you? Panther sweat, if that doesn't take the cake."

"Well, do you or don't you?"

"No. But I can get some easy enough. There's plenty of it back in second-class."

"Lead the way. But no funny stuff, understand? I'm not in the mood."

At that moment Lauren Howard appears, a stern expression glazed on her unsmiling face. The two women glare at each other. Irene maintains a defiant pose, slipping her arm around Ellis Wax's thin waist.

"Hello, Mummy," sings Irene. "Care to join us? We're just heading back to the second-class car for a quadrille. There's a fabulous orchestra playing, it's simply divine."

"I'm Lauren Howard. Pleased to make your acquaintance." She extends her hand and Ellis takes it. Irene slaps her forehead.

"How rude of me! Mother, this is my new friend Ellis Wax. It's spelled W-A-X and his people were once princes in Saxony. Mr. Wax, this is my mummy."

"It's my pleasure, ma'am." His voice changes from gruff to polite.

"What brings you to Florida, Mr. Wax?" Lauren Howard remains cool and collected, even as she steals disapproving looks at her wayward daughter, who seems to have been driven to utter ecstasy by her wanton gambol with this threadbare miscreant, who needs a new suit, a fresh shirt, a trip to the barber, and a soak in a tub of Lysol. "Business or pleasure?"

"A little of both, I hope."

"What line of work are you in?"

"I'm a collector."

"What is it you collect?"

"Jewels, right?" says Irene, examining her mother's face for a reaction. There isn't one. Not a hair out of place.

"Jewels, sure. Other stuff, too, from all over the world. I just returned from the Far East."

"That sounds fascinating," Lauren offers gaily. "Well, you must be extremely busy. Allow us carefree women to take our leave so you can attend to whatever masculine pursuits suit your fancy, Mr. Wax. I'm sure you have many pressing engagements. Come along, Irene."

"We're staying at the Soreno Hotel, wherever that is," Irene blurts, ignoring her mother's entreaty to leave. "Isn't that right, Mummy? Aren't we going there to get me some help?"

"I'm sure Mr. Wax would rather not hear the details, dear."

"I'm going to St. Petersburg, too," he says, eyes brightening. "I'd like to call on you there, if I might."

"Sure thing," Irene replies. "We'll have to have tea and scones."

"Irene, really. Don't put Mr. Wax in the uncomfortable position of having to call on us boring women."

"Speak for yourself, Mummy."

"Irene, we really must let Mr. Wax go attend to business. It was my pleasure, Mr. Wax." With a forceful tug requiring a great deal of exertion, Lauren Howard yanks her still-chattering daughter away as if she's some irascible toddler, almost causing the girl to take a tumble. Both stagger toward the parlor car, where rotund men sit in Chippendale armchairs reading newspapers from Jacksonville and Ocala, examining the real estate sections with pinched, fervid intensity. Buried in the agate type lie the impenetrable mysteries of the New World: plundered land that could be pawned off to the easily cozened.

"Ouch!" cries Irene, rubbing her arm. "That hurt."

"Good. What on earth were you doing with that vile little shark?"

"Talking. What else do you want me to do on this god forsaken train?" Irene speaks in a booming voice that draws attention away from the newspapers, but only for a few seconds.

"Don't yell." She yanks her daughter once more and herds her roughly into the parlor car.

"I thought he was cute in a rude way," offers Irene. "And anyway, it's time I got over Frank. He was no good for me. Right?"

"I see what you're doing, young lady."

"I'm not doing anything."

"I won't discuss this with you."

The two of them start off down the long vestibule that leads back to the private berths, and from the observation deck Ellis Wax watches them, jacket slung casually over a thin shoulder, shirt stained with half-moons of sweat at the underarms. He waits for them to get a good ways ahead, and then he starts to walk, following their path at a safe distance.

"Sir?"

"I'm just leaving," Ellis says, keeping his eyes down as he moves along.

"Next time I'll have you put off the train. This is for first-class only."

"Okay, okay. See me walking back?"

---

f rank's left leg has fallen asleep, but the rest of his body is still wide awake. The mail train rumbles through the night with a steady drone. They're in Georgia now, the middle of nowhere. But since they crossed the Mason-Dixon line, the train has stopped less often, probably because there's been no reason to. Nobody has any mail to send around here. These boobs might not even know how to write.

It feels like someone is pricking him in the leg with pins and needles. Yet that's not the only thing keeping him up. A pretty loud card game is going on in the back of the car, and each time he hears a shout or a groan he feels like hustling back there to see what happened. The thing is, he wants in. The players are an old guy in a black coat and two Negroes, and they all seem pretty well oiled. That's another thing: he could really use a drink but he doesn't have a drop on him. If they'll let him sit in, surely they'd pour him a snozzleful, too.

He shifts in the hard seat, trying to find a comfortable position. But Ginger's head is resting on his shoulder. She's getting some shut-eye but Frank just can't relax. He's got a little over a hundred dollars to his name. And that won't last long. Everything in Florida costs double this time of year, on account of all the "snowbirds" who come down to spend the winter. So a hundred bucks, that's chicken-scratch. He'll need to get his hands on more, because even if the Babe agreed to cough up seven thousand clams, it could take a while. The money would have to be wired down from a bank in New York. That's probably how it'll work. If it works.

Another howl of glee. Frank strains to look back, but he can see only cigar smoke circling above the game, like a ghost hovering above the seats.

I could double my money, he hears himself thinking. *Those guys are sitting ducks.*

No, comes another voice in his head. *Don't risk it.*

Frank doesn't like that last voice, the voice of caution. Not when it comes to cards. He grew up with a deck in his hands and he knows what he's doing. What the hell, why not sit in on a few hands? If he starts losing he'll pull out. He's not stupid.

He extricates himself from Ginger's embrace, lifting her gently off him and leaning her against his balled-up pea coat. Then he stands up and starts on back, limping as he walks. He needs to get the blood pumping again, and nothing does that better than the sound of cards being shuffled.

"I killed me twenty-five buffalo in one day, boys," Frank hears the old man rasp between shuffles. "You figure a dollar a head, that was real money in them days."

"You ever kill an Injun?" a Negro asks, eyes red from the booze Frank can smell heavy in the air. Whiskey. Bad whiskey. Better than no whiskey, though.

The old man wheezes out a fluttering laugh. "I killed six Cheyenne on Christmas Eve in the year of eighteen-hunnerd and eighty-six."

Three pairs of eyes fix on Frank, standing in the aisle as the train rocks to and fro.

"Can you deal me in?" asks Frank, trying to sound gullible, like he just wants to pass the time and barely knows how to play poker.

The old man scratches his white Vandyke beard, white eyebrows lifting thoughtfully. Then he looks at his two companions. "You boys care?"

"Nah, just so he got money."

"What's the ante?"

"Quarter ante, a dollar to open," the old man barks. "The name's Tumulty. This here's Gig and he's Buster. They're brothers."

"I'm Frank."

He drops down a quarter on the makeshift table of an empty orange crate. The old man scoots over and Frank wedges his long body into the seat. The old man starts dealing out a hand of seven-card stud, as Frank stares at the brown jug sitting between the brothers. They stare back at him, faces impassive but eyes alert now, regarding the newcomer.

"How much for a drink?" he asks, nodding at the jug.

Wordlessly they hand it over, and Frank tips it back. It burns his throat going down, and his eyes start to water. Once he's done he smiles and thanks them. Frank is starting to feel good now, but the feeling doesn't last long. He loses three dollars in the first hand when his three nines get beat by a full house, queens over jacks. The next hand goes no better, and the next is more of the same, slop. Ten minutes in and he's down five dollars. But he's had a few more nips at the jug, so all isn't lost.

"Okay," he says, clapping his hands, "time to get serious."

"Seriously beat, you mean," says Gig, dealing out a hand of five-card draw.

But this time Frank sees his luck change. He gets three deuces off the deal, and opens with a bet of five dollars. The brothers hoot like owls and fold, but Tumulty sees the five and raises Frank five. Frank matches but doesn't raise. He tosses in two cards and gets two back; Tumulty exchanges just one card.

"He be bluffing!" cackles Buster. "He ain't got shit!"

Tumulty doesn't say a word. He's got the eyes of a lion and the jowls of a turkey, and his skin is so white it looks like he's been bleached. But you can't read him. Maybe he is bluffing, but it really doesn't matter, because Frank gets another deuce, meaning he's got all four. Although he can feel his heart pounding wildly in his chest, his face shows no emotion. There's twenty-one dollars in the pot; time to see who's bluffing.

"Well," sighs Frank, "why don't we make it interesting." He pulls out a sawbuck and drops it on the crate. Tumulty stares at his cards and then snorts like a bull.

"Interesting? Interesting is when a Mexican señorita lifts up her dress and shows you her garter belt." He throws a ten on the pile, and then another ten. "Now that's interesting."

The brothers squeal like rusty wheels when they see Tumulty's bet. Frank knows the old man is bluffing, he can smell it from a mile away. Four deuces have to be worth another ten bones; he'd swear on his mother's grave the old man is bluffing.

"Okay, Indian killer," Frank growls, "here's your ten. I'll call. Show me your rotten cards."

Tumulty grins as he throws down his hand, and Frank blinks a few times to make sure he sees it right: four threes. Four fucking threes. Now he's down thirty-six bucks, leaving with what? Sixty bucks, more or less? How's he supposed to get by on that? He's got to win his money back, that's all there is to it.

"Your deal," Buster tells Frank, who keeps gazing down at the cards. "I was sho' he be bluffing. He been doing it all night."

"There's no such thing as bluffing, boys," sings Tumulty gaily. "There's just winning and losing."

Frank starts to gather the cards, his hands trembling slightly and his head filled with clanging, confusing thoughts, like somebody is beating him with pots and pans. He wishes he'd never come back here. He was doing fine until he got greedy. Now he's in worse trouble than before.

•   •   •

An hour passes, and then the game breaks up. Frank struggles to stand up; both his legs have fallen asleep and it feels like he could keel over.

"You're one lucky son of a bitch!" Tumulty spews drunkenly, pointing a wavering finger at Frank. "You hear me?"

"Yeah, I hear you."

"That last pot had fifty bucks in it!"

Gig and Buster have fallen asleep, so Frank doesn't bother saying good-bye. The sun is starting to come up. They've got to be near Florida now, it feels warmer, more tropical. He makes his way back to his seat, gently inching past Ginger's still slumped body. Some people can sleep anywhere. Frank could use some sleep, too. He'll need all the energy he can muster once they get there. As he settles into his hard seat, a smile escapes his lips. He can feel the money bulging in his pocket. Seventy-five bucks. He worked and sweated and bluffed to lose twenty-five bucks.

But losing never felt so good. Because at one point he was down to twelve bucks. Twelve bucks between him and total ruin. But he won a small pot and then a big one. He stared right into the eyes of his downfall and survived. He's a little weaker but maybe he learned a lesson: he needs to take things a little slower and not force the action, or he'll blow it just like he almost blew it tonight. He'll get one shot at the Babe, and he can't botch it.

Then Ginger's eyes blink open, and she sits up, startled. "What happened?" she asks him.

"Nothing," he tells her.

She starts looking around again, up and down the aisle like she's done a hundred times already. He reaches over and takes her by the hand. She feels cold, like not enough blood can get where it needs to. She smiles a little, or maybe it's not a smile. It's hard to tell with her.

"It's okay," he assures her. "I told you, we're safe. Nobody knows we're here."

"Aren't you nice for saying so. But I thought I was safe in Asbury Park."

She closes her eyes, and her entire body grows limp. Then she makes a sad sound that causes Frank to grow quiet. He's never killed anybody before. A broken leg, a busted jaw, those heal. But Ginger is putting herself through the wringer, and it's not like there's an easy way to cheer somebody up after they've been through what she has.

Ginger's eyes grow moist from tears that begin to fall in small droplets down her round cheeks. "This is all so terrible—I never meant for any of this to happen. I want to be a singer, that's all I ever wanted."

"I bet you're pretty good, too."

"Ah, who cares, anyway? I'll never get on stage again."

"Look, you don't have to tell me the dope on Sal Chiesa if you don't want to. It's none of my beeswax. There's plenty you don't know about me. We don't have to flip all our cards, we just have to collect that money from Babe Ruth. Once that's done, you can scram to any cave you want. But if you're in trouble, I can help you. But I have to know what's going on first."

"Nobody can help me, and I mean nobody. Not you, not anybody. The cops especially."

"Sal Chiesa wasn't a cop. He didn't carry no badge."

She smiles thinly, gently rubbing his arm. "It's nothing personal, Frank. I know you'd help me if you could. You already have, God knows. But it's just better if I don't say anything to anybody, ever.

That's just how it is. It's not that I don't trust you. I don't trust anybody."

"I guess that's the smart thing."

"Maybe one day, once this is all over, it'll make sense."

"Sure, one day you can tell me. As I said, it's none of my beeswax."

"Aren't you a nice boy."

She squeezes his arm reassuringly, and closes her eyes again. He should do the same. He'll need to get some sleep because he's going to hit the ground running when he gets there. It's like he's been storing up the energy for this moment for years. He's so agitated it's hard to sleep. He's going to Florida. He's getting a piece of the action, just like he always wanted. With a little luck he'll be driving a new Dusenberg just like one of the mutts in those brochures he collected. Anything can happen down there in the Sunshine State.

ASBURY PARK

William H. "Little Mac" McSwiggin is a young man with a bright future. At the tender age of twenty-four, he is the youngest Assistant State Attorney in the city of Chicago, and already one of the best. Last year he won nine capital murder cases, earning him the well-deserved nickname among the underworld of "The Hanging Prosecutor." Short but powerfully built, with the thick neck and the bulging biceps of the football player he was, Little Mac McSwiggin possesses an ease of manner and a quick wit, two traits that endear him to jurors. He is also fearless. He'll take on any mob in the city, including the Torrio mob.

He gets up early, before the sun rises. His mother then prepares a hearty breakfast of eggs and griddle cakes, which he devours. Then he is off to work, and no one will outwork Little Mac. His buddies from the neighborhood, they waste their nights chasing women, but Little Mac allows himself few luxuries. When taking on the Torrio mob, one must be willing to make sacrifices. That gang is bloodthirsty, so he must be vigilant. And he's got them on their heels. Torrio's top assistant, Alphonse Capone, hasn't been seen in weeks, not since he plugged six bullets into the skull of one Joseph Horn, in front of several eyewitnesses. With any luck, Al Capone will be swinging from the end of a rope before the snows begin to melt.

Every workday since the Horn killing, McSwiggin begins the morning by meeting with the chief of detectives, Michael Hughes, a fellow Irishman from the West Side. At this meeting Hughes updates Little Mac on the case. The two men have invested so much time into this homicide, as opposed to any of the dozens of others related to the gang wars that began with the passage of the Volstead Act, because they know that Johnny Torrio is grooming "Scarface" Capone to take over the operation. Torrio has purchased a home for his mother in Sicily, staffed with fifteen servants, and he and his wife have begun to spend more and more time in Palm Beach, Paris, and Rome, leaving Capone in charge of the bootlegging, prostitution, and gambling syndicates. And from the looks of it, Capone is a more dangerous hoodlum than Torrio, with the temper of a rabid dog and the morals of an unregenerate pervert. Plus, his apes are loyal to him. Why wouldn't they be? Take, for example, what Capone did for Jake Guzik, his bookkeeper.

Joe Horn and Jake Guzik got into a row over some dame at Heinie Jacobs's saloon on South Wabash. Now Horn was one tough slugger, and Guzik couldn't beat up a fly. So after Horn slapped Guzik around, the fat little butterball went whimpering to Capone, who as usual was holding forth at his own club, the Four Deuces, about a half-block away. Capone took one look at his bookkeeper and marched right over to Heinie's saloon to confront Joe Horn.

McSwiggin doesn't like the criminal element. Joe Horn was wanted for at least three homicides. On its face one would conclude that in this situation Little Mac would feel no pity for the deceased. But that simply isn't true. Joe Horn was much like McSwiggin himself, fearless and cocksure. Every hoodlum in Chicago was afraid of Capone and Torrio, but not Joe Horn, who routinely hijacked shipments of their beer and then bragged about it. So when Capone came in and asked Joe Horn why he'd given Guzik a knuckle sandwich, Joe Horn didn't back down. Joe Horn's last words were: "Go back to your whores, you dago pimp."

Capone pulled out a revolver and shot Joe Horn in the neck. After

Joe Horn fell to the ground, Capone plugged five more rounds into his skull. Then he walked out.

There were witnesses. Plenty of witnesses. George Bilton was a garage mechanic. He picked out Capone's mug shot and said that was the man who killed Joe Horn. So did David Runelsbeck, a carpenter. And so did the lounge singer at Heinie's saloon, a certain dish with the sonorous stage-name of Sally Serenade.

A few days later, George Bilton turned up dead, shot between the eyes as he sat in his car in front of his apartment building on Maxwell Street. All of a sudden, Runelsbeck can't remember anything. And Sally Serenade, whose real name she gave as Ginger Hoagland, is nowhere to be found. Though there's good reason to think she's not dead, but gone into hiding. An informant in the Torrio gang claims they're looking for her, too. The inquest is coming up next week. Without Sally Serenade, McSwiggin has no case, and Al Capone will get away with murder.

"Tell me some good news about the long lost Sally Serenade," says McSwiggin, sipping on a mug of hot coffee. It's the only warmth on this miserably cold morning.

"I'm not sure if this is good news or not," replies Hughes.

McSwiggin perks up, setting the mug of coffee down on Hughes's desk. "What's cooking, Mikey? Don't tease me this early in the a.m."

"We got a report that Sal Chiesa got shot last night."

"Yeah?"

"In Asbury Park, New Jersey."

"What in thunder? What was he doing there this time of year?"

"That's a good question."

"Did he have some dope on our lounge singer?"

"Our guy doesn't know."

"This is worth looking into. Sal Chiesa is a triggerman. They didn't send him there for a vacation."

"We need to talk to Fingers again." Fingers Finley was the piano man in Sally Serenade's act and, like Heinie Jacobs, he claimed to not have seen anything when Capone plugged Joe Horn. At least he could say his back was turned, sitting at the piano. Fingers is further insisting he has no idea where Sally is, but both Hughes and McSwiggin (and Capone, too, for that matter) think he's covering for her. Maybe Fingers will start chinning when he finds out about Sal Chiesa being filled with lead. Maybe next time Sally Serenade won't get so lucky.

"Yeah," says McSwiggin excitedly, "let's take a drive. This could be the break we've been waiting for. We might still bag Capone yet."

ON THE
PROWL

*f*rom where the men stand, they don't see the loggerhead shrike hopping along the sandy bank of the lake, a dead mouse hanging limply in its short, sharp beak. The stocky bird then takes flight, springing from the ground and landing on a nearby hawthorn bush, where it spikes its prey upon a thorn like a butcher would a cut of meat on a hook. A ribbon of black obscures its dark eyes, which scour beneath the willow and cypress trees for any sign of lizard, mouse, or dragonfly. The bird begins singing, a piercing shriek that gets the attention of the old man, whose leathery face grows soft in recognition.

"Shrike," he says, "damn good hunters they are. They'll about catch anything they can."

"Well, are we gonna catch a gator today or we just out here with our thumbs up our asses?" asks Babe Ruth. "My damn thumb won't fit with this bandage on it!" He holds it up and shows the group the injury, sustained yesterday during batting practice. It'll get better, the doctors say. But they urged him to rest. His cough has gotten deeper since he arrived from Hot Springs, because he's gone full tilt since he hit Florida. But Helen arrived late last night, so he'll slow up a little, on account of how she doesn't like people much. Or she doesn't like the same people he likes. She didn't want him to go on this hunting trip, for instance, but he wouldn't miss it for the world—hunting gators! It should be a blast!

Each time the Babe coughs, he produces a silver flask from inside his new hunting jacket and takes a nip of bourbon, compliments of his host, "Handsome" Jack Taylor, developer of Pasadena-on-the-Gulf and soon-to-be-owner of a fabulous hotel being built at the present moment. Handsome Jack is the one who hired the crusty guide, Cato Younger, for the entertainment of Ruth and some of his fellow Yankees, Whitey Witt, Ray Coombs, and Wally Pipp. It's a small price to pay to show these fellows a swell time, and no one's ever accused Handsome Jack about being shy with the loot, his or anybody else's. Already he's exceeded the budget his investors authorized for the hotel, because Handsome Jack wants his place, the Rolyat, to be something people won't soon forget, and people don't forget marble and brass and bas-relief. But even as the investors fret and sweat, Handsome Jack only has to remind them that he's married to a DuPont, Evelyn DuPont to be precise, who's pouring glasses of champagne back at her Daimler touring car (he drives one exactly like it) while Cato Younger leads the group into the dense hammock that surrounds Lake Maggiore, on a so-far futile search for alligators.

"Well, we'd stand a better chance without all this mess of yakking," says Cato, wiping some tobacco juice from his mouth. "Gator don't like the sound of a person's voice. Can't say I blame him."

"Yeah, shut up, Ruth," chimes in Whitey Witt. "You're scaring all the gators."

"How about I throw you in this pond and use your scrawny ass for bait?"

"I think they'd like your big old gut better, Babe," says Coombs, lighting a cigarette as his shotgun slumbers in his arms like a sleeping child. "How many hot dogs did you munch down yesterday at practice?"

"Not enough." The Babe looks through the woods back toward the car. "Where's that pretty wife of yours with them fish eggs?"

"She'll bring us some caviar and champagne," Handsome Jack

assures Ruth. "She's just getting it all ready. She likes everything to be just so."

For a few moments the men grow silent and stand still beneath the shade of the cypress trees. The only noise is the rustling of the wind through the trees and the patter of green anoles scurrying through the fallen needles in the underbrush. The delicate purple berries of a wild sage make a tempting meal for a lone cardinal, who plucks a few and then absconds when a starling chases him away. Far overhead soars an osprey, a silent messenger on a lonely trek through the blue sky. Somewhere off in the distance a pileated woodpecker hammers away at a tall cabbage palm, offering faint timpani to the gentle melody of the wind. Along the mossy rocks at the lake's edge turtles sun themselves like tourists, and anhingas sit with wings splayed as if exhausted from the effort of diving and swimming. A great blue heron watches the men from the shallows, but then removes herself to the other side of the vast lake when Wally Pipp approaches. The turtles go splashing into the water, causing all the men to look over.

"What do you got, Pipp?" asks Ruth excitedly. "You see one?"

"I don't know," the first baseman answers.

Moving like a ghost Cato Younger glides over, making no sound as he walks. His eyes narrow and then he smirks when he gets next to Pipp. "It's a branch," says the old man. "From a willow tree."

"Looked like a gator to me."

"You can shoot it if you wants to."

"I'll pay for the taxidermist, Wally," chuckles the Babe, blowing his nose loudly into an embroidered hanky. "We'll mount it in the clubhouse."

"We'll put it next to Gehrig's locker," adds Witt, an obvious jab at Pipp, who's been fighting off the strapping kid from Columbia College, the team's resident egghead, for the past two years.

"Why don't you put it up Gehrig's ass," Pipp snarls. "That way, when he's riding the pine this year, he can keep it company."

"The kid's sure swinging a good bat this spring, Wally," Ruth keeps

115

on, knowing it won't take much more to get Pipp hotter than a wop's stove. "He's really getting solid wood on the ball."

"When he's hitting, I always see the skipper with a big, shit-eating grin," says Witt, looking at Ruth for approval.

"To hell with you guys," Pipp spits in disgust, turning his back and walking along the lake's edge a few yards. At that moment the voice of Evelyn DuPont can be heard ringing through the pines. "Let's eat, boys!" she calls, standing on the running board of the Daimler and holding her hands to her mouth. She's an attractive woman, somewhere just south of forty or perhaps just north, it's hard to tell because her attire, midnight-blue satin dress studded with sequins, a stylish white cloche hat pulled tightly against her head, makes her seem a decade younger. She carries herself with the gregarious extroversion of someone not used to toil or drudgery, but as often is the case for such people, moments of reflection yield myriad disappointments. No one in her family was pleased with her decision to marry Jack Taylor, whose banking career in New York was marked by stock swindle and outright fraud; her father was so angry with Evelyn that he in effect cut her off from the family fortune, leaving her a trust fund that over the past four years has steadily been drained away. But one thing he couldn't take away was her name, and her name was as good as gold. "Champagne and caviar, boys! Come and get it!"

Ruth doesn't wait for the others. He starts off like a road grader, marching straight through railroad vines and spiderwebs. Cato Younger watches him go, his weathered straw hat pulled nearly over his eyes. He spits a rill of tobacco juice onto the sand and sits down on a stump. Soon the others follow Ruth back to the car, leaving Cato Younger to sit alone next to the lake he's grown up with. These city boys don't understand the first thing about Florida, he decides, gazing out across the water. They come down to play their games and get drunk, but they don't see what he sees. They don't see the raw power of destruction that teems everywhere, in the water, in the grass, in the clouds. They haven't seen a twelve-foot gator grab a two-year-old girl by the head and pull her under. They haven't seen what a bull shark can do to a grown man. They haven't watched a little boy die from a rattlesnake bite. Their houses haven't been blown away by a hurricane. To them, Florida's all fun and games. Point your gun at a gator and shoot. Take it on into town and get it stuffed. Hang it over the pool table back up north somewhere. But that ain't Florida. Handsome Jack can hire him out at a hundred dollars a day and Cato Younger appreciates the money, but it ain't the real Florida he takes people to see. That place died a long time ago.

Over by the drooping cypress tree that was hit by lightning twenty years ago he sees the long snout of a gator, a six-footer, plying through the waters, trailing not far behind a moor hen and her young. The gator'll likely pick off a few of the chicks, and it won't take much effort, either. That's the simple savagery of Florida, that's the courage it took for people to hew a life out of the soft, sandy soil. People like his father, whose hands got so tough that you couldn't cut the calluses with a knife. When he was coming up, the Seminoles were still at war with the white man. Now you get your picture taken with one. Cato Younger shakes his head and spits more tobacco juice into the sand.

"Dig in, boys!" Evelyn DuPont says, gesturing toward the black caviar piled high in chintz bowls sitting on a felt-covered card table. "And help yourself to a glass of champagne. You hunters must be famished!"

They set their shotguns down and stand a moment transfixed by the spread. Handsome Jack gives his wife a wink to thank her for another job well done. The woman is a born entertainer and could most likely get Vladimir Lenin himself to lighten up. Well-fed men make for happy men, and happy men make for good prospects when it comes to selling real estate. Champagne doesn't hurt, either. Handsome Jack knows to let his pretty wife flirt for a while to get the men oiled up and smiling, then he'll move in for the soft sell. She holds her glass aloft and proposes a toast, after everyone has had a turn at the caviar. "To the best team in baseball," she says, with Handsome Jack quickly concurring, although neither of them watch or even enjoy baseball, a boorish sport more suited for the unwashed. Nonetheless, as soon as they found out the New York Yankees were holding spring training in St. Petersburg, both of them started boning up a little, so they could make that all-important small talk that usually closes a deal.

After they all take a drink, Babe Ruth takes his turn. "To a real son of a bitch and his beautiful wife," he says, that playful twinkle in his eyes. "May Jack Taylor rot in hell for what he did to me on the golf course yesterday."

Everyone laughs and there's Evelyn, quick to refill empty glasses. As she's doing so, Handsome Jack sidles up to Whitey Witt, who's got a sheepish grin on his square face. Out of all of them, he's the best prospect, Handsome Jack has decided. Ruth'll take a lot of sword fighting, but Witt's ready to enjoy the good life. "Having a good time?" Handsome Jack asks, getting a vigorous nod of assent in return. Witt's just a plainspoken country boy agog at the splendiferous pleasures the Sunshine City has to offer, the glitter and the glamour. "I want you to enjoy yourself. Nothing like a little hunting trip to get the mind clear. I took Jack Dempsey out this winter—"

"Jack Dempsey, the fighter?"

"The same. He bought a house in Pasadena. I'll have to show it to you. And Bobby Jones, the golf champion, he lives next door. It's a good investment, to be honest with you. You don't have to pay state income tax in Florida. In New York, you get soaked to the gills."

"You do?"

"Sure, you do. I used to be a banker in New York. It's ungodly what you pay in taxes. Who handles your money?"

Whitey Witt snorts mirthfully. "Shoot, ain't enough to handle, seems like. I let the missus take care of everything."

"I see. Did you get enough caviar?"

"I sure did."

"That's great. Maybe we'll bag a gator yet."

"That'd be something."

Handsome Jack never stops smiling, never stops watching and observing the give-and-take going on around him. So, he misjudged this Witt fellow. That sometimes happens. But Wally Pipp's looking a little long in the mouth. Perhaps the idea of owning a piece of paradise on earth will shake the doldrums from his sad face.

MAKE A
KILLING

"Come on, get up, you bum! No sleeping on the benches!" A flattie pokes Ellis Wax in the ribs with a nightstick, causing an eye to blink open. "On your feet, or I'll take you in."

"What time is it?"

"Do I look like a clock?"

As a matter of fact, the copper did, with a round face, button nose, and moles spaced evenly apart on his cheeks. But Ellis holds his tongue. No sense angering a hardworking public servant in a new town. "What time do the stores open around here?" Ellis has swung his legs around and now sits up on the green bench beneath the cool of a tall oak tree. His first night in St. Petersburg was chilly and brief.

"Stores?" snorts the flattie in disbelief. "What on earth you need a store for, unless it's to rob it?"

"I'm just asking, officer."

"Move along, and don't cause no trouble in this town, or you'll be working on a chain gang before you can say jackrabbit."

"Oh, I'm not looking for trouble. I got in late last night and didn't feel like putting down the plunks for a hotel room."

"Were you on the Orange Blossom Special?"

"I believe so."

The flattie seems acutely excited by this fact. He starts smiling like he just heard an off-color joke. "Well, I saw a report that a lady had some jewelry stolen on that train. You wouldn't know anything about that, would you?"

"No, sir. I'm no thief, that's a promise."

"I'll be the judge of that." The flattie uses his nightstick to poke him sharply in the ribs. "Empty your pockets."

"What I do? Is it against the law to breathe in this town?"

The cop pulls Ellis up off the bench. "I said empty your pockets right now."

"Jeepers creepers, lay off me. I'll show you I'm on the level." Ellis starts digging his hands into various pockets, producing documents that the cop shows no interest in, letters of introduction from well-established friends of his family's vouching for Ellis Wax's character. He also has several blank sheets of letterhead, from various financial institutions located in Baltimore. He has a checkbook from the Bank of Catonsville. There is a Maryland driver's license with his name on it. He has five dollars in cash, and a few spare coins. Having shown the cop all of this, he throws up his hands. "See, that's all I got, until I get my feet on the ground."

"What about that pocket?" The cop taps him smartly on the backside with his nightstick.

"I emptied that one."

"Empty it again."

Ellis takes a step back. "Before I do, I want to make one thing real clear. I did not steal these from anybody on a train. These are my stepmother's, God rest her soul, and all I have in the world standing between me and a gutter."

"Hand it over."

Ellis reaches back and takes the diamonds from his pocket: a ring, a set of earrings, and a bracelet. His hands trembling like a leaf on a tree, he holds the gems up for the cop to inspect.

"Nice stuff," the cop chimes. "Let's have a look." With one big mitt he grabs the jewelry from Ellis and stuffs the whole ensemble into a pocket, grinning from ear to ear.

"Hey! I could report you for that!" Ellis warns, back stiffening.

"Sure you could. But you won't. I know your type. This is Florida. Garbage washes up on shore every day. We clean it up, but it just keeps coming back."

"Yeah, well, you'll feel like a heel when I tell you my stepmom passed away two days ago, and that was my sole inheritance, what you just took."

"Let me guess. You killed her and stole the goods, then went on the lam."

"Come on, what kind of fluter do you take me for? Listen, let's work something out. You keep the bracelet and we'll call it even."

The cop starts cackling as he saunters off, swinging his nightstick expertly like a circus performer. Ellis sets his jaw firmly and watches him leave, his mind racing a hundred miles per hour. Everything has changed now. Everything. One stupid cop blundered into luck.

Ellis stuffs the letters of introduction back into his pockets. He'll need those later, now more than ever. His stomach starts growling again. How long has it been since he ate a full meal? Three days? Drastic times call for drastic measures. The first step is finding Mabel Wright. He didn't want to play that card unless it was necessary, but now it is. He needs a place where he can clean up so he can hit the banks when they open.

———

Trucks from the Nu Grape Bottling Co. go rattling down Third Street South, sometimes careening wildly if the driver is in a hurry, late delivering crates of soda to the stores and restaurants of St. Petersburg. Also making that stretch of the street treacherous are trucks from the Farmer Concrete Works, which take many trips during the day at a breakneck pace, conveying the hexagonal blocks that make up the sidewalks of the glorious new subdivisions that have been springing up out of the pine flats in the southern wards of the city. The trucks from the two companies go speeding up and down, engines straining under the heavy loads. Adding to the frenetic character of the 800 block of Third Street are the hammering and drilling of the grimed-faced welders at Randolph and Dreiling's ironworks—not to mention the clamor coming from the Pinellas Machine Co. In short, this part of Third Street is not the kind of area where people live. But that's exactly where Frank Hearn and Ginger DeMore have rented lodgings for a week, from Mrs. Mabel Wright, who maintains a boardinghouse on the bustling corner of Third Street and Ninth Avenue, not far from a grungy-looking harbor.

"Come on, let's go." Frank slaps Ginger on the thigh, and she groans, rolling over on the creaky bed and curling into the fetal position.

"Now? I'm sleepy, Frank. We just got here."

"What the deuce you talking about? We've been here since this morning!"

"Aren't you in a rush. Let me get some beauty sleep."

"Look in the paper—'Yankees Hold Practice Today.' " He points to a copy of the *St. Petersburg Times* folded on a small table. A lingering odor of gasoline hangs in the unmoving air. They are staying in what was once a garage but, due to the demand for housing, has been recently converted into two rooms. Frank and Ginger had no choice but to take one because every hotel and apartment in the city of St. Petersburg was booked—or cost an arm and a leg. The landlords knew they had you by the short hairs and could charge the sky for a rotten hole-in-the-wall and get the asking price. It took them an hour to find this place, trudging up and down the streets. It was barely seventy degrees but it felt hot, and they wilted quickly.

"We're doing it today?" Ginger groans, still lying down, with no sign that she'll be getting up anytime soon. "I don't feel beautiful today."

"You look swell."

"I need to take a shower—and what am I supposed to wear?"

"Wear that."

"It's filthy dirty, Frank. No man in his right mind would give me a second look in this ratty dress."

"Didn't Paula give you a few things?"

"She gave me some feminine essentials, but nothing glamorous. And the Babe, I'm sure, likes his women to be glamorous."

"I want to start breaking eggs! You saw all them hustlers working the streets, selling real estate like it's going out of style. This town's on fire." True enough, because the evidence was everywhere they looked, from the crews of Negroes laying out the brick streets to the sleek-suited sharks hawking subdivisions on every street corner. Frank's blood is boiling now. Babe Ruth is somewhere in this city, and those seven thousand bucks of his are, too.

"Break all the eggs you want, mister, I need to catch forty winks. I'm tired."

"I didn't bring you down here to sleep. We got a job to do." He pulls on her leg but she kicks free.

"Let go of me, Frank!"

"This is the thanks I get for saving your life? Huh? Some two-timer you are."

"Leave me alone! I want everyone to just leave me alone!"

Ginger buries her face in a pillow. Frank stands over her helplessly. Now what's he supposed to do? He's confused by her tears, because on the outside she seems as tough as a blacksmith's apron—yet she's got a soft side, too. And so his hands trail down and land on her heaving back, and rest there a minute. He can feel her warmth through the coarse cotton of the blue dress she's been wearing the past two days.

"I'll buy you a new dress," he tells her, rubbing her shoulders as she stops crying but remains silent, inert, like a lump of clay. "Something that'll catch his eye."

She stirs a little. "Really? You think I can?"

"I know so. You got what men like."

"Yeah? What's that?"

She rolls over to face him. He grins, face turning crimson from the inflection in her voice. A minute ago he hated her, and she hated him. "I don't know, you look nice."

"Just nice?"

She reaches out and draws his large hands up to her breasts. He scoops them up and presses them together, before he leans down and kisses her passionately, deeply, her hands running through his thick brown hair. And something overcomes them both, an energy made from equal parts desperation, hunger, and a brush with death. They tear at each other's clothes, attacking each other with animal savagery. They do not make love nor do they pretend to. And yet, when it is over, and both are panting and sweating from the exertion, their nude bodies intertwined like railroad vines running up a palm tree, they laugh, unashamed by what just happened. Chips of paint have flaked from the low ceiling, and fell like a light snow while the bed rocked against the wall. Now the chips are stuck in Ginger's hair like baby's breath, and Frank begins to pick them out.

"It's like checking for lice," he cracks. She slaps him playfully.

"That's not a nice thing to say!" She sounds utterly delighted.

"I'm not a nice person."

"You try not to be. But you are a swell fellow."

"Enough recreation. Let's get moving."

He's putting on his shirt and she still hasn't gotten out of bed. She's lying there looking at something, not taking one step toward getting ready. "Well? Are you coming? Come on, get yourself all dolled up. You gotta catch the Babe's eye."

"I've got to wash my hair. I can't go around with paint in my hair, can I?"

"How long will it take?"

"Pour yourself a drink and read the newspaper. Isn't that what men do while their wives get ready?"

———

Mabel Wright scratches the back of her head, regarding the stranger standing in front of her with obvious suspicion. She's got her gardening apron on and wants nothing more than to go back to pulling weeds. "You knew Monk?" she asks again.

Ellis Wax nods his head in enthusiastic assent. "I did. He talked about you all the time, said you were the best woman he ever knew."

"Monk said that?"

"Sure he did. He said you were aces."

She breathes heavily a couple times, looking away as she brushes her hands against the apron. It's been many a moon since anyone ever reminded her of her days with Monk. Mostly she's been trying to forget. After all, she went to prison for the man. Five years for forgery, but he got a double sawbuck in the pen and never came out. He died last year. Got a note from his sister. "That's nice," she tells the kid. "Maybe you were pals with him, but what does that do for me? You need a place to stay, but you're a little short on cash. You'll get the cash but you don't know when. If I closed my eyes, I could swear I was talking to Monk."

"I know you're thinking the worst about me, and I won't lie. I made a mistake when I was a kid, but I'm on the straight and narrow now. I will—I swear to God—I will pay you every cent as soon as I get my feet on the ground."

"Feet on the ground? You're an ex-con. You need a job. They got jobs in this city, plenty of them, as long as you can lift a shovel or swing a hammer. I'll give you a week, back in the garage. You don't have rent by then, you're out on the street. No ifs, ands, or buts. I need paying customers. I'm no Salvation Army."

"Thanks a million! I'll have the money in the bat of an eye. I'm not afraid to work, and I plan on turning my life around. It's because of Monk, mostly. He helped point me in the right direction. He said you turned yourself around in Florida and I could, too."

"You have a week."

"I won't let you down, ma'am. That's a promise."

Mabel Wright sighs, wondering if she just made a big mistake. A friend of Monk's showing up out of the blue, fresh out of the can with not a cent to his name? That's a story that's not likely to have a happy ending.

And what do you know? An hour later she notices a kitchen knife has gone missing. She let Monk's prison buddy help himself to a sandwich, and what does he do? Pockets a carving knife. He'll deny he took it, so she won't even bother asking. Monk was the same way. A leopard doesn't change its spots.

Maybe she should place a toll call to Baltimore and speak to the one man who could figure some of this out for her: Detective Szymanski, who rousted her and Monk plenty of times over the years. Szymanski knows she went straight, and he won't mind answering a few questions about Ellis Wax. Might as well get to the bottom of it sooner rather than later.

(entral Avenue is the hub of the town. It runs due west from the bay, rising gently up and then straight out toward the gulf ten miles in the distance, its brick pavement bisected by streetcar tracks that disappear into the horizon of towering oaks and tall slash pines. St. Petersburg looks like it's been carved out of a jungle, like some men showed up a dozen years ago and just started hacking away at the dense foliage that encircles the city. It's a stark contrast, the way the jungle ends and civilization begins. From Sixteenth Street east to the bay, stores and businesses run down both sides of Central Avenue, and green benches line the sidewalks. On them sit old people, women attired in Victorian high-collared dresses and men in dour, dark suits— thousands and thousands of old people, it seems, as Frank and Ginger stroll past. Neither has ever seen so many gray heads in one place; it's as if someone has collected them from around the country and plopped them down on these green benches, where they sit with beguiling grins, holding canes and parasols and the morning edition of the *St. Petersburg Times*.

"What's this place, some kind of home for the aged?" mutters Frank, eyes roving about, from the green benches to the names of the businesses arrayed on the buildings. "I never seen so many gummers in my whole life."

"Everybody looks like my grandma," Ginger agrees.

This initial shock of the green benches, however, begins to fade as they walk down Central Avenue. Frank notices the signs: Boulevard and Bay Land and Development Co. Victory Land Company. Pasadena Estates. Louis Raquet, Real Estate Agent. Beach Park. Bender-Nichols. Square Deal Realty. Hawkeye Realty. Hoosier Realty. And on and on they come, the plethora of brokers, agents, developers, builders, and lawyers fueling the Florida boom Frank's been reading about. Here's the ballyhoo in all of its splendor, giving shape and substance to what Frank could only imagine from the brochures he collected. The boom is real and staring him dead in the face. The cars parked in front also hint at the money being made, gleaming new sedans that sit in regal display, awaiting their masters to hop in and speed off. It's got to be true: everybody's getting rich in Florida.

After just a few blocks Frank's step begins to quicken, propelled by the signs and an implacable desire to get in on the action. Ginger can barely keep up with him. She has to start running to stay even. "Look at this!" he says, passing by the oldsters on the green benches who regard his hulking frame with curiosity. "It's a damn gold rush! I gotta get my money and jump in!"

But Ginger's not next to him anymore. He stops and looks back. There she is talking to a man wearing white knickers that billow around his stubby legs, bright yellow knee socks, a navy blue blazer one size too small, and a straw hat perched at a jaunty angle. Under the man's arm is a briefcase, and his mouth is moving a hundred miles an hour. Ginger's just standing there, a pained expression on her face, like a child being scolded. When Frank gets close enough, he can hear the pitch:

"—a steal, ma'am. A regular heist and I'm not whistling Dixie— oh, is this the husband? Howdy, sir, name's Alberts, and I'm gonna ask you one question: how much money do you want to make today because I'm no busher when it comes to counting corn. Lakewood Estates is the place to make a killing in this market."

"We're not interested," Frank says without much conviction, because the truth is, he's very interested. Every word the man uttered cut through him like a knife.

"Let me show you our brochure." In the blink of an eye he's produced a document that bears all sorts of official-looking stamps and markings. "The X's indicate lots that have been sold this month alone. One of my clients, a nice old lady from outside Utica, New York—never paid me a dime—made six grand in a week. Lot Seven right there." With a pudgy finger, he points to an X. "She took that six grand and bought three more lots. Made another twenty." He folds the document and looks Frank dead in the eye. "That, my friend, is action, and it's at Lakewood Estates, the place to buy in St. Petersburg. In fact—" he takes a step closer as if what he's about to say is of the strictest confidence and not to be overheard by a passerby, "I hear Babe Ruth himself is about to invest heavily."

"So, he's in town?" asks Frank.

"Sure, friend! The Babe's in town! All the Yankees are! Now what do you say? Do you want to make a killing?"

"Are you selling binders?"

"I sure am!" booms Alberts. "You know what I'm talking about, eh? Smart man, smart man. I can spot one a mile away!"

"I've read of binders," Frank concedes sheepishly. He could use more information about them. Every little bit helps. "How do they work?"

"A binder means you intend to buy a piece of property within a period of time—say, two weeks. But you won't keep it two weeks, the way things are going at Lakewood Estates! I'll bet you nine and a half cents that you'll double your money before then!"

"Right. I thought it was something like that. Hey, thanks for the dope."

"You can't wait in this market, friend. Take it from me. Tomorrow the lots'll be five hundred more."

Frank waves and starts walking away, a wry smile fixed on his face. The sun high overhead feels warm against his skin; puffy clouds scud across an azure sky; a flock of seagulls goes squawking by; and for the first time in a long time, Frank Hearn knows, with every ounce of his being, that finally he's going to strike it big. He's in the right place at the right time. The invigorating smell of salt water fills the air. Everything in this town looks new, like it's just been born.

"Real estate's all the rage down here, isn't it?" Ginger observes as they lope along.

"That's why I'm here."

"You and everybody else in the world."

Frank sniffs derisively down at her. "I could dance circles around that dope, and all these other chiselers. You watch, I'll be sitting pretty in a month. I got pep, and pep is all you need."

"No, you need luck, too."

"You make your own luck."

St. Petersburg's quaint waterfront is spread out before them in a pleasant vista of sun-dappled pleasure. A few large yachts sway at anchor, and some sailboats bob near a long fishing pier. Lots of people have dropped a line in the water, and these anglers are pulling in hefty fish. Pelicans are flocked all around, waiting to be fed, flapping wings impatiently. Small boys tease the large-beaked birds, dangling pieces of fish in front of them.

"Look at that," says Frank, stepping aside to let a strange-looking vehicle rattle past. A Negro is pulling a two-wheeled rickshaw, its passengers taking in the splendors of the late morning.

"I could use one of those," Ginger groans. "I can't walk another step."

"You don't have to. There it is."

He points south to the baseball park, its wooden grandstand leaning over a sweep of sand and dirt, mixed with a few tufts of grass. It's hard to tell where the infield stops and the outfield starts. One thing is obvious, though: there aren't any ballplayers on it. The field is empty.

"What's this? Nobody is playing. The landlady said this is where they play."

They stand there for a few seconds, looking at the empty ballpark. Seagulls go squawking past. Frank's eyes narrow in bewilderment. How can this be? Is practice over already? Is this another case of him screwing up? He swallows, throat dry from the long walk and the salty air. He looks around for somebody to ask, but sees only old people sitting on green benches.

"That's bad luck," Ginger purrs. "I guess we have time to buy me a new dress, after all."

"**M r. Hamilton** will be delighted to speak with you, Mr. Gould."

"Thank you."

"Yes, sir."

With a final dismissive nod to the bank teller, Ellis Wax saunters over toward the glassed-in office of the bank manager. He doesn't feel confident about his chances on this one, because he doesn't like the looks of Hamilton, a red-faced Milquetoast with a crooked beak of a nose and a pair of bug eyes, the kind of yokel who's probably never heard of Yale. From the door Ellis carefully watches Hamilton handle papers with thick stubby fingers that look like smoked cigars. No, this isn't the right guy. This Hamilton, he's a jughead. Maybe he should try another bank. There are scads more on Central Avenue.

"May I help you?"

It's Hamilton, waving him in. Stay or go? Nothing ventured, nothing gained. He extends a hand. "Adam Gould," he introduces himself.

Hamilton remains a stoic in the face of this good-natured introduction. "I understand you'd like to cash a check, Mr. Gould."

"That's correct."

"Let's take a look, shall we?"

Hamilton leads Ellis to sit down in a high-backed chair with padded armrests. Then Ellis sees it: a framed photograph hanging on the wall, of Jack Dempsey, fists up, snarling at the camera.

Ellis nods toward the photograph. "You're a Jack Dempsey fanatic, I see."

Hamilton looks back at it. "I sure am. He's the best prizefighter there ever was."

"I heartily concur. In fact, not to feed you a gallon of applesauce, I boxed a little myself in college."

"That so? Where was that?"

"Yale."

"No kidding! That's a swell place. I know a Yalie, he's president of the Exchange Club in town. Name of Simmons."

"Lionel Simmons, perhaps? He was my year."

"Nope. He goes by Lawrence. Larry, actually. Oh well, it's a small world. So, what can we do you for?"

Ellis can feel the man's trust growing, can feel the worm turning. A bit more chinning and the deal will be done. Hamilton reads through the letters of introduction: one from the First National Bank in Catonsville, another from a prominent Baltimore attorney, and another from a well-respected priest, all of whom vouch for and recommend Adam Gould, a man of true character and outstanding morals.

"This all looks fine, Mr. Gould," says Hamilton cheerfully. "I just need some identification."

Ellis shows him the driver's license. Hamilton nods his head and hands it back.

"We should be able to have your account open in a week, after the check clears."

"A week?"

"At the earliest."

"That won't do. I was counting on getting some cash today."

Hamilton breaks into a whopping grin. "Cash in a day? Not in this town! Not with all the grifters floating around! Just last week someone tried to pass themselves off as Jack Dempsey's business partner! No, we're a bit more careful now. All the banks in town are, matter of fact."

"You can't be too cautious, I suppose."

"I'm glad you understand, Mr. Gould. This town sure could use a good stockbroker! Let me be the first to invite you down to the Exchange Club. All the young men with pep belong. You'll drum up some business down there, you can bank on it!"

"Bank on it. That's a good one. It was a pleasure doing business with you, Mr. Hamilton."

The two men shake hands. A few minutes later, Ellis Wax walks out of the bank with nothing. Monk was wrong about that: they don't cash checks in Florida at the drop of a hat. And Mabel Wright isn't some stand-up broad, either. He could try another bank but he's liable to meet the same response. If he couldn't bamboozle a dolt like Hamilton, he'd better try something else. But what? How's he supposed to get some money? Where did that rich skirt say she was staying? The Soreno Hotel? Irene Howard, wasn't it?

Then out of the multitude on the sidewalk emerges a man wearing a blue blazer, white knickers, and yellow socks. He's got a big smile on his squat face as he steps right up and says:

"Can I let you in on a secret?"

Ellis shrugs. "Sure thing, pal."

"Lakewood Estates is the best buy in the city of St. Petersburg. And I'm not whistling Dixie." His solicitous manner oozes out of every well-scrubbed pore, but to Ellis Wax, he's a bolt out of the blue.

"Is that so? I didn't catch your name."

"Alberts, with the Victory Land Company."

"My name's Smith, P. N. Smith."

They shake hands. Alberts's grip is soft and effeminate. He's fleshy, like an overstuffed turkey. "Well, Mr. Smith, today's your lucky day! I'm gonna make you rich!"

"You are? I guess it is my lucky day."

"You bet! Because the action at Lakewood Estates is thicker than a London fog! And the best part is, you don't need to pay me a cent. Not one plug nickel."

"I'm all ears, Alberts." This overgrown schoolboy wants to sell him real estate. If that's not the damnedest thing. Alberts launches into his canned spiel about the amenities and wonderments of Lakewood Estates, making it sound like the ninth wonder of the world. A golf course! A clubhouse! Paved roads! Ellis listens and tries to appear eager, punctuating Alberts's lines with enthusiastic grunts of approval.

"I'll be honest with you, Alberts," Ellis Wax confides in his new friend. "I'm eager to invest in this great little town."

Alberts nearly jumps out of his shoes. "We might be a little town now, but not for long! We'll become a top-flight city sure as I'm standing here. That's the honest truth. And you know what else? You stand to turn a handsome profit if you invest in Lakewood. One lady, she made a cool ten thousand plunks in a week and never left her apartment. Those lots in Lakewood, they're selling like hotcakes!"

Alberts's zeal shines out from his eyes like the headlights on a truck. He says what he believes and believes what he says. He's a young puppy straining at the leash. He doesn't fear anything. He'll go anywhere with anyone, as long as he can smell a buck in it.

"Well, let's take a drive and have a look!" Alberts sings like a lorikeet. "My car's just a couple blocks away!"

"I'm right behind you, Alberts."

A water tower rises up behind home plate like an ungainly ostrich whose legs can't support its weight. A strong gust of wind could knock it over, and boy, that would be news, because a lot of these cocky ballplayers would die in a flash. Each member of the New York Yankees, even the bush leaguers who won't get a whiff of the majors, swagger like pirates, chin held high, chest inflated, smirking at the world. They're supposed to be the best and they sure act like it. Like mockingbirds they chatter back and forth using their own language:

"Come babe, come babe, come babe. Attaway, attaway, attaway, come babe, come babe. . . ." A wiry old man with a leather face is hitting grounders to the infielders, who scurry about after the ball and kick at the sand in disgust when they miss it. In the outfield, men stand in small groups talking, some looking out at the cool, placid waters of Crescent Lake, ringed by cypress trees and thronged with long-legged wood storks and herons, while stubby ibises dig at the earth with their scimitar beaks.

And everywhere there are women. Sure, plenty of men and boys stand in slack-jawed awe as they gawk at their heroes, and even a few of the brave ones might yell something that the players ignore. But what gets Frank's goat is the number of broads all dressed to the nines and loitering around like a bunch of streetwalkers. Sure, hardly any of them can turn a man's head like Ginger can, but it's obvious this won't be easy. And worst of all, Babe Ruth isn't even out there.

"I don't see him," Frank finally admits. "You know what he looks like, right?"

"I've seen pictures of him," Ginger offers helpfully. "He's a big brute with short little legs, right?"

"That's the one." Frank keeps staring down at the field from their perch atop the rickety bleachers set up behind the Yankee's dugout on the first base side of the diamond. The sun beats brightly down on them, making Frank and Ginger sweat even more profusely. They just finished walking the fifteen blocks to the field after a kindly gent told them that the Yankees practiced at Crescent Lake—but will play their exhibition games at the Waterfront Park, the new downtown ball field that was empty.

"Let's get us a soda to drink," Ginger suggests, looking at the little concession stand beneath the water tower. "It's the least you can do, since you didn't buy me a dress."

"You look fine. You took a shower, didn't ya? And anyway, there'll be lots of new dresses once I get that money."

"So that's my cut? Some dresses?"

His eyebrows arch suspiciously, but then he smiles. "So you want a cut now?"

"I don't know, I suppose I might. I know you helped me out of a jam, but a girl needs to eat and put a roof over her head."

Frank considers her request. She does have a point. "Five hundred."

"A thousand."

"A thousand? Tell it to Sweeney. I'm the one doing all the work. All you got to do is, you know, wiggle and jiggle."

"If that's not work, then I don't know what is."

"Seven-fifty."

"Okay, I guess I'll just go on home." She stands up as if to leave but Frank pulls her back down.

"Okay, a thousand. But now you're gonna have to do some legwork. Use your charms and go get us some dope on the Babe. I don't see him nowhere out there."

"Some inside dope, coming right up."

She begins the descent down the bleachers, earning a few wolf whistles along the way. A few of the ballplayers are looking, too. That's a good sign, Frank decides. These red-blooded ballplayers will want to get their mitts all over Ginger. Too bad Ruth ain't the one doing the rubbering. He watches Ginger linger by the dugout, and she's playing it perfectly, pretending not to hear what some of the players are saying to her. At least three of them indecently proposition her, but she never flinches.

"Where's Babe Ruth?" Frank hears her ask.

The players all groan and wave at her, then turn away after the coaches start jawing at them. Ginger glances back up at Frank, who motions toward the concession stand. It's the little people in life who know the most about the big people. That old guy behind the counter, he might know where the Babe is. Ginger walks over and starts talking to him. Frank can't hear what they're saying, but the old man's face is lit up like a Christmas tree. He's grinning and chinning and guffawing, and Ginger looks like she's laying it on thick, too, handing him a quarter and letting her hand brush against the old man's.

"Well?" he asks her when she gets back. "What's cooking?"

"From what I understand, the Babe hurt his thumb yesterday taking a swing, so he's not at practice."

Frank scowls down at the field. It's just been one obstacle after another.

But then Ginger adds: "I did manage to get the name of the hotel he's staying at."

She winks at Frank, who nods back at her. Then he gives her a quick pat on the back. A thousand bucks is a lot of money to pay, but it'll be the best money he ever spent if this works out.

"Let's go," he tells her. "I'm getting my money out of you yet."

A car pulls up and parks along the sidewalk that skirts the eastern edge of Crescent Lake. Two men hop out of the rented Model T. Both are sweating like pigs, although both have removed the jackets of their dark suits and carry them slung over their forearms, as if to conceal something. They walk quickly and purposefully toward the grandstand filled with spectators. Other fans lean against the fences on both sides of the diamond.

Crack! A ball goes flying high up in the air toward the lake. Both men momentarily follow the flight of the ball with their eyes, and then keep walking.

"He's tall," Vecchio grumbles. "A real bruiser. And she's a real doll."

"I know what she looks like," sneers Musetta. "I seen pictures of her. A face like hers, no man can forget that. I wonder what kind of figure she's got. Hubba-hubba."

This kid Musetta is a know-it-all. Can't tell him anything. "I'm just saying. Be on the lookout. And remember, her real name is Ginger Hoagland. That's what she told the cops anyway."

"I know. I like Sally Serenade better. Sweet Sally."

They wade into the throng. The batter at the plate sends another ball into orbit, and despite themselves, both men stop and watch.

"That's the college kid. Gehrig." Vecchio keeps up with the teams. He pulls for the White Sox, but the Yankees, they're the best.

"I heard of the bum."

Crack!

"Sounds like a cannon, don't it?" Vecchio's heard enough batting practice to know when a ballplayer has it, and this Gehrig, he's got it in spades.

Musetta's face squinches up like he just bit a lemon. "He ain't better than Pipp."

"Nah, Pipp's a good player. Had a great year. Drove in a hundred and thirteen." Finally they agree on something. They begin to scan the crowd.

"Is that him?" Musetta asks.

Both men set their eyes like two hawks. Up in the grandstand is a tall man with dark features, scooping peanuts into his waiting mouth with absentminded pleasure.

"I don't know." Vecchio's squinting in the sun. This won't be easy. They got into Tampa last night but for a different reason. They came down from Chicago to take care of some kike jeweler Capone had a problem with. Then they get a call in the morning. There was a change of plans. Sally Serenade might be in St. Pete. That's another of Capone's problems—a much bigger problem. Vecchio sighs, still squinting. "I don't know."

"Could be him."

"Could be."

"Let's go."

"Wait!" Vecchio grabs the kid by the arm. Always in a hurry. These young fellas, they got no patience. This kid is supposed to be a good shot. Can hit a tin can from a hundred yards. But there's more to it than that. "See, you need to think. We know what she looks like. We should look for her first, on account of that. You know what Wise said. They're together."

"Unless they split up."

"Let's cross that bridge when we come to it."

"They might've split up."

"My gut tells me she's with him. You don't let a looker like that get away."

Crack! It's a pure sound, a joyous sound. It reminds Vecchio of being a kid playing ball in a vacant lot by the house. They'd play all day. *Crack!*

"For an egghead, Gehrig can sure hit," he says wistfully.

"But not like Pipp."

"Nah, not like Pipp."

"Look, if they ain't here, let's go get some food. I'm starving. I couldn't eat that food on the train. I need food. Then we can look for them."

Vecchio closes his eyes and sighs. The kid don't know what hungry is. None of these punks do. They think food grows in a refrigerator.

"**St. Petersburg's** got loads of potential, loads and loads," says Alberts in a mad rush of words. "This is a city that's going places. It's a great place if you're looking for action, lemme tell you. In a couple years this city'll be one of the finest in the entire world. And I can't wait. No sir, I can't. You know who's buying loads of real estate in this city? Miller Huggins, manager of the New York Yankees, just happens to be one of the biggest lot owners in Lakewood Estates. He's made a small fortune, too! Just don't tell him I told you!"

"I'll remember that," says Ellis Wax slyly. They're walking over to

Alberts's car, a 1923 Model T, and then they're going to take a drive out to Lakewood Estates. Ellis doesn't know what'll happen once they get there but he's keeping his mind open to all possibilities.

"Guess who my boss is playing golf with next week? Babe Ruth, that's who! That's something, huh? But that's the kind of burg St. Pete is. It's a high-rolling city of the future!" Optimism gushes from every pore of Alberts's body. He smells nice and clean, too. Like he's been dipped in bleach.

"That's why I'm here, friend. I'm banking on the future, too."

"You're in the right place!"

They come upon Alberts's car, and it looks just like all the others parked around it, one in a row of identical black machines. Just like Alberts himself: he's no different than the other hawkers working the streets in this town, eager young men who want to make a killing by selling the dream. Same plus-twos, polished shoes, colorful ties, and fast tongues.

"I just got her! Ole Henry Ford makes a swell car, huh?" Alberts puffs his chest out in pride.

"I'll say."

"Here we go! Hop in, Smith! Let's shake a leg!"

They start driving, the car bouncing over the brick pavement. Alberts explains how the next car he'll buy is going to be a Chandler, because they have excellent shock absorbers. "Better than a Ford even," he says, slapping the steering wheel.

"You think?"

"I know. Chandler makes the best car in the world!"

They head west, into the bright sun. Ellis holds up his hand to shield his eyes. After a few blocks, Alberts turns left and they drive south. After a few blocks, the streets are no longer paved. Dust and sand billow up from the road that meanders over a creek where a group of black children are fishing. Ellis suddenly realizes all the faces he sees are colored. Men and women walking up and down the street, a few older folks sitting on porches. Children everywhere. The houses sit tightly packed together and most look like they're ready to fall over.

"Just hold your nose," Alberts says. "They don't live past Twenty-second Avenue. Miles from Lakewood Estates."

"I thought you were taking me to Africa for a minute."

"Ha! That's a good one! But don't let them scare you away from Lakewood Estates! They know their place in St. Pete, that's a fact. Your women and children are safe in Lakewood."

"That's good." Ellis smiles, knowing Alberts has rehearsed these lines countless time before on his journey with customers. He still manages to make his promises seem genuine and spontaneous. He's a good salesman, not great. A run-of-the-mill sort.

"St. Pete has some crack, top-class boys in blue! Yep, our police keep the order, if you get my drift."

Alberts keeps driving, the car careening down a sandy, rutted road that snakes back into a broad, flat expanse of slash pines and cabbage palms, with houses spaced every hundred yards or so. It's a desolate stretch, and Ellis starts thinking: *This might work out after all.* No one's around, but Alberts doesn't pull over. He keeps racing onward, chatting about the advantages of Lakewood and the bright future of St. Petersburg.

Up ahead is the Lakewood Estates sign. A brick wall announces the entrance to a subdivision still in its infancy. Long stretches of sidewalk have been framed out by one-by-fours but not yet filled in. The main road is paved but the ancillary streets are still sandy. A golf course has been completed, but the houses abutting it haven't been, and sit like skeletons in various states of completion. Crews of workers scurry everywhere, awaiting trucks to bring more supplies and haul off piles of debris. Ellis is disappointed: too many people around.

"What's wrong?" Alberts picks up on Ellis's dissatisfaction.

"Nothing. It's just—I like privacy."

"Well, why didn't you say so? I'll show you privacy."

An osprey circles overhead, gliding with effortless grace before it lands on a stumpy pine tree. They turn left down a sandy road, with Alberts describing the wonderful improvements in the offing: paved roads, a sewer line, year-round golf. They pass by a construction crew standing around a cart pulled by a gaunt, haggard-looking horse. Some men are struggling to clear some fallen trees to make room for a house. Alberts gets a jolt of energy from the scene.

"See, the lots are big back down Alhambra Way! Your neighbors will be yards away from you!"

"What's up there?" asks Ellis, pointing to an area a half-mile in the distance, devoid of any building or men, a wide stretch of thick scrub that shields its innards with dense foliage.

"Oh, sure. Those are private!"

"Let's have a look."

"But those are so far from the golf course. You sure you want to be so far away from the links?" For the first time Ellis detects a trace of doubt in Alberts's optimistic trill. Does he finally suspect something?

"I love Lakewood Estates, I promise you. But I'm looking to buy a section of lots. I'd like to take a look if you don't mind."

"Nah, I don't mind. I guess it won't kill us to have a look-see!"

Ellis smiles. "Not unless we get attacked by alligators."

"We paid a man to clear them out of Lakewood. There're no gators back here."

So they drive where even the sandy road stops, and Alberts parks. They get out and take a look around.

"Sure is a nice piece of land. Must be fifteen lots or more." The excitement is back in Alberts's voice as he's probably already calculating his commission on the sale, but you shouldn't ever count your chickens before they hatch. That's the advice Ellis wants to give to the kid, but he won't be needing any advice where he's going.

"I like this," says Ellis cheerfully. "It's what I've been looking for. Lots of privacy."

"I'll second that. But I tell you, Mr. Smith, those lots by the golf course, just one'll turn your money around quicker than these fifteen."

"Mind if I take a closer look?"

Alberts is squinting in the sun. "Be my guest."

Ellis walks into the scrub, pushing back palm fronds to make his path. His feet crunch on the detritus, the fallen litter from years past that decays and rots on the ground. It's moist because of a recent rain and because the huge oak trees block out the sun's rays, creating a dark, cool canopy, the kind of place where a body could decompose without anyone ever knowing. Alberts trails behind, careful not to get his new duds dirty.

"We can drain that muck up there," says Alberts manfully, pointing toward a swampy area. "We'll bring a dredge in here and fill it up."

"That's good. Don't like to have muck around. What about these dead branches? I hate dead branches." Ellis picks up a branch neither dead nor alive, still green where something had ripped it from the tree not long ago. It's still got plenty of heft behind it.

"Oh, we'll bring a crew in. They'll clear it out. You saw those boys back there, didn't you?"

"With that dead-looking horse?"

"Yeah, that's a sorry creature."

"Somebody should put it out of its misery."

"Well, if you're interested in buying the whole kit and caboodle, let's see." Alberts stops and rubs his chin thoughtfully. "I can write a contract for a hundred thousand. As long as my boss approves."

"Sold."

"Now you're talking! We'll go write up what's called a binder. No money's due for thirty days. That way, you can sell it before then and hold on to your cash. It's standard business in this market." Alberts's face beams with an unfettered joy, the face of a child on Christmas opening a treasured toy, the one you've always wanted but never got. But you can't wait for people to give you anything in this world; you've got to take, without asking, like the big boys, the Rockefellers and the DuPonts. They do what they want.

Alberts turns around, his hair polish glinting where the sun has managed to penetrate into the forest. There's a bald spot right at the crown, like a little round target.

"Let's go back to the office and do the paperwork," Alberts chirps, the last words of his life. His head snaps sideways from the vicious blow, his skull crushed at the temple. Again and again the limb crashes against his head, because Ellis Wax is going to make sure. That's what Monk Eastman told him: *When you kill a man, kill him dead. Deader 'n dead.*

With hands trembling, Ellis fishes through all of Alberts's pockets, getting his wallet (with $105 in cash), his pocket watch, some loose change, the keys to the Model T, and his signet ring, from the Optimists Club. There's also a prescription from a doctor, for "medicinal alcohol."

This is getting better and better. Nobody has better booze than the pharmacy.

BREATHING

"Do you mind if I open a window?" Helen Ruth asks quietly, trying not to bother him. He's been in a foul mood ever since he got back from the hunting trip. He's complaining about his stomach again. He was supposed to get into shape at Hot Springs but succeeded only in getting sick. Although he hurt his thumb yesterday at practice, he got up early this morning and went alligator hunting when he should've been resting.

The sun has risen to its afternoon glory and shines right down into their room, the topmost suite of the Princess Martha Hotel. Every minute the room grows hotter, like they're trapped deep within a cave with no escape. She pictures Floyd Collins in that cave, gasping for breath, praying to God for deliverance.

"It'll get drafty then. I'm all stuffed up." He blows his nose into a handkerchief she's never seen before. White with fine lace at the edges, with his initials embroidered in black. Something he'd never buy for himself.

"But I can't breathe," she murmurs, sitting legs crossed on a loveseat.

"Neither can I. Listen." He wheezes and breaks into a fit of coughing. The cigars. He shouldn't smoke them. He shouldn't do a lot of things but he does them anyway.

"Drink your tea before it gets cold. That'll clear you up."

He looks at the tray of food they brought him. Pancakes piled high, strips of bacon, toast with strawberry jam, and a nice cup of steaming tea.

"Ah, to hell with it. Open your window then. You'll just mope around anyways. Enough to make a man half-crazy."

"I don't want to suffocate."

"Open the blasted window, Helen. You want me to call a bellhop to do it?"

"Yes. Call a bellhop."

He snorts in a tantara of derision, picking up a piece of bacon and dropping it into his eager mouth. She used to like watching him eat, the way he attacked food with a boyish gusto, savoring each morsel and describing his joy—he made everything fun, even a simple sandwich. *That was soooo good, I swear! The best piece of ham I've ever seen in my life! I could eat ten of 'em!* He was that way with her, too. Each night in bed he caressed her body with that same fervid energy, that effusive delight, making her feel like the most special woman in the world. She never doubted his love, because he was so open in displaying it, expressing it, not with words, which wasn't his way at all, but with his actions. He brought her gifts from the cities he played in, even sent her postcards. Sometimes he even called on the phone, never talking for long, but just to say he missed her. That he was thinking about her. That he wished she were with him.

"Okeydokey, I'll call a bellhop. Swanky digs like this, they got plenty of jigs down there." He sneezes, wiping his nose not with the handkerchief but with the sleeve of his white robe. He reaches for the phone, but then she stands up and throws open a set of French doors. A breath of fresh cool air kisses her face. She closes her eyes and drinks in the outside, then steps out onto a small balcony overlooking the street.

Why didn't she just head out to the balcony in the first place? Why did she have to talk to him at all? Why is she even here? These questions tumble in her mind as she sits in a rattan chair.

She's the one who asked to come to Florida, although she feared it would turn out like this. Yet a part of her heart hoped beyond reason that somewhere in the jungles and wilds of steamy Florida, they would rediscover that missing spark. That far away from the clamor of Manhattan, they would fall in love all over again, like that morning in 1914 when he stopped in at the diner and their eyes met—did she really think that, or was the truth more like this: she came to St. Petersburg only so She wouldn't. *She* being of course That Woman, That Tramp, That Whore, the one he's been seeing for months now. The one he really loves. Claire Hodgson. Fair Claire.

Down below, across the street from the hotel, a throng of old people has gathered in a pleasant-looking park. Some are playing checkers, it looks like, maybe chess, you can't tell ten floors up. Others are playing croquet, and others merely sit watching the activity. And she thinks: what a happy scene down there. Contentment. Fellowship. That's the way it should be when you get old.

She wonders if she'll become one of those lonely old women everyone feels sorry for. No, she won't let him do that to her. Never. She feels her jaw muscles grow taut in gritty determination. If he wants a divorce so he can be with Her, it'll cost him plenty. Helen has already hired a P.I. to follow him. She'll get the best lawyer in the city, and she'll get all the goodies she can. The farm in Sudbury. A nice Cadillac. And at least a thousand dollars a month in alimony and child support. She won't go without. She won't be laughed at or pitied.

She wipes a tear from her cheek. Why did she come? Why why why?

Turning her attention southward, she sees smoke billowing up into the crisp, clean air, its roiling blackness a stark repudiation of the surrounding tranquility. A fire. Her heart leaps into her throat. Somebody's trapped inside! She can feel it in her bones. Oh, how terrible, how awful! She stands up, gripping the iron rails of the balcony. She can feel the heat of the fire, the flames licking at her skin—to be trapped helplessly, is there nothing worse? But where are the fire trucks? Why aren't any sirens blaring? Maybe they don't know! Should she call and report it?

"What's burning?" He's standing there with a piece of toast, bread crumbs sprinkled on his face.

"See that smoke? It's a fire. I do hope someone's reported it."

"Sure they have, a fire that big."

"Someone might be trapped—like that man in the cave, the one who died in Kentucky a couple days ago. Floyd Collins, poor creature."

"That poltroon? Serves him right for going down a shaft without no backup help, is what the rube did."

"He didn't have to suffer! I swear, you can be so cruel!" The tears come in a great torrent now, and she turns away from him, sobbing, narrow shoulders heaving as he moves in behind her and touches her softly with a big paw.

"Helen, don't cry."

"I'm not crying." She makes herself stop, because he will not see her like this. No. She will not give him the chance to be nice to her. "I just hate fires. You know that."

"I know."

"How's the toast?" She turns and forces a smile, quickly wiping any stray tears.

"It's burnt. They burnt it."

"I can call down and have them bring some more up."

"Ah, don't put the boots to nobody on account of some burnt toast. Watch." He takes some of the blackened bread and crumbles it up, then sends the crumbs flying into the air, watching in delight as the particles fall earthward toward the old folks at the nice park. It's like he's spreading the ashes of some small creature, and she almost crosses herself in reverence of the dead. "Huh? Gotta feed them birds, right? One night, we wuz in Detroit, and Coombs and Whitey Witt got oiled up real good, I mean the two of 'em was so pie-eyed they could barely walk. Anyway, Whitey, he finds this dead bird on the street—what?"

"I don't know if I'll like this story, George."

"No, it's funny. The bird wuz dead, see, but Whitey makes like it's his pet. And he sticks it on his shoulder and starts walking up to people in the lobby, right? You shoulda seen the looks he wuz getting! Don't you think that's funny?"

"Sure."

"How come you didn't laugh?"

"I smiled."

"Ah, you used to laugh at my stories." With that last remark he departs, hulking back inside, bread crumbs on the tile floor the only reminders of his being there at all. She looks from the floor up and back out on the horizon, to the great plume of black smoke rising up over the roofs and trees like a slithery monster on the prowl. The fire department must have been called by now; a fire that size doesn't go unnoticed.

Does Claire laugh at your stories?

That's what she wanted to ask him. But the words never found their way into her mouth.

PEP

The lobby of the Princess Martha Hotel teems with life, like a fishbowl stocked with colorful tropicals. A bored woman in a slinky satin dress stands smoking a long cigarette, arms folded across her flat chest as she awaits her husband, who's explaining to a smiling bellhop why it's so important that he be careful with the luggage. An old couple, married fifty-two years, shuffles across the wood floor. A young man in a fedora watches them, and goes back to reading a newspaper. At the front desk, a squad of officious clerks stands ready to do the bidding of those who are lined up to make requests. Some are checking in, others are checking out; some want directions, others have a complaint.

Then a short, powerfully built man ambles in. He's wearing a cowboy hat and alligator boots, with a huge cigar wedged into the corner of his mouth. Gold rings flash on his thick, knotted fingers. He goes over and takes his place in line with the others, moving with the assuredness of someone who is familiar with being in charge. He walks in a straight line, expecting those in his path to get out of the way, which they do, once they hear the clack of his boots against the tile floor. Once in line, he waits impatiently, glaring dead ahead at those who impede him. He knows exactly what he wants, unlike the others from out of town who are searching for answers. What makes him even more restless is the excitement of what lies ahead that afternoon: he's going to take the great slugger Babe Ruth out on the hydroplane *Miss Ohio*, and if there's any justice in the world, the Babe will buy that boat, and the man in the alligator boots, T. W. Roland, will earn a considerable sum from the transaction. And why wouldn't the Babe want a boat like *Miss Ohio*? It's twenty-five feet of pure mahogany, with a pair of 900-horsepower, 12-cylinder Packard engines that can rev to 1,900 rpm at full throttle. It's big and loud and intimidating, just like the slugger himself—and that's exactly what T.W. plans on telling the Babe, too. Hydroplanes are for men, not boys. He'll say it just like that.

Out of the corner of his eye T.W. sees one fine-looking piece of female pulchritude, a curvaceous number in a low-cut dress and a set of juicy red lips—good enough to eat right out of the can, as T.W. likes to say. And damn if the little honey doesn't wiggle across the lobby and stand right behind him in line. If there's one thing T. W. Roland likes more than boats, it's women. He likes to ride both hard at full throttle, grabbing on to whatever he can during the ride. His whole life, he's collected both, with three ex-wives and boats enough to fill a warehouse outside Detroit, where he lives in the summer. As soon as something catches his eye, he can't stop until he gets ahold of it. That's how he came to buy the *Miss Ohio*, billed as the fastest boat in the free world, owned at one time by Sir Henry Seagrave, a fey Brit who swore the boat wouldn't break 100 mph, the ultimate goal being chased by Seagrave and the Wood brothers and T.W. himself, men addicted to speed on the water. Seagrave was right: the *Miss Ohio* wasn't the boat for the job. But it was still a hell of a boat, and only someone as rich and muddled as Seagrave would sell it for the price he did, so low that T.W. stands to double his money. With that profit, he can buy some bigger Packard engines, 1,000 horsepower, just like he knows the Wood brothers plan on doing. That's what it'll take to get to the century mark, 100 miles per hour: T.W. likes to repeat this phrase in his head like a silent mantra, reminding him of what's truly important in this world. That, and what's standing right behind him. Oh, she smells so nice, like a basket of fresh-cut flowers.

"Afternoon, ma'am," T.W. smiles, tipping his hat gallantly. He really can't help himself around beautiful women. "You're looking ever so lovely today."

"Thank you," comes her answer, inflectionless, eyes avoiding his, a signal most men would take as lack of interest in a conversation. But T. W. Roland can't accept that. She just doesn't know him yet. No wedding ring, either. Not that a ring means very much these days.

"Guess what I'm doing this afternoon?" he asks, suggestively lifting his furry eyebrows. The woman lets out a little sigh, as if burdened by every word out of his mouth.

"What?"

"I'm taking Mr. Babe Ruth out on my hydroplane and we're going to rip across old Tampa Bay out there at near one hundred miles an hour. You can tag along with us if you don't have any other plans."

Her eyes immediately brighten, as he knew they would. It's not every day a woman gets invited on a trip like that. Italian women, Puerto Rican women, Detroit women, they all succumb to a boat ride. "You're taking Babe Ruth out on a what?" she asks excitedly.

"Hydroplane. We're hopping on the *Miss Ohio*. That's my boat— well, one of them. I got lots of boats."

"I love boats," she purrs.

"I knew you did." T.W. hitches up his pants and sucks in his stomach. Sometimes life is as sweet as a big hunk of cotton candy. "That's why I asked you to come along. What's your name?"

"Ginger."

"Nice to meet you, Ginger. I'm T. W. Roland. *T*'s for Thomas and *W*'s for whatever you want." They're now standing at the front desk, and a slender young clerk with drooping eyes and a thin mustache awaits a query. T.W. clears his throat theatrically and booms: "Get me Babe Ruth's room, please." A hush suddenly falls; eyes seek out the speaker and take stock of the man making this audacious request. "Tell him it's T. W. Roland waiting for him down in the lobby."

The clerk picks up a black telephone as T.W. turns back toward Ginger and winks confidently at her. The clerk whispers into the phone and then hangs up.

"He's on his way down, Mr. Roland."

"Thanks, cowboy." T. W. Roland drums his fist on the counter for final emphasis, spins around, and offers his arm to Ginger, who giggles and takes it haltingly, watching Frank out of the corner of her eye. T.W. walks her over to a high-backed rattan chair next to a potted palm, and offers that she sit.

"Oh, stupid me." T.W. slaps his forehead. "Did you need to speak to the clerk about something?"

"No, it's not important anymore."

"There you go. Keep life simple, that's my motto. You are a beautiful lady, Miss Ginger."

"Oh, I bet you say that to every woman you meet."

"That's not my style. I like the truth. Lies are too hard to remember."

Frank is lurking by the entrance. She can tell by his quizzical expression that he doesn't know what she's doing, which makes perfectly good sense, because Ginger doesn't know what she's doing, either. Sometimes, though, luck drops into your lap almost like a spider. Some people stand up shrieking, scared by what they don't expect, while others, like Ginger, never bat an eye. The best-case scenario that she and Frank discussed on the way to the hotel involved Ginger somehow luring the Babe into a semiprivate spot, where Frank would confront him with the tattered IOU. But neither one believed that would happen. A more realistic outcome would have been for them to find out which room the Babe was staying in. Where they went from there was yet to be determined. Frank just wanted to be at the hotel, be near his prey. But this, this is beyond anything they ever discussed, and Ginger's just going to play along, hoping that Frank'll catch on and follow her.

"So have you ever ridden on a hydroplane before?" asks T.W. cloyingly.

"Can't say I have, Mr. Roland."

"Call me T.W. It can get awfully rough."

"I don't mind rough as long as it's fun."

"Me, either." He reaches down and gently clasps her hand, and, bringing it up to his lips, kisses it like some kind of cowboy courtier.

"Oh, T.W., you're such a gentleman," she giggles.

He's seduced a cargo hold's worth of women in his forty-three years, but none has fallen so easily, with so little effort, as this pretty little thing named Ginger. One more smooch on the hand and he might just have to go saddle her up, to hell with Babe Ruth. This mare needs to be ridden.

"I can be a tiger, too," he adds. "I can behave and I can misbehave."

"You're quite versatile, I'd say." Ginger keeps smiling breathlessly, but shoots Frank a quick look to let him know she's got a real lead here; he's no dummy, he'll figure it out.

When Frank saw the cowboy kiss Ginger's hand, he almost barged over there to break it up. He didn't, though, and a good thing too, because not a minute later does the lobby roil with near bedlam when a stout man wearing all white steps out of the elevator followed by a small army of newspapermen and fans and gawkers of every stripe. Babe Ruth himself has arrived. Frank's eyes grow big as saucers as he watches the Babe wave at the man with Ginger and, like Moses parting the Red Sea, wade through the throng in the lobby over to where Ginger is.

"What in thunder?" Frank mutters to himself, overcome by equal parts fear and joy at the scene taking shape before his eyes. The man in cowboy boots shakes the Babe's hand, pumping it vigorously and patting him on the back. Then Ginger shakes the Babe's hand, real lady-like, a coy smile appearing on her red lips. Again she gives Frank a quick nod, as if to show him that she's stumbled upon the jackpot. So that's what all the kissing and cooing was about! That cowboy is a friend of the Babe! Ginger's playing it perfectly, better than Frank thought she could. He decides to creep closer so he can hear what they're all saying. He edges up and takes a position behind the potted palm, and pretends to be looking out a window. He steals a glance every few seconds, as if he's looking for someone.

"—and so I asked this pretty little thing if she'd like to tag along with a pair of randy sailors, and she said she would," says the cowboy, who's wearing enough gold to choke a horse.

"Well, let's go, Roland. The good-looking ones get bored easy," the Babe snorts. Even his voice is large, and hearing it makes Frank grin. He sounds like a wally, like an overgrown kid. But he's bigger than Frank expected, like a bear through his chest and with arms the size of stovepipes. It won't be an easy fight. But hopefully it won't get that far. Hopefully the Babe'll do the manly thing and pay up.

"She's down at the pier, slugger. I'll lead the way. My dear?" Roland, the cowboy, again offers Ginger his arm and she takes it like a virgin schoolgirl on the way to a dance. People in the lobby now have stopped dead in their tracks at the sight of the mighty Babe, and stand watching his every move. The fans begin to circle him and ask for his autograph, and good-naturedly he starts signing baseballs and baseball cards and pieces of scrap paper, and Frank gets an idea: how about if he hands the Babe that IOU from Callahan and asks for an autograph. That would be a hoot, to show him up in front of all his adoring fans. But there's no need to rush anything, because he's got the Babe right where he wants him, thanks to Ginger, who once again gives him a little wink. He responds with a sly grin and a little shrug, careful not to alert the cowboy that his new girlfriend is playing him for a dunce.

"Okay, okay, I gotta go see this man's boat," the Babe announces, waving his arms to ward off more autograph seekers. "He says it's one of the fastest in the world. We'll see about that."

"Oh, it is, trust me it is."

With that, the group starts off, the Babe holding forth with a few sportswriters, Ginger walking with the cowboy, who's chomping on a

cigar like a cow chewing on cud, and Frank lingering behind the movable feast, walking with some fans who skip along in sheer delight.
Small boys have joined the gathering, dirty-faced and excited, scam-
pering about like little puppies. They walk down Fourth Street, past
the open-air post office and the Mitchell Realty Company, turning left
onto busy Central Avenue. Heads turn as pedestrians recognize the big
man in white, and flock to him. The crowd starts to grow larger; car
horns bleep; shouts of glee fill the air.

"A pool hall!" the Babe thunders, stopping in front of Ohio Bil-
liards. "What say, Roland, let's shoot us a game for your boat. You win,
I get the girl. I win, I get the boat."

"You ain't getting this little honey, slugger."

But the Babe isn't much listening. His face is pressed against
the glass of the window. "I'd love to shoot a game!" he barks. "Just one
game!"

"Well, damn it all, slugger. Let's shoot a game of pool."

By now the owner has come out and eagerly leads the Babe in,
handing him a cue stick out on the sidewalk as a kind of inducement.
The owner yells at somebody to get a camera so that a picture of this
momentous event will be memorialized and hung upon a wall. As in
the hotel, everyone in the pool hall stops playing and watches, mouths
agape as the Babe bounds in, telling everyone in there that as a bil-
liards player, he has few equals.

"My momma told me to stay out of pool halls," Ginger tells the
cowboy in a little girl's voice. The cowboy guffaws and gives her a pat
on the rump.

"You wait out here, sweetheart. I'll trounce this baboon and we'll
take us a ride."

Frank waits for the cowboy to duck into the pool hall, then sidles
up to Ginger, who's standing in front of the picture window and looking in, along with the rest of the crowd, so Frank does some pushing
and shoving to get a spot next to her. People yell at him and call him
rude, but a withering glare silences his severest critics.

"You're quick on your feet," he whispers.

"I had you going at first, didn't I?"

"I caught on pretty quick. Try to get the Babe alone."

"I'll try. It's not as easy as it looks. Scram, or you'll blow our cover."

Frank retreats from Ginger, wading back into the crowd watching Babe Ruth shoot a game of pool. The big man hovers over a table, cue in his unbandaged left hand, ready to break. Someone has fetched him a beer and a cigar. Each of his movements is applauded, every word out of his mouth sends his faithful into fits of laughter. When he misses a shot, they groan. When he sinks a ball, cheers go up like he's just clouted a homer in the bottom of the ninth. But the truth is, Roland is the much better player and runs the table on the Babe in short order. When the two reemerge, Ginger acts glad to see the cowboy, chirping hello like a little bird guarding the nest.

"You see me wipe the floor with the sluggard? Huh?"

"I sure did!" Ginger purrs.

The Babe waves a hand in disgust. "Ah, you got lucky, is all. Show me your stupid boat already."

A few pelicans descend on the deck of the speedboat, waiting to be fed. The cowboy shoos them away, and the Babe gives Ginger another squeeze around the waist and whispers something in her ear. She giggles like it's the funniest thing she's ever heard. "You're bad!" she squeals, eyes fluttering like an awestruck schoolgirl. She's playing it to the hilt, got to give her credit. Frank can't help but smile. Everything is working perfectly.

"Don't listen to him!" the cowboy booms, waving his arms over his head. "He's a liar as sure as I'm standing here. He can charm the stink off a skunk."

More giggles, more smiles. Frank, too. He's enjoying this immensely.

"Well?" the cowboy asks. "You gonna buy her or not?"

"The girl? Sure!" The Babe again throws an arm around Ginger, letting his hand slide down over her ass. "How much?"

"The boat, you old goat! You in or you out?"

"Hell, Roland. I'd kill myself in one of these death traps. And besides, I don't got the plunks for her. Wish I did. I should talk to Old Man Rupert about a raise."

"Oh, I know you're lying now! You make more than Coolidge!"

"But he don't have my wife! She's burning through my salary like there's no tomorrow!"

More chuckles and knowing grins and slaps on the back. Babe starts to make his way back to the pier, and Frank stands watching with a frown on his face. Ginger gives him a little look as she allows the two men to hoist her up onto the pier. She's done all she can. The rest will be up to Frank. And, all of a sudden, the gang begins to break up, and the Babe strides right by him, just a foot away—and Frank is seized by indecision.

What should he do? He's got the IOU in his pocket. Should he say something now? Should he wait to see what happens to Ginger? He feels his heart pounding in his chest, like he's on the dead run. One shot, that's all he'll get. He can't blow it. But this doesn't feel right. Everything is moving too fast. Too many people around. He remembers the card game on the train, how he almost ruined everything by being stupid.

Wait, he tells himself.

The cowboy and Ginger go strolling by, along with the rest of the group of onlookers. Frank follows the entourage back toward Central Avenue. The Babe is in the lead, dragging everybody along like a huge magnet. That's what it's like to be famous. You suck in everything around you. All eyes, all sound, all the air, too. Like he's commanding some army who'd do anything he says. Even Frank is mesmerized. You can't help but stare.

At the Princess Martha Hotel, the Babe bids all farewell and disappears into the lobby. Roland and Ginger are standing outside, alone now, except for Frank, who's pretending to window-shop in front of the hotel's gift store.

"So, young lady, did you have a good time?" the cowboy asks.

"I did. That was swell!"

"There's plenty more where that came from! I can take you to dinner tonight, anywhere you want!"

"Gee, I don't know what to say."

"Say yes! I'll pick you up at eight. What's your room number?"

"Oh, I don't remember. Have the boys at the front desk ring me."

"Do you need a pretty little dress to wear? I hear tell that this burg's got some nifty stores full of finery. Maybe we should go get you something to look beautiful in! And there's the dog track tomorrow night—you'll need two dresses! Twice the fun!"

"What dog track?"

"Didn't you hear him talk about it? They're running the Babe Ruth Cup tomorrow night! And you're gonna be my date. It's going to be a fancy soiree."

"That's awfully nice of you, but—"

"Come on, little lady. T.W. wants to shop!"

Out of the corner of his eye Frank sees the cowboy extend an arm, which Ginger takes with all of the daintiness of a fair damsel, and off they go prancing to raid the department stores on Central Avenue. There were lots of them. It should take them a couple hours at least.

So there's nothing for Frank to do now but wait for her to come back. If she comes back, that is. Because now Frank's starting to wonder if things haven't worked out a little *too well*. Ginger played it to the hilt, all right, but was she really acting? Or was she punching the bag with a sugar daddy? He didn't make her for a gold digger. But what if she was? What if she has her own plan? Why would she help him then? She wouldn't. Any rube could see that.

"**Y**ou follow him," Vecchio tells Musetta, "and I'll tail the skirt."

"I'll take the skirt."

"Don't whine. Just do your job. We'll meet back at the hotel after we figure out what's going on. We got lucky finding them this quick. Let's make the most of it."

So Vecchio heads off in one direction, while Musetta, frowning, goes off in another. Of course the old man wanted to take the skirt: she's got a ten-grand price tag on her head, and Hearn's worth just five. Vecchio sure likes throwing his weight around. Nobody told him he was in charge. All Guzik said on the phone this morning was *Get over to St. Pete and make sure that broad ain't there*. He didn't say Vecchio was in charge. But Vecchio's worked for Johnny Torrio for a long time now. He must think that gives him a leg up. But Joey Muse doesn't like taking orders from anybody.

So he'll tail this Hearn fella, because there ain't time to argue about it. But they'll have to discuss the situation later. Vecchio's an old-timer who's used to doing things a certain way, but the old ways ain't always right. Vecchio don't like to use a Tommy gun. Thinks those are for *burloni*, jokers who can't shoot. But if you want to get a job done quick, there's nothing better. Why use one or two bullets when you can use two or three hundred? They'll have to have a talk about that, too.

Musetta follows Frank Hearn down the main drag, keeping about fifty feet back. Along the way he pretends to be window-shopping. Looks at the oranges at the Sunshine City Fruit Company and some bowlers at the New York Hat Shop. Watches a woman making a dress and barbers cutting hair. Naturopath? What do they do? He ignores a bookstore, but lingers in front of a novelty shop. Like to spend some time in there, but Hearn keeps on going, down to the water, where they just were. That was some swell boat the Babe was checking out. It must be nice to make more money than the president—but neither of them bums makes a fraction of what Capone pulls in. Al could buy ten of them boats if he wanted to.

A steady stream of automobile traffic slowly creeps along in both directions. People have places to go and things to do, and they're in a hurry to get there. Horns blare, brakes squeal. It's pandemonium on the roads in this town. Nobody knows how to drive.

Hearn walks over to a park that runs along the waterfront. Concrete sidewalks wind through the swaths of sandy weeds, broken only by stout bushes, a few tall oaks, and stubby palms arrayed at water's edge. People are flocked along the water, fishing, sitting, courting, basking in the afternoon sun. Hearn finds a spot and plops down, letting his feet dangle over the side of the seawall.

Musetta traipses behind. A few nice-size sailboats are anchored in a harbor, rocking gently in the calm waters of the bay. The sun stands high overhead. The stubby palm trees rustle in the light breeze blowing in from the east. Musetta finds a green bench and sits down. Might as well enjoy the view. But he's dying in these clothes. They'll have to get some new threads and soon. He can't sweat like a pig all day.

A few minutes later Hearn lies back on a small patch of grass and closes his eyes. He's taking a snooze! It won't be hard to follow him now. Musetta looks around. There's a hotdog stand nearby. Talk about luck. It's all been aces so far.

When **Assistant** State Attorney William McSwiggin arrives back at his office after spending a frustrating day in court, he takes a call he's been hoping for. It's from Detective Hughes. The message is simple: Fingers Finley was finally home.

"I'm on my way!" Little Mac tosses his half-eaten sandwich on a stack of pleadings and goes rushing out. This is the break they need if they hope to find Sally Serenade before Capone's thugs do. Fingers Finley was her pianist and presumably her friend. If anyone can help them locate her, it's him. But he's been AWOL ever since the Horn murder. Maybe he thinks the coast is clear. Wait till he hears the latest news.

The address Hughes gave him is a ramshackle building on Belmont Street, just off Clark. Wrigley Field isn't far away, and it won't be long now until the Cubs are back in action, stinking up the joint. McSwiggin vows to take in a game on the first warm day of the year. He could use a break. He's been at it hammer and tongs for days on end. Mom says he looks pale. He'll rest once Capone is in college.

Hughes is waiting in the foyer. Together they walk up three flights of stairs, past the inconsolable wails of babies, the angry voices of cuckolded husbands, the aggravated cries of unhappy wives. "He's nervous," says Hughes. "He's spooked bad."

It's true. The first thing McSwiggin notices about Fingers Finley is how bad the old man is shaking. Every part of his body seems to be trembling, not just from the cold, but from something else.

"Something wrong?" McSwiggin asks the fragile pianist, whose long, slender hands seem almost comically feminine given his other pronouncedly masculine features, bulbous nose, large, elephantine ears, cleft chin, and thinning gray hair.

"Nothing some medicine won't cure."

"Got a good prescription, do you?"

Without answering Fingers Finley helps himself to a tumbler of scotch whiskey, legally obtained through a licensed medical doctor. The Volstead Act has a few loopholes, none larger than the medical exemption. Fingers may have obtained his prescription fraudulently, but that's no matter now. The good news is the drink calms the little man down. He stops shaking as badly as he was, and his two sad eyes regard the men with less malice.

"I told you I don't know where she is," Fingers says softly. "You trying to get me killed or something?"

"No," says McSwiggin, "but you can keep her from getting killed."

"How's that? If I told you where to look, word would get to Johnny Torrio by the end of the day."

"You have a low opinion of me. I keep secrets, Mr. Finley."

"That's Fingers to you, son. You know your problem? You're young. You think you can change things in this city. Well, the only thing worse than being young and stupid is being old and stupid. I may be old, but I'm not stupid."

"They know where she is."

The old man draws a sharp breath. "You're lying."

"They sent someone to kill her. In Asbury Park, New Jersey."

"Asbury Park?"

"Does that ring a bell?"

The shaking starts again, and Fingers Finley pours another drink, a double this time.

"They didn't kill her—this time," Hughes continues. "The trigger-man got it instead."

The old man's teeth start chattering, and he throws a blanket around his thin shoulders.

"There might not be a next time for her," McSwiggin interjects.

"How did they find her?" the old man asks feebly. "Nobody knows she went there except me. And I didn't tell those bastards nothing!" He starts coughing, his entire body convulsing as he does.

"Did she know somebody there?"

"No, I did. An old friend of mine from New York—he's a photographer there. Oh my God!"

"What?"

Fingers Finley brings a trembling hand to his open mouth. His eyes are wide and filled with horror. "He sent me a postcard last week. 'Greetings from Asbury Park. Ginger sends her love.' That's her real name, Ginger. Those bastards are reading my mail!"

ROUNDABOUT

Because Irene's skin is tender, the solarium's female attendant, Miss Cindy Hatchette, has decided not to expose the patient to the sun for any length of time, allowing only fifteen minutes of heliotherapy per hour. Thus Irene finds herself tossing a light medicine ball back and forth in the dank locker room, where the three shower nozzles drip, drip, drip against the bare concrete floor. The man who was supposed to lay the tile quit to take a better job as a land surveyor, and they haven't been able to find another tile setter. The same with the plumber: he never came back to fix any of the leaks after installing the pipes a few years back. Mr. Lawrence, the director, is a fine fellow, Miss Hatchette assures Irene, but he's not very handy. Now her fiancé, Daniel Ott, can fix just about anything he puts his mind to. In fact, he's building a garage for his father, at their house over on Burlington Avenue (wherever that is). They own the loveliest grove of orange trees you ever did see; soon they'll be blossoming and filling the air with the sweetest smell. It's heavenly to have a picnic back in the grove during early spring. But they need to start saving for their own house, although there's room enough at his parent's house. For a year or so anyway, and then it'll be time to start their own family—and you can't very well do that at his parent's house! How embarrassing!

Irene listens and agrees with everything Miss Hatchette says to her. It's remarkable how some people can find sheer delight in the smallest details, and wring from them every last drop of joy, making life a cheerful sponge soaked with trivial happenstance and frivolous fluttering. But there's a kind of gentle music in Miss Hatchette's fluid narration of her comings and goings, plans and hopes, that sounds kind of like a Gene Austin record, happy-go-lucky and brimming with good cheer. Nowhere in her chatting is there room for doubt and despair, for Daniel Ott to be a lying, womanizing loafer who'll say one thing and do another. They will be married and they will be happy, just as certainly as the medicine ball will fly through the air in a straight path and not veer wildly up toward the ceiling. Miss Hatchette's talking, though, passes the time, almost imperceptibly, and lets Irene forget for a few hours the ridiculous setting she finds herself in.

"Okay," Miss Hatchette announces, wedging the medicine ball beneath one of her plump arms, "now you should go back out under the sun for fifteen minutes."

"If you say so."

"Think how fit you'll feel in a week!"

Irene starts walking. It must be nice to have optimistic beliefs to guide you through troubled waters, instead of always kicking apart everything and thinking the whole world is bunco. As Irene reclines on the hard lounge chair, her robe splayed open to provide the only cushion beneath her, she closes her eyes and lets the sun rain down on her. Her naked flesh feels prickly and alive, her muscles relax beneath the deluge of heat, and to herself she mutters *Frank Hearn, Frank Hearn, Frank Hearn* like the dripping shower. He's probably having the time of his life in California with Miss What's-Her-Name. Frank always makes sure he has a good time. They had so much fun together, laughing like children, never a dull moment. If only she'd married him! Irene grips the sides of the lounge chair like it's falling through the sky.

"Okay, that's enough for the day," Miss Hatchette announces. "Time to go home. We'll see you tomorrow."

Irene lifts an eye. She doesn't want to move off her wooden chair, she doesn't want to leave the confines of these walls that block out the world. "Do I have to?"

"You don't want to burn. You're off to a good start."

Irene goes in and takes a long shower, soaping down every inch of her body and letting the warm water pound against her back. But Miss Hatchette chases her out of there, too, and practically dresses Irene herself, all the faster to shoo her outside where Mummy is waiting. Plucked eyebrows lift in obvious concern, but with a quick smile when Irene emerges.

"Hello, Mummy. I'm all better."

"Are you?" Lauren kisses her daughter gently on the cheek. Irene's face has become reddish pink, sunburned in a way Lauren Howard always tried to prevent. A woman's skin is her best asset and needs to be treasured like the gems in King Tut's tomb. Now her daughter looks like some common washerwoman too long exposed to the elements.

"Yep. I've decided I'm going to marry one of these Spanish-American War veterans. I think older, wounded men are very, very attractive."

Veterans come streaming out of the solarium, hobbling back toward their hotels with the same beet-red faces that Irene has. Except the men are smiling and seem rejuvenated, eyes sparkling and laughter rippling. That's it right there, Lauren Howard decides. Irene's problem is that she doesn't appreciate anything anyone's ever done for her. She doesn't know what it's like to struggle, to suffer, to sacrifice. Irene doesn't know because Lauren Howard has done everything in her power to make her daughter's life comfortable, stable, and structured.

A car horn bleats, and Irene waves. A spiffy black coupé pulls up to where she's standing, and Lauren watches as Irene skips over to talk to the driver. He looks a lot like that ruffian they met on the train. Wax. That's it, Ellis Wax. The same beetle-browed expression of un-mannered liberty, the same shifty eyes and careless smirk—what's he doing here? Lauren Howard hurries her pace, hearing the loud cachinnations coming from her daughter's delighted mouth. She sounds like a wounded bird. What a spectacle this is, from the frying pan into the fire. She threw herself at him on the train, all to get a rise. It's starting to work. Lauren feels her face growing hot.

"Irene!" Lauren Howard calls out. The car speeds off, the driver not even waving as he careens by. What kind of man calls on someone's daughter without the courtesy of a greeting to the mother? Unless his intentions are less than honorable, in which case it makes perfect sense for him to disappear like a thief into the night, absconding with purloined gems. The epitome of rudeness. Lauren comes traipsing back as if nothing in the world is amiss.

"Who was that, may I ask?"

"Ellis Wax. The nice gent we met on the train."

"Will he be calling on us?"

"No."

"That's too bad. I was so looking forward to his company."

"Ha, ha, Mummy. I can tell by the tone of your voice you don't approve of him. But you don't even know him." Irene's voice is loud enough that a group of men fishing nearby turns to look at what the fuss is all about. But nothing mortifies Lauren Howard more than public displays of incivility, so she allows Irene to have the last word.

"You're right, darling. Let's get something to eat," she says. "And then maybe we can go shopping."

When Irene was younger, before her troubles began, the two of them used to take the train into New York and spend entire days prowling along Fifth Avenue, visiting every store and trying on an array of outfits, chatting in that intimate shorthand that often develops between mother and daughter. Everyone always commented on not only how beautiful Irene was but also how well behaved she was, how well mannered and polite, with unaffected poise and charm mixed with the best parts of girlishness, giggles, curiosity, kindness, love of animals. Those trips to the city were so special.

"I hate shopping," replies Irene.

"Since when?"

"Since I learned that the poor creatures who make our clothes work in wretched conditions for very little money."

"Who told you that?"

"Daddy."

"Oh, nonsense."

"He did! He was proud of it, too! I didn't know we owned a textile plant in Virginia."

"And that's why women should keep their noses out of the affairs of men. It's not your place to know your father's business."

"So if I married Jimmy Woodman, and he got involved in bootlegging, I shouldn't say anything?"

Lauren Howard's heart nearly leaps into her throat. It's been months since Irene's even mentioned Jimmy Woodman's name, much less in context of marriage. Jimmy Woodman had been Irene's sweetheart until she stopped seeing him the summer she moved to Asbury Park to live with Tillie. Irene's abrupt termination of their courtship hurt Jimmy Woodman badly, but his mother has told Lauren that he loves her still and hopes that one day Irene will change her mind about their future. Jimmy Woodman is everything any girl could ever want, handsome, cultured, manly, wealthy, and kind. He attends Princeton and plays on the baseball team. He worshipped the very ground that Irene walked on, and she seemed to love him as well. Could she again? Could she become that person she was before she wrecks her entire life?

"Well, I'm sure Jimmy would never get himself tangled up in that," Lauren says happily.

"Ha! I guess you don't know him half as well as you think you do. Jimmy Woodman is just the biggest hootch hound at Princeton."

"I find that very hard to believe."

"Okay, fine. Don't listen to me. I'm crazy."

"You're not crazy." Lauren reaches out and brushes her daughter's sun-kissed cheek. "I don't want you to say that."

But like an unbroken mare her head recoils at the touch. "Ouch! That hurts! My face is on fire!"

"We'll need to buy some ointment. And you'll need a sun hat as well. I could use one, too. There wasn't much time to pack."

It's not hard to find reasons to go shopping. Life always springs surprises, needs constantly arise that you can't plan for. As mother and daughter walk back toward their hotel, so that they can hop on one of those wicker strollers, Lauren Howard hopes normalcy will return to her life. Return to normalcy: it's what President Harding promised. At least Irene mentioned Jimmy Woodman's name, and she's agreed to go shopping. Maybe this sun therapy will prove effective. Maybe there will be normalcy after all.

"I bet you're surprised, huh?" asks Ellis Wax as he gives Mabel Wright the rent he owes her. Fifty dollars, five sawbucks, crisp and new.

She looks up at him, kneeling in front of one of her flower beds. She puts down a spade, takes the money, and stuffs the bills into a pocket. "Nothing surprises me anymore," she says, turning away from him and resuming her gardening.

"I told you I had to get my feet on the ground," adds Ellis hopefully. "I'm turning my life around, and that's not balloon juice. Monk said you were the best, and he was right."

"Don't mention it. In fact, I'd really like it if you didn't talk about Monk to my other lodgers. I don't want them knowing any more about me than they have to."

"Roger." He pauses, watching her dig. "My mother loved to work in her garden. What's this?" He leans over to smell the fragrance of delicate white flowers blooming on a tangled vine. He closes his eyes and feels the warmth of the sun on his face. He's starting to like it here.

He's got money and a car, and a date with Irene Howard. He switched the license plates already, stealing one from a tin lizzie parked in an alley. He's home free. The cops'll never find him. No witnesses, no fingerprints, there's a thousand Model T's just like his in this town. A, B, C, 1, 2, 3.

"That's Confederate jasmine."

"It smells real pretty. My mother always had fresh flowers in the house. She would've loved your garden." He pauses a second, waiting to compose himself. "She died when I was young. But I'll never forget the flowers she grew."

Mabel stops digging and looks up at him again. "I meant to mention something else. Somebody took a knife out of the kitchen today. They don't grow on trees. So I'm telling everyone to ask me first before they use something." She tears at the earth with the spade, stymied by stubborn roots from a nearby oak tree.

"It wasn't me."

"I didn't say it was."

"I don't like knives. They're dangerous."

"Well, I'm just telling everyone about it."

Ellis departs, walking across the manicured lawn accentuated by a primrose path of stones, several birdbaths, and a scattering of tables, where Mabel's other renters sit playing cards or reading. Most are older, worn, decayed, withered: Ellis smiles as he passes by. He feels like being nice to the whole world today. A bottle of booze would be perfect right now. He could fill that prescription he's got, but it might be risky.

He walks into his room. He relaxes on the squeaky single bed, its springs sagging in the middle. He takes out the prescription for medicinal alcohol and looks at it carefully. If he could just change the name: Guy Alberts.

What about making it Albertson? Sure, that would be simple. Guy Albertson. Just add two letters at the end.

There's a way around every problem, if you just think about it.

"I got some information on Ellis Wax like you asked."

Mabel Wright sits down in a straight-back chair. She's been waiting for Szymanski to phone her back. But she's got pork chops grilling and potatoes boiling, and a bunch of hungry geezers waiting to put their dentures in their empty mouths. This isn't the best time to talk, but it'll have to do.

"Shoot, detective."

"He's a stockbroker, lives in Catonsville. White male, fifty years old, only a few speeding tickets. Is that your guy?"

It sounds like Szymanski is standing at the bottom of a well. She can barely hear him.

"Talk louder."

He shouts the same description. Mabel Wright hears him better this time.

"Nah, don't sound like it. My lodger is probably twenty-five, dark hair, wiry and thin. He says he knew Monk from the joint, and he came down here to start his life over."

The line starts to crackle, buzzing like a swarm of bees. Nobody says anything for a few seconds. Then Szymanski shouts: "Wait, I see here that Ellis Wax reported a burglary a couple of days ago. Somebody broke into his office, but it don't say what was stolen. It ain't nothing we're looking at too hard. This is the first I've heard of it."

Mabel Wright frowns. Szymanski sounds like he couldn't care less. "There's something fishy about this guy. He didn't have no rent this morning but he just paid me fifty bucks."

"Well, let me drive out and talk to my Ellis Wax when I get the chance. I'm pretty swamped now, but I'll do my best." The tone of his voice indicates he's going to hang up and forget all about it.

"I appreciate it, detective. I don't want no riffraff messing up my new life down here."

"We're real proud of you, Mabel, for turning things around."

"I better go before I burn supper."

Mabel Wright hangs up the receiver and rushes over to the stove. The kitchen now smells like burned pig. She picks up a fork and turns the chops over. A little singed on one side, but nothing horrible. Her eyes drift over to the utensils drawer. She thinks about the knife as she gazes out a window and back toward the garage. Ellis Wax took it but he returned it, didn't he? What if she's all wrong about the guy? Maybe she's blowing it all out of proportion. This Ellis Wax, whoever he is, maybe he's just some two-bit grifter who wouldn't hurt a flea. He played the C on some bank to get his dough—but then again, maybe he didn't. Still, it won't hurt for Szymanski to poke around a little. A hunch is a hunch, and she doesn't have a good feeling about her new tenant. He might be polite but polite people make her nervous. Those are usually the biggest liars of all.

DANCE
LESSON

After a quick snooze, Frank decides it's time to get up and see what else there is to be seen in this burg. The waterfront stretches for miles, so it'd be nice to take in all the scenery. He could walk south along the water and end up back near his smelly palace of a garage. At least it's near a big harbor, and earlier he saw some big boats there. Soon fishermen would be returning with the catch of the day: tarpon, kingfish, amberjack, those are the prizes the anglers seek. It'd be nice to book a charter and do a little fishing. He could chat with some of the captains and work a deal. Once he gets this business taken care of, he'll have plenty of time and money to do what he wants.

Frank walks a block and then stops to admire the yacht club. It looks like a trig building, tall windows opening out to spacious balconies. There's some high-hatters enjoying the view, the women dressed to the nines, the men in crested blazers. And everyone is drinking something. You won't see no flatties from the Prohibition Bureau breaking up that party. Different rules apply to the rich, and that's a fact. They're all so pleased and satisfied up there. They don't have to scrounge and beg and borrow—but they do steal, and steal plenty. Yet he'd trade places with any of them. To be rich for just one day! That's the life, never having to work, buying anything you want, traveling in first class. That'll be him up there one day, looking down on the rubes on the street.

Across the street from the yacht club is a little fish market, and he strolls over to see what's for sale. The fish look fresh enough. People crowd around to make purchases, and then they'll cook fancy dinners in fancy houses. Lucky for them. But he's got no one to blame but himself for being hungry. He thinks about the twenty-five bucks he lost playing cards on the train. Those bones would've bought him a nice meal, which he could use right about now.

A block farther south Frank comes upon the Fountain of Youth. It doesn't look like much, just a small concrete tub of funny-smelling water. Some old folks are splashing in it and even drinking it, and they couldn't look more delighted. Good for them. Why not live forever? There's nothing wonderful about getting old and losing your senses. You'd see some of them in Asbury Park, oldsters with stooped backs and leaning on canes, trying to get around, talking to no one. It's easy to see why so many of them head to Florida in the winter. Cities like St. Petersburg make it damn nice for the old folks. And if you can sell them a house, that just makes it even better. Good for business, these old people are.

Out of the corner of his eye Frank spots an ape in a dark suit. He's a swarthy-looking fella, and if Frank's not mistaken, it's the same person who was sitting on a bench back at the park. Now he's standing at the little fish market. Frank is suddenly seized with the idea that he's being followed. Not that there's any reason to think so. It's just old habits die hard. In a place like Asbury Park you learn quick to watch your back, because you can't really trust nobody else to watch it for you. But there's one way to settle this matter once and for all. Frank just needs to hop across the street and head west up one of these avenues, and see if the ape does the same.

He feels a little stupid when he crosses the street, darting through the heavy traffic that crawls along at a snail's pace. His mind is playing tricks on him. Why the hell would anybody be following him? He just got into town eight hours ago. And who even knows he's here anyway?

No one except Enrico, and he'd never tell a soul. But who else knew? Nobody—nobody. Frank's heart starts to beat faster as he cruises into the setting sun, its rays shining into his squinting eyes. Nah, don't panic, he tells himself. You're imagining things.

After he goes a block Frank stops and pretends to look into the window of a dress shop. He steals a glance back down the street, and damn if the ape hasn't crossed over, keeping the same fifty-yard distance. That spells trouble. Someone is on his tail. Frank's mind tumbles, trying to think of everything at once. Who it could be, what does he want, what's the next move? It's like juggling a bunch of knives. The first thought that flashes into his mind is somebody is going to a lot of trouble to find Ginger DeMore. She warned Frank that she was a target, and that he'd get it, too, if he helped her. Damn if she wasn't right. But he can figure all that out later. What should he do now?

It won't be hard to give this ape the slip. Frank's outrun plenty of flatties in his day. Duck into a building and head out the back door. Unless there's two of them. Frank swallows and glances back down at his pursuer. The fella is standing there, hasn't moved an inch in the last few minutes. But is outrunning him the right step? Maybe the best thing would be to turn the tables and see if the ape don't beat a fast retreat once Frank reverses field and walks back down the street. Yeah, Frank smiles, he should become the follower, not the followed.

So down the hill he marches, long legs devouring sidewalk with each stride. Little old ladies stand aside and let him pass. Frank keeps his eyes on the ape, who just keeps standing there. He's gawking at some flower shop. Flower shop! Who's he trying to fool? No ape like him ever buys flowers unless he's headed to a funeral. Well, two can play that game. Frank sidles right up next to the fella and looks at the flowers. The ape doesn't even flinch.

"Some nice tulips, huh?" says Frank, tapping on the glass.

"Those aren't tulips. They're violets. African violets."

"Jeepers creepers, you're some flower Einstein. What are those back there?"

"Roses."

"Yeah, I thought so. You can't figure out too much these days. Nothing is what it looks like anymore." The ape just keeps standing there, holding on to his jacket like a child clings to a teddy bear. Frank decides to take a more direct approach, since this fella is acting so cool. "You shopping for your girl?"

"No, afraid not. I'm going to a funeral."

"A funeral?" Frank almost snorts out a laugh but keeps it bottled up. This is getting rich. "Whose?"

The ape finally looks up at him, his big snout lifting up in anger, the way a dog bares its teeth at intruders. "What's it to you anyway?"

"Just curious, is all. Don't mean to pry. Just making small talk." With that last utterance, Frank lopes off back toward the waterfront, and the fella in the dark suit goes inside the flower shop. Some mixed-up world this is. You're always thinking somebody's after you. It's enough to drive a man to drink. And that's what Frank could really use. But where can he get some? Maybe his landlady will know of something. She didn't seem like a prude. But you can't be too sure, either. No sense getting tossed out on the street.

If she don't know anything, one of those old-timers will. So Frank beats it back double-time, hoping he doesn't get lost because he doesn't remember the address. It's on Third Street, that's all he knows.

It feels good to pass by face after face, not a single person knowing who he is. *Don't be so jumpy,* he tells himself.

K resky's is crowded as it usually is on a Friday after work. Every stool at the bar is occupied and so is every table. Excited voices clatter in the smoky haze as Detective Joe Szymanski elbows his way through the throng toward the back, where he knows he'll find his usual mates, fellow cops like himself who need a few drinks to unwind

after a long, hard week of keeping the citizens of Baltimore from ripping each other to shreds. It's not easy. It's hard enough keeping the
usual rabble in order, knife fights in Little Italy, Czech hookers working the Block, darkies selling dope on the Avenue, but when a rich
dame gets raped and killed in Mount Vernon, that's when all hell
breaks loose. Now you got the politicians breathing down the neck of
the brass, and the brass in turn want an arrest. Nothing should ever go
wrong in Mount Vernon.

A chorus of "Hey, Joe!" goes up when his companions spot him.
They've saved him a chair, and there's already a beer waiting for him.
He sits down and lifts the mug to his lips, draining half of it. Then he
wipes the foam from his mustache.

"Where's Carroll?" he asks, noticing that the usual group is missing a member.

"He's working the Marshall case."

"Anything breaking?"

No one answers, and Szymanski frowns. It's just a matter of time
before they pull him off Property and assign him to the Marshall case.
It's been three days now since the body of Freda Marshall was discov-
ered in the bedroom of her well-appointed home on Cathedral Street.
Her throat was cut from ear to ear, and she'd been raped. The only suspect is her stepson, Aubrey Marshall, who has seemingly disappeared
off the face of the earth.

"Carroll's talking to the other brother again," says Brodky, "for the
hundredth time. But they won't find this kid, Aubrey Marshall, if you
ask me. He planned this out for a long time, for a year, ever since Old
Man Marshall died and left Aubrey nothing. This was no spontaneous
thing. He plotted it out and got away with it."

"Hey!" sings Szymanski, eager to change the subject that has
dogged them since Tuesday, "guess who called me today? Mabel
Wright. Remember Monk Eastman?"

Laughter erupts from the table. Who could forget that pair? They
ran some of the most creative cons in the annals of Baltimore crime.
Monk was an expert forger, almost like an artist, and Mabel could talk

herself into anybody's house or office to steal whatever Monk needed. The best was the toilet scam: Monk sold bogus stock in a company that made toilets that flushed by themselves. "You don't need to lift a finger," he told his marks.

"Guess where Mabel's living now? Florida. She's got herself all straightened out and owns a boardinghouse."

The men shake their heads. One whistles. "Lucky dame. I wouldn't mind living in Florida. It's nice, I hear."

"They need cops down there, too."

"Wouldn't that be something? Huh?"

Szymanski finishes the rest of his beer, and volunteers to spring for the next pitcher. It's going to be a good night: at least now nobody's thinking about where Aubrey Marshall is hiding.

The sun's bleeding orange-pink in the western sky, hovering above the horizon, and soon darkness will fall. The coming of night always gives Frank an extra dose of pep. Daytime had never been his favorite. It's when people go to work to boring jobs and come home tired. Like his poor ma: that woman never knew what it meant to have a good time. Sure, Frank tried to bring in some cash, but how much can a kid make setting up pins at a bowling alley? Not much. So Ma worked for other people, doing the chores no one wanted to do, and he watched her suffer. Watched her body wither limb by limb until there was nothing left of her. She wanted so much for him to go to school, but Frank had other ideas. The night beckoned him. The night, when people took off starched collars and actually lived. After Ma died, Frank vowed never to let the daytime world grind him into pulp. He belonged to the night.

As he walks down the length of Third Street, he can see the tired men readying to leave. The drivers of the Nu Grape Bottling Company have finally delivered that last shipment. The Farmer Concrete Works has also called it a day, and the workers go trudging forth, carrying empty lunch pails back home, where they'll be filled by exhausted women who spent all day chasing around a brood of screaming children. And tonight they'll all dream of another life, tossing fitfully in their sleep, dreading the approach of dawn and another day of ceaseless toil. If Frank needed anymore reminding of what was at stake, these wan faces provided it.

In the lush courtyard behind Mabel Wright's boardinghouse, sitting beneath a kerosene lantern, the old folks are playing a spirited game of cards. Everyone looks up as Frank passes by. He nods politely to them, keeping an eye out for the landlady. He can smell chops being fried in the kitchen. What he wouldn't do for a hot meal. He should wash up first, before he turns on the charm. But a drink would be best of all.

Sitting alone at a table in front of the garage is a man in a white straw hat. He's young, unlike the other lodgers, with a pair of beady eyes beneath a jutting brow, shaped like he's got too much brains for his head.

"Evening," says Frank, passing on by, fishing a skeleton key from his pocket. The guy in the white hat gets up and follows him down the short and narrow corridor.

"I guess we're neighbors," the man chimes, extending a hand. "The name is Wax. Ellis Wax." They shake hands, and Frank stifles a laugh. This Wax fella is wearing a white coat that hangs on him like a sack, a white necktie, a white belt, white socks, and white shoes. Every item he's got on looks brand-new, with creases still running down the front of his white knickers. Wax looks like one of those binder boys that swarm the streets.

"I'm Frank Hearn."

"Nice knowing you. Say, some nice night out, huh? Those rubes up north are shivering but we're as balmy as can be."

"This is some swell weather." Frank's not sure what to make of this Ellis Wax. He talks kind of fast and seems real eager, and those clothes—he ought to buy a mirror, and soon. Truth is, Frank's not much in the mood for small talk. He wishes this little gnat would fly away. But then comes an interesting offer.

"Care to bend your elbow with me?"

Frank's face lights up like a kid on Christmas morning. "You got some booze?"

"Step into my office, Frank. Your nerves look shot. You could use a jolt of neuropathic ointment, in my humble opinion."

You should never judge a book by its cover. Happily Frank steps into Ellis Wax's room, the same cramped and smelly cave as Frank and Ginger have across the hall. It looks like Wax is traveling light: his only luggage appears to be a typewriter. But there is a nice bottle of vodka sitting next to it on the table. There's a basket of flowers, too. The booze is prettier.

"Yeah, I had a prescription filled this afternoon." Ellis winks at him. Frank smiles knowingly. Best booze you can get outside of Canada, pharmacy hootch. Ellis finds a couple of small glass jars, and they sit down in wobbly chairs. "Cheers," Wax offers, lifting his glass. "So, where you from, Frank?"

"Asbury Park, New Jersey."

"Great town! I love the shore!"

"Yeah, but it's all fixed. A man without pull don't stand a chance. But here—" Frank nods to indicate the lush environs outside their stinky abode—"here a man can make something of himself. You can pull yourself up by your own bootstraps. Especially if you figure out the real estate market."

"Is that your line of work, Frank?"

"It will be."

Wax snorts appreciatively, and pours two more drinks. Frank's feeling warm and loose now, weightless, like a raft on the ocean. This Ellis Wax is a good egg. A real straight shooter. Meet your neighbors and pour some drinks. That's how people should treat each other.

"You picked the right city, if my eyes are any judge," sings Wax. "It seems like you can make a killing here without breaking a sweat."

"What brings you to Florida?"

Ellis Wax's smile vanishes. He draws a deep breath and exhales while shaking his head. "I don't want to sound like a chump, Frank, but I'm here for one simple reason: I'm starting my life over. I've had some bad breaks back up where I'm from, and I just want to wash the slate clean. I know that sounds pretty stupid, but it's true."

Frank can't tell if Ellis is trying to pull the wool over his eyes or if he's just being honest. But since he's pouring the drinks, Frank's better off just assuming the latter. "Yeah, I know about bad breaks. But you can't let them weigh you down."

"I'm not, trust me. Oh, we're supposed to be getting greased, and I get all sappy."

Then Ellis Wax snaps back out of it, almost like he's got a switch in there he can turn on and off whenever he wants. "Let's have one more, friend. I've got a date tonight with a hot tomato I met on the train coming down here. Are your nerves calm? Is the medicine working?"

"It sure is. I appreciate it, too. I would've killed for a drink."

"No need for that! I can get more. Plenty more."

"That so?" Frank cocks an eye. This is getting very interesting. When you need to make a fast buck, nothing beats booze. "How much more?"

"How much do you want?"

Frank laughs and slaps the table. "A thousand bottles would about cover it."

Ellis Wax just nods his head. "It would take some money, of course."

This is all moving too fast. Frank barely knows this guy, certainly not well enough to start cooking up some caper. You can't rush the stew, his ma used to say, it'll be done when it's done. "Yeah, well, I know how that game works. But I'm a little short of cash at the moment. And anyway, I'm like you: I'm here to start over. I want to earn some honest money for a change."

"Here's to honest money!" The two men down their drinks.

The **door** opens. Musetta looks up from a chair with a quizzical expression, lower lip quivering in anticipation.

"Well?" he asks.

"I lost her." Vecchio's shoulders droop with apparent despair and defeat. He shuffles in slowly, uncertainly.

"Ha!" Musetta tosses down the magazine he was looking at, *True Story*. There's a good article on how easy French dames are. Enough to get your blood boiling but this, ha! This is even better. "You lost her? Who's the rube now?"

A withering glare. "Don't be a smart aleck. She got in a cab and they took off. I tried to get one, but by the time I did, they was long gone."

"That's a crying shame." Musetta picks up the magazine and pretends to start reading again, but he can hardly wipe that smile off his face.

"What happened with Hearn?" asks Vecchio. "Did you follow him back to his hotel?"

Musetta doesn't look up. "Nope."

Vecchio sinks onto a bed. "Rats! How did we futz this up? And why are you smiling? Don't you get it? That skirt can ruin us. All of us."

"She can ruin Capone, you mean. And that's too bad for him. But then Torrio'll need a new man to take that job once it opens up."

"Listen to me!" Vecchio wags a finger in the younger man's grimacing face. "Don't you ever say something like that to nobody! If Capone ever thinks you're disloyal, you'll go for a ride!"

"Don't yell at me!"

"Don't be stupid! We got a job to do and we better do it."

"If I'm so stupid, how come I know where they're staying?"

"You do? But you just said you lost Hearn."

"I didn't lose him. I said I didn't follow him back to his hotel because he ain't staying at one. He's staying at some house, back in the garage."

"He is?"

"I got the address right here." He pats the pocket of the jacket that's strewn across his lap. Vecchio springs off the bed and throws a brotherly arm around his partner's neck.

"Nice going, kid! You ain't as stupid as you look, huh?"

"Let's get to work." Musetta stands up and from underneath a twin bed pulls out a violin case. In it is a 1921 Thompson submachine gun, its serial number ground off, adding an extra thousand clams to the cost, but it was Capone who paid for it. He gets them from a kike in Philly named Goldberg.

"What are you doing?" Vecchio asks.

"Getting the Tommy ready."

"Ready for what?"

"Ready to blast that garage into bits, is what."

Vecchio shakes his head as if in agony. "Not that way, kid. Let's use our noodles first. There might be an easier way."

"This way is easy. You pull this trigger here and a couple seconds later, everybody's dead."

"Let's just drive over and see what the layout is."

"I done that already, Vecchio. I seen the place. We pull up in the alley, and *blam blam*, it's done. Then we drive away, over in five seconds. I done the Elf Man just like that, when he was shacked up with that skirt out in Cicero."

"You killed the Elf Man and who else? The skirt."

Musetta slams the case closed. "Fucking cares who else! Capone said take care of the Elf Man and the Elf Man got taken care of."

"But that ain't how it's done! You take one step at a time. First we scope, then we plan the getaway, then we shoot. She ain't there anyways. She's with the wally in the cowboy hat."

The kid's not listening to a word of it. "I'm bringing the Tommy, Vecchio."

When a man buys you two dresses, a gown of cerise georgette crepe and a voile frock that feels as soft as a glove, you also must let him take you out to dinner. When he tells you to get whatever you want, you don't dare insult him so you order oysters Florentine and lobster and let him fill your glass with pinot noir, all the while laughing and smiling with uninterrupted gaiety. And you don't remove his hand at once when it comes to rest on your thigh beneath the tablecloth. You wait a discreet few seconds and then shift positions, never wiping that smile off your face. It is in this happenstance that Ginger finds herself, dining with T. W. Roland at a very chic nightclub, wearing the voile frock he bought for her, along with a string of crystal beads and chiffon scarf that he also insisted she have.

"And so I said to Seagrave, 'Listen, you stupid son of a bitch, that's a five-hundred horsepower engine and it won't outrun a duck.' A duck!" T.W. bursts into uproarious laughter, as is his wont at the conclusion of a tale. He's not a bad fellow, though. He's got a certain charm, infectious self-confidence and implacable self-satisfaction, but he is about ten years past his prime. He likes talking about money and he likes spending it, not a bad trait, especially for that class of female who is on the prowl for a sugar daddy, as he most definitely assumes she is. Let him have his fun.

"Have another gallon of vino, honey," he says, refilling a half-empty glass. "You got to keep the oil changed if you want the engine to purr."

"Don't be bashful."

"Not to worry. There's not a bashful bone in this body."

Ginger slurps back the wine, and a warm feeling starts to spread across her face. She's laying it on thick, but at the same time, she's starting to get a little tipsy. The last time that happened, she ended up in bed with Frank Hearn. Oh, Frank. He must be wondering where she is. But she can't just cut out of here. T.W. is taking her to the Babe Ruth

Cup tomorrow, whatever that is, but Babe Ruth'll be there and that's the point. She's got a job to do and she's doing it.

"You like your lobster?" he asks hopefully.

"It's wonderful."

"Good. I like to make women happy. What other man would get married three times if he didn't?"

"I see your point."

"What about you, honey? You ever been in love?"

She wasn't expecting that kind of question from him. He's all bluster and braggadocio, and then out of the blue he accelerates into her past like one of his speedboats. "I've been married," she answers carefully. "It didn't work out."

"Why not?"

He honestly wants to know. He's got both his eyes on her and he's listening as if it matters what she says. Oh, just tell him. What difference does it make anyway? Ginger drains the rest of her glass, and he just as quickly refills it. "My husband bought a pig farm."

"A what?"

"A pig farm, in Temperance, Ohio. We left Toledo and our wonderful home and we moved to a pig farm. And I hated it. So I left him." She pauses a few seconds and lets this filter in. Then she grins at him and raises her glass. "He was much, much older than me."

"So?"

"I wanted some excitement."

"If it's excitement you want, sugar, you stopped at the right station. I might have a head full of gray but there ain't no rust in the crankshaft."

She laughs and closes her eyes, thinking of the day Lemuel Hoagland showed her that advertisement he ripped out of *McClure's*, its edges frayed: Turning Away from Anxiety, the headline read. About some auto executive in Detroit who chucked it all and bought an apple farm because he couldn't stand the pace of the "so-called modern world." That's what started it all. That's what led her to Chicago and all the trouble she's in now. Because she was happy in Toledo. She was singing on the weekends at the Vice Royal, Lemuel owned a successful advertising agency, and they had it all: a Lawson sofa with glazed chintz upholstery, a Crossley radio with crystal knobs, a fridge, a washing machine, Canadian booze, a Model T Roundabout—and they traded all that for pigs.

"You okay, honey?" He touches her on the arm.

"I'm just listening to the band." A lie, but then she actually starts to pay attention. They don't seem to be a bad group. The alto sax sounds real crisp, and the piano player has flair, too. They're playing a Duke Ellington number but they really need a better vocalist. "She's ruining the song," Ginger hisses. "Look at her! She's just standing there like a little girl waiting for the school bus. I'd love to get up there and show these people how it's done."

"You're a singer?"

Her face now feels flushed. She's drunk. Here we go. "I can sing a little."

"Professionally?"

"I've been paid to sing." Tell him, go ahead. Tell him how you dreamed of singing on Broadway. That's why you left Temperance and Lemuel Hoagland behind. Hopes and dreams turned into pig slop. Chicago the closest big city. You knew people there, musicians from Toledo who hit the big time and so would you. But six months later, you were lucky to have that gig at Heinie Jacob's saloon, crooning with Fingers Finley in front of a bunch of uncouth, drunken brawlers in an airless, smoky room that resembled a tomb. The big time? Hardly.

"I bet you're pretty good."

She rolls her eyes. "I don't know. I was popular back in Toledo, for what it's worth."

He pats her on the thigh. "Have I told you I'm buddies with the president of Columbia Records?"

"No, you haven't."

"Well, it's true. I sold him a boat last year. Want to meet him?"

"Sure." Composure gone. Don't jump on him like a dog. "I mean, if it's no trouble." Pretend like you don't care. Drink more wine, that's your ticket.

"Say the word and I'll take you to New York. I'll make you a star."

The room starts spinning. Put your arms on the table for support. "There's so much you don't know about me." Enigmatic smile. The Mona Lisa. But the room won't stop spinning. Look at you. You're going to fall face-first into your plate of lobster. Not that. Anything but that.

"Like what?"

"Oh, lots of stuff." Tell him how they're going to kill you. You saw a man killed, and now they want to kill you.

"I don't care about the past. I'm always moving forward, the faster the better. I don't judge people. I've made plenty of mistakes in my life."

"Do you mind if we go?"

"Now? Don't you like the lobster?"

"I'm getting tired. Sorry."

He is a gentleman. He throws some bills on the table and leads you out, holding you up like a rag doll until he puts you in the backseat of a cab and you fall asleep with your head in his lap.

NECKING

Lauren Howard waits for the porter to leave before she speaks, but Irene can tell when Mummy is upset. Her lips become pursed and she looks like she's about to explode. She never does, though. It's not her style to emote. She is in control at all times. An exquisite ice sculpture in rose Chanel.

"This is unacceptable," she fumes once they are alone in their new room, on the fifth floor. "We no longer have a view of the water. I've never in my life been asked to switch rooms in a hotel."

"There's a first time for everything." Irene flops down on a bed. Who cares about what room you're in? A bed is a bed is a bed.

Mummy walks over to look out the window. The city is arrayed before her. It's not a big city, more like a town, but there's bound to be exciting places. Ellis Wax will know. He seems like the kind of man who can put his finger on a corpse and feel a pulse. If there's action, he'll find it and take her there, just like Frank used to. What time is it now? She's supposed to meet him at eight, at the corner of Central Avenue. It took Mummy forever to pack up and vacate, and now she's running late.

"I better get cracking."

"Are you going out?" Mummy sounds like it's the most absurd notion in the world.

"I thought I might."

"With whom?"

"Nobody. I just want to have a look around."

"I know you're lying. You're meeting that man, aren't you? Ellis what's-his-name. Wax."

"So what if I am?"

"You're supposed to get your rest. We didn't come down here for you to gallop around with some piker."

Irene dissolves into laughter. "Piker? You slay me, Mummy. He's no piker."

"How do you know?"

"Because, I have special powers."

"Young lady, you are not well. If you could hear yourself talk, you'd cringe. You need rest, and plenty of it. You don't want to get all agitated and run down." But Mummy knows it's a losing battle. She can't hog-tie a full-grown woman. Poor Lauren H., she doesn't understand these modern times. How endlessly has she regaled Irene with the prim and proper stories of her own youth: women were always chaperoned, wore corsets, never smoked or drank, and, biggest of all, walked down the wedding aisle a vestal virgin. Irene knows the litany by heart.

"I'll rest when I'm dead," replies Irene coolly. "And anyway, I'm not going to sit around playing bridge all night."

"You could read a book."

Irene rolls her eyes. There's no point in this discussion. Might as well take a shower and get dressed. She heads off to the bathroom, thinking about what she'll wear. The red satin dress, with one long strand of pearls. Her white cloche hat would be striking. What about the dog collar? No, that would be too obvious. She could wear a wrist-watch around her ankle; some girls who went to Paris to study said it was all the rage in Europe.

When Irene gets out of the bathroom, she finds her mother speaking with a well-groomed and officious gentleman, who identifies himself as Collier, the hotel manager. He proffers a string of apologies and then leaves.

"What did he want?" asks Irene.

"He wanted to make sure our room was satisfactory. I told him it was not."

"I'll be home before too long." She kisses her mother on the forehead. Why does she wear so much makeup? It's plastered all over her face, and Irene has to wipe her mouth.

"Be home by eleven."

"I'll try. It depends on how much fun I'm having."

Lauren grabs her daughter's arm. "I don't like your attitude, young lady. I'd appreciate it if your were civil to me."

Irene rips her arm away. "I am civil. Good-bye!"

After she's gone, Lauren sinks into a chair and begins to curse her husband. Why did Seddon have to tell Irene about the trust fund? What good has it done? Now Irene thinks she can act any way she wants with no consequences. And that's dangerous. Very dangerous.

So much for normalcy. Now they're back at square one: Irene's cavorting with the wrong crowd again. When will it ever end?

"Here's to us."

Ellis lifts his glass, glancing around at the crowded nightclub. The Gangplank is supposed to be the hottest joint in town, or so said the clerk at the store where Ellis purchased his new suit, shirt, shoes, tie, and belt, all for the princely sum of fifteen dollars. But looking sharp in a new set of threads helped get them past the bouncer at the door, who was sizing everybody up and down like a priest searching for sinners. Lots of rubes were turned away. But the bouncer let Irene and Ellis right on through, to mingle with all the other swells and smarties sitting around white-enameled tables lit by rose-shaded lamps. The in crowd. The place to be. Waiters in white coats and black pants. A lively band belting out the jazz.

"So, Ellis Wax, tell me something." Irene is grinning like the cat that swallowed the canary.

"I'll try."

"You're a bootlegger, aren't you?" Irene traces the lip of her glass with her index finger, batting her eyes in a seductive manner. "Is that how you got that car so quick?"

"What, that thing? It's nothing special. A Model T like all the others."

She nods her head and sits up straight. "One day you're riding second-class on the train to Florida, the next you got a new car and plenty of loot. What's a girl supposed to think?"

"You could think: what a swell fellow. And it's not a new car. It's used."

"I stand corrected."

He shrugs his shoulders. "What if I was a rum-runner?"

She seems thrilled at the prospect. "I think it's a more honest way to make a living than what my father does."

"Which is what?"

"Oh, he owns a bunch of factories. I can't even keep track of everything. It's all perfectly dreadful if you ask me." She spits these words out venomously.

"Really?"

"Really. Be useful and give me a ciggy."

He takes out his case. It's all gnarled and scratched, and clashes with the crispness of his new clothes. He'll have to get a new one so he won't look like a wally. "Factories, huh? Your father sounds like a fat cat."

"Oh, enough about him. So, am I right about you?" She takes the cigarette. He strikes a match for her, and she leans across the table. One puff, and she falls into a violent fit of coughing. "That tastes terrible!"

"They're Turkish. I got them for you."

"You did? That's so sweet." She takes a quick puff. "It tastes better already. So are you?"

"What's that?"

"You know, silly. A bootlegger. Because I used to know a bootlegger."

"Know?"

"Okay, I dated him." She says this very proudly, like one might tout a family connection or a stock tip. "He took me to all kinds of places."

"I bet he did."

"What's that supposed to mean?" She's practically squealing in delight, flicking ashes almost into the tray. Most fall on the table.

"It means he took you places."

"Yeah, he did. He took me lots of places. Oh, I love this song!" She claps her hands, gazing longingly back at the Earl Gresh Orchestra, nine men attired in pearl gray suits with bright yellow neckties. They've broken into a rousing rendition of "Row, Row, Rosie," and the dance floor quickly fills with the nattily attired habitués of St. Petersburg's newest nightclub, the first in town with terrazzo floors that make for raucous and at times treacherous dancing. The couples skate along merrily, sliding gracefully to and fro. Irene jumps up. "Let's go!"

Ellis doesn't move. "Let's get a bracer of something good first. Some real scotch would taste swell, not this Bimini water."

"Promise you'll dance with me. I love dancing. It's the most divine thing in the world. Especially the Charleston. Don't you just adore the Charleston?"

"It's okay."

"They banned it at the stupid college I went to. They said it was immoral! But I abso-tively love dancing. We danced the Charleston anyway. Those stupid hens, what do they know? They think having fun should be against the law."

"You remind me of somebody." Ellis begins nervously tapping his heel beneath the table.

"Who's that? Is she pretty?" Irene sits back down, elbows propped up under her chin.

"She was."

"Was? Is she dead?"

"No."

"Who are you talking about?"

"My stepmother." He blows a plume of smoke into the air. It circles above them, and then drifts off into the swirl near the dance floor.

"Your stepmother? How are we alike?" She sounds as if she thinks the comparison is utterly illogical. She seems injured, in fact, that he could say such a thing. But there's a method to this madness.

"First of all, my stepmother was very young. We were only five years apart. So I am not talking about an old hag. I was fifteen and she was twenty when Father remarried."

"How are we alike?"

He shakes his head in discomfort. "I don't like thinking about her. She was a liar."

"A liar? Do you think I'm a liar?"

"No. Where's that waiter? He's ignoring us." Ellis glares angrily at their server, who's been kept busy by a very large party of young men sitting at the biggest table in the place. They seem to be ordering everything on the menu and most of the booze behind the bar. Other customers need attention, however. Ellis raises his hand and lifts his index finger, but all the waiter can do is hold up his hand in a gesture of mercy.

"Do you think I'm a liar? Why would you say such a thing?" Irene's face has turned white, and her lips are pursed angrily. She looks just like her. Same pout, same flashing eyes.

"I'm sorry I mentioned it. I meant to say you looked like her. You two are kind of alike. My stepmother loved dancing the Charleston, too. But Father was nearly sixty, so he wouldn't dance with her. That left me. I danced with her. She always wanted to dance with me. She'd grab me and haul me out there."

Finally the waiter comes over. He apologizes profusely. "That big party of ballplayers is keeping me on my toes! The New York Yankees made it to town after all."

"The Yankees, huh?" Ellis regards the big table again, trying to recognize faces. Then he grins over at Irene. "Huh? We're hobnobbing with the rich and famous. Is the Babe here?"

She glances at the table but doesn't seem impressed.

"No, he's not. What can I get for you?" The waiter seems distracted, like he's got something better to do.

"Do you have anything stronger than Bimini water?"

The waiter scratches his temple. "We have some nice Irish tea."

"What's that, whiskey?"

"We don't serve alcohol, sir. It's against the law."

Ellis holds up his hand. "I get it. Just bring a couple Irish teas."

"None for me, thanks," interjects Irene icily. The waiter scurries off.

"What? I thought you wanted to get pie-eyed tonight."

Irene yawns and stretches her arms. "I'm feeling a little tired."

"Tired? You wanted to dance a minute ago."

"It's been a long day."

"Oh, so you're sore at me. Listen, I didn't call you a liar. You just reminded me of somebody who is a liar. Who lied very badly."

"About what?"

"About me."

"What did she say about you?"

Ellis leans back in his chair, folding his arms across his chest. "What do women always lie about?"

"Their age."

"What else?"

"Their dress size."

"And one more thing."

Irene's eyes grow wide as saucers. Then the waiter brings the "Irish tea"—whiskey on the rocks—and Ellis gulps it down. "She lied about sex?" gasps Irene. "You and your stepmother?"

"She was a hateful person, one of the most callous and calculating women on the face of the earth."

"Why did she lie like that?"

"You'll have to ask her. I don't know how a sick person thinks."

How did they get on this subject? Ellis feels anger rising in his throat. It's because she keeps picking at him. This is one pushy broad, just like good old Freda, the slut. And murderer. When Father died last year, did the Baltimore police even suspect foul play? Hell no! Not the grieving Widow Marshall, who stood to inherit the house, his pension, his stock portfolio, and all else save the barest of crumbs left in an empty cupboard. Those doltish cops let her get away with it, too. No autopsy. Natural causes, they said. Heart failure.

"Do you mind terribly if we leave?" asks Irene. "I am getting awfully tired."

"Leave? You want to leave?"

"If you don't mind."

"No, sure thing. We can leave."

Ellis gets the waiter's attention and asks for the bill. Another fifteen dollars down the drain.

•   •   •

"Where are we going?" Irene asks as Ellis pulls the Model T off the paved main road leading back toward downtown. They first pass through a dense tangle of palmettos that stretches for acres in every direction. The land has been subdivided, and the survey stakes stand erect in the sandy soil like wooden tombstones. These lots are among the most prized in the city.

He smiles knowingly. "Somewhere nice."

"I thought you were taking me back to the hotel."

"I am. I want to take in the scenery first."

Of course, she's got to act like an untouched virgin. It's all part of the song-and-dance routine women perform like trained seals. *How dare you think I'd ever*—and then ten minutes later they're flat on their backs with their legs kicking up in the air. All of them lie about sex. Every last one.

He parks the car between two tall oak trees. Distant frogs and anoles fill the night with a symphony of croaks and grunts. Ellis sighs, pretending nature has a calming effect on him. There's no moon tonight, and the stars above dazzle with sparkling profusion. "Look at the sky," he says. "Isn't it something else?"

Irene purses her lips. She's not looking at anything. "You can see the sky from my hotel, too."

"I suppose you could." There's no need to pretend. She's the kind of rich girl who likes it a little rough. He slides over and nuzzles up next to her, but she pushes him away with a short shove.

"Not so fast, sheik."

"How about a kiss?"

"I don't think so."

She's really playing her good-girl act to the hilt, but she can't fool him. He's seen it too many times before. He takes her arms and presses them against her lap, and then leans in for a kiss. But she struggles, squirming mightily, trying to free her hands.

"Don't!"

They all are virgins, every last one. It's a miracle the human race has survived as long as it has, with all the virgins out there not putting out. She must think he's an idiot. He tries to pull her down onto the roomy seat, but she's pretty strong for a woman.

"Let go of me!"

"Cut the act, okay? We both know the score."

"You don't know anything! Let go!"

"Oh, you're a real gem, aren't you?"

She starts swinging her fists wildly, not even aiming, and somehow she delivers a blow right to his eye. He yells in pain, grabbing the eye out of reflex. Irene throws open her door and begins to run, not down the path back toward the paved road, but up the path, farther into the brush.

Blood is streaming down the side of his face, his nostrils flare with each angry breath. He sees her up ahead, galloping clumsily down the path. She looks back into the headlights, and in so doing, loses her balance and falls to her knees. It must be hard to run in those unbuckled shoes. But she quickly pulls herself up and keeps on going, trying to run faster. One shoe flies off, then the other.

Then Ellis leaps out of the car and begins to chase after her. But

Irene is faster than any woman he's ever seen. Her long legs propel her deeper into the thick, dark woods. But he isn't a slow runner, either, and he begins to close the gap between them. He bends down and picks up a branch. He holds it like a club as he sprints across the scrub, hopping over stubby palmettos like a rabbit. She trips and falls, but scrambles to her feet. He's even closer now.

"You stupid bitch!" he shouts.

But then he stumbles, twisting his ankle on a gopher tortoise hole, and crashes into a stand of cactus. He springs to his feet, drenched with sweat and stinging with a hundred pricks. He looks around. Where did she go? There's no sign of her anywhere. She's hiding behind a tree or some brush. He tries to stand perfectly still, to hear any noise she might make. The only sounds are of the wind whistling through the dwarf oaks.

The mosquitoes are thick now, so he can't stand there long. He's getting devoured, so he limps back to the car, its headlights the only illumination tonight. Particles of dust float in their beams, churned up from all the commotion.

He gets in and slams the door. He's calmer now, more composed. He turns the lights off and decides to wait and see if she reappears. His eye throbs from where she hit him. His hands burn from the cactus pricks. Despite the pain, a smile soon forms. An idea starts to take shape in his head.

"That's it," he says coolly. "That's what I'll do."

He starts the car and drives away.

The black car eases along the uneven pavement of the alley. Vecchio is driving, and Musetta is barking instructions. "It's on the corner there. That little hut, that's the garage. That's where Hearn is staying."

Vecchio doesn't believe it. Why would they be staying there in that dump and not some hotel? Joey Muse is still wet behind the ears, and he must've tailed the wrong guy. "You sure it was Hearn?"

"I followed who you told me to follow."

"The big guy, right? The one we saw talking to Sally outside the pool hall?"

"That's who you told me to follow, and I followed him here."

Vecchio grimaces. They need to make sure this is the right place. Since they don't have a picture of Frank Hearn, the only way they'll know is if they see Sally Serenade coming or leaving. "I guess we need to stake it out first. When we see Sally, we'll know."

"I know it's the right place."

Vecchio can hear the impatience of youth that can't bear to sit still for long. Already the kid is starting to get squirmy. He's got an itchy finger. Shoot first and ask questions later. Maybe Capone likes to do business that way, but Johnny Torrio sure never did. Vecchio sighs, contemplating the changes afoot. Torrio is getting out, the word is. Maybe he knows something. Maybe he's got the right idea.

"We can't just go shooting the place up. We got to be smart about it. We need to make sure it's the right time. We got to make sure we can get away."

Joey Muse gnaws on these words like a puppy with a steak bone. "We do it through the window there." He points to a small, rectangular window facing the alley. "Then we drive down the alley, hang a right, ditch the car, and head to the train station, a couple of blocks over."

"That might work."

"I'll see if they's in there."

"Stay put, kid! Just hold on. We don't gotta rush around. Let's use our eggs a minute." For some reason Vecchio thinks about Wally Pipp, the Yankees first-bagger. That bum can't hold off this Gehrig kid much longer. And it must feel lousy, watching the young bucks rise up and take your job. "We can't let nobody see us."

"It's dark!" Musetta sneers.

"People can see in the dark. Take a look around. What do you see?"

"An alley."

"Look behind you." Musetta twists around to look up the alley.

"I don't see nothing."

"Look left, look right."

Then a blinding set of headlights comes screaming right at them. Musetta reaches in and pulls out a .9 mm Mauser. A Model T screeches to a stop, kicking up gravel and dirt. A man in a white suit gets out and slams the door.

"If I see Sally, I'm shooting."

"You won't see her. That ain't the man in the cowboy hat."

"Rats," Musetta curses. "I had a clear shot!" He keeps the gun aimed anyway, then finally lets it drop to his lap.

Vecchio starts the car. "We better get out of here in case that guy saw us."

The dog's ears prick up and she rouses from her slumber at Cato Younger's feet. Out where he lives, beneath the whispering sibilance of towering slash pines, the farthest house a good mile away, no one ever pays him a visit, especially at night. He keeps a shotgun right by the door. He bolts up from the rocking chair his grandfather built and grabs the gun.

"Help! Please help!"

It's a woman's voice. Cato Younger puts the gun down and throws open the door to his rustic home, a two-bedroom box hewed from the same trees his grandfather felled in 1873.

A young woman is standing there, panting like a hunting dog, face stained with sweat and tears, eyes glistening with fright. She tries to smile. "I don't mean to bother you, sir. But I need some help. Someone is after me."

Cato Younger reaches back and grabs the shotgun, then marches outside. "Where is he?"

"I don't know."

"Go inside and shut the door."

"I ran as fast as I could."

"Get now. I'll take a look."

He whistles for his dog, Franny, and she comes bounding to him, a stout, sturdy bloodhound. He pats her reassuringly, and together they start off toward what Cato Younger calls Babylon, better known as Pasadena, the new subdivision being built a mile away, on the edge of the Younger property line. Until this young gal showed up, Cato's only visitors were Jack Taylor and his wife or one of their flunkies, all of whom had the same goal: to swindle him out of his land. They'll pay him a hundred dollars to take big shots hunting. They'll give him bottles of whiskey. They'll talk about how he could afford something nicer with the money he could make if he'd just sell. It won't work. He'll never leave this land.

"You smell anybody, girl?" he asks his dog, panting happily at his side. They stand and listen to the trees. A wind rustles through the long branches. If somebody was out there, you sure couldn't tell. Not on a night like tonight. "We better go check up on that gal. She looked mighty spooked."

rank springs up out of bed when he hears the car door slam. Maybe Ginger is finally coming home. He rushes over and opens the door, stepping out into the corridor just in time to see Ellis Wax walking in. He's got a pretty nasty scratch on his face, and his new white suit is all rumpled, bloody, and dirty. He's also limping a little. He must've had a swell time.

"What happened to your date?" Frank asks, trying not to giggle. It's obvious what happened, by the looks of it. She didn't put out.

"I was ambushed."

"Did you give her what-for?"

"It's not what you think. Let's have a drink."

They resume their stations around the table in Ellis Wax's room, sitting in the same chairs and using the same jars as before. Drugstore vodka tastes even better the second time. It's been a real snoozer of a night so far, sitting around and waiting for Ginger to come back.

"So what happened?" Frank finishes his drink quickly and slyly pushes the jar across the table for a refill.

"We were having a good time at the Gangplank, which I was told is the best nightclub in town. We were having a few drinks, and you know how things can go with women—my date had a few drinks too many, without any food."

"She got boiled."

Ellis nods his head vigorously. "She got boiled and so we had to leave. We were getting romantic anyway, and I had the choicest spot picked out down this path in the woods. It was all set. We were walking to the car and I was jumped."

"Jumped? By who?"

"Two men."

"Darkies?"

"No. Hired thugs."

Ellis pours Frank another drink, and he takes it greedily. "Hired? How do you know that?"

Ellis sets his mouth sternly, staring at empty space, wiping his scratch with a white hanky. "Because of what they took."

"What did they take?"

Ellis shakes his head sadly and tears well in his eyes. He looks like a little kid who got his lunch money stolen on the playground by some bullies. "Frank, I don't want to spill my guts like some fairy. Let's just say I have a very vengeful stepmother. We've battled over the years, but it's gotten worse since Father died. I left to get away from her, frankly. But apparently she's tracked me down like a dog."

"An evil stepmother, huh? Did your ma pass away?"

"When I was a kid. Our house burned down."

"Geez, that's tough. I lost my ma, too, so I know what it's like."

"It's torture. And when your father remarries, and to a lying whore, then the torture is even worse." He slams his fist against the table, nearly sending the bottle of vodka to the floor. Frank reaches over and catches it before it falls. "Sorry, I just can't believe she did this to me. I can't let her get away with this. I won't let her."

"Nah, you can't. But I mean, how do you know those muggers were hired by her?"

"Why would anyone take a key to a safe deposit box unless they knew what was in it?"

"That's what they took?"

Ellis refills Frank's jar. "It's a very long and winding story, but that's what they took. And I must get it back as soon as possible."

"How?"

"I have to find her."

"You think she's here?"

"I know she's here. Luckily the banks won't open until Monday, so I have a couple of days. Another?"

"Sure, why not? Doesn't look like I'm doing anything else to-night."

"Did you have plans?"

Frank frowns and slurps down the vodka. "Not really. I have a lady friend traveling with me, and she's off somewhere—working. She better be anyway."

"Working? Is she a waitress?"

"No. She's a singer."

"You don't feel like watching her perform?"

"It's complicated." Frank rubs his chin. Wax seems like a regular fella, but you shouldn't trust anyone. But there's a way of answering his question without tipping his hand. "She's helping me with a problem."

Ellis lifts his eyebrows. "We're in the same boat. You have a problem and I have a problem."

"Yeah, we're a pair of poltroons."

The two men share a cackling laugh. The bottle is almost empty and the night air has turned crisp, with the faintest touch of chill. It's perfect sleeping weather, and that's exactly what Frank wants to do. It's been a long couple of days. Might as well let the vodka do the trick.

As the elevator starts to lift up, Irene examines herself. Her dress now has a few minor tears, and her arms have a couple of scratches. Her legs took the brunt of the punishment, especially her feet. They are painfully tender, nicked and cut and bruised so that walking is quite excruciating. She's not wearing any shoes, something that won't escape Mummy's exacting gaze. Already Irene can hear the anguished sigh, followed by a concerned cluck and a million questions. And that's exactly what Irene doesn't feel like hearing right now. All she wants to do is curl up in bed and shut her eyes.

The corridor is long and narrow, and it takes Irene a long time to traverse it. She must keep a hand on the wall for support, allowing her to closely examine the fleur-de-lis pattern on the wallpaper. Mummy hated it when she first saw it. *Revolting,* she said. Nothing escapes her attention; she lets pass no opportunity to criticize. She's going to have a field day now; a dream come true: Irene messed up again.

Irene pauses at the door before letting herself in. She can hear voices inside—who is visiting this late? Irene frowns at the door, dreading her entry. Small talk will be torture. Better pretend to be sick and scamper off to bed as soon as possible.

Lauren Howard stands to greet her, and so does an older woman wearing a high-necked Victorian dress that reaches the floor. The room now reeks of cheap perfume, a heavy scent of lavender mixed with silver polish.

"You're home early," says Mummy. Then, turning to the guest: "Oh, this is Miss Kitty-Clyde East. This is my daughter, Irene Howard."

"My pleasure, dear." Irene curtsies and they shake hands very delicately. This one is an aging southern belle like Mummy. Haughty chin, sunken cheeks, long nose, thin lips, but shambling in ways Mummy isn't. The dress is from a consignment shop and the shoes look like they're as old as the pyramids.

"Miss East is from Richmond, Virginia. We met in the lobby. I asked her to come up and visit so I could catch up with the goings-on there."

Irene nods vacantly like a broken doll.

"Your mother is one strong woman," Kitty-Clyde purrs, "for marrying a Yankee."

"A handsome, dashing Yankee," Mummy reminds her.

"And generous as well. The Daughters owe you and your husband a great debt we can't ever repay."

"It's my pleasure." Then to Irene: "Miss East is the great-grandniece of General Lee. She's representing the United Daughters of the Confederacy as they raise money for Camp Zollicoffer, which will help educate today's youth about their southern heritage. It's a wonderful idea, don't you agree?"

"Sounds swell." But Irene isn't in the mood for this. The last thing she can stomach is Confederate small-talk.

"With your support, it will be."

Finally Mummy notices Irene's harried appearance. "What's wrong, dear?" she asks. Then her eyes trail down to her daughter's legs. "What happened to you?"

"Nothing."

"Where are your shoes? Your legs are all cut. You're bleeding. Let's get you a towel."

"I'm fine."

"I'll be right back." Lauren hurries away to the bathroom, leaving Irene alone with Kitty-Clyde.

"She's one strong woman."

Irene smiles blankly.

"I could never marry a Yankee, no matter how handsome or rich."

Then Mummy comes marching back. "Here you go, dear. Let's clean you up." She kneels down and begins wiping her legs with a warm, moist towel. It's been many years since Irene has required this kind of maternal attention, and it feels pretty nice, not what she expected. She reaches over and pats her mother's stiff hair, pulled back into a chignon.

"Thanks."

"Well, Miss East, we Howard girls must get ready for bed. It was a pleasure meeting you this evening, and I truly enjoyed our conversation. I stand in total agreement with you: this world needs something like Camp Zollicoffer if we are ever to hope for our young people to become decent and God-fearing citizens."

"I feel fortunate to have met you. Let's speak again tomorrow at tea."

"Yes, let's."

The two women take their leave at the door. Right after it shuts, Lauren wheels around and puts her hands on her hips.

"Tell me what happened."

Irene winces at the tone. "Nothing happened."

"Did he hurt you?"

"No. We had a swell time. We just went walking through a jungle, basically. Then we got bit by mosquitoes. Then I came home. Now, why did you let that woman con you?"

"She didn't con me. Don't change the subject. This is a world filled with dangerous men, and vulnerable young ladies need to take precautions."

"I can take care of myself."

"Ha! I swear, Irene, you are pigheaded. I don't know how you got so pigheaded, but you are."

"Send me to Camp Zollicoffer. Maybe that'll fix me."

"Don't mock me, young lady. I won't stand for it."

"I didn't make you come down here," huffs Irene, "and I sure don't need you to stay and baby-sit me."

"No, I should let you run off with the first scofflaw who comes along."

"Frank Hearn wasn't a bad person, for your information. He never did anything to hurt me, ever."

Lauren Howard stops dead in her tracks. "Has someone hurt you?"

"No."

Voice growing shrill. "Did that vile little man—"

"No. He didn't." Tears fall down Irene's pink cheeks.

"Oh dear God." She pulls her daughter to her, and they hug each other tightly. "I knew it, I knew it as soon as I saw you something was wrong."

Lauren strokes her daughter's bobbed black hair, softly, tenderly, cooing to her even as hot tears stain her Chanel dress. "There, there. It's okay now. It's okay. Are you hurt?"

"No, I'm fine. I really am."

"Do you see now why I worry so about you?"

Irene sniffles a sad laugh. "I know you do, but you never even met Frank. He's a nice person who's been through a lot and I loved him. He was always nice to me, always. I still love him, no matter what you or anybody say."

"Oh, I'm sorry, sweetheart."

Irene closes her eyes and listens to the wind blowing through the window. She just wants to go to bed. This hasn't been a drab night. Not at all.

EXPOSED

The next morning, a rap on the door stirs William Boyd, causing one of his bloodshot eyes to crack open. More knocking brings his head off the pillow, but nothing he sees seems familiar. It looks like he's in a hotel room, and not a very nice one at that. Then the room starts to spin, and Boyd's not sure whatever's in his stomach is going to stay down.

"Telegram for William Boyd," comes a voice from behind the door.

"Hold your horses," the sportswriter coughs out, having sat up. His head is throbbing, his throat is parched, and last night lasted a few hours too long. But that's how it goes in the newspaper business, especially when a legion of scribes gathers in one place to cover the greatest sports team on the face of the planet. When the New York Yankees hold a spring training, you can count on two things: good damn baseball and good damn booze. You file your story by noon and that leaves the rest of the day to make mischief until the wee hours. Last night's destination was some watering hole called the Gangplank, where scantily clad maidens paraded their exposed flesh and officious waiters poured snifters of just about every libation known to Christendom. They were all there, Pipp and Witt and Coombs and Dugan—well, everybody but Ruth. His wife came down to St. Pete with him, and she's got him on a short leash, so scuttlebutt has it. What a sad thing, to be the Bambino's wife! There's not a skirt around he doesn't go sniff under. And he doesn't even try to hide it. Not anymore, as far as William Boyd can tell.

Now he's standing. His legs are wobbly and the spinning hasn't stopped, but it has slowed. He manages to put one foot forward and miraculously begins to walk toward the door. He catches a glimpse of himself in the mirror above the small bureau. *Haggard*, that's the word that springs to mind. Sunken eyes, chalk-white stubble dotting a double chin, stooped shoulders, protruding stomach—he'll have to get some exercise while he's in Florida. Maybe go for a swim. At least a walk. Something before the team starts barnstorming back up north.

He opens the door and sees a fresh-faced, well-scrubbed young clerk with a pair of eager blue eyes and perfect posture holding a telegram.

"For you, sir," the clerk says officiously. "I came up as soon as I got it."

"I appreciate your diligence. Wait, let me—my pants. Where did I put them?" Boyd's muttering to himself even as he starts the search to find his pants, where he knows there's a nickel or dime or something in there for a tip. In town for less than three days and already his room is a sty, newspapers and books everywhere, clothes piled in every corner. Finally he locates a pair of twill slacks that made his balls sweat in this heat, and in a pocket he finds a quarter. Too much for a telegram, but under the circumstances, it'll have to do.

"Thanks, sir." The kid sounds like he means it, too. He closes the door on the way out and Boyd plops down on the bed to read this missive from Western Union marked urgent. He opens the envelope with some trepidation because his mother hasn't been feeling well, but he looks first to see whom it's from: Randolph Grayson, editor, *New York Evening World*.

RUTH GETTING SUED. $7000. TODAY'S P.M.

A twisted smile appears on William Boyd's face. Grayson has just tossed a big story into his lap. Immediately his head starts to clear. Nothing like scooping the other scribes to get the blood boiling. Nobody has gotten wind of this yet. There wasn't a word of it last night, and when everybody was as drunk as they were last night, the honesty was often brutal. Who was screwing who, who was going broke, who was in trouble with Huggins or Barrow—but not a word about the Babe getting sued. First thing to do is find the Babe and see if he'll talk. That's the angle there, to be the first one with the Bambino's reaction. That's the story Grayson wants for this afternoon's paper. Because by tomorrow it'll be on the wire and every Podunk hack will be on it.

William Boyd checks his trusty pocket watch: it's the ripe hour of ten o'clock. The Yankees started practice about thirty minutes ago, meaning Ruth will be leaving in another thirty minutes. That's the slugger's routine.

It's a good twelve or fifteen blocks from the hotel to the practice field at Crescent Lake, and if he weren't in such a big hurry, William Boyd would walk there. It's a picture-perfect morning, the sun's burned away the morning dew, leaving a sweet fresh scent. Only a few clouds hang in the blue sky, palm trees wave in the breeze off the bay, and flowers of every color bloom in pots that shopkeepers have placed along Central Avenue. He stands for a moment and lets the sun warm his face. New York and Grayson and the mad dash that is life up there seem to belong to another universe.

After the briefest of reveries, he hails a cab and tells the driver Crescent Lake. The cab speeds off down Central Avenue, then up Fourth Street, heading north. The city that passes by seems nice enough: friendly bungalow-style houses with inviting porches, tall oaks and pines providing cool shade, loads of parks where people loaf and play cards and sit looking at birds—would it be so terrible to buy a place down here? To get out of the rat race in Manhattan and spend a few years fishing and playing golf? Maybe find a nice girl who wants to pop out a litter—is that just a pipe dream? There's something about this town that makes you reflect and think. Maybe chasing after glory in Gotham ain't all there is to life. But soon the cab pulls up to the ball field, and William Boyd quickly falls back into panic mode. Got to get that story nailed down. He pays the driver and gets to work.

First, he's got to find Ruth. But that's not too hard, because the big gorilla is easy to spot. He's standing there beneath the water tower, holding a bat and waiting for his turn at the plate. And even from a good distance away William Boyd can hear that froggy Baltimore voice croaking away in nonstop chatter. "Geez, Whitey, put your back in it. I seen girls in grade school take harder swings. Better not let Huggins see you swing like that. He'll put one of these rookies in there—like that one. What's your name, son?"

"Johnson," the startled rookie responds, face covered in peach fuzz and eyes bigger than saucers. He pounds his mitt a few times as the Babe regards him.

"Johnson? That's the name of my best friend." Then the slugger grabs his crotch and looks down at his groin. "Hiya, Johnson, feeling good today? What's that? You want a kiss?"

And the laughter lifts up into the cloudless sky like the raucous cries of children on a playground, which isn't a bad analogy, William Boyd tells himself, waiting for the Babe to notice him. The rookie charges out onto the field, after getting a friendly pat on the back from Ruth, who squints as if he doesn't recognize the sportswriter who's been covering the squad for the past seven years.

"Boyd?"

"Hello, Babe."

"I thought you wuz dead and buried."

"Not yet."

"You look it."

"Thanks. You look good, too." But the Babe doesn't, not at all. He's even heavier now than he was last year, and he keeps coughing as he's standing there, eyes puffed out and watery, face bloated and skin chapped and dry like an old catcher's mitt left out in the sun. They say he's slipping, that his best days are behind him. That's what all the boys were jawing about last night, and maybe it's true. Maybe all that fast living has finally caught up with him.

"Did my lawyer wire you?" asks the Babe in a voice more businesslike than Boyd is used to. So this has been all planned out, a way for Ruth to get his side of the story out before the afternoon papers go bonkers. And William Boyd's thick in the middle of it—and it feels good.

"No, my editor did. What's the dope on that lawsuit? Who's suing you?"

"Some clown named Lichtenstein. I don't know the bum. I owe the money to Edward Callahan. Fast Eddie, that prick, was making a book at the track last summer and I fell into him for seven grand. He's a prick, I swear on my mother's grave, he's a prick."

Boyd nods politely as he scribbles down the words tumbling out of the Babe's mouth, his writing hand slightly trembling because this is a bombshell the Babe's dropping here, the scoop of scoops—but why me? William Boyd wonders. Why did they pick me? They could've funneled this to just about anybody.

"I told him I didn't have the money. I told him I'd pay at the end of the season when I get paid. And he said sure thing. This was in June, right? Then a couple months later he's back asking for the dough! What a snake in the grass! He said he'd expose me if I didn't pay, and I told him to go ahead. So he starts squawking that I welched! I would've paid him if he hadn't sounded off and called me a thief. I would've. Hell's bells, I make fifty grand a year, I could afford it. I did it on principle. They should keep that shark away from the track, the way he operates. Now people will say I'm broke."

The Babe's eyes rove over to the field, where Whitey Witt is still taking batting practice and smacking the ball pretty good now. "I ain't broke. I'd sure as hell have more if I didn't give so damn much of it away! Write that, how about it! Just the other day, I was in getting my thumb examined and into the doctor's office comes this cripple. I mean, he was lame, and he stank. So I gave him a dollar, just like that." He shakes his head in bewilderment. "I give away a thousand bones a year to people on the street."

It's not often that Ruth opens up like this, even though he seldom stops talking for long. This is different, and William Boyd realizes it. Something's really eating at the slugger. The lawsuit is one thing, but there's another, heavier weight, too. Maybe he's sicker than he lets on, because no athlete in any kind of condition should look so haggard, like he hasn't slept. Maybe it's true what the boys were saying last night: Helen is fed up with his tomcatting and she's ready to divorce him. She's hired a private eye, they said. She's got him dead to rights, since the Babe wasn't even trying to hide his fling with Claire Hodgson anymore.

"So you don't know this Lichtenstein character, right?"

"Never met him in my life."

And with that last statement, Whitey Witt's cuts are over and the Babe goes sauntering over to home plate, to do the one thing in the world he can do better than any man who ever lived (although some smart alecks talk about players in the Negro League being as good or better), stand in the batter's box and hit the round white ball a long, long way. Even though he's got a deadline, William Boyd can't help but watch the Babe take his swings. When he makes contact, the noise is different, more violent, a haunting impact that makes you wince. One after the other, the balls go flying toward the lake out in deep right field. A group of truant lads tries to shag them but a few end up splashing into the lake, sending cranes and herons fluttering away.

"What did Ruth say?"

Boyd turns to see Legs Rambo of the *Tribune* standing next to him, coffee stains on his rumpled white shirt.

"Not much," William Boyd replies.

IN

BLOOM

Two men come ambling up Central Avenue. Both are wearing panama hats and new seersucker suits, one powder blue and the other a jaunty tangerine. They spent an hour after breakfast at Boyer & Hayward, purveyors of men's clothes, trying on the latest warm-weather styles. A tailor on the premises hemmed the pants. At W. L. Tillinghast's shoe shop they selected white bucks to complete their transformation. Now they look like they're on vacation.

"Let's get a paper," says Vecchio.

They stop at a newsstand to buy the *St. Petersburg Times*, its pages crammed full of real estate advertisements, swelling the paper to a gargantuan size. Vecchio also buys a day-old edition of the *Chicago Tribune,* while Musetta selects a magazine entitled *Streets of Crime,* featuring on its cover a winsome gal in a ripped nightgown being menaced by a lantern-jawed thug.

"Why do you bother with that garbage?" Vecchio asks, knowing there can be no good answer.

"It makes me laugh."

"Well, you'll need something to read while we're staking out that garage today."

The fact is, they should've started that task long ago. But something about being in Florida takes the edge off. Laziness seduces you, invites you to take your shoes off and put your feet up, and whispers in your ear that nothing really matters. Everybody else is having fun, playing golf, boating, lounging in the sun. It's hard to feel urgency about anything.

They keep walking. Musetta hoots and whistles at every woman they pass. "You look lovely today," "Let me take you to the moon, doll face," "I think I'm having a heart attack!" are some of the offerings, combined with blown kisses, rude snorts, and smacking of lips. When you spend all your time with whores, you never learn how to address ladies. That's the kid's problem. He likes to waste his time at that squalid Hawthorne Inn out in Cicero, Capone's new whorehouse. You'd never find Johnny Torrio mixing up with those floozies, because Johnny Torrio's got class. He's a loving husband and a devoted father. Capone's got a long way to go if he wants to fill those shoes. These young hoodlums today, they're all too American. They were born and raised here, and they don't appreciate anything. They get some money and they can't wait to spend it. They get in a fight and they start shooting. Johnny Torrio never does business like that. Killing some lowlife in a bar in front of witnesses? Johnny Torrio would never do something that stupid. But Capone's got a temper on him. He doesn't think, and now he's in trouble. He's got the law on his tail, he got Sal Chiesa killed, and now this. They got to take care of this dame, all because Capone blew a fuse.

Maybe the kid's right. Maybe it would be better for Capone to go to college for murder. Better for the entire organization.

Their hotel is the Ansonia, a small, three-story building on Central Avenue. They get a key from the clerk and take the stairs to their room, number 205. The maid is cleaning it. She's a thin and leathery old black woman, who whispers to herself as she makes the two single beds. She doesn't speak to them when they come in. She keeps on flitting about, like she's an invisible bird flying around the room.

"I need to use the can," Musetta whines.

"So use it."

The maid dusts the two nightstands and the Tiffany lampshades.

She dusts the cracked mirror and the small desk beneath it. And it sounds like she's saying, "Lord, take me. Take me, Lord," but you can't tell with colored people.

Vecchio glances down at the front page of the *St. Petersburg Times*. "Babe Ruth Cup Tonight," it screams in bold lettering. Intrigued, Vecchio reads on. Turns out that there will be a big race at the dog track tonight, and presiding over it will be the Babe. There's a picture of him, wearing a suit and smiling.

Vecchio rubs his chin thoughtfully. *Bet you anything that Sally Serenade and her boyfriend will be there, too.*

The toilet flushes, and Musetta emerges from the bathroom right as the maid is leaving.

"I got an idea," Vecchio says. "It's better than staking out that garage."

"What's that?"

He tosses Joey Muse the newspaper. "The dog track. That's where we can nab her. She and Hearn'll be there as sure as I'm standing here."

The kid shakes his head. "That's horseshit."

"Yeah? They're tailing the Babe, pulling some con on him. They'll be there. We should be ready for them."

"I got an idea. Let's just fucking shoot the bitch and be done with it."

"Don't bust my balls, Joey. Let's take a drive and figure it out. You'll get a chance to shoot that Tommy gun, I promise."

***

The sound of a flushing toilet awakens her. Ginger blinks open an eye in time to see T. W. Roland walking out of the bathroom. He struts across the room and slips under the sheets next to her.

"Hungry?" he asks, gently stroking her shoulder.

"No." Her mouth feels like it's full of cotton, her throat is parched, and her stomach is gurgling in unpleasant ways. Her head throbs and even the dark of the room is too much light for her. Thick drapes have been pulled across the huge windows of what appears to be a luxurious suite.

"How about some water? Will that do the trick?"

"Aren't you a nice man—I'd love some water."

She closes her eyes when he hops out of bed, and then rolls over to face the other way. She sees her shoes on the floor—where's her voile frock? She lifts up the satin sheets. She's still wearing it. So, he didn't take advantage of her.

"Here." He taps her on the shoulder, offering her a glass. Ginger rolls back over and takes it from him, slurping down the tepid water like a man lost in the desert. "Whoa now, girlie. Go slow. Give your stomach a chance to acclimate."

"Thanks."

"There, now. T.W. will take care of you. We had ourselves a night, didn't we! Too much of a good thing is just enough."

"What time is it?"

"High noon. I could order us some breakfast. We could eat it in bed."

"I have to go."

"Ah, shucks, honey. What needs doing? I'll hire someone to do it for you."

She smiles. "You've done enough already."

"I've just started! I'm taking you to New York! I'm gonna make a star out of you! You bet I will! Wait till those pencil necks at Columbia Records hear you!"

She groans and covers her face with her hands. "I've got to go."

"Huh? I'm offering you the world and it ain't enough?"

"I need to go and do something, T.W."

"Don't forget about the track tonight. I'm picking you up at six."

"I promise I won't forget."

"That's a good girl. I could give you something to remember me by, if you want." He scoots over next to her, letting his hands explore her body beneath the sheet. She tells him to stop, not because it doesn't feel good, but because it feels too good. She likes being with him, and that only makes her even more confused. This is all happening too fast. She needs the world to slow down a little. She needs to talk to Frank. He's got to be worried sick. She can't enjoy herself knowing he's back at that stinking garage, wondering whether she's alive or dead.

But this mattress feels good. So do the goosedown pillows. No, get up, she tells herself. Go see Frank.

She rolls out of bed and pulls on her shoes. He's watching every move she makes, whistling approval. New York? To become famous? Hasn't she wanted that her entire life?

"Are you sure you won't eat first? I'm starving. I'm gonna call down and get some steak and eggs. There's a menu over by the phone. Get whatever you want."

She is famished. It won't kill her to eat something. Then she'll go talk to Frank and tell him what happened last night—she had too much to drink. She was tired. She's been on the run for so long, it finally caught up with her. He'll be mad, but he'll understand.

Who's she kidding? There's not a man alive who'd buy what she's selling.

———————

frank is staring up at the ceiling, his hands cradling the back of his head. A fly is buzzing at the only window, trying to extricate itself. It keeps bashing into the pane, over and over. Frank doesn't feel like getting up and killing it. He should, though. Stupid thing is making him crazy.

How long is he supposed to wait for her? It's past noon, and she's still not back. What the hell happened to her? He can only think of one thing: that she's lying facedown in some gutter, her body riddled with bullets. It's a horrible image he cringes at, but what else could have happened to her? On the one hand, they're as safe in Florida as they could possibly be, but on the other hand, there's always a remote chance that the apes who want her dead figured it out and got her.

He stands up. He rolls up a newspaper and starts for the fly buzzing against the window. With one swift whack he kills it, its lifeless husk falling to the floor. That's better. At least he can think.

But it's hard to think when you're starving. Even though he's running low on cash, he's got to eat. He should just pay the landlady to feed him; it'd be cheaper than eating out. A man who's hungry is a man who can't put all the pieces together. But it's not just the hunger. It's the not knowing where she is. Should he go look for her? Is she in trouble? Until he knows something, he can't plot out his next move.

Then he hears footsteps in the hallway. Ellis Wax has been coming and going all morning, but this doesn't sound like him. He throws open the door.

"Hi, Frank." It's Ginger, wearing some slinky new dress and carrying three shopping bags.

"Hi yourself. Wasn't sure I was gonna see you again. Here, let me take some of that." He reaches for the bags, and then he realizes that she's just standing there at the door, like she doesn't know what she wants to do. Come in, leave, sit, stand: she looks confused and moves carefully. It feels like she's paying him a visit but isn't planning on staying long.

"What happened last night?" he asks, setting the bags down by the bed. She won't look at him. She walks over to a chair and sits.

"I got fried. He kept filling my glass with wine, French wine. You don't want to hear about that."

"Sure I do. I want all the details. Was Ruth there?"

"No, I never saw him again."

Frank winces like she just pricked him with a needle. "What

should the next move be? I heard something about the dog track. It's in the papers. The Babe Ruth Cup. Is the cowboy taking you?"

She nods her head yes.

"Good. That's great." Frank's smiling but she isn't. She still can't look at him. He's no Einstein but it's obvious something is bothering her. "What's wrong, Ginger? There's something you're not telling me."

"Frank." That's all she manages to say before the tears come flooding out. He jumps up and goes to comfort her. He brushes her hot, wet face with one hand, and with the other he strokes her soft blonde hair. The sobs abate slowly, and with red eyes she finally looks up at him. "I'm going to New York, Frank."

"You are?"

"T.W. wants me to meet the president of Columbia Records. They're friends, or so he says. Maybe he's lying. I don't know."

Frank blinks a few times, like someone's just blown a thick cloud of smoke into his eyes. Then words come tumbling out of his mouth. "I'm happy for you. I know singing was your bag, before you got caught up in all this."

"I can't pass up this chance. I'd be stupid if I did."

"What, and leave all this?" Frank waves an arm to showcase their cramped, smelly room in a garage on an alley next to a row of garbage cans. "The mice, the flies, the stench?"

"You saved my life, Frank. That's what makes it so hard. I know you're counting on me."

"We never made any promises."

"The whole way over here, I wasn't sure what I was going to do. I still don't know if I'm doing the right thing. But I'm going to risk it. I've got nothing to lose."

"Right." He withdraws his hand from her hair and walks back to the bed.

"Frank, I didn't mean it that way. You think this is easy for me? It's not. I know we're not a married couple, we've only spent a few days together, but still, we're not exactly strangers."

"You could've fooled me."

Ginger stands up and walks over to gather the shopping bags. He watches her silently. "I want you to know something," she says, her voice cracking. "I know I'm a selfish person. I know I'm probably kidding myself with this pipe dream. But I'm not as callous as you think I am. I tried, Frank. I really tried to help you. I wasn't planning on any of this. It fell in my lap."

"Does he know?"

"Know what?"

"That people are looking for you."

"He knows a little. Not much."

"You should tell him, in case, you know, he buys the farm. Like I almost did."

She seems stunned by his words, like hearing them caused her physical pain. Then tears once again begin rolling down her cheeks, and she wipes them away, hands trembling, voice wavering between sorrow and resignation. "For the past month I've been waiting to die. Waiting and wondering, looking at every face I pass. Is he the one? How about him? It gets to you after a while. You see the world in a new light."

"You don't have to tell me. I shot a cop for you."

"I know you did. And I tried to help you get your money, Frank. You've got to believe that. I tried to make it right for you."

Frank springs off the bed and grabs her by the shoulders. "Try a little harder, how about it? One more night, one more shot in the dark. You're my best chance at this."

"Why?"

"Why what? It's seven thousand clams."

"But it'll never work. Never in a million years. Why can't you see that?"

Now it's his turn to feel like someone just punched him in the gut. It's one thing to have a broad walk out on you, and another when they tell you it was all a lie. She never believed. Not for one minute.

"Let me tell you what I see." His voice is angry and hurtful, but he can't help it. "I see my whole life going down the drain. I see me promising my best friend that I'll collect the money that's coming to us. I see a bunch of no-good cops setting me up. And I'm going to do something about it. That's what I see."

"Frank—"

Frank shakes his head. "Don't worry about it. You're in the clear. It's not your problem, it's mine."

"Oh, Frank." She brushes her hand against the stubble of his cheek. He grabs her arm and holds it tight.

"I'm still going out to the track tonight. I'm still getting my money from the Babe, with or without you. Just don't tip him off, that's all I ask."

"I feel sick to my stomach."

She closes her eyes and drops to the bed, the springs creaking under her weight. Frank sighs and sits down next to her. He picks up one of her hands. It feels lifeless and rubbery, like it belongs on a doll.

"Listen, I'm sorry I got all sore at you. I don't blame you for watching out for yourself. If you don't, who will?"

"I'm sorry, too, Frank. I want to help you."

"Fine. I just want one chance to talk to the Babe, man to man. I just want him to know I got the IOU and he can have it for half its value. I'm not going to be greedy."

"What if he says no?"

"I don't know. I guess I'll threaten to go to the papers with it."

Ginger's eyes brighten. "How about going to a lawyer? An IOU is just like a contract."

He grimaces painfully. "I don't like lawyers. They cost too much money. I want to see if we can't settle this the easy way first. After that, I guess I'll have to decide."

She runs her fingers through his thick, wavy hair. "If I can help you, I will. T.W. is picking me up back at the Princess Martha. I guess we're driving over with Babe Ruth and his wife." She yawns and rubs her red, swollen eyes. "Do you mind if I stay here and rest for a while? I'm still not feeling very good."

He grins down at her. "I'll never kick a woman like you out of my bed."

Ellis **Wax** is driving north on Ninth Street, a wide boulevard bisected by the train tracks that brought him here. He motors past large homes set far back off the road like country estates. Although handsome, they're not what interest him. So he keeps driving north for another few miles, until the brick street ends and the road becomes a sandy path winding into some orange groves. This is it, this is what he remembers seeing from the train, the fields that fan out across the flat landscape with paths barely wide enough for a car to fit through. He picks one and drives down it. The Model T bounces over the ribbed earth, sometimes sliding along the loose sand. If he gets stuck, he'll be in trouble. There's no one out here.

Which makes it perfect.

The emptiness stretches for miles, with just orange trees in sight. Ellis is looking for a place where he can stow her. A place where when she screams, only the buzzards will hear her.

Through the groves he drives, and sees nothing that would be useful as a holding pen. Right when he's about to turn around, he spots a wooden shack, set about a hundred yards off the path. It is not much larger than a shed, but it has a roof and a door. He stops the car, gets out, and looks around. He's far enough in the groves that he can't see the main road a half-mile back up the path. Nor are there any houses in sight. He goes and inspects the shed. It's not much taller than he is and one good gust of wind could knock it over. He pulls open the door and ducks his head to pass through the threshold. A heavy odor of mold hangs in the air and cobwebs descend from each corner. The floorboards sag and creak as he walks, as if the floor might give way. Lying about is some rusted equipment: a sickle, a hoe, a plow, a hitch. He'll have to get rid of those. She could use them to slice the rope that will be tying her down.

But how will he tie her down? He considers his options. There are no windows, only one door, and without the equipment, nothing in the shed that lends itself as an anchor heavy enough to keep a hale young woman from slithering away. Just four walls and a creaky floor.

He looks up. Two ceiling beams span the room. He reaches up and pulls on one. It seems sturdy. So does the other. Maybe he could use those. He could tie her arms to one and her legs to the other. She wouldn't go anywhere then. She'd hang there like a side of beef.

Pleased, he steps back outside. The blossoms on the orange trees fill the air with a sweet aroma. The wind rustles gently through the green leaves. Then Ellis Wax screams, as loudly as he can. He pauses a few seconds and screams again. He waits for someone to come see about the noise. Five minutes, ten minutes. No one does.

He plucks an orange from a nearby tree. It's not ripe yet, but soon it will be.

He needs to get a length of rope, so he can tie her up, and he needs to buy a gun. But even if he gets both of those things, he'll still need to get her in the car, and that might be difficult. He can't exactly invite her out for a ride. But he could try to force her in with the gun, but even then, he'd have to nab her near her hotel, which is located in the busiest part of the waterfront, meaning there'd be a lot of witnesses and traffic. Two people could do the job quick: one to grab her and shove her in the trunk, and the other to drive away. Two people could do it so fast she wouldn't even have time to scream.

He smiles as he walks back to the car. Frank Hearn will come in handy. It might take another bottle of vodka, but Guy Albertson has a few refills left on his prescription. A few drinks, a reasonable offer, and Frank will come on board. He seemed to buy his story last night, and even if he didn't, money has a strange way of convincing people to do things they wouldn't normally do.

Joe Szymanski has been a cop long enough to know when to expect the phone to ring on his day off, and so he's not exactly surprised to hear the garbled voice of his captain, asking if he wouldn't mind coming in to lend a hand with this Marshall case. He rubs the sleep from his eyes, checks his clock (1:11 P.M.), and smiles. The captain at least waited until he could sleep it off. The captain is a decent man, and hard to say no to.

"Sure thing, cap, I'll come in."

An audible sigh of relief. Everyone is feeling the pressure on this one. It's the lead story in the *Sun* again, and once again the paper is making the department seem like a collection of hopeless dopes: "Four days after the mutilated body of socialite Freda Marshall was found in her Mount Vernon home, Baltimore police are no closer to finding the killer today than they were when the investigation began. The lead suspect remains Aubrey Marshall, the murdered woman's stepson, and sources in the department claim that there are few if any promising leads."

Szymanski doesn't bother reading the rest. His headache won't allow it and there isn't time. He throws on the same clothes he wore last night, oblivious to the odors and stains clinging to the garments. A widower going on two years, Szymanski doesn't care how he looks. He's almost sixty, he'll retire next year with thirty years under his belt, and when that day comes, he won't draw a sober breath until his coffin is lowered into the ground.

Kids are playing ball in front of his Formstone row house on Biddle Street. It's chilly but they don't feel it, faces lit with glee, smiles a mile wide. Szymanski used to be one of those kids, but that was a long time ago. Baltimore was a different town then, and he was a different person. Why shouldn't he be? He's got to drive his car down to headquarters and help find some sick creep who killed his stepmother. After thirty years of this, who wouldn't want to stay drunk? When his own son said he wanted to be a cop, Szymanski had one reply: "Never." Danny was going to be a priest, but the Argonne Forest took care of that. What was the war for again? To end all wars? To make the world a better place? Safe for democracy, didn't President Wilson say that?

A foul mood has settled in like a dense fog. Thinking about your dead wife and your dead son on a day off, hungover and in dirty clothes, will wipe the smile off your face real fast. He drives past Kresky's saloon, and thinks: *I'll be there when it opens at noon and I'll be there when it closes at midnight.*

At the corner of Gremont and Eager he passes the state penitentiary, an imposing edifice of black stone that looks like a haunted castle. He doesn't get the same satisfaction anymore, seeing the pen and thinking of the hoodlums he's sent there over the past three decades. Not anymore. Not since the Volstead Act became the law of the land. Because now you can't tell the difference between a cop and a criminal. Last night he and his buddies committed multiple federal offenses, the same ones other luckless bastards got picked up for. It's a crock, is what it is, demanded by the same righteous boobs who thought war would lead to peace. Maybe so, but it cost the blood of a few million sons. Maybe Prohibition will improve the country's moral character, but it just might make it worse.

He cuts over to Baltimore Street and heads downtown. Soon enough he cruises past the Gayety Night Club, the Two O'Clock Club, a tattoo joint, a flophouse: but all is quiet on the Block this morning. The sailors are just waking up and realizing their money is missing. Too late: the hookers already gave it to their pimps.

One more year, he tells himself, parking the car on Fayette Street.

*   *   *

A half hour later, Szymanski gets his assignment: the killer, Aubrey Marshall, stole jewelry from the stepmom, so Szymanski, having worked Property for the last twenty years, must go around to the various fences he knows to see if anyone matching Aubrey Marshall's description tried to peddle any gems. If Szymanski gets a match, he's supposed to bring the fence in for questioning, and in the process ruin a valuable resource he's spent most of his career developing. Fences don't like to snitch, not unless there's money in it. A lot of money.

"Any reward?" he asks his captain, who's anxiously scratching his bulbous nose.

"Reward? I don't know."

"That family has money, the Marshalls are loaded. Answer me this question: If the stepson killed the stepmom because she got all the money after Pa died, who stands to get it now? The other brother?"

"I don't know. It ain't my case."

Szymanski shakes his head. Homicide is spinning its tires on this one. They need leads because they don't have squat so far. "Why do I need to burn my fences? If there's no reward, they won't talk. It's better to let me question them without hauling them down here and letting Homicide piss all over them."

"Joe, don't get mad at me."

"I'm not mad at you."

The place is a zoo, people coming and going, phones ringing, clerks hauling thick files, and the brass hovering over all, looking very worried. Police Commissioner Gaines himself has arrived, carrying himself like the general he was, back ramrod straight and jaw firmly set. He was going to clean up the graft and get the department in tip-top shape. He's patting his men on the back, like he wants them to go over the top of a bunker. *Keep your chin up. We appreciate all the hard work.* Most of the guys wouldn't mind seeing him get canned.

"I'll check on the reward," the captain says, standing up. "It's a good point. Fences won't sing unless they get paid to."

"Thank you."

They'll never find this Aubrey Marshall, just like Brodky was saying last night. It sounds like a lot of thought went into this murder, and unless the other brother coughs up some dope, there'll be no hope when the trail gets this cold. Szymanski will do his job, just like he always has, but he's not going to make it impossible for other victims to get their stolen valuables back. There is such a thing as common sense.

The captain returns with a smile on his pig face. "How does five thousand sound?"

"That might work," Szymanski shrugs.

Mother and daughter start walking back toward their hotel along the storm-damaged pier, its pilings slanted into the sandy bay bottom like little towers of Pisa. Off in the distance the dredges continue to devour the marshy shoreline to create new land for future development. Concrete seawalls will keep back the onrush of tide and when the walls crumble, as assuredly they will, crews will rebuild them, because that's the human condition in Florida: a never-ending process of reclamation and repair.

"How was it?" Lauren Howard asks quietly, her voice barely audible in the din of the dredges.

"It was okay," Irene replies. "I met this poor woman." She then explains how during her heliotherapy treatment she met a terminally ill young woman with a no-good husband, a little daughter, and an apartment without hot water. The poor dear was coughing like she had tuberculosis and didn't seem long for the world. The meeting seemed to have made a strong impact on Irene.

"It was terrible," Irene says helplessly. "To be dying so young— with no hot water! I can't imagine."

"Perhaps we could do something to help."

"You think?"

Lauren is proud of her daughter for feeling such empathy for the truly downtrodden. Maybe she'll join the Junior League yet. It's a start, at least.

As they walk toward the S&B Fish Market, they encounter a tow-headed newsboy, whose shouts of "Extra! Extra!" knife through the air with eerie urgency, making it impossible to ignore. Irene stops as the lad squawks: "Man found dead, man found dead! Extra! Extra!"

"Isn't that awful!" hisses Lauren disapprovingly.

"Hold on. I'll grab a paper."

Irene skips over and waits for her turn. Lauren sighs, annoyed by the sudden intrusion. They were having a nice talk, and now this. Reading the paper tended to agitate her daughter, when she needs calm above all else. Before it's too late.

When Irene comes back, her face is already buried in the paper, transfixed by the front page.

"You should let the fishmongers wrap the day's catch in that drivel," Lauren says. "That's all it's good for."

"You're the one who taught me to read."

"Your father was the one who encouraged you to read that nonsense backward and forward. Come, put it away. It's unseemly to stand in public gawking at the latest abominations." Lauren tugs at Irene's sleeve and away they go, with Irene gushing about the little she's read so far: a real estate broker was found murdered, beaten to death, and his car was stolen.

"Spare me the gory details." Lauren decides to change the subject. "Don't forget we've been invited to tea this afternoon with Miss Kitty-Clyde East."

"Have a good time."

"We were both invited. And I checked: she is the official ambassador of the UDC. She is not a con artist."

Irene rolls her eyes and walks ahead at a faster pace. Apparently her feet no longer bother her, because Lauren doesn't catch up until they reach the hotel. The porter opens the big glass door and they go in, Irene cruising across the marble floor of the lobby like some kind of circus performer shot out of a cannon. In the elevator Irene buries her face in the newspaper, holding it up like a shield.

"A Model T?" Irene asks no one in particular. The porter turns his head and glances at her. Lauren also gives her daughter a disapproving look, but Irene presses on. "The dead guy drove a Model T."

Lauren remains silent as the elevator ascends, eyes fixed on the mirrored panels. She's not sure the shoes she bought yesterday compliment the handbag. One is a light plum purple and the other a faint strawberry red. In the city this outfit would be considered garish, but nothing is garish in Florida, from what she can tell.

Irene starts crinkling the newspaper, and it makes an unnerving sound.

"Fifth floor," the porter announces, opening the cage-like door. They step into the hall and start walking toward their room. Lauren cringes at the wallpaper, a tacky attempt to suggest regal splendor.

"What I could never figure out is how all of a sudden he got a car," says Irene in a low voice. "One day he's riding on a train second-class and the next he's got a Model T?"

"Whom are we speaking of?"

"Ellis Wax."

The name sends shivers up Lauren's spine. It sounds like fingernails being dragged across a chalkboard. "I wouldn't know how that class of humanity operates, dear."

"Maybe it was Ellis Wax who killed the real estate agent. He killed him and stole his car, I'll bet my life on it."

This has become a dreadful conversation and, combined with the sight of her nicked and scratched daughter returning last night, Lauren is now quite afraid. They enter the room and suddenly it seems grotesque, sinister, evil. Shadows lurk menacingly, even as colors splash on every surface: the bright yellow pillows on the sofa, the irises standing in a vase, all pleasant, all false.

"I'm going to the police," Irene announces, her voice wavering, like a child who is angry but irresolute.

"To say what?"

"To tell them about Ellis Wax, that's what. You don't know what he's capable of."

The room starts spinning. Lauren steadies herself against the back of a chair. "I thought you said he didn't—"

"He didn't. But he tried."

"Oh my God, please, let's get out of this town! We'll take the first train we can! If he really is a killer, we can't stay here!"

"I'm not running away from him, Mummy. I'm no coward. The police should know about this creep."

And for the first time, Lauren sees a glimpse of the daughter she raised: strong, willful, determined. She is acting like an adult, accepting the responsibility thrust upon her without complaint, while she, Lauren, wants to run away and hide.

"Fine. We'll go to the police. But I do think we should leave here as soon as possible."

Irene greets this assertion with a shake of the head. "And go where? I know one thing: I'm not going back to Pearlman College. And I'm not going back to Greenwich, either. I've been doing a lot of thinking the last couple days, about what's important to me."

"And what is that?"

"There isn't time to explain it now. I'm going to the police."

"I'm going with you."

Irene puts her hands on her hips. "I can take care of myself."

Lauren holds her tongue. This from a girl who in the past week has dropped out of college, expressed a desire to kill herself, went on a date with a murderer, has been rude and surly, and wears dog collars around her neck. The last time Irene spread her wings, last summer, she fell in love with a bootlegger and nearly ruined herself in the process. Adventure?

"I'm going with you," Lauren repeats in a low growl.

"Fine. Let's go already."

•   •   •

Irene doesn't like the way the detective keeps smiling at her, looking very much like he's not taking her seriously. She's just a young, pretty girl with a story to tell—it's maddening. Maybe a swift kick to the shins would get his attention.

"Well?" asks Irene, palms outstretched across the cold steel of the table where they're seated, Mummy silently flanking her, though Irene can feel her glare. Mummy hates to make a scene. "Can't you have him arrested?"

The detective just keeps on smiling. She could tell him his stupid mustache was on fire and his expression wouldn't change. "Now where did you say he lives, this Ellis Wax?"

"I don't know."

"And he drives a Model T, is that correct?"

"Yes, he does. A black one."

He thinks that's just hilarious, but he manages to stifle a guffaw. "To be honest, Miss Howard, there just ain't enough information for us to arrest him with. You don't know where he lives, and there's a thousand Model T's in this town." The oil in his hair gleams beneath the bright lightbulb hovering over them. Each strand is perfectly combed in a straight line extending back from his brow like a vegetable garden. He must spend hours grooming in the morning. Irene has never cared for such vain men.

"But he's the killer! I know he is!" Irene hears her voice start to break, and she must sound exactly like the sort of frivolous girl he supposes her to be, one of those hysterical women who'll cry over anything. So she clenches her jaw and sits upright, staring into the cop's dull brown eyes.

"I appreciate you taking the time, Miss Howard." It's that smile she can't stand. Irene resists the urge to slap him across the face. "We need more concerned citizens keeping an eye out. We got your information on file in case we need it."

But the detective has barely written anything down, just the words "Ellis Wax," "Irene Howard," and "Soreno." They've been sitting at a table and jawing away; might as well deal a hand of gin to pass the time.

Mummy is growing restive and shifts her weight in the chair, causing its legs to squeak against the floor.

"Thank you, detective," offers Lauren Howard in a pleasant voice. "We've taken enough of your time."

"Are you going to look for him?" blurts Irene one last time. How could this cop be so closed-minded? Why won't he listen to her?

"Sure we will. We got it on file, like I told you. We'll call you if anything turns up."

●   ●   ●

Irene and Lauren Howard descend the marble steps from City Hall at a slow, mournful pace. At the bottom Irene stops and looks back, as if she might turn around and march right back into the building.

"The nerve of that man!" she hisses. "Did you hear him?"

Lauren takes her daughter gently but firmly by the elbow. They've done their civic duty, and now it is time to move on—literally—as soon as possible. She has no desire to spend another hour in this city lurking with hidden dangers and killers on the prowl.

"He was insolent! Did you hear him?"

"Come along, dear."

A few other patrolmen amble by on their way to police headquarters, and Irene glares at them as they pass. Given the state of mind she's in, she's liable to spew invectives and land them both in jail. So Lauren gives her daughter one last tug, and finally they depart. The wicker stroller is waiting for them, the driver standing beneath one of the three stubby oak trees newly planted in front of City Hall.

"Ouch! That hurts!"

"We shouldn't keep the boy waiting much longer."

"I know Ellis Wax killed that man, that Alberts fellow. I'll prove it, too, even if the police won't listen to me."

"You'll do nothing of the sort. You went to the police and that's that."

"Where to, miz?" asks the driver.

"The hotel," Lauren replies curtly.

The driver starts pedaling up Fourth Street toward Central Avenue. Lauren glances at her daughter: she looks like a stubborn two-year-old who can't get her way. What will she do next? Why won't she listen to reason? If Lauren could, she'd pick her daughter up, carry her aboard a train herself, and spirit her away to safety. Because going to the police was not enough; now she wants to do their job as well.

"I'll find him on my own. I'll prove he's the killer."

"You should listen to yourself. You sound like a lunatic."

"Maybe I am. But I know when I'm right. And I'm right about Ellis Wax. I'm not going to let that little creep get away with murder—I
could never live with myself."

As soon as we get back, Lauren Howard tells herself, *I'm calling the
train station and booking passage on the first line out of town.*

But when the driver stops at Central Avenue, Irene suddenly hops
out without uttering a word. Shocked, Lauren scrambles after her, calling out her daughter's name as she watches Irene dart across the busy
street, dodging a streetcar that clangs its bell angrily at her. Lauren
covers her face with her hands, but must wait until she can cross. By
then she has lost sight of her daughter, who's disappeared into the
throng like a penny lost on the beach. Lauren staggers around downtown like a drunk, not sure where to go or what to do, moving forward
and backward at once, knocking into passersby, keeping an eye out for
her beloved firstborn, and choked by fear that she'll never see Irene
alive again.

After a fruitless hour, Lauren returns to the hotel. She picks up the
phone at once and asks to be connected to the police. "My daughter is
missing," she stoically informs the voice at the other end of the line.

MIDNIGHT
JOE

inger is standing across the courtyard chatting with the landlady. They're looking at flowers and having a gay time doing it. Some of the old-timers invite Frank to sit in on a hand of gin. They wave at him pleasantly to come on over but he just shakes his head no. He's got too much on his mind to play a hand of cards. He's waiting for Ellis Wax to show up. They've got business to discuss.

Finally Ellis Wax comes scurrying down the sidewalk, head down and muttering to himself. Once he gets to the courtyard he stops, lifts his head, and begins to strut, tipping his hat to Ginger and Mrs. Wright. Frank scratches his chin and hopes Ellis Wax doesn't turn out to be a liar. But sometimes you just have to close your eyes and jump in.

"Afternoon, Frank," offers Ellis cheerfully. "Nice day to sit in the shade."

"Yeah, I suppose it is."

"It could be nicer."

"How's that?"

"A good shot of hardware never hurts." There's a brown bag beneath Ellis's arm. "Step into my office."

"You're talking my language."

The two men go inside the musty-smelling garage and sit on the same wobbly chairs around the same small table in Ellis's room. Ellis shows Frank the new bottle of vodka he's procured, the way a proud father might display pictures of his newborn. Then he pours two drinks.

"Here's to us," says Frank, lifting his jar. "I appreciate the generosity. This is some fine booze you got."

"Don't mention it. You can't beat good company."

The two men chug. The refills come quickly. Then Frank gets right to the point.

"Look, I got a business proposition for you."

"Is that right?" Ellis chuckles, slapping his knee. "I would very much like to discuss something with you."

"Why don't you go first then?" Frank offers. Ellis holds up his hand.

"No, you go. You're the guest. My mother raised me to have manners."

Frank shrugs. "Remember I told you last night that I have a problem that needs solving?" Ellis nods, and Frank draws a deep breath. "Well, the long and short of it is, I need somebody who can drive me someplace tonight, so I can take care of it once and for all. I don't know if you're game, and I know you got your own problems."

"No, of course I'll help you, Frank. Where are we going?"

"The dog track."

"Okay. Do you know where it is?"

"Yeah, it's on the road to Tampa."

"That sounds easy." A dilute smile appears on Ellis's lips. "I'm glad to help you, and it just so happens I need some help myself."

"With your stepmother, right?"

"I found her. It wasn't hard, she's staying at the nicest hotel in town. The Soreno."

"Did you talk to her?"

Ellis shakes his head. "No, no, not yet. I'm waiting for the right moment. The banks don't open until Monday, so I have a little more time. But I've got a plan, if you'll go along with it."

"Sure, you know, depending on what it is. I don't want to get involved with nothing too deep."

Ellis's face betrays no hint of emotion. He's one cool customer, Frank has to admit that. "I need you to drive, that's all. I'd never ask anyone to fight my battles for me."

"Sure. That sounds fair. But I don't have a car."

"You could drive mine while I talk over things with my stepmother."

Frank smiles knowingly. "We're taking her for a ride?"

"I need to get that key back. It's worth fifty grand."

Frank's ears perk up. He whistles as Ellis pours another drink. That same warm feeling is returning. "That's some real mazuma."

"Yes, it is. What I'm saying is: I'll make it worth your while if you help me."

"You'll pay me?"

"If I get that key back, I'll pay you five grand."

"If you don't?"

Ellis shrugs. "I'll be in trouble."

Frank considers this offer. On the face of it, there doesn't seem to be much he can lose. "You drive for me tonight, and I'll drive for you tomorrow. I guess that's tit for tat."

"That's how I see it. Here's to the start of good friendship."

The two men shake hands and finish their drinks. It could be Ellis Wax is a liar and a damn good one. But what difference does it make as long as he drives him to the dog track tonight? Tomorrow is a long way off, and Frank'll cross that bridge when he comes to it. By then he might be a couple thousand clams richer, and he won't need Ellis Wax for anything.

"If I'm wrong, I'm wrong," Vecchio growls as Musetta shifts uneasily in his seat, picking at the imitation leather upholstery. "But I don't think I am. They'll be headed to the dog track tonight, you watch."

They're parked on Ninth Avenue, about a half block away from the garage apartment they've been staking out for the past hour. Vecchio has a pair of small field binoculars to keep tabs on the situation. It's getting on toward six o'clock now. Things should start stirring soon, and Frank Hearn and Sally Serenade ought to be heading to the dog track.

"Any minute now," Vecchio says.

"Then what?" Musetta sounds skeptical. No big shock there. The kid has bitched and moaned all day. They drove out to look at the track and scout out the roads. It's perfect. There's a road that runs behind the track that leads all the way out to the Gandy Bridge, which takes you to Tampa. Or you can go the other way and head back to St. Pete. Vecchio thinks Tampa is the best bet. Once they take care of Sally and Hearn, they can hit that jeweler and head back to Chi-town, splitting twenty-five grand between them. But Joey Muse thinks the whole idea is baloney. "They go to the track and then what?"

"I told you a million times. We'll get them on the way there, and then head to Tampa. You can use that Tommy gun of yours."

"We could get them right here, right now."

"It'll be easier once we get further out of town. Where do we go from here? We're in a city, people all over, crowded roads. Near the dog track is perfect."

Musetta sighs. Vecchio decides to let it go. Some lessons in life can't be taught but must be learned. The kid will figure out soon enough that it's easier to do less work than more. That your brain grows stronger as your body grows weaker. That sometimes you need only to give the cue ball a tap, not a wallop.

"Here we go," Vecchio announces when Sally and Hearn emerge from the garage, along with a strange-looking guy in a white suit. The three of them hop into the flivver parked in back. Mr. White Suit is driving.

"Who's that?" the kid asks, voice dripping with fake concern.

Vecchio keeps his cool. "He must be in on it, too. Three for the price of two. But they're right on schedule. It's going down just like I said it would."

Musetta perks up. "She's dressed to the nines, huh?"

"She sure is."

Sally looks ravishing in the slinky dress she's got on, white cloche hat pulled tight against her head, moist red lips pouting.

"Too bad we got to kill her."

"Yeah."

Vecchio has never rubbed out a dame before. He's not looking forward to it, either. He keeps thinking about his mother, his wife, his daughter—maybe they can just nab Sally and put her on ice till the inquest is done with. Those aren't the orders, though. And if you don't follow the orders, your number gets called next. That's how Capone keeps everybody in line.

The car heads north on Third Street. The dog track is located a good five miles outside town, a straight shot up Fourth Street. They should swing over in a couple blocks, that's the way to go. Except they suddenly turn left onto First Avenue North and stop in front of a big park. Vecchio drives past, slowly. "What's going on?" he demands, angry at this unexpected detour.

"She's getting out."

"Really?"

"They dropped her off. We should grab her now!"

"Hold your horses." There are no parking spaces available in this crowded part of downtown, so they must drive on past the Princess Martha Hotel. Musetta keeps an eye on Sally.

"She's headed this way! Pull over, pull over!"

"Shut up! It's not the right place, kid."

"She's going into the hotel up there!"

Finally there's a place to park. Vecchio is breathing hard, flummoxed by this sudden alteration. The kid is ready to do something stupid. "We need to stay patient and figure out what's happening." He tells his partner this as they make their way down the sidewalk toward the lobby of the Princess Martha, which is crowded with the sort of well-heeled dandies who stay at the Carlisle in Chicago. They spot Sally sitting alone in a wicker chair over in front of the elevators. Vecchio walks past her and into the lounge.

"Well?" Musetta asks.

"She's going to the dog track. She must be meeting someone, probably that man she was with yesterday. He knew the Babe."

"We blew it! We shoulda nabbed her back there."

"Shut up. We'll have our shot later. Just be patient, how about it?"

Whenever a man looks like Woodrow Wilson's sickly younger brother, that's not a good sign. Dwight Yoder is not hopeful, sitting across the desk from Pete Allen, head of investigations in the St. Petersburg office of the Prohibition Bureau. Allen has a pinched, narrow face, round spectacles, grim mouth, and graying temples to go with a neatly pressed flannel suit and Knights of Columbus cuff links. His office is a picture of order and discipline, with not even a paper clip out of place. His walls are covered with plaques from the service organizations he belongs to, including the Ku Klux Klan and the American Protective Association. This rube would last about ten seconds in the Trenton office, Yoder thinks, before everyone started taking up a collection to have him bumped off.

"So Agent Yoder, am I to understand that you have been sent to my district to apprehend a suspect in a New Jersey bootlegging ring?" Allen sounds like a constipated Sunday school teacher. "A man by the name of Frank Hearn?"

"Yeah. Isn't that in the transfer there?" Yoder points to the paperwork he had Sonja type up. It took him a day longer to get out of town because some big brass from D.C. came for an inspection, and he didn't want prying eyes sifting through his business. It was bad enough explaining the bandage on his nose and several fingers from the frostbite he suffered courtesy of Frank Hearn. He's starting to mend but he won't feel completely healed until Frank gets what's coming to him.

Lichtenstein wants to make sure Hearn doesn't futz everything up. He's already filed a lawsuit against Babe Ruth and he doesn't want Hearn trying to collect the IOU he stole. By tomorrow the newspapers should have articles about the lawsuit. Ruth will fork over the cash to kill the bad publicity. So now isn't the time for Frank Hearn to go running around with an IOU signed by the Babe. Yoder will gladly make sure that won't happen.

Allen leafs through the paperwork. "It is in here, plainly stated. Nice work."

Yoder smiles triumphantly. It took him an hour to figure out what forms he needed to have to make this work, but Allen seems like he knows the handbook inside and out. "Yeah, this Hearn is someone we want real bad."

"What I don't see is an official Request for Intrabureau Cooperation. Those require a signature at the regional office."

"Yeah, well, there really isn't time for that. Hearn is a flight risk."

Allen's face puckers up like Yoder just told him the pope likes little boys. "I believe there was a memo about increasing intrabureau teamwork. The left hand must know what the right hand is planning."

Yoder titters helplessly. "I just go where they tell me to go. We have reason to suspect that Hearn will attempt to buy contraband down here in Florida and transport it to New Jersey."

"Oh. Then what you need is an Emergency Waiver."

"If you say so."

"I can provide one for you, but first tell me about this Frank Hearn. Why do you think he's here? We conducted a major raid last night on various establishments along Central Avenue, and we didn't arrest any Hearn."

"We came across information from an informant. Hearn boarded a train and headed your way. So I hopped a train last night and here I am. I haven't even checked in to my hotel yet."

"Good work, Agent Yoder. That's the sort of dedication everyone in the bureau should have."

Allen again begins reexamining the paperwork Yoder handed him.

Now what's he going to bitch about? That he didn't use the right kind of typewriter ribbon? This wally is a true believer, one of those zealots who really are determined to stamp out alcohol from the face of the earth. Not that anybody's complaining: business has never been better. The Volstead Act has been a gift from God. It wasn't that long ago Yoder was running errands for Ed Callahan. Now he gets to spend summers in Maine. Allen probably takes a hammer to every bottle he's ever seized. His men must be sick of his act. You can't live on the pittance they pay you. The only way to get ahead is grab a piece of the action for yourself.

"Agent Yoder, I will grant you an Emergency Waiver. You can have one of my men to help you. This is a town filled with illegality, much of it overflow from the Cubans and Italians across the bay in Ybor City, and I can't spare a soul and keep up with my responsibilities. I don't know how things are done up in New Jersey, but in my office we take our duties as assigned to us by the great citizens of the United States very seriously. Drinking is a scourge and the reason this country teeters on godlessness."

"I'm doing all I can to take as much booze as possible away from bootleggers." Yoder stands and manfully extends a hand. Allen grasps it and looks him dead in the eye.

"God bless you, Agent Yoder."

"No, thanks for your help. With some luck, Frank Hearn won't be poisoning our children ever again."

"Park over there," Frank tells Ellis Wax, pointing vaguely toward a palm tree. Too late: another car pulls in before he can react. So they keep circling the shell-and-limestone parking lot of the Derby Lanes dog track, which is teeming with cars and people and children darting in and out. Frank just shakes his head in bewilderment. He wasn't expecting this throng. But as soon as they got onto Fourth Street heading north, he started to worry. It seemed like everybody and his brother was moving in the same direction, toward the dog track, located out near the new Gandy Bridge, practically halfway to Tampa. The road after about Fortieth Avenue started to really fill up, and traffic slowed to a snail's pace.

"There!" Frank shouts. "Grab that one."

"Got it!"

Ellis eases the Ford into a narrow spot between a Roundabout and a Packard. Frank opens his door carefully, not wanting to scratch the gleaming Packard, with chrome and whitewall tires and leather seats. It's the kind of car the big shots drive. The kind of car he could afford if this all works out. And make no mistake: if he gets within ten feet of the Babe tonight, he's taking his shot.

"The idiots have come in droves," Ellis says, slamming his door. "Nothing like a cheap amusement to stir the masses."

"You don't like gambling?"

"Oh no. We used to go to the horse races at Pimlico. Father would get us a box for the Preakness. It was wonderful."

"I used to go to cock fights as a kid. I guess it ain't the same thing."

They're parked about as close to the dog track as they can be, as if God created this spot for them. Maybe that's a good sign. From the looks of it, this is one swell place. A big grandstand rises up from a grove of palm trees, and the infield is lush and tropical, too, from the little Frank can see of it. But it's classy and brand new, and dolled-up skirts are everywhere you look. Under different circumstances, he could see having a ball tonight. But there's work to do. The first order of business is figuring out where the Babe's party will be.

Kids with dirty faces and eager eyes come up and try to sell them tip sheets. Frank spends a quarter on one, buying it from a big, raw-boned youth who reminds Frank of himself. This kid is a hustler, spewing out names of trainers and times like he wrote the bible on dog racing. But that's what you got to do if you're on your own.

Ellis buys a different sheet from a smaller kid. He looks it over as they merge in with the throng. "This one claims the winner will be Midnight Joe. Well now, who am I to disagree?"

"I guess I got to go with Racing Ramp."

"Let the best puppy win."

As they wait in line to get in, Frank starts to get a funny feeling, like he's being watched. He takes a couple of surreptitious glances over both shoulders, but all he sees are faces, hundreds and hundreds of faces, mouths all yakking away excitedly about the race and seeing Babe Ruth and how nice the air feels tonight. He's letting his mind play tricks on him, just like when he thought he was being followed yesterday. Turned out the guy was headed to a funeral. It won't be long now and this will all be over. He'll either get paid or he won't. Why wouldn't the Babe pay to get his IOU back? Hell, it's the smartest thing in the world. They just need to have a talk, is all.

Again he looks behind him. It's a good thing he brought the .38 with him. Otherwise he'd be feeling very vulnerable right now. At least this way he can put up a decent fight. Not that he'll have to.

Now they're at the admission window, and Frank pulls out a dollar, getting fifty cents in change for the two tickets. Not many bills remain in his money clip, not enough to bother counting. In they go, just in time for a bell to ring, announcing the start of one of the preliminary races.

"Too late to get money down," says Ellis.

"I'm not here to gamble. I got a job to do."

Frank tries to get his bearings. The Babe wouldn't come through the main gate with the rest of the horde. There's a side entrance somewhere for VIPs, and then they'll whisk him away to some private party up in a box. Frank surges through the crowd to get a look at the grandstand. In front of him, a pack of dogs goes tearing around the first turn, and a few stumble and fall. The crowd in the grandstand roars as the dogs head into the backstretch. A man next to Frank begins jumping up and down, waving his wager ticket. "Get up, three! Get up, you mangy cur!" The speckled dog does hop up and keeps running, lagging far behind the leaders, smiling at the joy of the chase, without a thought about winning and losing. Then the dogs in the lead sprint down the straightaway and through the finish line, finally converging on the mechanical rabbit they had been chasing. Number three came in last. "He was the favorite!" the man tells no one, crumpling up his ticket in dismay.

Frank pushes past him, heading now against the flow of people stampeding away from the track and toward the betting windows located behind the grandstand. The next preliminary race will start in ten minutes. Frank scans the grandstand. There are sections that have been roped off on the second level. There's also a glassed-in box right at the finish line where the judges sit. That might be a likely spot for the Babe and his entourage. Ginger ought to be having the time of her life. This all worked out well for her, considering how things might have turned out if he hadn't saved her skin. But he can't blame her for jumping ship, just like he can't hold a grudge against Irene Howard. What has he done with his life so far to make a woman think he'd be worth sticking it out with? In six months things might be different.

"So do you see your friend?" It's Ellis Wax, standing at his elbow.

"No, not yet."

"I think I'll go put some money down on the next race. Let me know if you need my help."

"I will."

Ellis wanders off, and Frank decides to keep poking around. He's got to find out where the Babe will come in, so he can figure out the next move. The slugger will be surrounded at first, like a king wading through his adoring subjects, so there's no need to jump in then. Ginger could really smooth things out if she would just help Frank get past the goons who are going to be keeping the general public away. Maybe she will. The jury is out on that one. She said she'd do what she could without messing up her play. Whether she meant it or not, who knows?

Frank keeps walking around the track, until he reaches the staging area, where the dogs for the next race are getting weighed in. They look like friendly animals, but real excitable and jumpy. Probably haven't been fed, some of them. They'll feed the ones they want to run well. Irene Howard wouldn't go to the track in Atlantic City. Said it was barbaric. He teased her about it, but she had a point. She was like that, always rooting for the underdog.

Enough of Memory Lane—time to think. There're a few flatties milling around a gate behind the scales. That's worth keeping an eye on.

T.W. **Roland's** left hand rests solidly on Ginger's right thigh as the Chrysler Six limousine inches along Fourth Street. What a mess of traffic there is, giving T.W. even more time to snuggle up next to her. She doesn't dare move his paw. Not yet anyway. Not till they get to New York.

"Well," says Thomas L. Weaver, the track's owner, from the driver's seat, "I'd say we have a full house."

"Thanks to the Bambino!" shouts T.W. gaily.

Mr. Weaver is nattily attired in a white suit gleaming in radiant luxury, announcing to the world his success. As the track's owner, he has an obligation to maintain a certain image, a task he takes seriously, from his polished shoes to his slicked-back hair. Every detail of his appearance was probably overseen by his wife, sitting at his right elbow in queenly silence, garlanded with gold and diamonds, ruby-red lips pursed in stately remove. Mr. and Mrs. Weaver both have accumulated that fullness in face that comes with the arrival of middle age, paunch and flanks courtesy of gobbling heavy meals at fabulous galas and sundry dinner parties, no two of which were ever alike or ever different. But not tonight: no, tonight is unique because tonight is the running of the Babe Ruth Cup.

"Me?" the Babe snorts. "I haven't done nothing."

"You don't need to, slugger."

"I don't care what you say, Roland, I ain't buying your boat off you. So you can stop feeding me the applesauce."

"Ah, keep your hair on, slugger. I'll find some sucker to pay me my price. How about you?" T.W. playfully slaps Ginger's thigh. "You want her?"

"Oh, I don't think I could afford it," sings Ginger, sounding every inch the awestruck ingenue. The other women, Mrs. Ruth and Mrs. Weaver, glare hostilely at her. They're giving Ginger a bad case of the jumps. It's like they can see right through her, can detect the insincerity—because they know how a woman acts when she's smitten, and how she acts when she's just trying to get something.

"Well, you play your cards right," says T. W. Roland, "maybe I'll just give you *Miss Ohio*. Huh? Would you like that, doll?"

"Sure!"

"She's easy to please!" the Babe roars. "You hear that, Helen? She's happy with a boat. And it's a small boat."

Mrs. Ruth smiles thinly and keeps looking out the window. There's a marriage headed for Splitsville. Ginger feels sorry for the woman. Being his wife has to be harder than eating glass. Men think they can buy you nice things and you'll love them forever for it. But what good is a new sofa if you sit on it alone every night, waiting for your husband to come home? No, Ginger's not falling for that trap again. Frank was right: if you don't look out for yourself, no one else will.

Frank: there's got to be something she can do for him. She'll keep her eye out. She owes him that much.

The limo pulls up to a side entrance. Ginger can see a gaggle of photographers running over to snap pictures that will run in every newspaper in the country tomorrow, letting those goons back in Chicago know exactly where she is. She can't be in those shots. She ducks her head down low.

"What's wrong, honey pie? You afraid of cameras?" T.W. has moved his hand from her thigh to her back.

"A little."

"Let T.W. take care of it." He takes off his jacket and lets her use it as a shield, as they are hustled from the limo and into the track. *Pop! Pop! Pop!* she hears as she scurries past, letting T.W. lead the way.

A few in the crowd shout "Babe! Babe!" as if he's standing far away and can't hear. But such intrusions never bother him. A smile, a wave, a wink, a tip of the hat: he truly thrives on the adulation, the constant attention. Most likely because he didn't get it as a boy. That's what Helen has decided about her husband, that's what always makes her choke up when thinking about him. How hard he had it as a lad. How he sat in that orphanage year after year with nobody coming to visit him. How neglectful his mother was. How unloved he had to have felt. He used to tell her such things when they were first married, open up his heart for her to see.

"We're throwing a little party up in the judges' box," Mrs. Weaver tells Helen. "I hope you like caviar."

"Who doesn't?"

"Do you like caviar, Miss DeMore?"

"Sure, that sounds swell." She now has T.W.'s coat draped over her head like a shawl.

"Are you cold?"

"No, I just don't like cameras."

"Wait till you get older. You'll loathe them."

"We should go on up," Weaver announces with the gravity of a czar. "They're waiting for us."

"Just so there's enough to drink," the Babe says with a wink.

"Oh, I believe there is, slugger. You won't be disappointed."

Look at the sweat dripping down his face, thinks Helen. He's killing himself a little bit each day, and he doesn't even care.

"Okay, folks, the show's over," says Weaver proudly. "Time for us to go watch the race. Better go get your wagers in. You'd hate to miss this one!"

With that, the group is led away by a cop with a nightstick and a stern expression of contempt. T.W. puts an arm around Ginger and guides her through the mob, flashbulbs still popping away, people yelling and gawking. She feels like a horse with blinders on. She can see only what's right in front of her, namely the cop. Then they go up a flight of stairs to the judges' booth, which the Weavers have fashioned into a sumptuous parlor with a spread of food that makes Ginger's eyes bug out. There's the best booze, the best caviar, the best cuts of steak, the best Belgian chocolate, the best of everything for Ginger to partake.

"So, doll, having a good time?" T.W. has slipped his arm around her again. Ginger smiles and nods, unable to speak because of the delicious bite of potato au gratin she's eating. "I'm glad. Drink up. There's plenty of everything."

Ginger swallows and puts a hand on her hip. "Are you trying to get me boiled? You know it won't work. It didn't work before."

"You're a good sport. You don't get all crabby like some dames."

"The only thing that'll happen if you get me canned is that I'll start singing."

"You better save your voice for when we get to New York. You still want to go?"

"Of course I do. More than anything in the world."

"Good, I'm glad. But sugar plum, I need to know something."

She can tell by the tone of his voice that he wants The Truth. It's what all men want from their women: The Truth about Their Past. It's not that he doesn't deserve some explanation. But not The Truth. Not yet anyway.

"What's that?"

"What are you hiding from?"

Ginger doesn't skip a beat. "Oh, some of this and some of that. Does it scare you?"

"Nothing scares me."

"Okay then. Finish your drink and get me another one. I'm very thirsty tonight."

"You're something else. That's all I got to say."

As he skips away to the bar, Ginger looks over at the Babe. He's holding forth with a drink in one hand and a plate in the other, face smeared with cream sauce, voice booming, sweat streaming down his brow, while his poor wife is just standing there, silent as a church mouse, holding her handbag in front of her with both hands. The scene makes Ginger a little mad. Maybe Mister Big Shot could use a glass of cold water tossed in his face. But how can she get Frank up here? The least she could do is have a quick chat with him, if she can find him.

T.W. brings her another drink.

"Oh," she giggles. "I better use the powder room. I thought I saw one downstairs."

"Hurry back now. I want to ask you a few more questions."

She frowns at him. "We'll see about that," she pouts at him playfully as she leaves.

The agent Yoder was assigned is named Cooper. He's real quiet, a middle-aged man who's been in the wars long enough not to care much beyond punching a clock. He's just collecting paychecks and trying to stay alive. He won't care if Yoder wants to take Hearn for a ride. At least that's the impression Yoder gets. But he's got to be sure before this gets too much deeper. They might find Hearn here at the dog track, and what happens next depends on Cooper's attitude. Given that his boss, Pete Allen, is a true-blue believer who does everything by the book, Yoder can't assume Cooper will look the other way.

"See my face?" Yoder asks him once they enter the track.

Cooper shrugs. "What about it?"

"My nose got frostbit, thanks to this Hearn ape. You follow me?"

"Let's find him."

"Yeah, that's why I came down here. But if we pick him up, I need to have some time with him alone, so I can get some answers out of him."

"I don't care what you do to him."

"He left me for dead, understand? I ain't no slut. I do my job the way it's supposed to be done. But it's personal between me and him."

"I heard plenty about the Trenton office. I'd love to transfer up there, but Allen won't sign off on it."

"It's a good place to work."

Cooper guffaws, patting Yoder hard on the back. "I could retire after a year!"

"Well, if we find Hearn, I'll make sure you get your share. That's how we do things in Trenton."

"Let's go then. Lead the way."

Finding Hearn won't be easy, not with this crowd. People are packed in like sardines, bumping into one another, shuffling along at a snail's pace. The betting windows have long lines snaking from them, spilling into the walkway beneath the grandstand and clogging it up.

"We're not the only ones looking for Hearn," Yoder explains as they make their way to the rail. "He's with some skirt, and she's got the Torrio mob after her."

"That's a rough outfit."

"Tell me about it. I don't know what's happening. I would've left yesterday but the chief came from D.C. All I know is I got tickets to the Yankees game tomorrow, and I'm going."

A bell rings, and six dogs go tearing out of the paddock, chasing a mechanical rabbit. The roars go up, and Yoder's eyes lift upward, too, back toward the grandstand and the judges' box in the middle of it. And unless he's seeing things, there's Babe Ruth himself, standing right at the glass, waving his arms frantically.

And right next to him—is that Frank Hearn?

Yoder gives Cooper a poke in the ribs, and points up. "That's him next to Babe Ruth."

Cooper clenches his jaw. "Yeah, so what's next? You wanna go up there?"

"Damn it! I got here too late."

"Is he selling booze to Ruth?"

"No. Son of a bitch. Let's go. I'll explain later."

The two men walk quickly toward the judges' box.

The Babe is jumping up and down like a little kid, waving a betting slip in his big paw of a hand. He's made a few people spill their drinks and his poor wife dumped a plate of food on her dress when he bumped into her. He doesn't even notice. He keeps on jumping and cheering like a maniac. "I won, I won! I won, I won! The long shot came home!"

Weaver sidles up to him. "Okay, Babe, how much are you hitting me for?"

"Just a grand, Weaver. I'm on fire tonight! Wait till the big race comes up. You better call your banker! I'm putting the whole thing on Racing Ramp!"

Ginger shoots Frank a look. He's been staying on the sidelines ever since she brought him upstairs and introduced him to T.W. as her cousin. Frank played it perfectly, and T.W. seemed to buy it. But the longer Frank stays, the more nervous Ginger gets. Something's bound to happen. She's really risking it with T.W. because this little ploy might blow up in her face. Then where will she be?

"I'm going down to collect my money!" the Babe shouts. "Don't go anywhere, Weaver. I'll be back in a flash."

Ginger thinks: *Now.*

As the Babe goes walking past, she again glances at Frank. He doesn't tip his hand in any direction. He finishes his drink and very casually falls in behind the Babe, like it's the most natural thing in the world. "I've got a winner, too," she hears him say.

"That so?"

Then they are gone. Ginger closes her eyes, feeling relieved and much lighter in the head. She feels T.W.'s arm snake around the small of her back.

"Your cousin seemed nice," he tells her. His voice has a harder edge now. Maybe she's imagining it.

"Oh, he is. I haven't seen him in years! What a coincidence."

"It sure is. So he's your mother's sister's son?"

"No. He's on my father's side."

"I thought you said mother's."

"Did I? The things that come out of my mouth!" She laughs nervously, bringing the glass to her lips. She bats her eyes at him coquettishly. He has an expression like he's trying to find the right words to say. A change of subject would be a nifty idea, if she could just think of something.

But the Babe comes bounding back up the stairs, and then points right at her. Everyone stops talking at once. "Hey, doll face! Your cousin just got arrested!"

277

Ellis Wax hurries over to his car, parked between the Roundabout and the Packard. He just saw Frank get picked up by two gorillas from the Prohibition Bureau. They led him out in cuffs and tossed him in the back of a Chrysler. One of them hopped behind the wheel and the other stayed behind. That's trouble. Big trouble. Frank can't die or it'll ruin everything Ellis has planned. Stupid, meddling apes, sticking their noses where they don't belong.

Ellis hops in and floors it. He saw the Chrysler was heading east, toward Tampa.

"Where are you taking me?"

Frank is sitting in the back of a sedan with a pair of handcuffs digging into his wrists. So this is how it will end, with Dwight Yoder killing him in St. Petersburg, Florida. He knows Yoder is planning on killing him because Yoder left the other agent back at the track, so he wouldn't witness anything. There's no doubt now. This is it, the last stop.

Frank keeps on struggling against the cuffs, but they're not budging. His hands are wedged behind him, cutting painfully into his wrists. The car is screaming down a dark road. In the distance he can make out the faint glow of lights rising up into the night sky. That must be Tampa.

"I'm taking you for a nice ride, just like you took me." Yoder sounds almost happy. His voice has a gleeful ring to it.

"I knew you were coming, I just didn't think you'd get here so soon," Frank says, mind racing, turning over the possibilities. Time is running out, though. He's got to think of something.

"I'm like God. I move in mysterious ways."

"I didn't kill you, Yoder, when I had the chance. I know what you want. Just take it already and let me go."

"Take what, Frankie?"

"You know, the IOU. The one from Babe Ruth."

Yoder starts giggling like someone is tickling him. "Oh, Frank. I'll get the IOU—and plenty more, too, once we get where we're going." Then his voice becomes solemn, like a teacher scolding a naughty pupil. "I warned you to stay out of it. You didn't listen. You left me in the cold. That was a mistake."

"You stole my booze."

"No, Callahan stole your booze. You should've come straight to us, Frank. Callahan is a bum."

"He was like a father to me."

They stop and pay a toll, and now they're driving across a bridge, the car shaking when it passes over gaps in the concrete. "Frank, there is something you need to understand. Life is simple: either you're smart and you win, or you're stupid and you don't. Maybe you had more muscles than me, but I was always smarter. That's why I went places and you didn't."

"I just wanted my share, Yoder. I didn't hijack nothing from you and I got the IOU right here in my pocket."

Yoder chuckles again. "I like you, Frank. You're a fighter. You just picked the wrong fight."

The car continues on, going up an incline before it starts to slow down at the top. Time is running out. They're in the middle of a bridge. *Think of something, think of something.* Frank stares at the back of Yoder's egg-shaped head, mottled from the passing streetlights. It's a very inviting target, but for what? He's only got use of his legs. But this sedan has a pretty roomy backseat. He leans back, bringing his legs slowly up, knees bent, arms aching from the awkward positioning of his body. All his weight is ripping at his shoulders, and he grits his teeth. Beads of sweat dapple his brow, and the veins in his neck pop out in bold relief. Higher his legs go, until they now hover above the seat.

"Do you like to swim, Frank?" asks Yoder, turning his head to glance back at the prisoner. That's when Frank unleashes a crushing kick to Yoder's right temple. The impact creates a sound like rotten fruit hitting a sidewalk. Yoder slumps down, and the car begins careening over into the opposite lane of traffic, the accelerator floored under the weight of Yoder's body. Frank bolts upright and is trying to climb over the seat when the Chrysler slams into the north side guardrail. The impact sends Frank flying back-first through the windshield, ejecting him from the flipping, spinning car. Both splash into the cold water of the bay.

Frank is submerged for a few seconds, and then his head breaks the surface of the water. Since his hands are still cuffed, he's having trouble staying afloat. He's kicking wildly and trying to maintain his balance. He manages to roll onto his back and kick toward the bridge, but he's starting to get tired. His lungs are burning, he's gasping for breath, and he's not sure he can last much longer. It's impossible to swim with your hands cuffed behind you, but he's a strong swimmer, having grown up on the shore.

Then he hears a voice. "Frank!"

He can't see who it is. He hears a splash, and seconds later, Ellis Wax swims over to him. He's got a piece of wood from the guardrail to use as a float.

"Are you hurt?"

"I don't think so."

"It's a miracle you're alive."

The Chrysler has sunk to the bottom. There's no sign of Yoder as Ellis pulls Frank back toward the nearest bridge piling. They swim from one piling to the next, until they reach the shore on the St. Pete side.

There they rest a minute. "Wait here until I go get the car," says Ellis. "It's best if you stay out of sight. I can pick those cuffs once we get back home."

Frank sits shivering by the banks of the bay, looking out over the still, black water, the moon's glow reflected on its smooth surface in long tendrils of gold. Still no sign of Yoder. He went down with the car and got what he deserved. One less thieving cop to worry about. Good riddance.

But what about Ginger? If Yoder found him this soon, then the apes will be on her, too.

Vecchio presses down on the ignition switch. The Model T coughs a few times and sputters.

"Pull on the choke a little more," Musetta advises, anger dripping from his voice. Vecchio won't even touch the choke. Because that's giving in. He presses again on the ignition switch. The car won't start.

"It's the choke!"

"It's not the choke! It's the damn starter, kid!"

"It's the choke, I'm tellin' ya."

"You wanna drive? Is that it?"

"Yeah, let me drive. She's getting away!"

They switch places. Vecchio sits in the passenger seat, breathing heavily, sweat pouring down his brow. The kid pulls on the choke. The car won't start. Now they're stuck out in the parking lot of the dog track. The races ended nearly fifteen minutes earlier, and Sally is getting into the same limo that brought her here. It pulls away and snakes out of the parking lot.

"Great! This is great!" Musetta screams. "We shoulda nabbed her hours ago!"

And for the first time in his life, Vecchio feels spent and useless. He stares at the dashboard, at the gauges that register nothing. "Try one more time."

The car sputters again, coughs like an old smoker, but the engine catches. Musetta throws it into first and spews rocks and shells as he speeds across the parking lot. The limo has about a one-minute lead on them, but cars jam the roads again, just like on the way out to the dog track. That's been the story so far, people everywhere.

"Now we're cooking," Vecchio says. But Musetta still hasn't calmed down.

"This is horseshit! We keep missing chances and eventually we'll run out."

"No, be patient. We'll follow them back into the city."

"I've been patient. Real patient."

Neither man speaks as they creep along in bumper-to-bumper traffic. Musetta is snorting like a bull ready to charge. He'll do something stupid unless he pulls himself together. Anger has no place in this business. You keep your cool and do the job. Nothing goes perfect. No point telling the kid that.

"Is it because she's a skirt?" Musetta asks, never taking his eyes off the road.

"Is what because she's a skirt?"

"You don't want to kill her."

"I don't want to be stupid."

The kid just smirks. So now he's a coward for wanting to be careful. These young idiots today, they all want to act so tough. Pull out a gun and shoot, doesn't matter who or where or when. Just shoot.

Vecchio shakes his head. "You don't spend ten years with Johnny Torrio by being a coward," he says to the window. "Sometimes the best shot is the one you don't take. It's called playing it smart."

"Come on!" Musetta yells out the window. "Move it, pops!"

"That draws attention. Don't draw attention."

Musetta replies by swinging the car onto the grass shoulder and flooring the accelerator. Now they're passing all kinds of cars, and who knows, maybe a copper. This kid is reckless. He's not long for this world. Some people get their ticket stamped early and don't realize it until it's too late. Capone's the same way. He'll get his and bring everyone down with him. Torrio's smart moving back to Italy. Vecchio shakes his head. What he wouldn't do to go back. He doesn't remember much, he was just a little boy when they left. There were goats he played with. He helped Mama feed them.

"There they are, right up there," announces Musetta triumphantly, easing back into the traffic amid a fanfare of blaring horns. The limo is about four cars in front of them. "We're doing things my way now."

Weaver drops off Babe Ruth and his wife first. The Babe's not feeling so swell, complaining of his stomach killing him and God knows it should, the way that man eats and drinks. He was putting something in his mouth every time Ginger looked over at him. He gets out of the limo slowly, carefully, his wife holding on to him with her nice satin dress stained like she's bled all over it. They'll get into a fight once they are alone. At least they should. Or maybe she's the type who gets walked on.

"Well, sport," says Weaver dryly, "better luck next year. Maybe you can recoup some of that."

"This whole thing was a setup to fleece me. Babe Ruth Cup my leg! I'll get you yet, Weaver!" Still jovial right till the bitter end, even though his face is bloated like a frog's and it doesn't look like he could hit a fly, much less a baseball.

Ginger watches him stagger toward the hotel, and with him goes a strange chapter of her life. What happened to Frank, she has no idea. But that's not the biggest problem she's got right now. Fences need mending between her and T.W., who hasn't exactly been friendly to her since the episode with Frank. He hasn't mentioned New York and he's been acting cold and distant, like he's not so sure about her anymore.

"Where to?" asks Weaver.

Ginger lays her head on T.W.'s shoulder.

"Aren't you getting out here?" he whispers to her.

"I'm not tired yet."

T.W. rubs the back of his neck thoughtfully. "Let's go have us a talk. We better clear the air about a few things."

"How about your place?"

"Sure. But I want some answers from you. Honest ones. You can't con a con." Then he leans forward and tells Weaver to take them to the Hotel Alexander. Ginger gazes out the window as the limo pulls off. There's the Babe surrounded by well wishers once again. His poor wife's been shoved aside and she stands there with a blank expression, the fronds of a potted palm reaching down like a giant claw to scoop her up.

The limo stops in front of a hotel on Central Avenue.

"They're getting out," Vecchio says. Musetta pulls around the limo and stops fifteen yards away.

"Shoot her!" he snorts. Vecchio has the better shot, right through his open window.

Vecchio lifts his gun up and aims. He's got a clear shot, nothing in the way. She's walking toward the hotel, the man she's with a step behind. As he squeezes the trigger, though, a porter springs to her side. Vecchio watches him crumple to the sidewalk. He squeezes the trigger again, but the cowboy pushes Sally toward the hotel. A bystander, shot in the leg, falls to the ground, writhing in pain.

A streetcar rings its bell from behind.

"Just go!" Vecchio yells.

"You idiot!"

Musetta goes tearing off down Central Avenue. Vecchio keeps his eyes dead ahead, staring at the red brake lights in the distance. Traffic.

"Turn right," he barks.

Musetta hangs a sudden left, tires squealing like the high-pitched wail of an angry child.

The injured have been loaded into ambulances, but the blood remains pooled on the sidewalk in front of the Hotel Alexander. Irene's never seen so much blood at one time, and although it makes her queasy, she can't pull herself away from what she's just witnessed: a man and a woman stepping out of a limo, and shots ringing out from a moving car that sped off into the night. A porter was hit, and so was another man.

Irene had been across the street in a pool hall and was just walking out when the scene unfolded in front of her. It didn't take long for the cops to arrive, and Irene watched as they led the man and the woman into the hotel. She watched the wounded being tended to and then carted off. Neither had died, although both were badly hurt.

She tells herself to leave but doesn't. A mixture of shock and curiosity keeps her there, the unexpected onslaught of raw, wanton violence involving a smart-looking couple that must've been the target—but who was after them? What's the story? These questions don't have answers, and Irene starts to feel foolish for lingering at the scene. She should move along now. But right when she's about to depart, the man and the woman from the limo come out of the hotel. They walk a half-block down the sidewalk and stop, but they're not standing very far away from Irene, who wanders toward them, straining to hear their voices.

"Okay, you can cut the baloney now," the man says. "Why don't you level with me?"

"You heard what I told the cops," the woman replies, voice so low that Irene can barely make out the words. "I don't know who would shoot at me."

"I covered for you back there. I could've mentioned the photographers, how you hid from them."

"I wasn't hiding from anyone. I just don't like my picture taken."

The man snorts in disbelief. "What're you gonna do now? Huh? They'll find you again. They might be waiting right around the corner."

Irene starts to look around, pulse racing. The street is crowded with Saturday night traffic, it's impossible to tell who's who.

"Where will you go?" the man asks, trying to hold the woman's hand. She pulls it away.

"Away from here."

"If you're in some trouble, those cops back there can help."

"The cops? Are you off your nut?"

"Well, then I can help, if you'll let me."

"No, you can't. You're a nice man, and you should run as far away from me as you can. Good-bye, T.W."

The woman hails a cab and gets into it without saying another word. It then goes creeping away, inching along with the other cars on Central Avenue. The man stares at it for a minute, shakes his head, and pivots with stern precision, turning his back both literally and figuratively. Irene watches him march past. The cops who are still loitering about give him a glance but say nothing. It's over, but the mystery remains.

Irene then starts for the Soreno Hotel.

She can't help thinking about the woman. Who was she? Why were they trying to kill her? How did she get herself in this position? Irene isn't jealous, exactly, but she imagines the woman leads a glamorous life, full of excitement and intrigue. Sort of like when Irene was with Frank. You never knew one day to the next what was going to happen. He always had some scheme in the works. Looking for an angle, an edge, an opportunity. Laws didn't scare him and neither did dying. He did what he wanted when he wanted, and what he wanted most of all was to have a ball.

Frank is with his other woman now, out in California; she's probably an actress or a singer, a starlet hoping to break into the movies. They're probably in Hollywood. Frank is wheeling and dealing, trying to get himself established. He's gone down to Tijuana and brought back cases of booze. Irene can almost picture it perfectly, the wonderful insanity that swirls around Frank Hearn.

Her feet feel heavy and still a little sore. She's walked miles over the course of the afternoon and night, stopping at every hotel and roominghouse she could get to, but there's been no sign of Ellis Wax. He's not registered under that name anywhere, and he wasn't in any of the pool halls or blind pigs or speakeasies she managed to get to. She knew it was a lost cause but she kept on anyway because the search itself was interesting. She met some rather distinctive individuals today: lorry drivers, carpenters, house painters, barkeeps, Italians, Poles, Jews, Greeks, old men with bright eyes, young men with deep scowls, and everywhere women giving her the up-and-down, like she didn't belong. But she'd been to such places before, with Frank. She wasn't slumming it, like Jimmy Woodman and his crowd liked to do, packing into a Marmon for a trip to Harlem. No, it wasn't like that. It was a taste of the life Irene wanted for herself. Trips to the unknown corners of the world.

I won't let myself be bored again.

That's the promise Irene makes as she approaches the Soreno, where on the fifth floor a wealthy society woman from Greenwich, Connecticut, is pulling her hair out. They'll have to have a talk about the future. Things won't be the same again. Irene knew that the minute she crawled out of her dorm room window. She's left that life behind forever.

---

f rank's arms and wrists feel like they've been worked over by a mallet and a pickax. He's got a deep gash on the back of his head from the windshield and his legs are wobbly from the kicking and thrashing in the water. This has been a bad night, but it could've been worse. It could've been him on the bottom of the bay.

"How about a drink?" offers Ellis as they walk from the parked car to the garage.

"Sure, maybe one."

"You're living on borrowed time now, so you might as well enjoy it."

"Look, I appreciate you saving my life. God knows I owe you one."

"Sure thing, friend. You'll pay me back tomorrow, when we do that job."

"That won't exactly make us even. I'm a goner without you."

They walk down the narrow corridor that separates their rooms. Ellis enters his and Frank promises to join him as soon as he strips out of his wet clothes. He then realizes he doesn't have a key to his room. Along with everything else, it went down with the car—everything but his life, that is.

"I'm locked out," he chuckles to himself.

Then from behind the closed door he hears: "Frank? Is that you? Oh thank God!"

Ginger cracks open the door and peers through. He becomes worried. "What happened?" he asks. She doesn't answer; instead, she throws open the door and leaps into his arms. He feels something hard pressing him in the back. He carries her into the room and quickly discovers the gun she's holding.

"Expecting trouble?"

"They found me, Frank!"

"Where?"

"They followed me from the track, and they tried to kill me! But they missed!"

"Did they follow you here?"

She shakes her head and wipes the tears from her eyes. Frank lets out a deep sigh of relief. Then he turns on a lamp and dull light renders the darkness a murky mist of beige. Ginger collapses onto the bed with the gun still in her hands, makeup smeared all over her face, eyes puffy from crying, and her new dress soiled from their embrace.

"I took a cab here," she explains as he starts pulling off his wet clothes. "I told the driver to make sure no one followed me. I paid him all the money I had, Frank."

He hangs his shirt on the back of a chair. "Join the club. I'm busted, too. And wouldn't you know, they found me at the dog track and took me for a ride. We're a pair of rubes, huh?"

"Oh Frank, what are we going to do?"

"I need to dry off. I went swimming."

He takes his pants off and hangs them on another chair. Then he removes his socks, undershirt, and underpants, and takes the blanket off the bed and wraps himself in it. He sits down next to her and pats her ankle.

"Swimming?" she repeats softly.

"With the cop who stole my booze, Yoder. We went for a swim, but he never came up for air."

"You killed him?"

"I wouldn't say that. It's more he drove us off a bridge and into the bay. I made it out, he didn't." He nods his head toward the door. "Ellis Wax over there saved my life. He followed me from the track once he saw I got nabbed."

"Thank God you're alive!" She reaches over and wraps her arms around his neck. She's shaking, too, and feels cold.

"Back at ya, sister. Sounds like you dodged a few bullets yourself."

"You're the only person I trust, Frank. The only person in the world."

"We've got to get out of here."

"I know we do. But where can we go?"

He frowns. "If we're going to get out of here, we need money fast."

"Sounds like you have a plan. Do you, Frank? Please say you do!"

He shrugs and forces a wry grin to make it seem like he's got it under control but it's an act and she probably knows it. "There's something Ellis needs help with. He's got some problems with his stepmother, I don't know. He might be lying about it. I don't care, as long as he pays me for it tomorrow. Then we can hop a boat for Cuba."

"Cuba?"

"It's close by. I saw charter boats that go there."

She lets her head fall on his chest. "Are you sure you want to stay with me? I'm the kiss of death. It was horrible. They shot two people." She starts crying, and Frank rubs her back gently. "I don't know if I can take much more of this. I really don't."

"Somebody is going to a lot of trouble to find you."

"I know. They'll finish the job one of these days."

He waits for her to regain her composure. The tears stop falling in time. He dabs at her eyes with a corner of the blanket. "Feel better?"

"No."

"Maybe you will if you talk about it."

She laughs bitterly. "How about if I just start at the beginning?"

"That would be nice."

"Okay, you asked for it." Ginger takes a deep breath. "It all started when my husband came home one day and said he had just bought a pig farm."

Nothing.

That's exactly what Joe Szymanski has come up with so far. He's shown pictures of Aubrey Marshall to just about every fence he knows and to a man no one has ever seen the guy before. Which means that Aubrey Marshall was probably planning on selling those gems he stole in the city he escaped to. The most likely scenario runs something like: 1) He killed his stepmother and 2) He left town. He didn't dally around Baltimore trying to fence stolen property.

The question is, what's the next assignment he'll get stuck with? It's getting late and Szymanski is getting thirsty. The clock inside his head is clanging loudly. His regular Saturday evening seat at Kresky's bar beckons him; it's time to put the Marshall case in the unsolved pile, along with the scores of others already there, the dead bodies nobody much cares about. But Freda Marshall gave money to the Peabody Conservatory, to Johns Hopkins, to this, to that, she was rich and white and lived in Mount Vernon, so the commissioner won't let up. They'll have something else for him. If not today, then tomorrow.

Since he's on the west side of town, Szymanski stops at the Pine Street station to call headquarters and tell the captain about the zilch he's got. If Szymanski doesn't physically show up downtown, there's a chance they'll let him go home.

He finds a phone and calls. He waits while they connect him to the captain. That's one hardworking Scotsman, like a mule. Szymanski feels bad about not wanting to stick around when he knows the captain will be there most of the night.

"Anything else?" Szymanski asks after he gives his report.

"Not tonight. Tomorrow, though, you could do something for me."

Szymanski cringes. "What's that, cap?"

"There's somebody out in Catonsville we want interviewed. His house was broken into about a week before the murder, and the guy keeps calling and insisting there's some connection. I mean, half the city is calling with tips. You know how that works on something like this. Everybody wants to be a hero."

Not everybody, Szymanski thinks bitterly. "So why him?"

"Well, he's not your typical crank. He's the head of the bank out there, and he knew the Marshall family. He thinks the kid broke into the house and stole some blank checks and other documents. There might be something to it. There might not."

"Catonsville, huh? On a Sunday? He must be a churchgoing man, being a banker."

"I don't know. I guess you should call first."

Szymanski takes out a pad to write down the number. "What's his name?"

"Adam—I can't read this. Gould. G-O-U-L-D, I think. Anyway, here's the number."

Szymanski scribbles it down. "I'll call him, cap."

Before he folds the notebook up and slips it back into his frayed tweed jacket, he notices the name "Ellis Wax" printed in block letters on the opposite page. He won't have time to check into that character for a good long while; Mabel Wright of all people will understand. She knows more about how the department operates than most of the cops who work in it.

MOUND
BUILDING

His clothes still aren't dry, and although it's a warm morning, a damp shirt doesn't feel good. Frank scowls as he gets dressed. Looking down at Ginger lying nude in bed, it reminds him of a morning just a few days ago, when he woke up next to her for the first time and vowed never to be cold again. No one ever gets cold in Florida, he was sure of that. Well, here he is, right where he wants to be, and he's cold. And just like in Asbury Park, there's not a hell of a lot he can do about it.

One thing is certain, though: no one ever, ever gets cold in Cuba. That's the next stop, once he does what he has to with Ellis Wax.

"Frank?" Ginger stirs, the bed creaking as she sits up.

"You awake?"

"Are you leaving?"

"For a while."

"I'm scared, Frank. I don't want to be here alone."

He sits down next to her. After what she told him last night about that thug Al Capone back in Chicago, he doesn't blame her for being scared. Anybody who works for Johnny Torrio is dangerous, and Capone sounds rougher than your usual wop racketeer.

"Listen," he calmly tells her. "Don't go anywhere till I get back. I mean anywhere. Don't take any chances. You got that gun, you used it once already—use it again if you have to. I'll come back, hopefully with enough dough to buy us a trip to Cuba. What happens after that, I don't know. I'll worry about it later."

"You'd be better off without me."

"Don't say that."

It was a constant refrain last night as she recounted the story of her life, from Toledo to a pig farm to Chicago, where she got mixed up with Capone. *You're better off without me. I'm weighing you down.* "Now's not the time for self-pity. One mistake can get us both killed," he reminds her sternly.

She looks him straight in the eye. "It's true, and you know it. I'm nothing but trouble."

"No one's killing me, understand?" He wags a finger at her. "Yoder had his chance last night, and he missed. So it ain't time for me yet. You either."

"You don't know that."

"Let's just cut the hokum." He stands up and pulls on his damp pants. "I got a job to do, and we'll figure things out later. Just don't go anywhere."

"I won't." It doesn't sound like she means it.

He leans down and kisses her on the neck. She doesn't kiss him back. He lifts her chin up to look at her face. She closes her eyes, but then clutches his hand with hers. It makes him feel a little better, like she's not going to go off the deep end. If they can just get out of St. Petersburg, they'll be fine.

"I'll be back as soon as I can," he says. Then he leaves and goes across the hall to knock on Ellis Wax's door.

•   •   •

When things don't go as planned, you have to grope through life like a blind man. You touch things you shouldn't, because you can't help it. Either that or smack face first into a wall. This might be one of those times. Frank doesn't know much about what Ellis Wax wants him to do. But when a man saves your life, you can't exactly turn down a favor. Ellis Wax pulled him out of the water. He didn't have to. They're just neighbors, barely more than strangers passing in opposite directions on separate journeys.

Frank owes him his life. He wished he didn't, but he does.

"Good morning," chirps Ellis as he opens the door. "I was just coming to get you."

"I was getting dressed." Frank pats his arms. "Clothes are still damp from last night. They stink, too. Like fish."

"If it all goes as planned today, I'll buy you a new suit of clothes."

"So what is it we're doing anyway?"

Ellis leads him by the arm down the narrow corridor. "Let's talk in the car."

Out they go into the balmy March air. The old-timers have already congregated around the tables in the courtyard, some dressed for church and some dressed for fishing. The landlady is fiddling with her flower beds as usual. Ellis goes over and has a word with her. A few of the oldsters wave at Frank. He smiles and waves back.

"Got some big plans, do ya?" one calls out.

Frank cocks his head. "Wish I did. Nice day, huh?"

"Oh yeah. It's twenty degrees back in Detroit. Saw the paper today." There's some general murmuring among them. It's a spry group. One of them brought home a trophy yesterday. Won it playing shuffleboard, whatever that is.

Finally Ellis comes back. "It always pays to be nice to the landlady. You never know when you'll need a favor. Okay, Frank, let's shove off."

During the other six days of the week, Third Street bustles with traffic, but Sunday all is quiet. The shops aren't open and the street is basically deserted. Sunlight streams through the towering oak trees, creating a lattice of shadows on the brick pavement. A flock of parakeets goes screeching overhead and lands atop a palm tree in front of a barbershop. Fragrances float serenely through the clear air, because flowers are in bloom. These are sad reminders of why Frank wanted to come here. He can't enjoy himself. He's got more clawing and scratching to do. These were going to be his salad days in the sun. Now Frank's down to the last card in the deck.

They walk over to the Model T and hop in. Ellis gets behind the wheel, which is interesting. That wasn't the plan they discussed last night.

"I thought I was driving," Frank says.

"Well, I want to talk to you about that."

Frank raises his eyebrows. "I'm listening."

Ellis places his fist in front of his mouth and breathes heavily through his nose. Then he drops his hand to his lap and sighs. "I haven't been completely honest with you. But don't get mad. I just didn't know how to explain everything at once. It's a very complicated situation I'm in, Frank. It goes back many, many years."

Some alarm bells start going off, but he should hear the whole story first. "Okay. Just answer me two questions: What do you want me to do, and how much does it pay?"

"Five thousand dollars."

Frank nods his head and bites his lower lip. "Five grand? For what?"

"Putting a woman in the trunk of this car."

"Your stepmother?"

"Yes."

"I need the money up-front."

"I don't have it at the moment. But I will by tomorrow."

"When you get the key to the safe-deposit box?"

"Yes. I will get the key and I will get the money. That is a solemn vow."

Frank laughs uneasily, tracing his finger along the black cardboard of the door panel. "So you're kidnapping her."

"I'm dispensing justice."

"You're kidnapping her and stealing this key."

Ellis reaches into a pocket and pulls out a hundred dollar bill. He hands it to Frank. "That's a C-note. I won it at the track last night. I was coming over to tell you when I saw you get rousted by those cops.

I followed them, Frank, because I knew you were in trouble. Now I'm the one in trouble, and I need you to follow me. Take the money. I'll get the rest to you."

The bill feels crisp and cool in his hands.

"Are you in or not? That's the job. You grab her and put her in the trunk, and you stand to make five thousand dollars."

Frank lets out a deep, forlorn sigh. "Yeah, I guess I'm in."

The breakfast dishes sit on a silver tray by the front door, and the morning's *St. Petersburg Times* is strewn about the floor in front of the sofa. "Man Shot on Central Ave." is one of the headlines, along with "Midnight Joe Victorious" and "First Game of Season Today." Lauren and Irene Howard are hanging in limbo and are running out of ways to pass the time. Irene has read through as much of the paper as she can stand, including the sports section, which admittedly had an interesting article about Babe Ruth getting sued for seven thousand dollars. Apparently Mr. Ruth has gotten himself into hot water with loan sharks, a charge he denied, but since men are born liars, Irene doesn't believe his plea of innocence. As gripping as the story was, it has done little to stymie the main irritant grating Irene on this beautiful Sunday morning in March: boredom.

The sun is out in all its glory, the sky is a peaceful blue, with little cottony clouds here and there, the air is clean and fresh, and she is stuck in a hotel room until five o'clock this afternoon, when they will depart by train to New York. Irene agreed to leave, but under one condition: that she be allowed to go study in Europe, never again to return to Pearlman College.

"Mummy," she yawns, stretching her long arms, "let's do something today."

Lauren looks up from her book. "We are, dear. We're leaving."

"Not till five. We have all day to kill."

"Go downstairs and window-shop."

Irene bolts up from the sofa. "No! Come on. This is our last day in Florida and we haven't seen anything yet. We can go somewhere, can't we? I know you're worried about me and you're still sore, but we shouldn't just sit around being bored. Life is too short. Let's have some fun."

Lauren rests her book on her lap. "Where do you propose we go?"

Irene happily claps her hands. "I'm glad you asked that question. I was leafing through a guidebook, and I ran across something that caught my fancy."

"Dare I ask what?"

Irene goes and gets a small paperbound booklet called *Seeing St. Petersburg*, its cover featuring a washed-out engraving of a pelican perched on a pole. She flips through its dog-eared pages until she finds the one she wants. "Listen to this! 'The Alligator Farm. St. Petersburg Alligator Farm, owned and operated by A. H. Baker, is located at Big Bayou on Pinellas Drive.' "

"Irene, please."

"Wait! There are six hundred alligators, snakes, monkeys, birds, foxes, coons, insects—"

"Oh my heavens! It sounds dreadful, like my worst nightmare! Snakes, insects, alligators? Not in a million years."

"Mummy! You're such a stick in the mud! This is Florida. You do junk like this when you're a tourist."

Lauren looks severely at her daughter. "Decent people do not gawk at frightful creatures. Next you'll want me to take you to Coney Island."

Irene breaks into a gleeful grin. "That was so much fun! I went last summer with Frank. We ate cotton candy and rode on the Ferris wheel." She drops the guidebook and pitches forward dramatically, landing on chintz-patterned pillows. "It was so much fun being with him. I miss him so much."

"Oh now, let's not discomfit ourselves. Pick up that guidebook and see what else there is. Getting out for a few hours might do us some good before the train ride back home."

Irene complies with this request. Her enthusiasm dampened, she turns a few pages with little interest, but then stops at one that brings a nod of approval. "Here's one I was wondering about. 'Indian Mounds. See the world of Florida's first inhabitants. Tours daily from Soreno Hotel. Dr. Hubert Moore, noted anthropologist.' Well, how about that?"

"Indian mounds?"

"I took a class with a teacher at college who actually spent time out west with a tribe. I forget which one. But it was interesting."

"Fine. Let's take the tour, but only if it returns in time for us to make it to the train station."

"Okay. I'm game, too. Anything's better than sitting around here all day."

There's not much traffic on a Sunday morning, so Edmundson Avenue is clear all the way out to Catonsville. Adam Gould has agreed to meet with Szymanski because Adam Gould doesn't go to church on Sunday morning; he goes on Saturday night, being a Pentecostal something or other. Now what exactly Adam Gould knows about the possible whereabouts of Aubrey Marshall is anyone's guess. He's called the station repeatedly and claims to have important information. Now it's put up or shut up time.

Szymanski is feeling a bit cloudy this morning, having spent the night at Kresky's with the usual crowd, none of whom think Aubrey Marshall will ever be found. Too intelligent, too cunning, too cold-hearted. This is the story everyone was chewing on last night:

When little Aubrey was six, he burned down the family house on St. Paul, killing his mother (it was an accident). But apparently that disturbed the boy, as it would any kid. His father never forgave Aubrey, who was packed off to boarding school after boarding school, expelled from one and sent to another, while his older brother got to live at home and went to Gilman Prep. More fuel to the fire, and by the time Aubrey got into his teens, he was becoming a monster. He got charged with a couple of rapes, but the family paid plenty to hush everything up. When Aubrey turned eighteen, though, and caught an adult rap, the old man didn't lift a finger and Aubrey went to the pen. By then Mr. Marshall had married Freda Jenkins, who had worked in the house as a servant of some kind, and was thirty years younger than her new husband. This didn't sit well with Aubrey either, but what could he do, locked up in the pen? The year he got out, 1924, Mr. Marshall passed away suddenly, and in the will he made no provisions for Aubrey (the older brother got a million, Freda got the rest). So Aubrey Marshall plotted and waited, schemed and scoped, and then pounced when he had all his ducks in a row. He slipped into the house Marshall built after Aubrey burned the other one, crept up the carpeted stairs to the bedroom where Freda slept, put a knife to her throat, raped her, and then killed her. There were no servants at home (Monday was their day off) and no witnesses saw him enter or leave. They never found the murder weapon but they did find his blood type on the sheets of the bed. That was the only physical evidence linking him to the crime—his flight from Baltimore told the world he was guilty. He was last seen by his landlord on Monday morning; no one has seen him since.

Now Szymanski turns right onto Beaumont Street and drives past the large country estates of Baltimore's leading citizens, who liked to spend the summers out here. Most of the mansions are unoccupied, immense brick edifices that tell the true story of America: the few prosper at the expense of the many. Szymanski has the heart of a Socialist, the son of a Polish ironworker who admired Kropotkin and hated the excesses of capitalism. That's one reason why Joe Szymanski became a cop: so no fat cat would ever suck him dry, like they did the old man, who died at forty-nine with the body of a man twice that age. Bankers were the worst of all, and here he is, getting ready to pump one for information. And if Adam Gould shows even a scintilla of disrespect, Joe Szymanski will show him what he thinks of bankers who live in luxury on Beaumont Street.

Ah, calm down, he tells himself as he finds the address. Adam Gould lives in a spiffy colonial-style house, with an impeccably manicured lawn, two towering elm trees, an inviting front porch, and a brass knocker engraved with the word *Gould.* Szymanski is about to use it when the front door swings open. Greeting him is Adam Gould himself, fiftyish, bald, short, with a vigorous handshake and a grim smile.

"Thanks for finally coming," he says curtly.

"We've been pretty busy chasing down leads. I understand you might have some information related to the Marshall case."

"I do. I think Aubrey Marshall broke into my house and stole some checks from me. He might be trying to cash them."

"Why do you think it was him?"

Adam Gould rubs the back of his neck. "I don't know exactly. I certainly can't prove it, but the Marshalls own the place next door and I thought I saw him there the weekend before, you know, he killed Freda. We don't have much crime out this way, so when my house was robbed last Friday night, I became suspicious."

Szymanski takes out his notebook. There might be something to this after all. "Did he take anything else?"

"An old driver's license, and strangest of all, a letter of introduction I was writing for a business associate. Ellis Wax is his name."

Szymanski stops writing. "Ellis Wax?"

He is staring at the name he'd written down a couple days ago, after speaking with Mabel Wright about that tenant of hers who showed up saying he knew Monk Eastman. Claimed they'd been in the pen together, or some such. The only thing Szymanski found out was that there was an Ellis Wax living in Catonsville.

His mind starts racing. This can't be a coincidence. Didn't Aubrey Marshall serve time in the pen for rape? Maybe he's passing himself off in Florida as Ellis Wax. He could've met Monk inside, maybe even shared a cell with him. He looked up Mabel so he could get a roof over his head. This could be the break they've been needing.

"Can I use your phone?"

"Sure, detective. It's in the kitchen."

They're parked on Beach Drive, just in front of the Chess and Checkers Club, where a flock of stooped and weathered old men has gathered beneath a fabric canopy to stare at each other, smoke cigars, and curse in God knows what language. Some of those guys can barely move around, leaning on their canes for total support. One slip and they'd be flat on their faces. But that's true at any age.

"So how long are you planning to sit here?" asks Frank, not attempting to mask the irritation in his voice. "Because we've been rubbering that hotel over there for an hour, and she ain't come out of it yet. How do you know she's even in there?"

"She's staying there." Ellis Wax doesn't look over at Frank in the passenger seat. "I know that for a fact. She likes to spend money. She likes to pretend she's some highborn princess. There's no more pathetic sight in the world."

"I wish like hell she'd hurry up. I can't sit here all day looking at these big boats." That's the part driving Frank nuts, having to look at the watercraft anchored in a protected basin. Some are large yachts, clean and sleek, and on them a couple real dolls are lolling around, swinging their long legs off the gunnels and expecting the world to drop dead. The easy life, the life of idle pleasure. It's what every man dreams of.

"It'll all be over soon enough," Ellis quips. "It'll be the easiest money you ever made."

"There's no such thing as easy money. Every dollar is hard to come by."

"Unless you marry it, like this stupid cunt did."

There's a hard edge to his voice Frank's never noticed before. Ellis can't talk about his stepmother without getting all balled up. On the surface he's all smiles and pats on the back, but underneath it there's some real savage hatred. It's like his mind can only focus on one thing, how bad and evil and manipulating his stepmom is. He can't let it go.

"She'll get her due," he adds quietly. "Do you know she tried to fuck me?"

Frank doesn't know what to say. He's getting tired of the subject. "No, I didn't."

He watches a truck drive by, its payload filled with dirty-faced workers sternly regarding the world. Grime clings to their sweat-coated bodies. It's another truck in a procession of trucks on the way to the big hotel being built at Beach Drive and Fifth Avenue. Guys working on a Sunday. Doesn't seem right.

"She always wanted me to dance with her, since Father didn't dance. She would tell me I was light on my feet and graceful—things you don't tell a young boy, especially your stepson. But it's not like she could help it. She was a whore. She wasn't even pretty. I don't know what Father saw in her."

"Yeah, sounds pretty confusing."

People are starting to stream toward the ballpark a couple blocks south. The spring training game between the New York Yankees and the Boston Braves must be getting ready to start. He knows those were the teams because old men holding signs advertising the game have walked past, up and down Beach Drive.

"It's starting to fill up around here," Frank offers pointedly. *Just get out and walk away*, he tells himself. But he doesn't move; it's like he's been glued to the seat or something.

"It doesn't matter. You'll hustle her into the trunk and I'll drive off, right down First Avenue like I told you."

"But there's a thousand witnesses."

"Just grab her and throw her in the trunk, that's it."

"What if she doesn't get in? What if she starts screaming?"

"I guess you'll have to shut her up."

"How?"

"Put your hand over her big, fat mouth."

Now Frank looks over at the oval-faced little man whose nervous hands grip the steering wheel as if it is anchoring him to the seat, keeping him from flying off into outer space. He can't be serious. This must be the worst plan ever devised in the history of scams. None of it makes sense. Why don't they just go up to her room? Why can't they wait until tonight, when at least it'll be dark?

"Why don't you just pick another time and another place?" asks Frank, his words gathering momentum like stones rolling downhill. "This is all wrong."

"No, she'll come out eventually."

A silence falls between them. Frank can hear a voice: *Don't do anything stupid.* But he's done lots of stupid things, starting with grabbing Yoder and throwing him out of the car without his clothes. After he did that, he couldn't stick around town, so he went to Ginger. That created another disaster, her shooting Sal Chiesa and him shooting a cop. Even after all those blunders, if he'd just gotten money for that IOU, he'd be home free. But he missed his chance there. He had Babe Ruth in his sights down at the pier two days ago, and he balked. He waited for a better shot, but there wasn't one. That was it. He should've pounced. Now he's here, in this car next to a man who saved his life—but who appears to be a lunatic. Sure, Frank owes him, but this is just baloney.

He's got the C-note in his pocket. He doesn't have to stay. Ginger's alone back at that garage. That's not right, either. They need to get out of here.

"I think I'll go grab a paper," says Frank matter-of-factly. "I'm getting bored out of my mind."

"There she is!"

"Where?" Frank squints, trying to make out the target.

"That tall dame with black hair! That's her."

"In the blue dress?"

"Bingo. Just grab her and throw her in the trunk."

Frank opens his door and steps out. This is sick. This is the lowest you can go. This is the kind of thing only sick bastards do, pathetic people who got nothing else going for them. This is how failures get by in the world, grabbing women off the street. What's next? Children? Newborn babies? Frank's stomach twists in knots as he walks away from the car, intently studying the tall young girl in the blue dress. She's with a group of people walking out down the semicircular drive in front of the hotel. Something about her seems familiar, the way she walks and carries herself: with dignity, like she's got class but doesn't try to flaunt it. How the hell did somebody like that get mixed up with Ellis Wax? There must be a story there. Frank suddenly realizes who the tomato looks like: Irene Howard, his sweetheart from the Jersey shore. That could be her twin, as a matter of fact.

The group keeps walking toward him. The closer she gets, the more he thinks that it is actually Irene. But that's screwy. It can't be. Yet his eyes don't lie. It's *her*. No, he tells himself. His heart starts pounding like a jackhammer and his lungs burn with every breath he takes. What's he supposed to do now?

"Grab her," he hears Ellis say. Ellis has pulled the car around to the opposite side of Beach Drive, closer to the hotel.

"Forget it," Frank says, gravely shaking his head.

"What do you mean?" squeals Ellis.

"I ain't touching that dame."

"You must be off your nut! Come on, don't get yellow now!"

Frank reaches through the open window and grabs Ellis by the lapels of the white jacket he's wearing. In one motion he pulls Ellis's body nearly out of the car so that now the two men, like lovers at a petting party, are face-to-face. "I ain't scared of nothing, understand," Frank growls, eyes blazing with implacable fury. "You better shut that trap of yours before I shut it for you."

"Let go of me!"

Frank tosses Ellis into the steering wheel with such force that he yelps in pain. Clenching his teeth, eyes the size of saucers, Ellis snarls: "You'll pay for that, Hearn! Mark my words, you'll pay for that!"

"Do you think we'll see any savages?" asks a rotund woman in a floppy white hat festooned with peonies. She minces up next to the tour guide, Dr. Hubert Moore, a dour, deeply tanned man of forty with a bushy brown mustache and a missing left arm.

"Not around here, ma'am," he answers her politely. "Perhaps down in the Everglades you might encounter some Seminoles, but all the Indians native to Florida have long since perished."

The group has gathered around in the lobby and is preparing to depart in a jitney bus for a three-hour tour of various local Indian mounds, luncheon included. That means they'll be home by two o'clock, with plenty of time—too much time, in Irene's opinion—to pack up for their journey homeward. It's not something Irene is looking forward to, but she won't be in Greenwich long. As soon as she can, she's jumping on the S.S. *Berengaria* and heading for Europe.

"Are there any skeletons in these mounds?" the rotund woman continues.

"Human bones have been found within them, yes. But mostly they are middens, or in layman's terms, trash piles."

There is general grumbling with this explanation. Three hours looking at garbage? Dr. Moore anticipates this reaction. His voice assumes an air of authority. "Much can be learned from studying what a people discard. We can know how they hunted and fished, what they ate, what they used to cook with, how they carried water, and basically conducted society. We have gleaned a great deal from these middens, some of which rise to thirty feet in height. They are quite impressive, I assure you."

"I hope we don't see a skull," the rotund woman exclaims. Dr. Moore ignores this comment and leads the group from the lobby to the outside. A porter holds the door open for them, smiling pleasantly as the tour of well-fed white women troops past, arrayed in a dizzying collection of pastels. Some carry parasols and some have bonnets, tokens of their own girlhood in the previous century.

The jitney bus is parked at the end of the front driveway. The bright sun makes Irene squint. She holds up her hand to shade her eyes.

"He'd better have us back by two," Mummy grouses as they march along the sidewalk toward the bus. But Irene isn't paying attention, because up ahead she spots a very handsome man standing by a car. He's a tall, rugged specimen, with a strong jaw and a cleft chin, and could be a dead ringer for Frank Hearn. Of course, it's not, because Frank's in California, but the resemblance is striking. Irene keeps watching the man; he seems to be having an angry conversation with the driver of the car. In fact, the brute reaches in and grabs the driver by the lapels and tosses him into the steering wheel. Irene winces at the blow, and has yet another shock of recognition. The driver looks like Ellis Wax, with that beetle brow and rat's nose. She brings a hand up to her mouth. It can't be, can it? But what if it is? Irene feels the muscles in her face and neck grow taut, and then her legs start to move, just as the car also pulls away.

"Excuse me?" Irene calls out to the man she first saw. He's watching the car drive off with his back to her, so she doesn't get a clear look at his face until he turns around. She gasps when she sees him. "Frank? Is that you?"

"Irene?"

She doesn't know what to say or do. The stupidest thing leaps out of her mouth: "What are you doing here?"

"I could ask you the same thing."

"Murray Redd told me you were in California!"

Frank's eyes narrow quizzically. "Why would he say that?"

"Oh Frank, I thought I'd never see you again!" She throws herself into his waiting arms, and it feels like she's returning to the safest, snuggest place she's ever been in her life. She buries her face in his chest, pulling him close to her, closing her eyes, fighting back tears she doesn't want him to see. She takes a deep breath, even as he runs his hands along her back and through her hair. She's never wanted to kiss a man more, but there's not time for that. She looks up at him. He seems sad, burdened by something.

"Irene! What on earth are you doing?" It's Mummy, aghast at this display. She's got a stern expression on her face. Irene has created a spectacle in front of the entire group, who stand muttering in confusion as they observe the sequence of events.

"It's Frank! Frank, this is my mother." Irene still has her arm looped around his waist. But enough of the introductions. There's a more important question to be answered:

"Who was that man you were talking to?"

"Oh, him? Some klunker I never want to see again."

"Irene, they're waiting for us." Mummy's voice cracks with disbelief. She knows she's not in control anymore. Too much is happening too fast, and Irene holds her ground. She's not letting Frank get away this time.

"I'm not going anywhere."

"Let me tell the others. If you'll excuse me." Lauren turns and saunters off, doing her best to maintain that cool exterior.

"That wasn't a fellow named Ellis Wax, by chance?" Irene asks, blinking in the bright sun.

Frank frowns down at her. "You don't know that rube, do you?"

"I met him on the train coming down here."

"You should stay clear of him, Irene. He's a no-good bum." Irene lets go her embrace and steps away from him. Thoughts are racing through her head. She's got to find out more.

"Frank, this is important. Do you know where he lives?"

"Yeah, but—"

"Then I need you to take me there."

"But you don't understand."

"Sure, I do. He's a bad man. He might be a murderer. But I don't care."

"A murderer?"

"I think he killed someone, and I'm going to prove it."

Lauren returns and taps Irene on the shoulder. "I need to have a word with you, dear."

"Mother, I need to talk to Frank in private. Please let us have a moment alone."

Lauren's mouth drops open but she doesn't press her case. "It was a pleasure meeting you, Mr. Hearn. I'd ask you to join us for luncheon, but we're due to leave today."

"Mother, please. I need to speak with Frank—alone." She takes Frank by the arm and leads him away from the hotel.

"You shouldn't be mixed up in this, kid." Frank sounds sincere but she's not buying it.

"It's too late for that. Come on."

He doesn't budge. She puts her hands on her hips and shoots him a withering glare. Still he doesn't move.

"I'm sorry, Irene. There's no way I'm taking you anywhere near that fluter. I'll be damned if I'm going to let him hurt you."

"He won't. Come on, there's not a second to spare!"

Most men think they know what's best for women, whom they assume can't handle danger and will shrivel up under pressure. But Frank Hearn isn't like most men. He's taken Irene to plenty of places where men carried guns wedged in their belts. He never acted like she couldn't handle herself, he never promised to protect her. So why is he starting now? Can't he tell how important this is to her? Still he won't move. He seems agonized, unsure of himself, even a little frightened. These are all sides of him she's never seen before. He usually exuded total confidence. Now she's the one who has to assure him.

"Nothing will happen to me, Frank. You'll be there."

"That won't matter if he's got a gun. I won't let him hurt you, I swear to God I won't."

Irene smiles at the warm sound of genuine tenderness in his voice. It's hard to get mad at somebody for caring about you. "I just want to get the address and call the police. That's it. He doesn't have to know we're even there."

"The address? It's on Third Avenue South."

"Third and what?"

"I don't know. Tenth? Ninth?"

"Come on. Show me where it is and then I'll call the cops and they can take over from there if they want to."

"What about your mother?"

"We won't be gone long. I'll hash it out with her later."

———

When **Vecchio** gets back with the new rental car, he walks into the hotel room just as Musetta is hanging up the phone. "You talking to the boss?" he asks, dropping a folded-up newspaper on the twin bed closest to the door. They checked into the same fleabag motel in Tampa where they spent their first night in town, before they got the order to head over to St. Pete. The drapes smell like wet cigars, the wallpaper is buckling, and God knows how many hookers have ridden these beds.

"No. I called a couple rental car places."

"You checking up on me?"

"You been gone all morning."

"There wasn't a car to be had in this town. Had to wait two hours before I could find a place."

"Is that what took so long?"

"Yeah, but it's taken care of."

They ditched the other rental car after they made it across the bridge. They couldn't afford to keep driving it in case a witness made their plate number.

Musetta belches out a laugh, and then unfolds himself from the chair he's been slumped in. He picks up the violin case and begins to assemble the Tommy gun.

"I know what you're thinking," says Vecchio carefully. "I want this over as bad as you do. But we can't be stupid."

"You don't know what I'm thinking, Vecchio." Musetta walks over to the closet and takes out his coat, his back to Vecchio, who keeps pleading his case.

"Okay, kid. I know you're steamed. But we shouldn't panic. That's the worst thing."

"Panic? We don't know where she is. The cops probably got her. She could be on a train back to Chicago, for all we know." Musetta has his coat on, with the Tommy gun in one hand, and he walks back toward the center of the room.

Vecchio holds up his hands like he's trying to ward off a flurry of blows. "That's what I'm talking about, kid. You can't think with a cloudy head."

Musetta sucks on his cheeks, nodding his head slowly. He's standing about two feet away. "Let's go," he says.

The small bag is packed. There's not much in it, a few belongings, some toiletries. It's just like that morning when she left her husband: it felt like she was standing on the edge of a cliff, ready to jump off. But Ginger had been planning that move for months. This is different. She doesn't want to leave Frank. But she can't get him killed, too. Enough is enough. It's time to do what she should have done a long time ago.

Those hoodlums in Chicago never understood. They went to a lot of trouble over nothing. She had no intention of testifying against Al Capone, none whatsoever. Not if it was going to cost her. Fingers told her you've got to be selfish if you want to see your name in lights. He told her she should go back and lie to the cops like he did. He saw Capone clear as day but he'd denied it.

She couldn't do that. She ran instead. If only she hadn't—one lie, on top of all the other lies she's ever told. Why didn't she just lie? She wouldn't have gotten those men shot last night. She wouldn't have shot Sal Chiesa. She thinks about how he just showed up at her door like some monster from the deep. She opened the door because she thought it was Frank. But she had the gun in her hand, just like Fingers told her.

We need to talk.

About what?

Joe Horn.

He tried to grab her, but she shot him in the heart instead. And it was terrible, the worst day of her life. Last night is a close second. Too much blood. Watching the blood and the life drain out of another human being. The way the eyes grow vacant and the arms twitch. She didn't stick around to talk to the cops last night, because she doesn't know who's in on it. There're only two people she trusts: Frank, and the prosecutor back in Chicago. McSwiggin. He seemed nice but he couldn't keep her alive. But she can't keep running forever. She's got to face up to these heartless thugs before somebody else dies. She's got to go back to Chicago.

She should leave Frank a note. It would be a thoughtful gesture. He'll worry when he comes back and finds her gone. She goes outside and borrows a pencil and a scoring sheet from the card players, and the old gents very solicitously offer her whatever she might want. She thanks them and then returns to the little wobbly table she tried to cheer up with some cut sunflowers. She tries to think of what she could say to him, and she can't put into words what she feels. She starts:

Dear Frank,

   I'm leaving. Thanks for everything. You saved my life and now it's time for me to save yours. I'm going to do what I should've done from the start.

   I love you.

She frowns at the hurried scrawl of the last sentence. Does she really love him? Or is she just feeling guilty about all she's done? Writing the word *love* won't excuse anything. In fact, it looks rather stupid. So she scratches out that line. But what fool couldn't see what she's written beneath the black lines? Now she's botched the whole note, just like she's botched everything else, and in the same way: too much emotion, not enough self-control. She married Lemuel Hoagland to get out of her father's house. She ran away from Lemuel Hoagland to get away from the pig farm. She ran to Asbury Park because she was afraid of dying. But there's something worse than dying: getting someone else killed.

And then she hears the door in the hallway open—is that Frank? She jumps up, startled and anxious. The door slams closed, followed by the sound of footsteps in the narrow corridor. A lump the size of a tomato forms in her throat. What is she supposed to do now? If she sees him, she might change her mind. She might not be strong enough to leave—and leaving is what she should do, she must do.

Someone knocks. Ginger freezes. "Anybody home?" a voice calls out. It's Ellis Wax, the neighbor.

"Coming," Ginger answers. She opens the door and is greeted by a short man whose face is pale, eyes bulging out, a thin sheet of sweat slimed across that protruding forehead. Ellis Wax looks truly disturbed and menacing, although he's smiling, hat in hands, like everything is fine. Ginger doesn't know what to think, although she grows suspicious that all is not well.

"Sorry to bother you," Ellis says meekly, shifting his weight nervously from one foot to the other, like he needs to use the bathroom.

"No bother. What can I help you with?"

"I have some news for you."

"Oh?"

"It's about Frank. Can I come in?"

She steps back and lets him in. "What happened? Is Frank okay?"

"Going somewhere?" He motions to her bag, prominently standing in plain view.

Ginger coughs and clears her throat in lieu of answering.

"Me, going? No, afraid not." Ginger suddenly doesn't think it wise to share any information with Ellis Wax, considering his state of mind and his forward manner—and his refusal to say where Frank is, which only makes her even more cautious and afraid of him. They were supposed to be doing some job together. Something bad has happened. She can feel it in her bones.

"It looks like you're all packed up."

"Just cleaning up. So what's your news about Frank?"

"I hate to be the one who tells you this, but there're things about Frank you might not know."

This is not the answer she was expecting. It just breeds more questions. She doesn't even know where to begin, so confounding is the scene she's encountered. Ellis Wax is acting like a bratty little boy who knows a secret but won't reveal it. Why is he playing this stupid game with her?

"What on earth is going on, Mr. Wax?"

"I know I shouldn't stick my nose in other people's business. But he told me to come back to tell you, so I'm the messenger. Like Western Union."

"What's the message?"

"Well, it's like this. Frank ran off with another woman."

"A woman? What woman?"

"Her name's Irene. That's all he told me. He saw her today down at the pier."

Ginger shakes her head like she's warding off a buzzing fly. "I can't believe that."

"Are you calling me a liar?" The solicitous tone is gone, replaced by a seething hostility that seems to have burst forth from deep within his heart. Frightened, she takes a step back away from him.

"No, of course not."

"It sounds like you did."

"No, I just can't believe Frank would do that." Ginger keeps backing away. Ellis Wax stands there with a malevolent smile. He's really enjoying himself.

"You are stupid, aren't you? You called me a liar and I'm telling you the truth. Just like a woman."

"Come one step closer and I'll scream!"

She sees the gun now as he pulls it from a coat pocket and points it at her. She feels every muscle in her body tense up at once.

"You open your mouth again and I'll blow your brains out. Do you think I'm lying now? Huh?"

"What's happened to Frank? Where is he?"

The tears feel hot against her cheeks. She's backed all the way against the wall, beneath the sole window located at eye level and the width of a Crossley radio. It's too high up and too narrow to fit through. So she's trapped. And she's having trouble breathing. She might pass out, and fall face first right on the floor.

"I liked you the first time I saw you. You're pretty, for a whore. I'm glad you're all packed up." He kicks the bag. "Because we have someplace special to go."

"No, please. Don't hurt me, Mr. Wax."

"I won't. I'm not that kind of man." He waves the gun at her, eyes blazing with such hateful fury that Ginger knows he'll kill her, no matter what she does. Her purse is on the table, next to the flower vase. She put the gun in there while she was packing. He notices her looking over at the table. He grabs the vase, assuming Ginger has designs to use it.

"Shut your mouth and do what I say, or I'll break this bottle across your face. You won't be so pretty then."

"What do you want with me?"

"We're going to get in my car and go for a drive."

"Where to?"

"A special place. Come on."

She just needs to reach into that purse. It worked once before, maybe it can again. "Let me grab my purse."

"Your purse? You won't need that."

"But if I leave my purse and my bag behind, Frank'll know something is wrong."

He considers her request. "You're a clever little cunt. Grab your purse and your bag. That's a good idea, now that you mention it."

She tries to evince no hint of emotion as she walks over to retrieve her purse. But he's standing right next to the table, and to her horror he puts the vase down and picks up her purse. A look of suspicion appears on his oval face, his eyes darkening like storm clouds and his mouth twisting in confusion.

"This is heavy for a handbag."

"If you don't mind."

She tries to swipe it from him, but he levels his gun at her. "What's in here?"

"None of your business."

She tries grabbing the purse from him, but she loses her balance and knocks into the table. The empty vase crashes against the concrete floor and shatters.

"What was that?"

Irene looks up from the Model T she's been briefly inspecting. It's parked in an alley behind the garage where Frank said Ellis Wax lives. They had just arrived by taxi and were starting to take down information about the car when Irene heard the noise, the crashing sound, coming from inside the garage. Frank must've heard the same thing, too, because his eyes have become two slits of concentration as he stares back over his shoulder.

"I don't know," says Frank guardedly. "You better get out of here. Let's call the cops."

Irene is about to agree when she hears a more sinister sound coming from the garage—like a woman yelling.

"And what was that?"

"Stay here!" Frank implores before running back around to the front of the garage. Irene follows right behind him, because she's not afraid of Ellis Wax, and she wants that little pervert to know she's not afraid. Plus, Frank might need her. It's like when you're sailing and you hit a squall line. The boat starts to keel, and the cry goes up: *All hands on deck!* That's what it feels like now.

They go running inside the garage, down a narrow hallway. Frank stops at a door and tries to open it, but it's locked. They can hear a fight going on inside the room, muted sounds of a fearsome struggle.

"I told you to stay back!" he cries, not angrily, but sorrowfully. Like he's blaming himself for putting her in this position. Then he stands back and rams a shoulder into the door. The hinges come splintering from the wood and the door itself splits in half. He rushes in, and Irene follows a step behind. But then Frank stops, and Irene runs into him. She can't see around his broad back.

"Leave her alone!" she hears Frank bellow.

"Go to hell, you coward!"

Irene leans around Frank enough to see the most frightening scene she's ever laid eyes on: Ellis Wax has a gun pointed at some poor woman's head. But then the little pervert lifts the gun and points it at them, the woman still prostrate at his feet, with broken glass everywhere. Irene feels like screaming but nothing escapes her lips. Because it doesn't seem real. Ellis Wax looks like a child outfitted for Halloween. The gun resembles a toy, it's so small in his hands. But his eyes are filled with animal rage. He's looking right at Irene now.

"I don't care about your whore Ginger here," he snarls. "Give me the girl."

Frank tries to push her away. "Run, Irene. Go!"

"If she moves, this one dies." Meaning the other woman, Ginger, the one on the floor. Irene covers her mouth with her hand; she will not run from this man, gun or no gun. It's three against one.

"You'll never get away with it," says Frank, like he's giving a neighbor advice on how to fix a leaky sink.

"Don't be stupid, Hearn. She's not worth dying for." Ellis Wax is still looking right at Irene. She clenches her fists, ready to strike out if she gets the chance.

"Put the gun down before the cops get here." Frank sounds calm and relaxed, like his old self.

Ellis Wax curls his nose in disgust. "I don't have time for you anymore, Hearn."

Then there's a gunshot, with a report that pierces Irene's eardrums. Frank surges forward toward Ellis Wax but staggers and eventually falls from the second shot that hits him in the face. Irene screams just as the woman beneath the table springs up and jumps on Ellis Wax's back, grabbing him around the neck, gouging at his eyes with her long fingernails. This sudden attack also stirs Irene from her state of shock. Enraged and emboldened, she jumps over Frank's fallen body and picks up a jagged piece of glass off the floor, the long neck of a broken flower vase, its sharp edges now a deadly weapon.

"I'll kill you, you stupid bitch!" screams Ellis Wax, firing a shot that hits the ceiling. Ellis Wax keeps trying to throw the woman off, but she's strong and has a good grip on his face, her fingernails digging into his skin. Then Irene, unthinkingly and fueled by pure adrenaline, plunges the piece of broken vase deep into Ellis Wax's groin. He emits a blood-chilling groan of exquisite pain, dropping the gun as he crumples to the ground, both hands covering his injury.

"Get the gun!" the other woman shouts. But Irene is frozen: never has she intentionally hurt someone before. She stands immobile, the bloody piece of glass still in her hand. The other woman scrambles over and picks up the gun, pointing it at Ellis as he writhes whimpering at Irene's feet.

"Check on Frank!"

"Frank! Oh my God!" Irene tosses aside the piece of glass and goes to him. His still, supine body lies atop a pool of gathering blood. "Somebody call a doctor!" she cries, her composure regained. A group of old men has gathered in the doorway.

"We already did," someone says. "And the police."

"Is he dead?" the woman asks, still aiming the gun at Ellis Wax. Irene feels for a pulse, on one wrist and then the other.

"I don't know."

"Do you feel a pulse?"

"I'm not sure. There's so much blood—I've got to stop the bleeding. Give me a shirt!"

The old men quickly remove theirs and stand with bird chests heaving as Irene presses their starched garments against the wounds in Frank's stomach and face. A medic from the Civil War kneels down to help her, although he's eighty-five and terribly arthritic, barely able to apply much pressure. But his voice is reassuring and he tells Irene she's doing a wonderful job. Inwardly, though, he thinks about the terrible day at Antietam Creek, with the bodies piled up and the men groaning like the fellow Wax over there who's holding his privates. No one's helping him much. But since Miss Ginger is aiming that pistol at him, he mustn't deserve much help. Wax didn't seem like a nice man. He told everybody he cheated at cards and made a fortune doing it. What kind of man cheats at cards and brags about it? A fool, assuredly. A damn fool.

"I'll drive," barks Musetta, like somehow he's got to prove he's in charge now on account of what happened last night. Like somehow Vecchio's lost his stripes because he shot the wrong guy, while this kid thinks nothing of spraying a restaurant with that Tommy gun, killing five to get one. He wants to be in charge, fine. Be in charge. Come up with a plan.

After they pay the toll for the bridge, Vecchio asks the obvious question: "Where are we going?"

Musetta shrugs. "Got to find her."

"How? Where? The train station? The police station? We're spinning our tires here, kid. We can't get in a lather."

"We'll go to the garage."

"Where Hearn is staying? Sure, let's go there. That's not a bad idea."

Musetta grunts. It's like he's forgotten how to talk all of a sudden. One thing is sure: he's telling Torrio when they get back to Chicago that he won't work with this goof again.

They pass by the dog track they were at last night. Looks like they're running a Sunday matinee, cars are starting to fill up in the parking lot. That's a tricky move: going from church to the track. Might feel luckier that way. But luck's got nothing to do with it. Those rubes think they can beat the system but Vecchio knows the fix is on; how else could Torrio afford a house in Italy?

About fifteen minutes and five words later, they're back in downtown St. Pete, and back in the traffic that never seems to end. They park out on Ninth Avenue, across the street from the alley where Hearn is staying. Vecchio picks up a pair of binoculars to get the lay of the land. He's not expecting to see much, but that's not the case. Almost immediately sirens start to wail in the distance, growing more strident as the cops and the ambulance get closer. The two men look at each other.

"What should we do?" Musetta asks.

"We ain't breaking no laws sitting here."

Then all the flatties start arriving in black-and-whites, a whole squadron of them descending on that garage apartment. Through the binoculars Vecchio sees a couple of bodies being brought out on gurneys, both of them covered with blood. Then he sees Sally Serenade and some other nice-looking dame being led away. And none of it makes any sense at all.

"What in deuce is going on over there?" Musetta sighs.

"I wish I knew, kid. I wish I knew."

"What are we gonna do now?"

"Shoot her. She's right there. You can get a clean shot through the police car."

The kid actually starts to lift the gun, but Vecchio grabs his arm. "I didn't mean it! You got an itchy trigger finger, kid. It'll get you in trouble one day."

"You think this is funny, huh?" Musetta asks, voice squeaking like a rusty hinge. "I called Jake Guzik this morning. He don't think it's too funny. They want that dame dead."

"Nobody said it's funny."

"You know what he told me to do?" The kid is sneering, biting his lower lip and squinting in the bright sun.

"What's that?"

"This."

The kid lifts the gun up to the older man's face and fires a shot between his eyes.

"**I** better get that," Mabel Wright tells the officers who've crowded her lovely backyard, which has become a shooting gallery. She skips away to answer the phone, not because she's expecting anyone to call, but because she could use a little break from the horrors that have taken place on what should've been a quiet Sunday. Frank Hearn shot in the face; maybe he'll live, maybe he won't. The other one, Ellis Wax, he'll live but he won't be having children. Her garage is full of blood.

The boarders seem agitated; a couple from Canada has already packed their bags. Others might follow.

She'll answer the phone and maybe linger awhile in the kitchen, fix something to drink, settle her nerves.

"Mabel?"

She can tell from the thick Baltimore accent that it's Szymanski. She smiles and shakes her head; he didn't forget about her after all. But it's a little late now.

"Is that you, detective?"

"Mabel, listen. You should be expecting some St. Pete cops soon. I don't want you to worry, though. But that Ellis Wax you called me about, we think he might be armed and dangerous. Just get your tenants to stay inside. You, too. I'm sorry I didn't call you back sooner but I'll explain after we catch this bum."

She cackles, despite her frayed nerves. "They got him already!"

"They did? We just called down there!"

"You always were a little slow, Szymanski. No wonder it took you so long to bag me and Monk."

PUBLIC
RELATIONS

I t's such a beautiful day, too. There's just enough crispness in the air to make each breath invigorating, but the sun is warm in the cloudless sky. It would be a perfect afternoon for a picnic, beneath the shade of an oak tree, a blanket spread out over a swath of freshly mowed grass. The kind of day you could lie back and watch your small children play and frolic in the happy fields of childhood.

Instead, Helen Ruth has packed most of her belongings into the cherrywood trunk George got for her in Chicago years ago. She brought clothes enough to Florida to last a month; that's how long she was planning on being gone. But plans change.

For some reason she thinks about the day he told her he was sold to the Yankees. She cried, because she didn't want to leave home, their comfortable little home in Boston they'd made together. It wasn't a big place, and it wasn't fancy, either. It was a little flat off Newton Street, and the kitchen didn't even have a refrigerator. She had to go shopping every day to buy his favorite food. She didn't mind. He seemed to appreciate it.

But then in New York he stopped loving her.

Her train departs at five, and she'd like to tell him in person that she isn't staying. Leaving him a note is too impersonal, but she's ready to do it. God knows where he is. God only knew where he was last night. He went back out after they returned from dinner. Said he was going to a boxing match with Witt and Pipp. Pointedly, he didn't invite her. He just went. He came crashing back hours later, staggering around, knocking over lamps, before he passed out in his clothes on the sofa. He woke up this morning complaining again of a sick stomach. It's been bothering him for months but he won't do a thing about it.

She would've told him then, before he left for today's exhibition game, except he was rushing around, moaning about being hungover, about his stomach, and he wasn't paying her much attention. Nothing new, that. But she'd already made up her mind the night before, sitting alone in the darkened room, that she couldn't save this marriage. He hadn't touched her since her arrival. He treated her like she was one of those matrons at his reform school who watched and criticized his every move. He certainly didn't act like she was his wife. He was miserable, she was miserable, so why prolong the agony? Why spend your life cooped up in sunless caves waiting for a love to bloom that has long since withered on the vine? Pulling the weeds, watering, pruning, nothing will save the flower of this marriage.

How could she possibly tell her mother? The news will probably kill her. She hasn't been well, and the only thing that sustains her, it seems, is going to Mass. Her mother's belief in the church is like a flame burning in the furnace of her heart, and should it ever go out, she'll quickly grow cold and die. Divorce is for whores, so whores can please themselves by spurning God. That was her attitude. Helen tried to tell her that the marriage was in trouble, that he was being unfaithful. "God never meant for marriage to be easy," was her response.

Behind her she hears a door open and then slam closed.

"Helen?"

He's come home at last. And not a moment to spare. "I'm out here."

She hears him lumbering across the floor. The entire building seems to shake when he walks. He joins her on the balcony. His face is red and his suit is rumpled and stained with ashes. A lock of hair falls across his forehead, hanging there boyishly. His breath reeks of bourbon whiskey and stale cigar smoke, but he doesn't try to kiss her.

"Sorry I'm late. A few of the boys were having a card game," he says excitedly. "I had to let them have a chance at winning their money back."

"Aren't you the lucky one," she says quietly.

"You know what they say—lucky in cards, and—" He doesn't complete the aphorism. So she does it for him.

"Unlucky in love?"

"Well, I guess it ain't true in my case. I'm lucky in both!"

"I suppose you are." She fights back the tears she feels growing hot behind her eyes. She will not cry. She's cried enough. Last night for hours. The time for tears has come and gone. Still, he's not making this any easier, acting like the uncorrupted man-child brimming with that innocent joy at life's pleasures. That used to be his sole personality, and the one she loved. But there've been additions to this humble cottage of a man, towering garrets she's never been allowed in, and secret, dark, windowless rooms of his soul.

"Did you come to the ballpark? I didn't see you there."

"No."

"You didn't come to the game? Why not?" He sounds hurt. "I left four tickets for you at will-call. And I clouted a homer. They booed me when I didn't play yesterday against the Braves. Not bad, huh?"

"You're quite a player."

"So why didn't you come? You always come."

"I just needed to think—I needed to think, George."

"About what?" He sounds very suspicious of her, like she's one of those incessant real estate pitchmen on Central Avenue trying to sell him a parcel of swampland. But she looks him right in the eyes.

"About what I want to do."

"I don't get it."

She sighs. "I'm going back to New York."

He seems genuinely surprised by these words, as if he couldn't imagine the reasons why she might feel this way. He shakes his head in disbelief. Then he smiles, but it's not mirthful, but angry.

"That's super, Helen. That's just super. Why'd you come down here then if you're not interested in giving it another try?"

"I tried, George."

"Ah, come on! You tried nothing. I know about the P.I. you got tailing me. And you know something? I don't give a damn. Hire ten dicks if you want."

She could mention the seven thousand dollars he's getting sued for. She could mention the paternity suit last December. She could bring up Claire, she could throw it in his face. But she doesn't get angry. No, sadness sweeps over, calm sadness like the sea after a violent storm. "You've become a mean person, George."

"Yeah? If I'm so mean, why am I going to the hospital to visit that guy who got shot saving that flapper's life?" He's referring to the brave Frank Hearn, whose courageous story was splashed on the front page of the local paper this morning. He was shot saving a woman's life.

"That's awfully sweet of you." And it was. He'd help anyone in pain, except her.

"I don't have to go see him. I'm doing it because I want to."

"I'm sure he'll be glad to see you."

"Well, maybe. But he's in a coma, so I doubt it."

"It's the thought that counts."

"You don't give me any credit."

Helen is about to reply when suddenly his face turns ash-white and contorts in obvious and acute pain. He staggers over to the sofa, doubling over and grabbing his stomach. He groans like a bear that's just been shot by a rifle. Sweat is streaming down his cheeks, and his eyes are clenched like two angry fists.

"Let me get you some water," she says calmly, worried that this time he's pushed himself too far. She runs into the bathroom and fills a crystal glass out of the tap. By the time she gets back he's sitting up, holding his head between his hands. "Here, drink this."

He gulps the water down.

"Slowly!"

He drains the glass dry, and wipes his mouth with the back of his hand. She helps him remove his jacket and presses her hand against his forehead. He doesn't feel feverish; if anything, he's a little clammy.

"You can't leave me, Helen," he says, taking her hand and kissing it. "I need you. Who else can take care of me like you do?"

"You need to see a doctor about that stomach of yours."

"I will. I promise I will."

"You need to rest."

"Don't leave me, Helen. Please don't leave."

She pushes him back onto the sofa so that he can lie down. He's still gripping her hand when he closes his eyes. She sits next to him, rubbing his temple and cooing. She even starts to sing a lullaby. It's just like getting an infant down for a nap.

William **Boyd,** of the *New York Evening World*, reaches into his jacket and fishes out a pack of cigarettes. He's standing in front of a tall hill of bones and shells, made by some Indians a long time ago. It's located not twenty yards from the hospital where Babe Ruth is supposed to show up and visit a fellow who's in a coma. Ruth goes to hospitals all the time, usually without any reporters tagging along, but this time, Barrow, the Yankees' business manager, made sure all the scribes got wind of the visit. It's not hard to see why: the Babe could use a dose of good publicity right about now, considering the stink of that gambling-debt lawsuit still hangs in the air. A drop-in to sit beside the Hero Who Saved the Flapper will generate the kind of photographs Barrow wants. Ruth at his most caring. The thing is, the big lug does care, especially about kids.

As usual Ruth is running late, and so the newshounds have convened around the big shell mound to smoke and gossip and wait. The freelance photographers are huddled together, exchanging tidbits on whimsical editors and prices on Kodak film. The reporters talk mostly about the comely nurses staffing the hospital. Something about a woman in white that gets the blood boiling. But William Boyd doesn't join in. Instead, he wanders off alone, gawking at the mound of bones. There's nothing like this in New York, where the old is discarded in favor of the new. New buildings going up, old ones coming down. New reporters taking the place of the ones who lose a step. It's hard to get your bearings in the city. But this mound, it's ancient, a thousand years old. Sure, it's the work of the red man, but still—it makes you think. What's so important about following an overpaid extrovert ballplayer around? What difference does it really make in the world? Would anyone in a thousand years remember Babe Ruth?

Probably. But would anyone remember William Boyd? He inhales deeply and blows a smoke ring, pensively regarding the pile of sun-washed whiteness.

"There he is!"

"About time!"

William Boyd turns around. A limousine has arrived, and out of it emerges the familiar sight of the most famous person who's ever lived. The Babe smiles and waves dutifully, wearing a navy blue, pinstriped suit with a garish yellow tie and black-and-white patent leather shoes. God, the sap looks awful, worse than when he left for Hot Springs. He's smiling, sure, but his eyes look like they belong on a dead fish. He's pale to boot, his skin a sickly sallow color. If you were from Mars, you'd think that fellow was checking into the hospital, not visiting a patient in one.

William Boyd tosses his cigarette to the ground and stomps it into the sandy soil. He hurries over to join the others who've already formed a circle around the Babe, like he's a king or something. Which is what he is, in a way. The closest thing in America you'll ever see. The Babe could declare war on Germany tomorrow and by the end of the week, the ranks would be swelled. Poor Woodrow Wilson, he had to draft men to fight his war.

A gaggle of doctors and nurses greets the movable feast as the entourage enters the lobby. There are smiles aplenty, and Ruth is polite and cordial and makes everyone feel warm beneath the glorious sun of his fame. Barrow, at the Babe's side, is all business. No surprise there. The team's business manager is singularly mirthless.

"We really appreciate you stopping by today, slugger," says a doctor, a man of fifty who suddenly is acting like a boy of ten.

"It's the least I could do for the poor guy. Is he any better?"

"I'm afraid not."

"Let me go see if I can wake him up!"

And just like that, laughter resounds down the halls where death begets mourning, where people wonder how they will ever get along again. But Babe Ruth mocks death. He is indestructible (so they think). His gargantuan self seems to give life. Why couldn't he bring the guy out of the coma? With him, anything is possible.

So they ascend a flight of stairs, the retinue having grown even larger, doctors, orderlies, nurses, even other patients garbed in gowns that barely conceal their sickly bodies, drawn to the great force of life bursting and abundant, even as William Boyd notices how stiff the Babe is moving, like an old man. The pain is obvious in each step. The reporters know he's been ill, and it will only be a matter of time before something goes terribly awry.

Barrow tells the photographers to scurry ahead, and the flash-bulbs start popping as the Babe approaches the room. The doctors and nurses step aside so the members of the press can get a front-row seat, crowded together in the private room where a man lies in a bed, his face heavily bandaged, his body motionless, oblivious to the commotion all around. Standing by the bed, one on either side, are two dames, pretty in different ways. One is tall with bobbed ink-black hair, the other is shorter, more shapely, with blonde hair. Both are real lookers. One must be the flapper the guy in the coma took a bullet for. The tall one with the bobbed hair is the most likely candidate.

The Babe sits down in a chair by the bed.

"So this is the fella who saved a woman's life, huh?" the Babe asks. "That's what I call hitting a home run."

"Shake his hand, Babe!" a photographer calls.

Babe Ruth reaches down and grips a limp left hand. Bulbs pop brightly and loudly. Barrow beams proudly, arms folded across his barrel chest. There are more likable men in the world than this prevaricating fool who didn't have the good sense to let Babe Ruth play every day when he managed the Red Sox. But he landed on his feet, the lucky bastard, getting hired to run the best team in baseball after Boston canned him.

"Make sure you get that, boys," Barrow chirps as the Babe grins away. It's a scene William Boyd has witnessed and written about countless times, just the kind of sidebar piece editors love because it makes the reader feel good.

"What's his name again?" the Babe asks.

"Frank Hearn," comes the answer.

"You get well, Frank. We're all pulling for ya."

It's a heartwarming performance, but then something out of the ordinary happens. The shapely one steps forward, and with hands on her hips says matter-of-factly: "Do you remember me?"

The Babe looks up at her helplessly, then over to Barrow.

"Should I?"

"I introduced you to Frank at the dog track. He wanted to talk to you about an IOU."

Barrow swoops in and grabs the Babe by the arm. "Okay, let's visit the children's ward," the business manager intones.

"Not so fast," the skirt says. "I want to talk to the slugger."

"I never seen this man before in my life," he says without much conviction.

"Let's go," barks Barrow, pulling on his charge with greater force.

Those assembled begin buzzing about the sudden challenge that has waylaid the carefully scripted benevolence. The Babe mutters in bewilderment as Barrow hustles him out the door, through the crowd in the hallway, which parts to let the addled slugger pass. The photographers and the reporters, amused but ever dutiful, follow at heel.

"He was trying to help you out!" the skirt yells at the departing press conference.

Some grim-visaged orderlies tell her to pipe down or else face a bum's rush to the sidewalk.

"Leave her alone," the Flapper commands. "I'm paying for this room and I decide who's allowed in here."

A doctor comes over and shoos the orderlies away. William Boyd watches this as he backpedals away. There's got to be a story in all that, he decides. The Babe gets sued for seven thousand bucks last week, and now that woman is saying the fella in the coma had an IOU from the Babe. Coincidence? Doesn't matter. Grayson won't run anything like that. So William Boyd trundles along toward the children's ward, where Babe Ruth will bring smiles of joy to some sick kids. It's what the big slugger does best of all.

"I tried," **says** Ginger once everyone leaves. "You can't say I didn't try."

Irene nods her head. Ginger is a fighter, there's no doubt about that. She's one of those determined, hell-bent women who grab life by the horns and won't let go. It's not hard to see why Frank was smitten. She's tough, beautiful, sultry, and confident. She's had to be, to endure all she's been through. They stayed up last night talking, sleeping on cots next to each other, hoping and praying that Frank would wake up. A bullet passed through his left eye and is lodged in his brain. The doctors don't know how severe the damage will be. He might not live; if he lives, he might never recover his faculties; and there's a chance, no one knows how slim, that he'll pull through this with minimal problems, save the missing eye.

"Ah, Frank," Ginger coos to the motionless patient, "we finally got him right where we wanted him. You slept right through it."

Irene allows a faint smile. There hasn't been much to be cheerful about lately. "You two embarked on quite an adventure."

"We did, didn't we? It's over now. Time for me to go face the music." Ginger shakes her head. "I'm sorry, Frank." She reaches down and squeezes a limp hand.

"It wasn't you," Irene quickly corrects her. "It was Ellis Wax."

Ginger brushes away a tear. "It was me. I got those people shot, and now this. All because I was a coward."

"No! They were going to kill you!"

"You're a sweet kid." She brushes Frank's face, at least the cheek not bandaged. "You picked a good one here, Frank. You should keep her."

"Me? He's in love with you."

Ginger turns and glances at the door. "Where is that detective anyway? I thought he was eager to haul me down to the train station."

The St. Pete cops have arranged for Ginger to return to Chicago so she can testify against the gangsters who wanted her dead. Ginger's life is glamorous, complete with exotic tales of show business, smoky saloons, corrupt cops, and handsome bootleggers. She left her husband and ran off alone to Chicago, and then got tangled up in a big mess. She's had one adventure after another, stared death down, and now will testify against a Chicago gangster. Irene can't help but feel awed.

"Listen, tell Ducky I said good-bye," winks Ginger.

The two women start giggling like grade-schoolers. Last night they gave the doctors nicknames, and one was Ducky because of his waddling gait. Ginger noticed how often Ducky and Valentino, he of the oily black hair, kept "checking on the patient," when their real interest seemed to lie in her and Irene. Ginger has that ability to laugh at life's absurdities. Irene will miss her company.

"Ginger, I want to ask you something. I know you're leaving for Chicago, but what should I tell Frank if he asks for you?"

Ginger smirks. "Honey, if he says anything, we should jump for joy."

"I know, but we haven't talked about—everything."

"Irene, listen up. Frank and I, we had a few yuks, but mostly we just had desperation. He needed me, I needed him, so we fell in together. It wasn't what you two had, real love."

"You think?"

"I know. You two are meant to be together. Fate brought you here. Don't mess with fate. Don't end up like me."

"Oh! Don't say that! You're wonderful! I wish I could be just like you!"

They share a hug, ending when someone knocks. In comes a detective, named King, who has turned out to be a nice man, unlike many of the other cops they've dealt with in the last twenty-four hours. King seems to know what he's doing and didn't mind trading gossip with Irene about the oiled-hair detective who didn't believe her story about Ellis Wax (he's on the way out because he's crooked). Irene trusts that King will arrange it so that Ginger will make it back to Chicago alive.

"How's he?" he asks, nodding toward Frank. "Any change?"

"No," answers Irene heavily. "There's not, unfortunately. How about Ellis Wax?" She isn't sorry she stabbed him but she doesn't want him to die from her blows, either. She doesn't want that on her conscience.

"He's recovering. I think tomorrow he can get transferred to a jail cell, where he belongs. Hopefully we won't see the likes of him again. A true deviant and a cold-blooded killer. But he won't be bothering any women again for a long time. They'll put him in the electric chair for what he's done."

Ginger pats Irene on the back. "Way to go, kid."

King clears his throat. "It's time we shove off. You say your goodbyes?"

Ginger nods.

"Okay, well, let's go. I've got uniformed officers posted outside the hospital, and a patrol car is waiting downstairs. We'll take that to the train station, it's just a few blocks from here. We have reason to believe you're still under some danger."

"Big surprise, detective."

"Whoever's been shooting up this town is still out there. He might be watching us now. He might get on the train with you. You'll have Pinkerton detectives with you the whole way to Chicago. They're well-trained and know what they're doing. You'll be fine."

Ginger shrugs her shoulders. Nothing seems to bother her. "I know it won't be a walk in the park, but I'm not afraid of those thugs anymore."

King nods, and then turns to Irene. "Miss Howard, thanks for all your cooperation. I just wish I could've prevented yesterday from happening. Our department let you down, and I'm sorry."

"I'm sorry, too."

"I saw your mother in the lobby. Should I send her up?"

"No. I want to be alone for a while." She gives Ginger one last hug before they depart. Into her ear she whispers: "I want you to write me as soon as you get there."

"If I get there, you mean," Ginger whispers back.

Musetta has been prowling around the grounds of the hospital like a caged animal, keeping a steady gaze on the entrance. Sally is in there, holed up in a room with Frank Hearn, who's lying in a coma. And that other dame is always in there, too. The Flapper. That's what the newspapers called her.

It's too dicey to spend too much time inside the hospital. A nurse is liable to make him. No, it's better to wait out here. You got this big pile of shells and bones, thirty feet tall, a perfect place to squeeze off a shot. That's risky, though. Killing her would be no problem. She'd be a sitting duck the minute she walked through the front entrance. But could he get away? There're witnesses all around. Flatties come and go all the time. He's got the car parked nearby and he could make a run for it. The big mound of shells would give him cover, shielding him as he ran.

On the other hand, he could wait her out. She'll have to go somewhere eventually. She can't stay in there forever. When she does come out, he could follow her. She'll go back to that garage apartment. Her clothes are there. She's got to be pretty ripe. Skirts like to stay fresh. Some of them, anyway.

Musetta sighs warily. He's standing in the shade of a tree, at the base of the shell mound. This won't be easy. Those mugs in Chicago, they better appreciate what he's doing. And with no help. Vecchio was an idiot. They said he was the best but it was obvious he'd lost his nerve. He wanted to coast. He wanted to go shopping for new clothes. Vecchio won't be shopping no more where he is. No, they better appreciate it, all the work he's done for Capone. And them that don't, he'll do them the same way as Vecchio. There's nothing a bullet won't take care of.

Musetta starts to walk up the stairs leading to the top of the mound. Capone says he wants his men to be loyal. To do what he tells them. Killing a skirt, that's no easy job. Not everybody can do it. No, they better appreciate it. There better be a reward. Something plum. His own whorehouse would be nice. You rake in the dough and screw anything that moves. He'll talk to Capone about it when he gets back. First thing.

He takes his position against the rail. He can see straight down to the main entrance of the hospital. He watches, just like he has been for most of the day. People come, people go. Some are crying, some are smiling. That's life in a nutshell. Everybody pays the piper, it's just some pay later than others.

Then he sees her.

"What's this?" he mutters. Waltzing through the main entrance, a cop on each arm, is none other than the skirt herself, Ginger or Sally or whoever she is. It won't matter soon enough. The coroner can figure all that out at the morgue. But kill her now or wait? He bites his lower lip, eyes fixed on the target. Kill her or wait?

He can hear Capone thundering: *Way to go, Joey! You made us all proud down in Florida!*

He reaches into his jacket and grabs his gun. He lifts it steadily, like the hands of a Swiss clock. He wants to do it right. One shot, and run like hell.

Then behind him he hears footsteps. A voice soon follows:

"The Indians of Florida were of the Stone Age. They used no iron or bronze whatsoever. Theirs was a simple technology, pointed rocks for breaking up shells, sharp bones for hooks, and so forth. If you look closely, you might even see some crude implements mixed together among the shells and bones."

He quickly slips the gun back into the shoulder holster. A one-armed guide is leading a group of tourists up the stairs. Each member of the party gives Musetta a friendly nod or wave as they step onto the platform. The one-armed man keeps on jabbering about the Indians.

He hears Capone's voice again: *I'm disappointed, Joey. I gave you a job to do and you didn't do it. I'm very disappointed.*

Musetta turns and heads back down the stairs.

WHITE

POWDERED FACE

The man in the pea-green suit saunters up the stairs of the Criminal Courts Building. It's another cold day in Chicago but the man wears no overcoat. Snow has been piled in great mounds that have turned a shade of dirt brown. Pedestrians go scurrying along the sidewalk huddled beneath thick jackets, while the man keeps a white fedora cocked at a jaunty angle. A marquise diamond glitters in his tiepin, and over his protruding stomach hangs a platinum watch chain littered with more diamonds. On the middle finger of his left hand he wears an eleven-carat, blue-white diamond. Some say it cost him over $50,000, but no one dares ask him to his face. Standing a shade under six feet and weighing in at a heavily muscled (though pasta-and-wine inflated) 255 pounds, the man is known to possess a volatile temper, capable of inflicting remorseless punishment. His shoulders are bulky and massive, supporting a short, thick neck and a head shaped like a bowling ball. His fat, purple lips are chapped from the cold, and his gray eyes water from the wind whipping off the lake. Across his left cheek, from ear to jaw, runs a scar, courtesy of a knife fight in his youth. Two more scars disfigure his face, and he is touchy about the subject. Sometimes he powders his face to hide the scars, giving him a ghostly hue, as if he has been sent from the land of the dead to torment the living.

The cop who has driven the man to the Criminal Courts Building opens the door for him. Together they go in, and walk silently down a series of narrow corridors back to the office of Assistant State Attorney William H. McSwiggin. They sit in stiff wooden chairs while the dew-eyed secretary alerts her boss of the sudden and unexpected visit. She knocks on the door of the inner office and sticks her head in.

"Alphonse Capone is here, sir." There is a pause, and she shuts the door. "He'll be right with you, Mr. Capone."

"Thanks. I hope we can clear this up."

The secretary says nothing. Al Capone examines his fingernails as he waits. The cop looks straight ahead, like his head has been bolted in place. A few minutes later McSwiggin throws open the door and asks Capone to come in.

"I heard you're looking for me," Capone says as he stands up. "I have no idea what for."

"We'll talk about that. Please, sit down."

"I'm an antique dealer, Mr. McSwiggin. I run an honest business."

Four hours later Al Capone reemerges from the office and shakes hands with the prosecutor who wants to charge him with murder. But Capone acts like McSwiggin has just thrown him a lavish dinner party, thanking him profusely for taking the time to discuss these matters. "I'm sorry I can't be more help to you," Capone says. "I really am. Whoever killed Joe Horn should pay."

"We'll see you at the inquest, Mr. Capone."

"Sure, I'll be there. I'll do the best I can."

Then the cop drives Capone back to the antique store located next to the Four Deuces club on South Wabash Avenue. The cop knows there are no antiques in there, just boxes and boxes of papers and account ledgers that fat little bookkeeper, Jake Guzik, maintains with meticulous care. During the ride Capone is morosely silent, staring out at the passing bustle of Chicago's Southside.

"I don't know what happened," he says finally. "I thought it was taken care of."

"They don't got no witnesses," the cop answers. "You're in the clear."

Capone's eyes grow wide, and his purple lips quiver with boiling anger. "There's a witness! The broad! Sally Serenade! She's coming back from Florida surrounded by Pinkertons! What the hell happened, that's what I want to know. How hard is it to rub out a dame?"

Somebody has been standing outside her berth ever since the train pulled out of St. Petersburg. It's either the tall and thin one or the short and fat one, and sometimes both. They're obviously hired dicks and they're keeping a close eye on Sally Serenade. Musetta has passed by plenty of times on his way to the observation deck. He hasn't said anything to either one yet. He's smiled and been friendly. The thin one looks mean, with fierce black eyes and a hawk's nose and twitching jaw muscles. He's not the one to mess with. The fat one, he might be an easier mark. But how? That's what Musetta hasn't figured out all these hours and miles that the train has rumbled, bringing them ever closer to Chicago. So he's got to make his move if he's going to make one. They've passed through Louisville and are somewhere in Indiana. Just a couple hours left, and then it'll be too late.

He stares out into the cool passing night. The air is crisp and clear, and he can see his breath floating away from him. The cigarette is warm against his face. A thousand stars hover above, shining brightly in the black sky.

"What's the next stop?" he asks a conductor getting some fresh air.

"Indianapolis."

"When's that?"

The conductor checks his watch. "Twenty minutes."

They're going fast now, too fast for him to jump off. But once they get closer to the city, the train will slow down. And that's when he should do it. There's no other choice: he'll have to go in guns blazing. The fat one is standing outside the door now, and it won't be hard to take care of him. A smile will be enough to freeze him, and he'll be dead before he knows what hit him. The fat one isn't the problem. The thin one is the trouble. He's inside the berth, guarding the skirt. Somehow there's got to be a way to lure him outside.

Musetta takes one last drag off the cigarette and then sends the butt flying into the night. It sparks against the ground before disappearing into oblivion. He'll shoot the fat one, and a silencer will muffle the shot. He could stand over the fallen body and shout, "Help! Help!" The thin one would come out, and presto, he'd be dead, too. Then the skirt. Then he jumps off the train.

"You getting off at Indianapolis?" the conductor asks.

"I think I might."

Musetta says good night and starts to walk back, through the parlor car filled with cigar smoke and wealthy men. He keeps going, through one car of private berths, and another. Then he stops. Through the small window of the door separating the cars he can see the fat dick standing outside the door. The train starts to slow, and its brakes begin to squeal ever so slightly. It takes a long time to get these things to stop.

He takes out his gun and screws on a silencer. He slips the gun into the side pocket of his jacket. He pushes open the door and smiles at the fat man, who smiles back. Why shouldn't he? They've seen each other plenty of times already. Musetta nods his head and keeps walking past, slipping his hand in his jacket when he reaches the door at the other end of the car. He grips the gun and wheels around.

But Musetta never fires a shot. The first bullet catches him in the chest and throws him back against the door. His gun goes clanking to the steel floor. He can see the fat man pointing the pistol at him, just a glimpse, because the second bullet pierces his forehead and all becomes black.

The **bed** has been made and fresh towels hang in the clean bathroom. The radiator fills the small room with warmth, and Ginger kicks off her uncomfortable pumps and flops down face first on the soft mattress. They'll bring her food from the kitchen, and they'll take away the dirty plates once she's done. She's getting the royal treatment at the Drake Hotel, a taste of the life the stars lead. Fanny Brice must spend her days lounging in bubble baths in places like these, sipping on mimosas, seducing eager young bellhops.

Ginger chuckles at such impure thoughts. And she feels guilty for enjoying herself so much with poor Frank in that hospital down in Florida. She knows Irene is taking good care of him, but still it seems to be awfully selfish of her to dream about her future when Frank lost his saving her from Ellis Wax. He's done so much for her, and he might never be the same.

What to order, what to order—she certainly earned a delectable dinner, given what she did today. She got on the witness stand and told the grand jury that she saw Al Capone shoot Joe Horn. If the grand jury indicts Capone, McSwiggin, the cute prosecutor, said he'll book her as a material witness and keep her in jail until the trial. That way, she'll be safe from Capone's killers. Not an exciting idea, spending a couple weeks locked up, but it's one Ginger has accepted. So she might as well live it up now.

If the grand jury doesn't indict, though, it's all over. Capone will be in the clear and Ginger will hop on the first train to New York. What happens after that? Fame, fortune, hotels like this one, handsome men vying for her love.

And then maybe she'll get elected president!

First, she must eat dinner. And with dinner, wouldn't wine be lovely? A place like the Drake, there's plenty of booze. The porters will know what to do. *Just put it on my bill,* she'll say. McSwiggin, he's Irish. He won't mind.

*   *   *

The ringing of the phone awakens her. Night has fallen, and the darkened room momentarily frightens her. Lights from the street below cast a strange glow on objects she can barely see. She fumbles for the telephone, answering on the third ring.

"Hello?"

"Ginger? It's Bill McSwiggin."

She groans, still half-asleep. The bottle of champagne she drank with dinner went straight to her head and zonked her out. Now her throat is parched and her head aches. "I was dreaming this was all over."

"Sometimes dreams come true."

"What?"

"You are completely relieved of all civic responsibility in this matter."

She sits up, nearly knocking over a bedside lamp when she reaches to turn it on. "Don't lie to me, McSwiggin. I'll sue you."

"You'll never have to testify in this case ever again. The grand jury reached a verdict. They found that Joe Horn was killed by 'one or more unknown white male persons.' Capone got away with it."

She listens to him breathing, because she doesn't know what to say. "Wow," is all that comes out of her mouth.

"Ginger, I must say, you did wonderfully on the stand. I really do appreciate your courage. The other witnesses were scared. They said they didn't see who killed Horn."

"You can't blame them."

"No, I don't blame anybody. That Torrio mob is powerful in this city, and it'll take some time to clean up this mess Thompson left us."

"Who?"

"The previous mayor. Oh, I don't want to bore you, Ginger, with stupid Chicago politics."

"You're not."

"Capone is somebody I'm keeping my eye on. I might get another crack at him down the road. We'll have to wait and see."

"But won't Capone take another crack at me? It seems like the creep really wants me dead."

"I guarantee you'll be fine, Ginger. He's in the clear and you're nothing to him anymore. The case is over. You'll never testify. He won't make trouble for himself by coming after you when there's no reason to. He's not that stupid."

"You think?"

"I know. So you'll be headed for New York in the morning, I suppose. Will you be resuming your singing career?"

It seems like an odd question now. So many people have died, lives ruined, for nothing. Now Ginger will try to sing silly love songs for money. Sometimes life doesn't add up. "I'll give it a whirl. It seems kind of pointless, in a way. But it's all I ever wanted. That ain't saying much, is it?"

"Great singers can lighten a heavy load. I know for me I have to unwind with some Jessica Dragonette or Ruth Etting. It helps me relax. No, singers are important. It's not pointless at all."

"You're a nice man for saying so."

"No, I'm just being honest."

"Maybe one day you can relax to one of my records. That would be something, wouldn't it?"

"I hope I get to live that long."

"Hey! I'll have a record out before you're married, you watch."

They share a good-natured laugh, these two who have worked so hard only to come up short. But McSwiggin's last words will resound in Ginger's ears when, six months later, living in New York, she happens to walk by a newsstand on Broadway on her way to an audition for a bit part in an upcoming musical and she sees a week-old Chicago paper with the headline McSwiggin Gunned Down. She stops in total disbelief and, with trembling hands, lifts the paper up and begins to read about how a passerby chanced upon the bullet-riddled body of William McSwiggin, star Assistant State Attorney, found dead outside the Pony Inn. Detectives investigating the case had no suspects.

TATTERED
AND TORN

An alarm clock clangs loudly next to Frank's ear. It's seven o'clock in the morning but already it's hot and sticky. Summer isn't the time to be in Florida. It cools off for about ten minutes after a thunderstorm but then the heat comes roaring back. An electric fan helps a little—if you can afford one. That's why the snowbirds migrate back north after Easter. The humidity, the mosquitoes, the lightning that rips in huge bolts from the black sky—who'd want to hang around for five or six months of that?

"Honey?" he calls out, reaching over and feeling the emptiness of where she slept. The shower is running and it sounds very peaceful. A wistful grin appears on his sleep-creased face. He can smell her perfume lingering in the air, a gentle reminder of what he's going to miss. He sits up and grabs his eye patch from the bedstand. He puts it on quickly before she can see him. Hell, he doesn't like looking at his mangled eye socket, either. So he doesn't. He takes off the patch every night after the lights are out and puts it on first thing each morning.

She says he's being silly. She says it doesn't bother her. She claims she's gotten used to it. After all, it's been four months, almost five, and she's hardly left his side. She sat with him in the hospital, held his hand and read him books, bought him a radio and paid for every single cent of the bill, the total of which she refuses to tell him. *My treat. You saved my life, after all.*

The shower stops. Frank leans back on a stack of pillows and listens to her getting dressed. He hasn't slept over very often, but last night was special. The landlady knows they aren't married because Mrs. Howard made sure of that when she rented Irene the room. The Mann Act isn't something to play around with. Mrs. Howard would call the cops in a heartbeat if she got word that he and Irene were playing house without a marriage license.

We could get one.

No, Frank. I'm not eloping. When we get married, it's going to be a gala event. The biggest party ever.

So Frank spent most nights back at the same garage he rented on the day he arrived in St. Petersburg. Mabel Wright had it painted, but the beds were the same, lumpy and squeaky. Irene begged him to let her rent him a nicer place but he put his foot down. She's done too much already. Mrs. Wright is letting him stay for free until he gets well enough to start working. He's been out of the hospital for a month, still regaining his strength by taking long walks along the waterfront. Irene was always with him, step for step.

He's almost fully recovered. Today he starts work at a hardware store on Central Avenue. The real estate business won't get hopping until the winter. But he won't be around to join in.

"Are you awake?" she asks, stepping out of the bathroom. She's wearing a blue satin robe that falls to her ankles. Her wet hair shines as the morning sun rises above the stumpy orange tree outside the bedroom window. She smells clean and pure, and her skin is tanned from their long, languid strolls. He catches himself feeling sad and he doesn't want to be sad. She'll start crying again.

"Yeah, the alarm clock blasted my eardrums. I guess I better get used to it."

"Not for long."

He grimaces, glancing over at her suitcases, all packed up and ready to go. Today she's getting on a train for New York, and next week she sails for Europe, where she's going to study and travel. Her parents think it will keep them apart, but Irene wants him to come over and travel with her. She's even offered to buy his ticket. He won't let her, though. He'll come once he earns enough money for the trip.

"No, not for long," he sighs. Then he forces himself to brighten up. "I figure four months, tops."

Her body sags like someone dropped a sandbag on her shoulders. "Four months! I don't want to wait four months!"

"I can work two jobs and get there quicker."

She stomps her foot. "No. You're still getting better. One job will be plenty, Frank Hearn. But I don't like your stubbornness. You could leave in a month, you know, if you'd let me buy you a ticket."

"I know."

"Oh, Frank!" She runs over to him and falls into his arms. Together they tumble back onto the bed, their lips locked and tears streaming down their wet cheeks. He doesn't want to cry. He tries to make himself stop. "Please come with me! I love you! I don't want to leave you."

"I swear on my mother's grave I'll be over there before Christmas. I got to do this my way, honey. I got to."

"Okay. But I don't like it."

"Me neither." He pulls himself away from her. Time is getting on and he's got to be at work. He stands up and dresses quickly. Irene is curled on the bed in the fetal position, dabbing at her moist eyes with her robe. On the bedstand are his billfold and a crumpled piece of paper, the writing on it long since faded. The IOU from Babe Ruth is tattered and torn but Frank keeps it with him everywhere he goes. It cost him an eye but gained him something more valuable than 7,000 clams.